There are no secrets that
time does not reveal.

–Jean Racine

MYSTERIES *of* LANCASTER COUNTY

IN PLAIN SIGHT

MYSTERIES *of* LANCASTER COUNTY

DeAnna Julie Dodson

Guideposts

Danbury, Connecticut

IN PLAIN
SIGHT

CHAPTER ONE

The February wind whipped over the cemetery as Bertha Shetler's simple pine coffin was lowered into the ground. Mary Classen Baxter pulled her coat a little more snugly around herself and closed her eyes, letting the words Bertha's eldest son was speaking sink deeply into her mind and heart. He spoke in Pennsylvania Dutch, but Mary could pick out enough of the words to recognize the quote from the fifth chapter of the book of John, the words of Jesus:

"Verily, verily, I say unto you, he that heareth my word, and believeth on him that sent me, hath everlasting life, and shall not come into condemnation; but is passed from death unto life."

She nestled a little closer to her boyfriend, Bill Richmond, as much for comfort as for warmth, and he gave her the slightest of smiles, the crinkles in the corners of his eyes making him look more than ever like a middle-aged Harrison Ford. She wasn't here alone. Her sisters, Martha and Elizabeth, had come to the funeral along with Elizabeth's fiancé, John Marks, but it was still nice to have someone who was there especially with her.

The minister began reading a hymn, again something Mary recognized even if it wasn't in English, and she knew the service was coming to a close. It had been as simple and unadorned as the headstones that stood in dense rows in the field. As quietly plain as Bertha Shetler herself. She had lived a long life and was beloved by family and friends alike. Mary would miss seeing her sitting on her front porch knitting or shelling peas or out tending to her garden. Her large family would miss her much more.

They stood together at the side of the hand-dug grave, her five sons and three daughters, elderly now themselves, her fifty-nine grandchildren, and Mary didn't know how many great-grandchildren, many of them blue-eyed and very blond. Standing next to Verity Shetler, Bertha's nineteen-year-old great-granddaughter, was the young woman who worked for the family, Katura Stolfuz. Verity's parents, Mervin and Iris Shetler, had hired Katura to help Verity and Iris with the many chores around the house, while Mervin and three grown sons did the farm work. She was as dark as the majority of the Shetlers were fair and noticeably quiet even for an Amish girl.

After the grave was filled in by the pallbearers, Katura walked with the family, blotting her tears with a plain white handkerchief. She stumbled, and Verity steadied her with an arm around her shoulders as they walked with the others to their buggies and drove away. They were followed by the rest of the congregation, the women in their long dresses and crisp white *kapps*, the men in black coats and black broad-brimmed hats, who left in the order they had come in, designated by numbers chalked on the side of each buggy. Those who had come in cars followed, to join the others at the family home to share a simple meal and to remember their time with Bertha.

"I'll miss her apple cake," Elizabeth said over her shoulder as she and John walked arm in arm to his car with Martha, Mary, and Bill trailing behind.

"And her advice," Martha added. "She always had a practical solution to whatever the problem was."

"It was good to see all the family," Mary said. "Poor Katura, I'm sure she'll miss Bertha. The dear woman treated Katura like one of her own."

"I thought she might not come," Elizabeth said. "She's so shy."

"She could hardly stay home for the funeral," Mary said. "Bertha was very good to her."

"Bertha was good to everybody," John said. "Did you see how many *Englischers* came today?"

"And how many people came back to town for the funeral." Bill looked around as they walked. "Hey, I think I know that guy."

Mary looked up to see a man a few feet from them who had been standing with Jedidiah Bontrager and his son Eli during the service. He was dressed conservatively, as befitted a funeral, but like an Englischer all the same, though his dark hair and eyes were reminiscent of both Bontragers. He was taller than either of them.

"Dan," Bill said, putting out his hand. "Daniel Bontrager, right? I haven't seen you in years."

Dan shook hands with him. "Good to see you, Bill. How are you?"

"Good. You remember Mary Classen and her sisters, don't you?"

"Of course. Mary wasn't around much when I lived here, but we met a few times when she came to visit her family. How are you, Mary?"

"I'm sorry," Mary said, feeling like she ought to know the man but not remembering him at all. "I'm afraid I don't quite—"

"Dan used to work for me after school when I could afford the help," Bill said. "You know, sweeping up, doing some finishing work, painting, that kind of thing. It was when I was still getting my business going way back when. I thought I had me an apprentice, but he decided he'd head out to the big city."

"Oh," Mary said, only vaguely remembering him. "My parents knew your grandparents. And of course, we know your father and brother."

"Right." Dan shook hands with all of them, and then John introduced himself.

"John Marks. I work for the East Lampeter Police Department."

"John's about to be a member of our family too," Mary said, making Elizabeth turn a little pink.

"Well, congratulations to you both," Dan said to John and Elizabeth. "Yeah, I left here about eight years ago now." He shrugged. "My father and I didn't see eye to eye about some things back then, but I've been thinking about coming back lately. And when I heard Bertha Shetler had passed away, I knew I had to come to the funeral. She was good to me."

Mary didn't know how well Dan had known Bertha, but like John had said, Bertha was kind to everyone who came her way. Then again, Dan had family in Bird-in-Hand, and maybe the funeral was simply an excuse to come home.

"Are you still living in Philly?" Bill asked.

"No," Dan said. "I moved out of state."

"I can see why you might want to come back to a quieter, simpler life."

Dan chuckled. "I'm not ready to give up my car and my phone quite yet, but maybe it's time I cleared some things up with my father and Eli." He looked over the well-populated field of headstones. "You never know how many chances you'll get."

They stood silent for a moment, watching the last of the numbered buggies pull away.

"Bertha had quite a family," Dan said. "I never could keep up with them all when I lived here, and there sure has gotten to be more of them since I left. Who was that dark-haired girl though? The one who almost fell down."

"She works for them," Mary told him. "Has for the past three months or so. I don't know all that much about her. Do you know Rachel Fischer? She knows the Shetlers. She says Katura is pleasant and works hard but mostly keeps to herself. Katura's been to our shop once or twice."

"She's pretty shy," Elizabeth said. "She and Verity are good friends."

Dan grinned. "Verity was only a button-nosed kid when I saw her last. And what about her uncle Hannes? He and I used to hang out when we were in school."

"Hannes has his own rather large family now," Martha said. "But he came for the funeral. He'll be at the house, I'm sure. Are you coming?"

"I was hoping to." Dan's forehead wrinkled. "Do you think it'd be okay? I know I haven't been back here for a long time. I haven't had a chance to even say anything to anyone in the family."

"I know they'd be happy to have you," Elizabeth said.

"Funeral pie," Mary added with a smile, making Dan smile too.

"You know, I always thought that was an awful name for a pie, but it sure is good."

"A more interesting name than raisin pie," Mary said.

"Not easy to forget anyway."

"See you there?" Bill asked, shaking hands with Dan again. "I know your father would love to spend more time with you."

"He and I'll do that for sure," Dan said. "But yeah, I guess I'll come along to the house for a little while. If nothing else, I'd like to pay my respects to Bertha's family."

Martha smiled at him. "I know they'll be pleased you remembered her."

"All right then," Dan said. "I'll see all of you there."

The Shetler home, a white-painted farmhouse that was at least a hundred and fifty years old, was crowded to overflowing with family and friends. There was a table set out in the living area with a simple meal of ham and cheese sandwiches, noodles, potato salad, and mixed fruit. And, of course, there was funeral pie. Knowing they wouldn't be staying long, Mary went straight for the raisin-filled custard treat, and so did her sisters. Bill and John had sandwiches first. All of them chatted with members of Bertha's family and their other neighbors.

Dan, Mary was interested to see, spent most of his time close to the food table, helping himself to a little of everything, making conversation with young Verity Shetler. Verity and

Katura both seemed a little uncomfortable at the attention, and Dan finally went to talk to Bertha's son Jedidiah. It seemed Dan still remembered his Pennsylvania Dutch.

Mary went over to the table to get a napkin.

"How are you girls?" she asked.

"We are well, Mary," Verity said, answering for Katura as she often did. "Everything tastes good?"

Mary swallowed a bite of her pie, savoring the sweetness that melted in her mouth. "It's wonderful. Thank you. You must have been working for a long time to make food for everyone."

"All of us prepared it," Verity said. "It was not hard with so many hands to help."

"You look tired, Katura," Mary said, smiling at the dark-haired girl.

Katura ducked her head. "No," she said in her soft voice. "I am well. I miss Bertha, but I know I should not grieve for her. She is with *Gott* now, and for that we give Him praise."

"She told me several times what a good worker you are," Mary said, trying to cheer her up, "and that she was so glad you were able to come here to stay."

"I cannot thank her enough for taking me in. I did not—"

Katura stopped suddenly and moved over a little so she could slice some more bread, her eyes carefully on her task. Then she stopped again, got her inhaler from her pocket, and breathed deeply from it.

"Do you have asthma?" Mary asked sympathetically.

"It is all right," Katura said. "It has been a long day for us all. Please excuse me. I must get more sauerkraut."

"She does look tired," Mary said to Verity as Katura hurried to the kitchen.

"Since she does not have any family of her own, this has been very hard for her," Verity said. "*Grossmammi* Bertha meant a great deal to her. As well as having this place to come to when she had need of it."

"I'm sorry. I know it's hard to lose someone who's been so kind. If we can do anything to help, please let us know. It's always good to have more friends."

Verity smiled a little. She and her family were known by nearly everyone in Bird-in-Hand. Katura was harder to get to know. When she came to the shop, she was always polite, but she didn't say much. Mary was curious about what had happened to her family, but she didn't want to pry. She just wanted to be friendly.

"There," Katura said when she returned with the sauerkraut and then quickly turned her attention again to the bread she had been slicing. "Now everyone will have plenty."

"Are you feeling better now?" Mary asked her.

"Yes, thank you, Mary," Katura said meekly. "I have had asthma for a long while." Before Mary could reply, Katura abruptly put down the bread knife and brushed the crumbs from her hands. "I will see if there is more ham in the kitchen."

Mary raised her eyebrows as Katura hurried away again. There was a full platter of sliced ham on the table already.

"We will need more soon," Verity said serenely. "My brothers and cousins are coming this way."

Mary turned to see several teenaged boys headed eagerly for the food table. Beyond them she noticed Dan Bontrager looking toward the kitchen door. When her eyes met his, he looked away and struck up a conversation with one of Verity's uncles, who seemed somewhat startled by the sudden attention.

She went over to her sisters, who were talking to their neighbor Rachel Fischer.

"Jedidiah said they were surprised when Dan said he was coming to the funeral," Rachel was saying. "He has not often heard from Dan."

"I'm sure he's happy to have Dan come back," Mary said. She took another bite of her pie and swallowed it before saying, "Even if it's only for a little while."

"Any father would wish to have his son return," Rachel said, sympathy in her dark eyes. "I know it has been difficult for him since Daniel left."

"I wasn't surprised when he did," Elizabeth said. "You and Martha weren't living here then, Mary, but Daniel was always eager to try new things and see the world. He wanted to be everything from a policeman to an architect to a nuclear scientist. I don't know what he settled on, but I'm surprised to find he's even considering coming back to Bird-in-Hand."

"Maybe he got tired of the big city and wants some peace and quiet," Mary said. She took another bite of her pie and noticed that Dan was again trying to talk with Katura, who was clearly uncomfortable with his attention.

The Bontragers kept a few sheep and a few cows and sold wool, dairy products, and meat. After Dan left, Jedidiah hired a single Amish man to help out. The man lived in a couple of rooms above the barn, but he had been saving for a place of his own, and everyone expected he would be marrying and leaving the Bontragers before too much longer.

"And then what will Jedidiah do?" was the nearly universal question.

"Too bad Daniel did not stay," was the nearly universal reply.

"Now that Daniel has come to visit," Rachel said, "perhaps he will consider coming back to live."

"Has he said anything like that?" Mary asked.

She could understand that the Amish life wasn't for everyone, but she did hope that, after all this time, he could mend the rift between himself and his father and brother. Maybe all she was seeing now was Dan's awkwardness with being back with the Amish and trying a little too hard to fit in.

"He has not said," Rachel answered. "But it would be nice for his father and brother, I think."

"Mary," Martha said, "did you know Katura is a painter?"

"Really?" Mary shook her head. "I hadn't heard that. How do you know?"

"I went to get a pen out of my purse from the room where everybody put their coats and things and noticed several small paintings on the easel in the corner. Did you see them?"

"I did. I thought they were lovely. I meant to find out more about them, but I guess I got distracted and forgot. That's Katura's?"

"That's what Verity said when I asked."

"I have to go talk to Katura about them. Maybe I'll go have another look at them too." Mary finished her last bite of pie and went to the kitchen where Katura and Verity were tidying up what was left of the food after all the teenagers had plowed through it.

"My sister tells me you're an artist, Katura," Mary said as she put her plate and fork into the sink.

Katura turned a little pink and ducked her head. "*Ja.* It is something I enjoy."

"I'm a painter too. I didn't really get a chance to look at your paintings. Will you show them to me?"

Katura glanced at Verity, who smiled. "You should," she said. "Mary has been painting for a long time. Remember we saw one of her paintings in her shop? The one of the sea? It was very nice."

"I remember, and it was very good," Katura said, "but I do not know if it would be right for me to show my own work."

"Gott has given you His gift," Verity said, "and it is not for you to keep hidden under a bushel basket. And you are using His gift to help others. I will see to things here."

Katura led the way to where everyone had piled their coats and other belongings. The paintings of several songbirds were not large, but they were beautifully done and boasted intricate detail.

"They're really gorgeous," Mary said, studying one more closely. "This looks like it could fly off the canvas."

Katura blushed. "I am glad you like it. I have painted several of them for the children's nature study at school. Their teacher says they are quite helpful."

"I'd love to hear about how you did those feathers on the cardinal. The shading is exquisite."

Katura bit her lip. "I do not feel I made the wing tips just right."

"I think they're fine." Mary turned her head a little to one side. "The legs are very realistic, but you don't have as much detail on the beak."

"I should do more work on them." Katura's slight smile was hopeful. "Maybe one day you could show me what you would do to fix them."

"Would you like to come paint with me sometime? Then we could both learn something."

"I would like that," Katura said, touching the painting wistfully and then glancing toward the door. "Maybe we can talk about it sometime later. I am certain Verity will be needing my help now."

"Sure." Mary walked with Katura back down the hallway. "And it doesn't have to be anything very involved. Just stop by the shop whenever you're ready to make plans."

"I would like that very much. And I—" Katura faltered when they reached the living area. "But—but we are here today to remember Bertha and the goodness of Gott and not to think of ourselves."

She hurried back to the kitchen.

"Let me know," Mary called after her, and then she went back to her sisters.

"What did you think of the paintings?" Elizabeth asked.

"They're really well done. I'm impressed."

"I thought you would be," Martha said. "I had no idea that Katura painted."

"I'll have to make sure to check her work out before we leave," Elizabeth said. "But where did Katura take off to? She looked like she just got caught with her hand in the cookie jar."

Mary shrugged, but she noticed Dan making his way into the kitchen too. Maybe he just wanted more pie and coffee. She promised herself she'd ask Bill to tell her more about Dan later. There was probably nothing at all to wonder about.

CHAPTER TWO

That evening, Mary and Bill sat in the Classen living room enjoying an after-dinner cup of coffee and each other's company with Tinkerbelle, the sisters' dachshund, snoozing at their feet. Pal, their border collie, was stretched out in front of the fireplace, and Butterscotch had made his feline way up to the top of the bookshelf. They were sleeping too. Martha had made a delicious chicken pasta casserole because she knew it was one of Bill's favorites, and Bill had shown his appreciation verbally and by how much he had eaten.

"You know how to make that too, right?" Bill asked Mary while Elizabeth and Martha were still in the kitchen cleaning up.

"Yes, I know how to make that too," she told him. "It's really very easy. Do you want the recipe?"

He rubbed his stomach. "Maybe not. If knew how to make it, I'd probably make it all the time. And then I'd gain fifty pounds within a week or two and wouldn't fit into my clothes."

She slipped her hand into his, laughing softly. "You might be right. Maybe we'll keep that for special occasions."

"Speaking of special occasions, we're still going out Sunday night, right?"

He looked at her expectantly, and she felt a touch of warmth come into her cheeks. She was a grandmother now, but sometimes he made her feel like she was a girl again.

"That's what I'm planning on," she said.

"Good. I've had the reservation for a couple of weeks now."

She squeezed his hand. He always made her feel like she was something special.

"Where are we going?

"That's a secret. You be ready to go at seven and leave the rest to me."

"All right. Should I wear a ball gown or a bathing suit?"

He grinned. "Well, February is a little cool for swimming in Lancaster County, and I'm afraid Bird-in-Hand doesn't have any grand balls scheduled for the foreseeable future."

"That's too bad," she said with a melodramatic shake of her head. "I guess my Sunday best will have to do."

He squeezed her hand. "You always look nice. Just remember it's not a burger joint."

"Not a burger joint," she said thoughtfully. "I'll remember that."

"And we're still going to see the philharmonic on Tuesday."

"Tuesday?" She frowned, scrambling to remember what date that was supposed to be. "This coming Tuesday?"

"This coming Tuesday. That would be the sixteenth."

"No, it can't be the sixteenth. Really?" She shook her head. "I guess it must be. I've been thinking that's at least two or three weeks away. I hope I have it on my calendar right. Hang on a minute."

She got up, waking Tink, and went into the kitchen with the dog at her heels. There, she grabbed her purse, gave her sisters a quick wave in answer to their inquisitive glances, and went back into the living room. Tinkerbelle jumped up on the couch, and Mary sat next to Bill again and started rummaging in her bag for her phone.

"Ugh. Everything I need always seems to sink straight to the bottom."

He was wise enough to only give her a sympathetic and slightly concerned glance as she started unloading everything.

"I had it this morning before the funeral," she said. "I checked the temperature when I was getting dressed." She put her wallet and makeup bag on the coffee table. "I'm sure I put it back in my purse after that. I always do. Will you do me a favor?" She added an envelope full of coupons to her stack. "Would you call me? Maybe I left it in my room or somewhere else in the house."

"Sure." He called her number and waited. "It's ringing."

Mary hurried up the stairs to her room. Hearing nothing, she walked back down and listened for a few seconds in the hallway. "I don't hear it anywhere. You picked me up—do you think it could have fallen out in your car?"

"Maybe. Want me to check?"

"Would you mind? Please?"

"No problem." He slipped into his jacket and went outside.

"Is Bill leaving already?" Elizabeth called.

"No, he's just seeing if my phone's in his car." Mary went into the kitchen, again with Tink right alongside her. "It's not in my purse, and I didn't hear it ring anywhere in the house."

"I didn't hear it," Elizabeth said, putting the last of the dried dishes into the cabinet.

Martha shook her head. "Did you have it at the Shetlers' after the funeral?"

"I don't know," Mary said. "I didn't check or anything. The last time I remember using it was before we left here."

"It'll turn up," Elizabeth assured her. "Where else did you go?"

Mary thought for a moment. "After we were at the Shetlers', Bill and I went to the grocery store for some things, and then we stopped by Mrs. Knepp's because it was on the way back and she had made some applesauce cake as a thank-you for Bill fixing her porch rail for her. We didn't stay long, but she does like to talk."

"It doesn't seem likely you'd have left your phone there," Martha said.

"I didn't even put my purse down while we were there."

"And at the Shelters'?"

"I don't know." Mary considered a little more. "I left it on the bed with everyone else's things. I don't think anybody there would take something from someone else's purse. Do you?"

"I wouldn't think so," Martha agreed.

"But it could have fallen out," Elizabeth said. "You're not always careful with it."

"I know."

Mary sighed and hurried back into the living room when she heard Bill come back in.

"Sorry," he said, taking off his coat. "I called your number again but didn't hear it ring in the car. I looked under the seats and in them and in the door pockets and everywhere else I could think of just in case you had the ringer turned off. It's not there. Any other ideas?"

"Maybe it fell out of my purse over at the Shetlers'," she said. "Do you think it's too late to go ask about it?"

He glanced at his watch. "It's not even eight yet. You want me to drive you over?"

"I'd like that. Thank you."

She let her sisters know where they were headed, told Tinkerbelle they'd be right back, and a few minutes later they pulled up to the Shetlers' sprawling white farmhouse.

Verity answered the door. "Mary. Bill. Come in. *Maam,* we have guests."

They were soon surrounded by a host of neighbors and their visiting family members, all inviting them to have coffee and some of the pound cake they'd just had with their dinner.

"You really should," Iris Shetler said, a welcoming smile on her round face. "We have more than enough."

"Oh, no," Mary said. "Thank you. We don't want to be a bother."

"And we're both stuffed already anyway," Bill added, making them all grin.

"We only came by to see if I left my phone when I was here earlier. Has anyone found it?"

Katura looked up from where she was clearing the table and shook her head.

"We can all look," Verity said. She looked around at her brothers and cousins. "Go make yourselves useful. Come on, Mary. We will look in my room. Did you put your purse and coat in there with everyone else's?" She gestured to Katura. "Come help us."

The dark-haired girl looked uncertain for a moment, and then she nodded and followed Mary and Verity into the back of the house while Bill stayed to help the others search the living room and kitchen. In the end, even though they searched in the most unlikely places, they found nothing.

"We are very sorry," Iris said. "But we will continue to look, and we will make sure to let you know if we find it."

"Thank you," Mary said. "I'm sorry to have bothered you."

"Maybe you will find it soon," Verity said.

"Maybe it is in the cemetery," one of her teenaged cousins said, his blue eyes alight with mischief.

"You behave yourself, Amos Glick," Verity said with a shake of her finger.

Mary laughed. "I could have dropped it there, but I'm not going to look for it out there tonight."

Mary and Bill made their farewells and drove away.

"They sure have a lot of company right now," he said, glancing back at the Shetler home. "Seemed like even more cousins than there were this afternoon."

"Those boys sure liven things up. Poor Katura doesn't have a chance."

"She's awfully quiet, isn't she? I don't think I've heard her say more than a handful of words in the time she's been here."

"We've talked a little. Mostly when she and Verity have come into the shop. Verity pretty much speaks for her most of the time. I guess it's because Katura's so shy."

"Seems like it," Bill said, his tone thoughtful. "Even Dan asked me if she ever talked. I told him I've only seen her keeping to herself and Verity's family."

"Did he know Bertha that well? I mean, to come to her funeral and everything?"

"Well enough. You know how she was. She never met a stranger." Bill glanced at her then. "But Dan didn't come back just because of her. Like he said, he's going to spend some time with his father and brother now that he's here. He didn't say it outright, but it seemed to me he was wanting to stick around for a while. Maybe try to rebuild some bridges."

Mary was silent for a while, trying to remember what she'd heard about Dan Bontrager since she'd come back to Bird-in-Hand. Very little, it seemed.

"What happened between him and his father? Did you ever hear?"

Bill shrugged. "Not really. All I've ever heard, and it seems pretty likely, is that Dan wanted more of the Englischer world than his family thought was right. Once his mother passed away, Dan decided he wouldn't join the church, and he moved to Philadelphia. I'm sure his father wasn't too happy about that. Or his brother. Eli told me at the Shetlers' that Dan hasn't been back to Bird-in-Hand more than a handful of times before now."

"And now?"

"Now maybe he's testing the waters. Funerals always make people think, don't they? A lot of people regret not spending more time with family until it's too late. How many of them do anything about it before then?"

She sighed. "Not enough. I know I still feel bad about not being with Daddy and Mama before they went."

He reached over and squeezed her hand. "I guess we always see things we could've done better, no matter how close we were to someone we've lost."

"Dan is smart to try to fix things now, if he can. If Jedidiah will let him."

"Yeah, that's the question. He can be pretty stubborn at times. Eli might be a little more open to welcoming him back again. Of course, that's if Dan's come to stay and not merely to visit."

"You mean, as in join the church and really be Amish again? Did he say he was thinking of doing that?"

"I don't know. We talked for only a few minutes. I'd be interested to know what he has in mind, but if he's not cut out for that kind of life, it's better he and his family realize it. He's already been gone a long time. Even if he did want to be closer to his family, that doesn't necessarily mean he wants to go back to the Amish lifestyle."

"True. And if he's tired of big-city life, I could see how someplace like Bird-in-Hand would appeal to him. I hope that, whatever he decides, he works things out with Jedidiah and Eli. It's hard to do that with family sometimes, and the longer the estrangement lasts, the harder it is."

They were back at the house by then.

"I'm sorry to have wasted your time," she said when he slowed the car to a stop.

"Being with you is never a waste of time," he said softly.

"Even if we didn't find my phone?" she asked.

"I'll drive you out to the cemetery tomorrow if you'd like and help you look for it."

"You don't have to," she said. "I know you're busy."

"Never too busy for you, Mary."

They got out of the car, and he took both her hands.

"I really enjoyed tonight," he said.

Somehow, even in his old jeans and a worn coat, he looked very handsome right then, especially with that smile.

"Even though we didn't do anything but eat and talk and not find my phone?"

"Even not finding a phone is a good way to spend time if it's with you."

She put her arms around him. "It was pretty nice, wasn't it?"

"You're pretty nice." His voice was soft, and he traced one gentle finger along the line of her jaw. "Mary?"

She could feel the low rumble of the word in his chest, and for some reason, she couldn't seem to catch her breath. "Yes?"

"You know..." He tilted her face up. "You know I love you, right?"

In spite of herself, her eyes filled with tears, and she nodded.

"I mean, you really know?"

For the life of her, she couldn't seem to say a word, but she ducked her head against him and nodded again, holding on more tightly.

"I've been wanting to tell you that since we were kids," he murmured against her hair. "I should have told you years and years ago. It's always been true. I love you, Mary."

She laughed softly, mostly in amazement to know that he really meant that and, more, in amazement that after her disastrous marriage and divorce, the idea didn't terrify her. In fact, it felt like the most natural and comfortable thing in the world.

For another moment she stayed right where she was, and then, once she was sure her voice wouldn't betray her, she lifted her eyes and cupped his face in both hands. "I love you too, Bill." Her voice broke anyway, and those tears that had pooled in her eyes now ran down her warm cheeks. "I wish I had realized it long before now."

With a low laugh of his own, he pulled her closer and leaned down a little as she stretched upward, their lips meeting in a warm, tender kiss.

"Mary," he whispered against her cheek, holding her tighter, and then the porch light came on.

"I guess I ought to go in," she said. She grinned as she pulled away from him, feeling as if she were sixteen again.

He walked her to the door. "So should I call you tomorrow about going out to the cemetery?"

"You'll have to call Martha or Elizabeth. Or call the shop phone. I'm supposed to work tomorrow, but maybe around lunchtime I can get one or the other of them to take over for me for a little while. And then you can take me someplace cheap for lunch."

"It's a date. I'll be in touch. Oh, by the way." He kissed her again. "I love you."

"I love you too," she said, wanting to laugh and cry both. "Oh, Bill, I can't even—" She shrugged helplessly, not knowing what she wanted to say.

"Yeah," he said, his eyes warm. "I know. I feel the same way."

He touched his lips to hers once more, gave her a quick wave, and drove away.

Somehow she managed to get into the house without her feet touching the ground.

"Did you find it?" Elizabeth asked her as Tinkerbelle hurried over to sit on the floor beside her.

"Hmm?"

"Your phone. Was it at the Shetlers'?"

"Oh, that. No, it wasn't there."

Martha and Elizabeth looked at each other.

"I thought you'd be a lot more upset about losing your phone than this," Martha said.

Mary smiled. "It's only a phone. I'll look again tomorrow. Bill and I are going to go back to the cemetery to see if I dropped it there."

"Okay, Mary." Elizabeth put both hands on her hips. "What aren't you telling us? And don't give us that 'Who, me?' look."

"Nothing's going on," she said, smiling more. "I found out something a few minutes ago."

Her sisters looked at her expectantly.

"Um, Bill just told me he loves me."

"Oh," Martha said, going back to the recipe she was cutting out of a magazine.

Elizabeth shrugged. "Everybody's known that for ages."

Mary's face fell. "Uh—"

Elizabeth grabbed her and hugged her tight. "Everybody but you, honey."

Martha stood and threw her arms around them both. "I'm so happy for you, Mary. Bill's such a good friend and such a good man. I can't think of anybody who'd be better for you."

"He is pretty wonderful, isn't he?" Mary said, beaming at them as she pulled away. "I'm sorry I didn't see that a long time ago. Maybe I wouldn't have wasted so much of my life on Brian."

"You leave Brian in the past where he belongs," Elizabeth said. "Bill isn't anything like him."

"I know, and I'm so thankful for that."

"And I'm glad he's our friend too," Martha added. "It's always so comfortable to be around him." She grabbed Mary's hand. "You do love him, don't you, Mary? I mean, not only as a friend."

"I do. I think I didn't want to let myself think about it too much, in case he didn't feel the same way, but he does. I know he means it, and I do too."

"Good. That's so good. Lizzie's right. Don't let what happened with Brian sour what you have with Bill. Just enjoy being really loved. I had that with Chuck, and you deserve nothing less."

The three of them hugged again.

"I'm supposed to mind the shop tomorrow," Mary said then, "but I told Bill it would be okay for us to go out to the graveyard and then go grab a quick lunch."

"Not a problem," Elizabeth said. "I'll be there anyway."

"And I can pitch in too, if we're busy," Martha added.

"Are you sure?" Elizabeth looked her over critically. "You've seemed a little tired lately."

"Oh, I'm fine," Martha said, waving her off. "I'll go to bed early tonight."

"You've been doing that a lot anyway."

"Not a lot. Once in a while. Sometimes it's nice to snuggle into bed and read."

"Are you okay?" Mary asked, studying Martha's face.

"Of course I am. You're both being silly. I'm absolutely bursting with health."

Martha did look her usual blooming self, but she had been going to bed earlier than usual off and on.

"Go on now," Martha said. "And don't worry about the shop. Elizabeth and I will see to everything."

"Thanks, both of you." Mary picked up the dachsie. "You like Bill, don't you, Tink?"

Tinkerbelle panted happily.

"Do you think you ought to go out early to see if you can find your phone?" Martha asked. "I don't think we'll have snow or anything tonight, but if it's out there, you don't want somebody picking it up."

"I doubt anyone will be out there," Mary said. "It might not even be out there anyway."

"Where else could it be?"

"I don't know, but I'll find it. Or somebody else will, and they'll bring it back."

"Maybe so."

Martha didn't look entirely convinced, but Mary was too happy to mind.

Secondhand Blessings, the Classen family's thrift store, was busy the next morning. They usually were on Saturdays, but today it was crazy. There were lots of customers, many of them with questions about the merchandise. Besides the previously owned articles the store carried, it featured handmade items made by local craftsmen, furniture and clothing, quilts, various kinds of needlework and woodwork, even baked and canned goods. Mary and Elizabeth were kept busy showing people what they had, telling them what was made by the Amish and what by their other neighbors, what was made in Bird-in-Hand, and what came from other places nearby. Even Dan Bontrager and his brother, Eli, had been in to see what woodworking tools they had available. And five of the rowdy Shetler cousins came in a short time after that.

"Whew," Elizabeth said when there was a momentary lull. "We're not usually this busy this time of year."

"I know." Mary dropped into a chair and looked at her watch. "It's after eleven. Mind if I call Bill and find out when he's coming?"

"No problem. I'll go see if Martha is going to be ready to come help out here when you're gone."

"Great. Thanks."

When Elizabeth was gone and the store was empty except for one young couple looking at a set of antique flatware and two Amish women going through the baking pans, Mary called Bill. He answered on the first ring.

"Hey there. I was about to call you. We still on for lunch?"

"Yeah," she told him, smiling just to hear his voice. "It's been a zoo here at the shop, but things have calmed down a little now, so I thought I'd see when you want to go."

"Is now too soon?"

"Elizabeth just went to check with Martha, but I think now would be perfect."

"I'll be right there." He paused for a second. "Uh, Mary?"

"Yes?"

"Love you."

She realized she was blushing again and, glancing at the couple looking at the flatware, she lowered her voice. "Love you too. Can't wait to see you."

He picked her up a few minutes later, when both of her sisters were back in the shop, and they drove out to the graveyard. It was a clear, sunny day, but the wind was brisk, and Mary huddled in her wool coat as they walked the way they had the day before from the road out to the newly turned earth of Bertha Shetler's grave.

"I don't see anything," Bill said after they'd looked around awhile.

Mary could still see the signs of the crowd that had been out there for the funeral. There were lots of footprints jumbled together and even the distinct marks that showed where the coffin had sat before it had been lowered into the ground. But there was no phone.

"Well, it was just a possibility," she said with a disappointed smile.

Bill put his arm around her and turned her back toward the car. "It's freezing out here. How about some lunch to warm us up?"

"That's a good idea." She nestled against him, letting him shelter her from the wind as they walked. "Maybe somebody found the phone wherever I lost it. All I need to do is tell our friends it was lost."

"The Shetlers know," he said. "That's a start."

"I'll tell Rachel too. She knows everybody. If somebody found a phone without an owner, she'll probably hear about it. Or isn't there some way the phone company can ping it or whatever they call it and tell me where it is?"

"Yeah, I guess there's that. Let's get some lunch, and then we'll check into it."

They hurried back to the car, and Bill turned on the engine and then the heat.

"What'll it be?" he asked. "Burgers? Chinese? Home cooking?"

She rubbed her gloved hands in front of the vent. "Anything as long as they have hot coffee and their tables are out of the wind."

"That shouldn't be too hard to find."

He was just pulling away from the curb when, from the depths of her purse, her phone rang.

CHAPTER THREE

Mary looked over at Bill in disbelief as a second ring sounded. She dug through her purse till she came up with the phone.

"Hello?"

"Ken?"

"I'm sorry," Mary said. "I think you must have the wrong number."

There was a long pause.

"Oh," the other person said finally. "Uh. Sorry."

The call ended abruptly.

Mary laughed uncertainly and clicked off the call. "Only a wrong number. But how in the world did my phone get back in my purse?"

"Are you sure it wasn't always there?" Bill asked.

She gave him a look. "You called it last night. If it had been in my purse then, we would've heard it. Besides, I took everything out right in front of you. It wasn't there."

"Did you recognize the person?"

She shook her head, checking her phone for the number. "I don't even know where this area code is from. It's not local."

"Was it a man or a woman?"

"A man. Sounded kind of young. I mean, he sounded grown-up, but maybe in his early twenties."

"What did he say?"

"He asked for Ken. Or, I should say, he thought I was Ken. Do I sound like a Ken?"

Bill chuckled. "Not like any Ken I ever met. That's very weird about your phone though. Somebody had to get it out of your purse and get it back in without you noticing. Have you left your purse someplace where somebody could get into it?"

"I don't know. Maybe. The only time it wasn't with me was when I put it with the coats and purses at the Shetlers' after the funeral. I always leave it behind the counter at the shop. I've never had anybody bother it there, but obviously I can't stand around and watch it all the time either. There were a lot of customers in the shop this morning."

"And when do you remember using your phone last?" he asked her, thinking again.

"Right before the funeral. I called you to see if you were on your way to pick me up."

"Yeah. So sometime between then and now, somebody got your phone out of your purse, presumably used it, and then put it back."

"Well, it couldn't have been put back before last night, because that's when we found out it was gone. And it wasn't at the Shetlers'."

"Okay. To be more precise, it was taken sometime between when you called me before the funeral yesterday and when you found it was gone last night. And it was put back, most likely, sometime this morning at the shop. Does that seem reasonable to you?"

"I suppose. Do you think somebody simply wanted to use my phone? Why?"

"I dunno. Maybe whoever it was doesn't have a phone. Or theirs wasn't working or something."

"Then why not just ask to borrow it?"

"Yeah," Bill said. "It's very strange. Whoever it was would've had to know your password and all that."

Mary winced. "I don't usually lock it."

He glanced over at her, one reproving eyebrow raised.

"I know I should, but it's such a nuisance to unlock it every time I use it. Besides, isn't it supposed to lock itself after a while?"

"Depends on how you have it set. You'd better look it over and see if there's anything on it you didn't put there. And check your outgoing calls. Maybe we can figure out who took it based on what number was called."

As they continued to the restaurant, she checked the things he suggested.

"I don't see that anything was downloaded onto it. I checked my browsing history. The most recent thing on there was a recipe I looked up. And I don't see that any calls were made after I called you about going to the funeral." She bit her lip. "But that doesn't necessarily mean anything. It's easy enough to delete numbers from the list of recent calls."

"Maybe whoever it was got it by mistake. You know, thought your purse was somebody else's, somebody he or she had permission from to use their phone. Then maybe the person was too embarrassed to give it back to you, or you left before they could put it back."

"I guess that's possible. It still seems a little strange. But I guess it's no big deal. Doesn't seem like any harm was done."

"And your mystery caller?" he asked archly.

"People misdial all the time. And he was polite about it. I doubt it has anything to do with my phone being missing."

"Yeah, probably not."

"And, yes, I'll make sure it's more secure from now on," she said. "It seems kind of silly in Bird-in-Hand though. I mean, we know almost everybody."

"It's still a good idea. Next time might not be so harmless, you know? You wouldn't want somebody getting your personal information from it."

"You're right. I'll be more careful. It's too bad we can't feel like our things are safe wherever we go."

"It's only wisdom to protect your property, even if it's just from simple mistakes."

She gave him a smile. "I sure am glad to have it back. Now remind me about that concert again so I can make sure I have the right date on my calendar."

"It's Tuesday. This coming Tuesday, the sixteenth. And tomorrow night we're going out too."

"I'm not about to forget that," she said, reaching over to pat his arm. "Not now that I have a real valentine."

He laughed low. "Happy?"

"Yes. More than I can even start to explain. It seems like this couldn't be real or it shouldn't be me."

"Why shouldn't it be you? You're an amazing woman. You're smart and talented and beautiful and funny and easy to be around and—"

"And you might be the tiniest bit biased," she said with a laugh.

"But it's true," he protested.

"I love that you think so. And I love you."

She squeezed his arm. He was good for her. She'd known that for some time now as far as his friendship was concerned, but knowing that he truly loved her made it even better. Now she had to make sure she didn't do anything to mess it all up.

They spent longer over their "quick lunch" than Mary realized, and she made a big show of tiptoeing back into the shop after Bill dropped her off.

Things were crazy busy again, but Martha and Elizabeth didn't seem to mind.

"We're just glad you're back," Elizabeth said while Martha went to help a customer with a particularly nice piece of ruby-red Depression glass. "Did you find your phone?"

"I did, actually," Mary said, putting her purse into the drawer below the cash register instead of merely tossing it behind the counter as she usually did.

"That's great. In the cemetery?"

"Nope. In my purse."

Martha came back to the counter in time to hear what they were talking about. "In your purse? I thought—"

"No, it wasn't in there last night. Yes, it's in there now. No, I don't know how it happened. And yes, it seems perfectly fine."

Her sisters looked at each other, clearly mystified, and Mary told them what she and Bill had discussed and about the call she had gotten.

"So you think it was somebody at the funeral or at the Shetlers' house?" Martha asked.

"Seems like it must have been," Mary said. "Like I said, I didn't put it down at Mrs. Knepp's or at the grocery store yesterday. Besides, Mrs. Knepp wouldn't even dream of using someone else's phone without their permission."

"True."

"So if somebody took it," Elizabeth said, "somebody must have put it back, right? Who would have had the opportunity to do that?"

Mary thought for a moment. "I didn't have it last night, and the only place I was today besides at home up until Bill picked me up was here in the shop."

"It was busy enough in here that almost anybody could have dropped it back into your purse." Elizabeth looked around the still-buzzing shop. "But who had the chance to put it back this morning who would have also had the chance to take it yesterday?"

Just then, two women came up to the counter with some antique books and Amish embroidered pieces and looked at the sisters expectantly.

"I'll take care of it," Mary told Martha and Elizabeth. "Be right back."

As she rang up the purchases, Mary tried to picture who had been in the shop that morning. Most of them had been friends and neighbors, some of them better known than others, and a few had been strangers, tourists probably.

By the time she was finished helping her customers, Martha and Elizabeth were busy with others, and it was late afternoon before the three of them were able to talk again.

"I've been thinking about who was in the store this morning," Mary said, keeping her voice low and her eyes on the customers still browsing around the shop. "Eli Bontrager was here looking at tools. His brother Dan was with him."

"I remember," Elizabeth said. "But neither of them bought anything, and I don't remember them being up at the counter."

Martha looked around the store for a moment. "But it was busy, right? You don't know for sure they weren't up here."

"Not for sure," Elizabeth admitted. "But why would one of them take Mary's phone? Jedidiah wouldn't even think of it, and Dan has one of his own. I saw him with one at the Shetlers' yesterday."

"So did I," Mary said. "But maybe he found mine at the Shetlers' and didn't know whose it was until later."

"So he sneaked it back into your purse instead of simply returning it?" Martha asked dubiously.

"That doesn't seem very likely, does it?" Mary shook her head. "Well, I'm not going to worry over it anymore. It's back. Nothing bad happened. I've got better things to think of."

"Like your Valentine's date tomorrow night?" Martha asked, her eyes twinkling.

"Exactly. You're both going to have to help me decide what to wear. Bill won't tell me where we're going, but I'm sure it's someplace very nice."

"Speaking of Valentines," Elizabeth said, handing Mary a flash drive, "here are those pictures we were talking about. Are you sure Cindy won't mind?"

"Pictures?" Martha asked.

"My friend Cindy Martin does beautiful scrapbooks, so I thought I'd get her to make one for John and Elizabeth with pictures from early on in their relationship up to their engagement," Mary said. "Then, after they're married, I'll get her to make one from their engagement to the wedding and the honeymoon. And no, Cindy won't mind. I'm paying for the materials, and even though she said she wouldn't take it, I'm going to pay her for her work too."

"That'll be a great present. Something they can always look back on."

"It's a wonderful idea," Elizabeth said. "John and I are going to Paradou for Valentine's Day, by the way. It's going to be fabulous."

"Oooh, French cuisine for Valentine's Day," Martha said. "So romantic. And I'll stay home and watch old movies like Chuck and I used to do on Valentine's Day."

"Are you sure you don't want to get together with a friend or two and go out?" Mary asked her. "I hate for you to be home alone."

"I won't be alone. I'll have Pal and Butterscotch and Tink. Really, I'll miss Chuck, but I'll still have a wonderful time. He left me with so many good memories. And I'll be very comfortable too. It'll be a great evening."

"That does sound pretty nice," Mary admitted. "And no having to get all dressed up."

With the help of her sisters the next night, Mary decided on a slim-cut silk dress in a soft turquoise that brought out the same color in her eyes. She wore candlelight pearls in her ears and around her neck and on her wrist, and a gold-and-pearl clip in her hair. When Bill knocked on the door, she opened it for him and then stepped back to see what he thought of her all dressed up.

"You look wonderful," he said, giving her a tender kiss on the cheek and then presenting her with a dozen red roses.

"Oh, Bill." She took the flowers in her arms and closed her eyes, breathing deeply of their heavenly fragrance. "Thank you so much. Let me put these in something, and then we can go."

Martha came in from the kitchen looking comfortable in her jeans and T-shirt and carrying a bowl of freshly popped popcorn.

"I'll take care of the roses," she said, putting the popcorn on the coffee table and taking the flowers from Mary. "Oh, they smell wonderful. Now, you two had better go before you miss your reservation. Bill, you look very nice."

Bill smiled, only faintly embarrassed. "Thanks."

It didn't matter that they had gone to church together only that morning. Mary's heart quickened as if she hadn't seen him in a very long time. He looked more than "very nice." His dark suit hung very handsomely on his muscular frame, and his dark hair was neatly in place. He didn't dress up often, but when he did, he did it right.

"Are you ready to go?" he asked, offering her his arm.

She took it, enjoying being treated like she was something special.

"I could get used to this," she said, smiling.

His dark eyes were warm. "I hope you do."

Martha was already settled on the couch with Tinkerbelle and Butterscotch, and Tink was sound asleep.

"Have fun," Martha said with a yawn. "I'll try to stay awake until you and Lizzie get back home."

Mary gave her a little wave, and she and Bill got into his car and drove away.

"I hope I'm dressed right for wherever we're going," she said, for some reason not sure what to say. They'd been out many times before. Just because this was a little fancier than usual, she supposed, didn't mean it was that much different.

"You—" He swallowed down the catch in his voice and started again. "You look amazing. I don't know exactly what you did, but you seem brighter or something."

She smoothed the silken folds of her skirt. "Martha and Elizabeth tell me this dress is good for my coloring. The right color can make such a difference on someone. Or maybe it's only that I'm really happy."

"Yeah, maybe that's it more than anything."

"Are you going to tell me where we're going?" she asked after another minute or so. "Elizabeth said she and John are going to Paradou."

"That's a nice place," he said.

"So you're not going to tell me."

"Nope."

"Will you tell me if I guess right?"

"Nope."

"Okay," she said with a laugh, "I'll be patient."

"I'll tell you that I don't think you've been to this place before. At least you haven't told me you have."

"Oh? Have you?"

"Once. A couple of years ago. I think you'll like it."

They drove into Lancaster and finally pulled up in front of an upscale steak and seafood place called the Russell Whitman Grill.

"Oh, this is great," she said. "I've heard lots of good things about this one. And no, I haven't been here before."

"Good."

He parked the car and came around to open her door for her, and then they walked up to the restaurant hand in hand. There were a lot of couples waiting for tables, but Bill and Mary were right on time for their reservation, and they were seated right away.

"This is perfect," Mary said once the waiter had taken their drink orders and given them menus. "It's a lovely place, and everything on the menu sounds so good. I was afraid, since it was Valentine's Day, you might have picked one of those places that serves a bunch of things I've never heard of and can't pronounce."

He shook his head. "I didn't think you'd enjoy that."

She reached across the table and squeezed his hand. "Thank you. It's nice to be with someone who knows what I like."

"And likes the same things. I know I wouldn't be comfortable in a really fancy place either."

"That's what's so nice about being with you, Bill. I can be myself and be comfortable. When I was with Brian, I always felt I had to say exactly the right things and look exactly the right way, or he wouldn't like me. It's a hard way to live every minute of every day."

"You know you can be yourself with me," Bill assured her. "Yourself is exactly who I love."

"Oh, Bill." There was a familiar sting behind her eyes, but she managed to smile. "We'd better decide what we're going to eat before I make myself look silly."

They ended up having steak and lobster and all the trimmings and the most delicious crab-stuffed mushrooms Mary had ever tasted.

"I'm so full," she said, "but everything was fabulous. Thank you."

"But you have to have dessert," he protested. "It wouldn't really be a proper Valentine's Day date if you don't have something lavish for dessert."

"Oh, no." Smiling, she shook her head. "I think I'd burst at the seams if I ate another bite."

"Aww, come on. Just a taste of something. I'll split it with you, how would that be?"

"Only if you eat most of it," she said. "And I mean nearly all of it, okay?"

"Okay. I know you like cheesecake, and theirs is the best I've ever had. What do you think?"

"Well…"

"It's got strawberries."

He looked at her hopefully, and she couldn't possibly say no.

"Actually, that sounds delicious. Okay."

He called over the waiter and placed the order, looking as if he had won the lottery or something.

She shook her head. "If we do this too often, I'm going to have to buy a whole new wardrobe."

"Not often," he said. "But this is a very special occasion, don't you think?"

"It is, but it would be even if we were only eating at home. You make it special."

"You're special to me, Mary. Wherever we are and whatever we're doing. I don't want to lose that." There was a sudden gravity in his tone. "I feel like I've missed out on so much being without you all this time."

She felt the same way. Now that they had both admitted how they felt, she knew he was the one she wanted to always be with. But did he feel the same way? She believed he loved her, but what exactly did that mean to him? Just dating or…

"Your dessert, ma'am," the waiter said, bringing her an enormous slice of cheesecake.

"Oh, no," she protested. "That's not just for—"

She caught her breath when she looked at the plate. Then she looked wide eyed at Bill, and then at the grinning waiter.

"I think that's yours, ma'am," he said and, with a slight bow, he left them alone.

"Bill…"

He was looking at her hopefully, fighting a smile.

She looked down at the plate, once more reading the words that were drizzled on it in strawberry glaze, and now she couldn't keep her eyes from filling with tears.

Will you marry me?

"You're crazy," she said, laughing as she dabbed at her eyes with her napkin.

His face fell. "You mean the answer is no."

"Oh, no!" She reached around the gleaming plate and grabbed his hand. "Of course I'll marry you. It's a crazy way to propose, but I love it. And I love you. Yes. I will definitely marry you."

"Mary," he breathed, and he brought her hand briefly to his lips. "I wasn't sure if it was too soon. I mean, it hasn't been more than a couple of days since we said—"

"But we've both known it for a long time now. Only I wasn't sure you'd be ready to propose yet."

"I was ready to propose on Friday night," he admitted, still holding her hand in his. "But I thought you deserved something special."

"You're so sweet to do this for me."

"I would have bought a ring," he told her, "but I thought maybe you'd like to pick it out yourself."

"I'd love for *us* to pick it out. Together."

He nodded. "I knew you'd want that. We can go look whenever you're ready."

She blinked hard and dabbed at her eyes once more. "I'd like that." She glanced down at the cheesecake and smiled again. "That's too beautiful to eat."

"What if I take a picture of it for you?"

She nodded. "Perfect."

He took a picture of the dessert by itself, and then he took a picture of her with it. She was sure she looked ridiculously happy in it, but that was okay. She was ridiculously happy. Then the waiter, who must have handled many such occasions before, came back to the table and offered to take some pictures of the two of them together. It was so much fun, she even enjoyed the indulgent smiles of the people from the tables around them.

By the time they were ready to actually eat the cheesecake, she really was unable to eat more than a bite. Bill took three or four, and then they had the waiter pack up what was left so Mary could take it home.

"We can have a little more privacy somewhere else," he said as he paid the check and left the waiter a very generous tip.

She was quiet on the way back, holding the box containing the cheesecake in both hands, thankful for that tangible proof that the evening hadn't been only a very vivid dream.

"Is it too soon?" he asked her after a few minutes.

"No. Really, Bill, it isn't. But you did surprise me. I thought you might want to talk about our future some, but I didn't think you'd jump right in there and ask me." She leaned over and kissed his cheek. "I'm so glad you did."

"Have you thought about when you'd like to get married?"

Okay, she really wasn't ready for that.

"I haven't thought that far ahead," she said. "I mean, Elizabeth and John ought to get to have their wedding first, right? And then we can decide what to do."

"That's fine. Things have moved kind of fast the past couple of days."

"Maybe that makes up for how long it's taken for us to finally get to this point since I moved back to Bird-in-Hand."

"As long as we got here," he said, "I'm good."

"Yeah. Me too."

She'd do better this time around. She wasn't a foolish and naive young girl anymore. She'd learned a lot from her mistakes with Brian. Bill was a totally different kind of man. A good, dependable man, who truly loved her. And she loved him so much more than she had ever thought she loved Brian. He was someone she could be herself around, knowing that, even if she wasn't perfect, his love wouldn't change. She was ready for this.

Wasn't she?

CHAPTER FOUR

Mary was glad Bill took the long way home. She hadn't been quite ready for him to drop her off yet. They stood a long while on the front porch, talking about nothing and everything, and then he finally pulled her closer to him.

"I guess I'd better get on home," he said softly. "Your sisters are going to be wondering where you are."

"I'm sure they know we're out here. Do you want to come in and tell them about us?"

He shrugged and shook his head. "Do you mind if I don't? You can tell them, and then next time I'm here you three will already have gotten through all the questions."

"Coward," she said with a grin.

"Guilty as charged." He leaned down to touch his lips to hers. "Are you going to miss me?"

"Always," she murmured, putting her arms around his waist, still with the box of cheesecake in her hand. "Call me tomorrow?"

"Promise." He kissed her one last time and then stepped back. "Sweet dreams."

"Good night."

She leaned against the porch railing and watched him walk to his car and drive away. Then, with a soft, happy sigh, she went into the house.

As she had promised, Martha was waiting for her. Elizabeth had already gotten home too.

"We were starting to wonder where you were," Elizabeth said, glancing conspicuously at Mary's left hand which was adorned by nothing but her to-go box.

"Now, it's not that late," Mary said, and she reached over to brush away some kind of faint yellowish residue from Martha's sleeve. "What did you get into?"

Martha shrugged and brushed the remainder away. "Who knows? There's always something in the house or the shop that has dust or whatever on it. Now what about your dinner?"

Mary told them about the restaurant and what a good time they had.

"I could have stayed right there and talked all night," she said, "but we decided since it was Valentine's Day and people were waiting for tables, we should go. We went for a drive instead and talked a lot."

"We thought that, after Friday, you might come home with an engagement ring," Martha said knowingly.

Mary kept her expression perfectly innocent. "No, no ring. No more than a partly eaten piece of cheesecake." She opened the little box to show them. "But you should have seen it when they first brought it to the table. It was amazing. Wait, we took pictures."

"You took pictures of your dessert?" Elizabeth asked dubiously.

"Just wait till you see."

She got out her phone, dutifully locked this time, and accessed the pictures Bill had sent her. First she showed them the one that showed her delighted face as she looked at the dessert.

Martha laughed. "I know you've seen cheesecake before."

"Not like this," Mary said, swiping over to the picture that clearly showed the words written on the plate in strawberry glaze.

"Oh!" Martha gasped, her smile a mile wide.

Elizabeth was smiling also. "Mary, you sly thing! You said yes, didn't you?"

"I did. Wasn't he sweet?"

"That's a cute way to ask." Elizabeth looked more closely at the picture. "I would have thought he would do something more traditional. With a ring and everything."

"He said he would have bought a ring, but he thought I'd like to pick it out myself."

Elizabeth nodded. "That's practical."

"And, he didn't say this, but I think he asked me this way so he wouldn't lose his nerve at the last minute. He must have had it all set up ahead of time. I should have guessed something was up when he insisted I have dessert."

"Oh goodness," Martha said. "There's so much to be done, especially with the two of you getting married now."

"No there isn't," Mary said firmly. "Bill and I haven't even talked about a date or anything else. Well, nothing but shopping for rings, but that's all. And neither of us wants to interfere with what Elizabeth wants to do for her wedding."

"You could never interfere." Elizabeth gave her a warm hug. "John and I haven't figured out exactly what we're going to do yet either. We did look at a couple of houses though, just to see what's out there." She winced. "Judging by the prices, the sellers are sure proud of them."

"Ouch," Mary said. "That's something else Bill and I are going to have to discuss before long."

"See?" Martha said. "And of course John and Bill both already have houses, so there's that to consider."

Mary patted her arm. "Give us a day or two to get used to being engaged before we nail down all the details."

"Okay, I won't worry about it if you're not going to. But I'm really happy for you both, and Bill will be the perfect addition to the family."

"Thanks. And I promise if there's anything you can do, I'll let you know right away, okay?"

"Okay."

Mary was showing them the pictures the waiter had taken of her and Bill when her phone rang. She couldn't think who it would be besides Bill. Frowning, she answered anyway.

"Hello?"

"Could I talk to Ken?"

"Who is this?"

"Sorry. I thought maybe—I guess it really is a wrong number. Sorry."

The call ended.

"Who was it?" Elizabeth asked.

"Somebody asking for Ken. I'm sure it was the same guy who called before."

"That's strange."

"You should block his number," Martha advised.

"He was very polite," Mary told her. "More than anything, he sounded kind of desperate. This Ken must be somebody he really wants to get in touch with." She checked the number of the man who had just called then googled it. "Well, I'm not paying to find out who owns a private number, especially since it was probably only a mistake, but the area code is Portland."

"Oregon?" Elizabeth asked.

"Maine. I'm simply not going to worry about it. I'm sure it was a mistake."

"You know how it is," Martha warned. "With cell phones it doesn't necessarily mean that person is calling from that area code or that he lives there."

"I know. But he probably won't call again. Now, come on, Elizabeth. I'm going to get my pajamas on and then I want to hear how your date went."

Once Mary had changed, the three of them chatted until it was late, and then they went to bed.

"Come on, Tink," Mary said, picking up the sleepy dachshund and carrying her up to her room.

While Tinkerbelle snuggled against one of the pillows, Mary stood looking at herself in the mirror. This was the Mary Bill would see more often than not once they were married. No makeup, looking tired and every one of her fifty-plus years at the end of the day. Once the honeymoon was over and they were living their normal lives, would this Mary be enough?

"Don't be silly," she told herself firmly. "Bill's not that way. He's not like Brian."

Over time, Brian had gotten to be more and more critical of her clothes and her hair, of the decisions she made and the things that were important to her.

"Like marriage vows," she muttered to her reflection.

She studied herself again. She didn't look bad for her age, but Bill thought she was beautiful. She smiled at the thought, and her image smiled back at her, and for a moment maybe she was beautiful. Happiness did that to people.

Bill wanted her to be happy. She was sure of that, as sure as she was that she wanted him to be happy too. They were happy together. They were going to be happy together.

She crawled between the cool sheets, tugged the blankets over herself, and pulled Tinkerbelle into her arms. Tink sighed and didn't wake up.

"Dear God," Mary whispered as she began her prayers, "please don't let me mess this up."

The shop was busy the next morning, and Mondays usually weren't, but Elizabeth was glad for the work. Mary seemed almost jittery, but it wasn't unnatural to be a little jittery when you had just made a big decision, especially when you'd made it so quickly. But Elizabeth knew Mary loved Bill and wanted to marry him. They'd work out the rest as they went along. Like she and John would.

She smiled at the thought of her fiancé. She was proud of the work he did as an officer of the East Lampeter Police Department, proud that he did all he could to protect people and help them when they were in trouble. She was looking forward to when they would begin their life together as husband and wife. Through the years, she had sometimes imagined what it would be like to be engaged again and how much fun it would be to get a chance to plan the parties and the showers, the honeymoon and the wedding itself. Her first engagement had come to an end so quickly.

But now that the time to make decisions about those things had come, she realized there was more to it than she had expected. And throwing Mary's engagement into the mix made her hesitate even more. She and John had talked about getting married in the next two or three months, and if that was going to happen, she would definitely have to make up her mind.

"I know you and Bill haven't started making any real plans yet," she said when there was a lull in business right before lunchtime. "But have you two talked about when you might want to get married? I don't mean setting the date or anything, but whether you expect to do it soon or wait awhile or anything."

"Not yet," Mary said as she got herself a cup of coffee. "Sooner rather than later, I think. Why?"

"No reason, except I don't want anything John and I plan to get in the way of what you want to do."

"I thought you two wanted to get married in April or close to that."

"That's what we talked about, but if you would rather have your wedding then, we can move ours back to the summer. Or the fall, if you'd like."

Mary shook her head, her smile indulgent. "What would *you* like? You don't always have to let everybody else have first choice, even if, like the big sister you are, that's what you've always done. Sometimes it's okay to say what you'd prefer."

"I do," Elizabeth said. "But I want you to have what you want too. I think Bill is perfect for you, I want you both to have the wonderful wedding you deserve. You didn't have much of one the first time."

"But you've never had a wedding at all yet," Mary protested. "I know Martha agrees with me that you should have things exactly the way you want them to be. You and John were engaged first. You pick whatever time and place you want. Bill and I won't plan anything that will interfere. Besides, we haven't even picked out rings yet. We're way behind you and John."

Elizabeth sighed and got her own cup of coffee. "But there's so much to consider. Who to invite and who might be upset if they aren't invited. Where to have the wedding and how much to spend. I don't want to leave anyone out who wants to be there, but sometimes I think something small and intimate with just our immediate families would be lovely too."

"What does John think?"

"He's not being any help at all. He says he wants me to have whatever I want."

Mary grinned. "How selfish of him."

"Very funny. You know what I mean."

"I think it's very considerate of him. You've never been married before. You should have the kind of wedding you want. I can't see you doing anything really crazy anyway. Isn't there anything you've ever dreamed of for your wedding?"

"I don't know. Anything elaborate seems kind of silly at my age."

"Not if that's what you want," Mary said stubbornly.

"And anything elaborate would cost a lot of money that we could use on something more practical and long lasting."

"True."

"And I'm not really wild about having something that's all about me," Elizabeth said. "Like I was some kind of bridezilla."

Mary laughed. "I don't think you could be a bridezilla if you tried. Really, you should do whatever makes you happy. I know Martha and I will go along with whatever you want. But don't ask us to dye our hair strange colors or expect us to have nothing but rice cakes and water for the month leading up to the wedding."

"Don't worry about that," Elizabeth assured her. "But I suppose, if John and I are going to get married in a couple of months, I really should start making actual plans."

"Probably. Depending on how fancy you want to get. A simple wedding at the church could probably be planned in a few days."

"Not if your kids and Martha's are going to come. They'll have to make travel plans and everything. And if they're in the wedding, they'll have to get clothes. That's a lot of money to spend, especially including the grandchildren."

Mary had two children and only one grandbaby, a little boy, but Martha's three kids had five children between them. It would be expensive getting them all to Bird-in-Hand.

"But you know they'd all want to come see Aunt Elizabeth get married."

"And then they'd have to turn around and do it all again when you have your wedding," Elizabeth said. "I want them to come, of course. All of them. And I'm sure they'd want to come too, but I hate to make them feel like they have to come. I feel like it's a lot to ask, and everybody seems to be a little short on cash these days."

"You're right," Mary said. "It would be easier if everybody lived close. Maybe when you get married, we could have a nice little party for me and Bill too, so people won't have to come back for our wedding."

"That doesn't seem fair to you two." Elizabeth sighed. "See what I mean? I can't just do what I want and not consider everyone else, especially you and Bill."

"Maybe we should have waited," Mary said. "To tell people we were engaged, I mean. Really, this should be your special time, and I'm stepping right in the middle of it."

"No you're not," Elizabeth assured her. "You don't have to put your life on hold because I'm getting married in a couple of months. That's exactly the kind of bride I don't want to be."

"We can keep our engagement between you and me and Martha, if you'd like."

"You can't keep this from Michael and Jennifer," Elizabeth said. "Haven't you already told them?"

Mary grinned. "I haven't yet. It was pretty late by the time we went to bed last night, so I decided to wait until after dinner tonight to call them. I mean, a mom can't just text her kids and say she's getting married."

"You could send them that picture of your cheesecake," Elizabeth teased. "They'd get the idea."

Mary laughed. "That ought to get me a call back at any rate."

"At least Bill doesn't have any kids he has to take into consideration."

"John's kids like you. I know they do."

"I know," Elizabeth said. "And I want to make sure they keep on liking me, especially Tina. I don't want her to feel like she's being left out of any of these decisions. It'll probably feel at least a little awkward for her when we're all living together, and I want to make sure I don't do anything to make that any harder than it has to be."

She liked Tina and knew how hard it must have been for her to lose her mother when she was so young. She didn't want to make her feel like she was losing her father too. Jonathan was older, in college already, and more prepared to be on his own. But Tina still needed her dad, and Elizabeth didn't want to be thought of as a rival.

"You ought to talk to John about that," Mary suggested. "Or maybe the three of you should talk."

"Maybe Tina and I should spend a little more time together, just the two of us. Maybe lunch and some shopping or something. This is going to be a big change for everybody, and I want us all to be on the same side."

"You're sweet, Lizzie, and so is Tina. I'm sure you'll work everything out. But just because you have some things the way you want them, that doesn't mean you're a bridezilla. You're going to be a bride. That means it's your day."

"And John's."

"And John's," Mary agreed. "And, plain or fancy, you should have it exactly the way you want it to be."

"Well, the way I want it to be is for as many people to be happy about it as possible."

"Then I'm sure you and John will figure it all out. And you know Martha is just dying to help you with whatever plans you make."

"Speaking of Martha, do you think she's really okay?"

"She says she is." Mary put her hand on Elizabeth's arm. "Do you think something's wrong?"

"I'm not sure. She seems fine, but it's not like her to sleep so much and still seem tired during the day. I know she's stayed up at all hours before when she particularly wants to get something done and then been tired the next day. But it's not usual for her to be tired after she's gone to bed early."

"Maybe she should see a doctor just to be sure."

"I suggested that. She reminded me she had her annual physical not very long ago and that everything was good. She even offered to let me look over her test results."

Mary bit her lip. "I hope I'm wrong, but you don't think she's upset because we're both about to be married, do you? I mean, because she doesn't have anyone."

"No. Martha's not the jealous type."

"I don't think she'd be jealous, but maybe she feels sad. You know, left out."

"No." Elizabeth smiled. "You heard what she said. She's happy for us to have what she had with Chuck. Maybe she misses him a little, but she would no matter what we did or didn't do. No, I think she's happy exactly the way she is. Do you think she looks unhappy?"

"No, not at all. She's buzzing around as usual, and I know she's eager to get on with planning whatever wedding festivities we want." Mary hugged Elizabeth suddenly. "And so am I."

"You're both wonderful. And as soon as I make up my mind, I promise to put you both to work. For now—"

At that moment, the shop door opened. Mary put on a cordial smile.

"Hello, Dan. Is there something I can help you with this morning?"

CHAPTER FIVE

Good morning." Dan gave Mary and Elizabeth both a very charming smile. "You were so busy when Eli and I were in here before, we never did get what we were looking for."

Mary remembered the two brothers had been in the shop looking around on Saturday morning, and then she hadn't seen them anymore. Had they been behind the counter? Surely Eli wouldn't be in on such a thing. It was impossible to know for sure. Still, she had her phone back. Nothing had come of it being…misplaced.

"We were pretty busy that day," she said. "What was it you were looking for?"

Some other customers came into the shop right then, and Elizabeth excused herself to go help them.

"Eli told me he talked *Daed* into making some hand-carved pieces for sale," Dan said, "and that they had brought some here."

"Yes, they brought in several things a while back. Most of what we have like that is over here."

Mary walked him to the table that held carved toys and boxes and other decorative items.

"We didn't see any of his work when we were looking around before," he said.

"I'd have to check our records to tell you who made each of these, but if you'd like—"

"No, that's all right. Even after all this time, I'd know one of his if I saw it. I don't see any of his here."

"We have moved things around some in the past couple of weeks. We wanted to try some new arrangements and just freshen up the place," Mary told him. "It could be that something of your dad's got moved out of this area or to the back. Why don't we look around?"

"Thanks." Dan followed her as she walked. "You left Bird-in-Hand for quite a while too, right? Was it hard for you to come back?"

"I came back when my mother died. I don't imagine that I'll ever leave again."

He sighed. "Yeah, but you're Englischers."

The way he pronounced the last word betrayed his Amish heritage. It was definitely different for those who had been raised in the Amish church and in the Amish way of life. Since Dan had never joined the church, he wasn't shunned by the Amish community. But not joining the church, not staying in Bird-in-Hand and working the family farm as Eli did, had clearly left a rift between father and son, and even between brother and brother.

"Whether or not you come back for good," Mary told him, "I don't think you'll be sorry you tried to reconnect with your family."

"I hope that Daed will give me a chance. Eli is trying."

"That's a start."

They didn't find what Dan was looking for where Mary thought it would be.

"Would you like to come into the back and see if there's anything there? As I said, we've been doing some rearranging, and it's possible that something of your father's ended up there."

"If it's okay, yeah," Dan said. "Thanks."

They looked around in the back and still found nothing.

"I'm sorry," Mary told him after they had gone through a box of assorted items from the top of a crowded shelf. "We must have sold it all. Maybe if you asked your father—"

Dan shook his head, a touch of regret in his smile. "When I moved out, I deliberately left behind the things he had carved especially for me. Now I wish I still had them. He's not so old that he couldn't make more, of course."

Not much older than I am, Mary thought, hiding her own smile.

"But nobody's guaranteed any particular lifespan," he continued. "I just thought that, in case we can't work things out just now, I'd like to have something of his, made for me or not."

"You don't think he brought us anything that was yours to sell, do you?"

Dan shrugged. "I'm not sure. It's been so long, all that stuff could have been out of the house years ago. Then again, knowing Daed, maybe not. I haven't had the courage to ask yet. Actually, I haven't done anything but make small talk with him at the funeral and then the one time we've eaten dinner together. I did go to church with him and Eli yesterday."

"That's a start."

"It just reminded me how much I hated sitting that long on those backless benches."

"That can be a challenge," Mary said with a low laugh, all the while wondering what it was about him that made her wonder if he was exactly who he said he was.

"Anyway, I appreciate you taking the time to look back here."

"Sorry we couldn't find what you were looking for. If anything turns up, one of us will get in touch with you. Are you staying at your dad's?"

He shook his head. "I don't think either of us is ready for that. I've got a room at a B and B in town. It's not far from the farm. Who knows? Maybe I won't have to keep it long. Anyway, thanks for trying to help."

He gave her a little wave and walked back into the front part of the shop. She stayed behind for a moment so she could put the box back up on the shelf it had come from. When she left the back room, she was startled to see Dan up at the front counter talking to Katura. Elizabeth and Verity were on the other side of the store chatting and laughing, evidently discussing the handmade quilted items they had there and the quilting group that met at the store every Thursday. Elizabeth had really gotten good at her hand quilting, and she was always eager to interest everyone else in it too.

There were several other customers in the store now, so Mary didn't immediately go over to Dan and Katura, but she did wonder what they might be talking about. Katura hadn't seemed very friendly when Dan was around her before. Of course, she had never been very outgoing in the first place, but

222222222222

he had seemed to be watching her when everyone was gathered after the funeral.

Mary kept a discreet eye on them from where she was. She couldn't tell what they were saying, but it was definitely in English and not in Pennsylvania Dutch. It was also very intense, almost as if they were very quietly arguing.

"Katura!" Verity said from across the room.

Then she said something in Pennsylvania Dutch, and motioned with her hand.

"Ja," Katura said, and with another low word to Dan, she went over to where Elizabeth and Verity were standing.

Elizabeth looked at Dan inquiringly, and then, smiling, she started talking to the two girls about the quilting circle and how much fun the ladies seemed to have every week.

"I didn't know you two were friends," Mary said, coming up to Dan.

Dan shrugged. "We're not really. She was already in Bird-in-Hand when I came to the funeral on Friday. Does she come here often?"

"Not very often. I think this is only the second time since she's been in Bird-in-Hand."

"Pretty much stays home?" Dan asked. "Not a lot of friends?"

"I don't know," Mary said, not sure what he was getting at. "I've never seen her with anyone but the Shetlers, or at least Verity. But she seemed to be having a lively discussion with you just now."

"Yeah, well." Dan chuckled and shrugged. "I just thought I'd ask how the family was doing now that Bertha is gone.

Evidently Katura was very attached to her. She didn't feel much like talking about her just now."

"That was thoughtful of you anyway," Mary said, though it seemed more logical that he would have addressed that question to Verity rather than Katura. "I'll be on the lookout for anything your father made. Is there anything else I can do for you?"

He gave her that charming smile again, and his dark eyes were warm. "Thank you. That's it. I remember this place from when I was growing up. Nice to see you back in business."

"My sisters and I are happy to be here together again. Tell your father and brother hello for us."

"I will." Dan waved at Elizabeth and Verity and Katura as he went to the door. "Take care."

Mary went over to Elizabeth and the two girls. "Hello, you two. When are you going to come paint with me, Katura?"

Katura blinked at her. "Uh, yes, we must do that soon. For now, I am sorry, we must go. I will come back when I have more time. Will that be all right?"

"Sure. Whenever you have a chance. I'll be looking forward to it."

Katura hurried Verity out of the shop. Neither of them bought anything.

"That was odd," Elizabeth said when Mary came over to her, keeping her voice low so none of the customers overheard her.

"It was," Mary said. "I think Katura seems nervous around Dan, and that makes me nervous. I took him into the back to look for anything his father made, and then when he left, I stopped for a minute to put some things back where they belonged. When I came out, he was talking to Katura. I didn't even know she was in the store."

"She and Verity came in because Katura wanted to talk to you about painting, and Verity is curious about the quilting group."

"It seemed to me that Dan and Katura were arguing about something. I didn't want to outright listen in. Okay, I *did* want to listen in, but I knew that wasn't right, so I made myself stay where I was, but I could tell by their body language and the tone of voice they were both using that it wasn't a casual conversation. I don't know what the two of them would have to argue about. They're practically strangers."

Mary picked up her coffee cup, took a sip, and immediately put it back down. "Ugh. Cold. Anyway, I'm wondering about Katura now. I never have heard where she's from specifically. I hope she'll come paint with me. She seemed excited about it when we talked after the funeral."

"Maybe Verity will come quilt with us on Thursday and bring Katura along. That will give us an opportunity to get to know them both better."

Their conversation was ended when a large party of tourists came into the shop. Mary and Elizabeth helped them find what they were looking for, but that was only the start of another busy afternoon. Mary sighed when the phone rang at exactly five o'clock.

"We're closed," she told the phone, but she put warmth into her voice when she answered it. "Secondhand Blessings. This is Mary. How can I help you?"

"You can come have dinner with me."

She couldn't help smiling. "Hi, Bill."

Elizabeth grinned and resumed her sweeping.

"Hi, sweetie," Bill said. "What do you think?"

"I'd love to go, as long as you don't think you're spoiling me taking me out every night."

"Well, I'm sorry to say this dinner probably won't be as posh as the one last night. You won't mind too much, will you?"

"Not at all. A burger would be fine as long as I get to see you."

"I knew you were the right girl for me. But besides dinner, I was wondering if you wanted to go ahead and look at some rings. Or would you rather wait?"

Mary hesitated until she saw Elizabeth was locking up the shop.

"You want to hear my guilty secret?" she asked Bill.

"What's that?"

"I was looking at engagement rings online earlier today."

"Did you see anything you like?"

"Well, I decided I definitely don't want anything big and flashy."

"I kind of thought you'd feel that way."

"What do you think about wedding bands? Or would you rather not wear one?"

"I absolutely want one," he told her. "But, again, nothing elaborate. Something solid and uncomplicated."

Solid and uncomplicated. Just like him.

"That's what I was thinking too. I saw some really pretty ones on the website for a place in Lancaster. I can show it to you when you come get me. They're really classic looking and simple. Something that will never go out of style. That's what I want for my engagement ring too."

"I like it. I like it a lot. So what time would you like to go?"

"If I don't have to dress up," she told him, "you can come over whenever you want. I'll be here. We're closing up the shop right now. Oh, and I need to drop Elizabeth's pictures by Cindy Martin's on the way, if you don't mind taking a quick detour."

"No problem. I'll be there as soon as I get cleaned up a little so you can stand to be in the same room with me."

She giggled. "Have you been working hard?"

"Nope. I've been useless all day, just thinking about this cute little blond I know."

"I guess you'd better come over and tell me about her then," she said. "So I can let you know whether or not I approve of her."

"You'll love her," he said earnestly. "I promise."

"And how do you know that?"

"Because I do. See you in a little bit."

Before she could say anything more, he was gone.

After a few seconds, Elizabeth came up to her.

"You can stop smiling now."

Mary ducked her head and felt the warmth rise to her cheeks. "He's so sweet. Oh, that was Bill, by the way."

"Yeah, I kind of figured out that part. How is he?"

"He's wonderful."

"Ah," Elizabeth said wisely. "Young love."

That made Mary laugh. "We're going to go eat and then look at rings."

"Oh, that sounds fun. Do you know what you want?"

Mary told Elizabeth about her online shopping as they finished locking up and walked back to the house. As soon as they stepped inside, Mary heard Martha's bedroom door open and close.

"Home already?" Martha called from upstairs.

"It's not much of a commute," Mary called back.

"Sorry." Martha padded swiftly down the stairs. "I guess I lost track of the time." She pushed a wayward piece of hair behind her ear and brushed thread from her blouse. "I haven't even thought about dinner yet. Any suggestions?"

Elizabeth gave Mary a "see what I mean" glance, and Mary had to admit to herself that it was unusual for Martha to not have everything at least planned out for dinner by now on the days she didn't work at the shop.

"Bill and I are going ring shopping," Mary said quickly, "so we'll grab something while we're out. Do you want us to bring you something?"

"No, that's all right," Martha said. "You'll probably be out a while."

"Why don't I make something simple?" Elizabeth suggested. "How about grilled cheese sandwiches and tomato soup?"

"That sounds quick and easy," Martha said, looking relieved. "And good for a cold night. That would be great, if you don't mind."

"You deserve a night off."

"No more than anybody else, but I'll be glad to have one. You know, maybe you and John should have dinner together too."

"We just did that last night," Elizabeth protested.

"Well, you're going to have to get used to that eventually anyway," Martha said with a grin.

Just then Elizabeth's phone rang.

"Excuse me," Elizabeth said, glancing at the number, and then she answered. "Hi, John." She started chuckling as he talked. "All right. No, not at all. I think that's a great idea. We just closed up the shop." She listened again. "Okay. Bye."

Mary and Martha looked at her expectantly.

"Looks like you get your wish, Martha," Elizabeth said. "Tina ended up going to work on a school project with one of her friends, and John doesn't want the lasagna going to waste, so he invited me over. Do you want to come along?"

"Oh, John would enjoy that, wouldn't he?"

"I'm sure he'd love to see you."

Martha gave her a look. "You go on and have a good time. I enjoyed my quiet evening last night, and I'm sure I'll enjoy this one. I'm a big girl now. I'll be fine. And I can make my own sandwich too."

By the time Mary freshened her hair and makeup, Bill was there to pick her up. Elizabeth walked out the front door with them on the way to get into her car.

"Why do I think Martha wants us both out of the house?" she asked once the door was shut behind them.

"Because that's basically what she said?" Mary asked.

Bill chuckled.

"Elizabeth," Mary said, stopping for a moment, "she looked fine. She seemed like she was in a good mood, and she certainly doesn't look sick. I'm sure if there was something wrong, she'd tell us about it."

Elizabeth didn't look quite certain.

"I tell you what, I'll talk to her after Bill brings me back tonight. How would that be?"

"You can try, I guess. Maybe you'll have better luck than I did."

"Or it could just be nothing," Mary said. "Now don't worry. Everybody needs a little time alone once in a while. We'd all get cabin fever if we never talked to anybody but each other."

"All right. You two have a good time. Pick out something pretty."

"I will," Mary said. "You and John have a good dinner. See you in a little while."

Elizabeth got into her car and drove away, and Bill and Mary were right behind her.

"Is Martha okay?" Bill asked as he and Mary drove toward Lancaster.

"I think so. Elizabeth thinks she's been a little tired lately, but Martha says it's nothing. She has been going to her room a little earlier than usual most nights, and she seems to really like it when she has the house to herself."

"Maybe she's just getting ready to be on her own again. You and Elizabeth will both be moving out before too much longer."

"I suppose. I don't like the idea of leaving her alone, but it doesn't seem to bother her at all. And I expect we'll all still be working at the shop, so we'll still see each other a lot."

"That'll be good." He took advantage of a stoplight and leaned over to kiss her. "What would you like for dinner?"

"How hungry are you?"

"Not a whole lot yet, but I will be. What about you?"

"I think I'm too excited for food right now. Do you think we could go to the jewelry store first and then eat?"

"I don't know why not."

It didn't take long for them to get to the jewelry store. Mary was a little bit dazzled by the enormous selection of rings and then the seemingly infinite number of diamond solitaires that could be set into them. They finally settled on plain gold wedding bands with a short inscription inside each.

The engagement ring looked good with the wedding rings. It was made of two slender gold bands twined together, simple and elegant, with a setting that let the diamond nestle between them. The diamond itself was brilliant and clear, not ostentatious but very good quality and decently priced. It was exactly what she wanted.

"Are you hungry now?" Bill asked her when they left the jeweler's hand in hand.

"I think so. I'm still a little overwhelmed. Do you like the rings?"

"I think they're great," he assured her, not for the first time. "I didn't want anything flashy, and those are just right. Are you sure you didn't want a bigger diamond?"

"Absolutely," she told him. "What I got is just perfect. I just wish I could wear it home tonight."

He smiled and opened the car door for her and then got behind the wheel. "It won't take long for them to size it and set the diamond. And you'll have a long, long time to wear it after that."

"Thank you," she said, leaning over to kiss his cheek as he started the engine. "It's just perfect."

"I'm glad you like it. Now where to? Anything in particular you're hungry for?"

They finally settled on a casual seafood place off the highway. There was a short wait, and they sat side by side on one end of a bench.

"How long did they say it'd be?" Mary asked, taking off her coat.

Bill glanced at his watch. "Five or ten minutes. Is that okay? Or would you like to try somewhere else?"

"No, that's fine, and I doubt anyplace else will be any better right now." She gave him her coat to hold. "I just wanted to make sure I had time to go to the ladies' room."

"I'm sure you do. I'll be right here."

With directions from the hostess, Mary made her way to the farthest corner of the restaurant, past the kitchen and down a long hallway. When she got back to the waiting area a few minutes later, Bill was still sitting on the end of the bench, but a tall redhead had taken the place beside him.

CHAPTER SIX

Mary froze for a moment where she was. Bill hadn't noticed her yet. The redhead hadn't noticed anything but Bill. She was smiling a lot and leaning toward him. Mary couldn't help feeling some satisfaction to see that, while he was listening to her and nodding, his smile was only polite. She was talking to him, but he didn't seem to really be talking to her.

"Did they call our table yet?" Mary asked when she was a few feet away from them.

He gave Mary an apologetic, almost relieved smile and stood up. "I figure we'll be getting our table in a couple of minutes. You go ahead and sit down until we're called."

She sat down in Bill's place, and the redhead looked slightly pained.

"He didn't tell me he had a friend."

Mary smiled faintly and wished again that she already had her engagement ring.

"Anyway," the redhead said, looking up at Bill, "I'm just meeting a couple of girlfriends for dinner, but I don't really have to stay long, you know, if you wanted to get together for dessert."

"No," Bill said politely. "Thanks all the same."

The hostess told them their table was ready, and Bill gave the redhead a cordial nod. "You and your friends have a nice dinner."

The hostess seated them in a corner booth, took their drink order, and told them their waiter would be with them shortly. As soon as she was gone, Bill reached across the table for Mary's hand.

"I'm sorry about that out front."

She smiled at him. "She was kind of pushy, wasn't she?"

"I was just trying to be polite when she sat down and started talking to me, but she did come on pretty strong. And I did tell her I was with someone. She just decided not to hear that part."

"Don't worry about it, Bill. Really. I know what kind of man you are, and I trust you. If I didn't, we wouldn't have been shopping for rings just now."

He chuckled. "I guess not. And I guess I'd be pretty stupid to start something with a woman like that—like I could ever be interested in a woman like that—when I knew you'd be back in less than five minutes. Now, what are we having?"

The waiter, a tall young man with bleached blond hair, brought them water and menus and recommended the stuffed flounder. They took his recommendation and added green salads, baked potatoes, and steamed broccoli.

"So tell me how your day was," Bill said when they were alone with their drinks.

"Actually, I was meaning to tell you about that. Dan Bontrager came into the shop again. He said he was looking for anything his father might have carved and then put into the shop for sale."

"I know Jedidiah's a woodcarver. I didn't know he sold his stuff."

"Not a huge amount," Mary said. "But he's brought stuff to us once in a while. Elizabeth said Dan sounded like he wanted to patch things up. I know you said he didn't want to be a farmer or stay in the Amish community, but I'm wondering if there was more. Did he and his father have a real falling out?"

"I can't say what might have happened between them in private, of course, but I never heard anything more than that. Any Amish father is going to be disappointed and upset to see his son openly reject the culture he was raised in and not join the church. They haven't exactly been in touch from what I've heard, but maybe Dan can salvage some kind of a relationship with him and with Eli."

"Dan and Eli were in the shop Saturday, so maybe they're making some headway together."

"That's good to know," Bill said, and then he frowned. "What?"

"What do you mean, 'what'?"

"You suddenly looked, I don't know, suspicious or something. Why?"

Mary shrugged. "It's just that when Dan was in the store today, Katura and Verity came in too. Dan and I were in the back, looking to see if anything his father made had gotten put back there. We didn't find anything, and I stayed behind another minute or so to put away one of the boxes we'd taken down. When I came back into the shop, he and Katura were by the front counter talking."

"And?"

"Well, from what I could tell where I was, they seemed to be arguing. At least they were talking low and fast, and Katura looked upset. I don't know what the two of them would have to argue about."

"That does seem strange, unless they've met before. I've never heard of anybody who knows much about Katura," Bill said. "Have you ever just come right out and asked about her?"

"I haven't wanted to be pushy. I did ask Iris about her when Katura first came to live with them. All she said was that Katura was going through a difficult time and wanted to keep to herself. I thought we had connected some over her painting, and she really is a good artist, but she seems to clam up when Dan's around."

"Has Dan done anything in particular that makes you suspicious?"

"Just her reaction to him. I know Katura is old enough to be on her own, but she's still very young. Too young, if you ask me, for someone Dan's age."

"Well, Dan's not old by any means, but you're right about him being too old for Katura. Not just age wise. Katura's got to be what? Eighteen? Twenty?"

"I'd guess about that, though as shy as she is, she seems younger. That's really what bothers me about Dan being interested in her."

"Are you sure he is?" Bill asked. "I guess there are different kinds of interest."

"True, but apart from the obvious, what kind of interest could he have in her? I can't imagine what they'd have to argue about unless he was being too forward with her."

Bill frowned. "That doesn't seem much like Dan Bontrager. Granted, I didn't spend a lot of time with him when he lived in Bird-in-Hand, but he did work for me. And word gets around, especially in a small town like ours." He considered for a minute. "Where was Verity when this happened? When I was at the Shetlers', she seemed to be doing most of the talking for both of them."

"She and Elizabeth were on the other side of the store talking. Usually Verity and Katura stick close together when they're in public, like Verity is looking out for Katura for some reason. Of course, Dan and I were in the back when they came in, so they didn't know he was there at all."

"I don't know what she and Dan could have been talking about, but it's probably—"

Bill stopped short when the hostess came by their table. Behind her was the redhead from the front of the restaurant along with two other women, presumably the friends she had been waiting for. The redhead gave Bill a little wave but walked on without slowing down.

Bill shook his head when she was gone. "Mary, I—"

"I know. I know." She smiled even though seeing that woman again definitely rankled. "You can't help it if you're irresistible."

He shook his head, chuckling. "Anyway, I don't know what Katura and Dan could have been talking about or even arguing about, but they're adults. If Katura was in trouble, there was a store full of people right there."

"You're right about them being adults. I don't exactly think Katura is in danger or anything. But it feels...uncomfortable to me. Like they knew each other before she came to Bird-in-Hand."

"He didn't act that way at the funeral."

"No," she admitted, puzzled, and then she smiled at him. "Did you have an interesting day?"

He shrugged. "Just a normal workday, I guess. The most exciting thing that happened, up until I called you, of course, was I got a wrong number call from Utah. Probably just misdialed."

"That's funny. I got another one—from the same person as before. Both of them from Portland, Maine."

"How do you know that?"

"After the second one, I was curious and looked it up. The number was private, but the area code was Portland."

"They weren't from somebody named Carlisle, were they?" he asked with a grin.

"Carlisle?"

"You've heard about that big murder trial that's about to start in Portland, haven't you? The rich guy, Carlisle?"

"Oh yeah. He killed his girlfriend."

"So they say. I feel bad for the woman's family, and I feel bad for the guy's wife. I read that he lost his wedding ring at the scene, or at least he lost it somewhere. He couldn't account for it to the police."

Mary raised her eyebrows. "Maybe he typically took it off when he and his girlfriend were, um, visiting."

"His wife must be devastated."

"True. It's bad all the way around, especially with him saying he's never going to be convicted. I wouldn't want to be on that jury."

"I know what you mean," Bill said. "Supposedly he's not just rich, he's got connections to the underworld. I'm surprised he killed that woman himself when it would have been easier to pay to have it done."

"Maybe it was a spur-of-the-moment thing," she said.

"Guess so."

She shuddered. "I'd rather not talk about something that sad tonight. I'd rather talk about us getting married."

"Me too," he said, reaching over to take her hand.

The waiter brought their meals and refilled their drinks, and the conversation turned to more commonplace things. As she ate, Mary thought how nice it would be to spend every evening with Bill just sharing the events of the day and enjoying each other's company. She forced herself to not think about the red-haired woman anymore. Bill was clearly not interested.

She took a bite of her fish, scolding herself. Bill wasn't Brian. She knew that. She was over Brian. He didn't matter now.

"Is your food good?" Bill asked her.

She nodded, forcing her expression into more pleasant lines. "Delicious. I don't usually like to cook fish at home because it tends to be smelly, but I love it when someone else cooks it."

"I'll remember that. And, speaking of remembering things, you remember we're going out tomorrow night too, right?"

"I haven't forgotten. I'm looking forward to it. But you're going to have to let me fix dinner for us to make up for all the times we've gone out lately."

"Sometime," he said. "Tomorrow, we'd better go someplace. You're going to be dressed up, and I'm sure you don't want to cook in your nice clothes or mess up your hair and makeup."

"Okay, that's true. I don't mind where we go as long as we're together. But if this keeps up, my sisters are going to start asking who I am when I come into the house."

"Tinkerbelle will vouch for you."

She smiled to herself as the meal went on, enjoying his company as she had for so long, finding it better because she knew they were going to be married. She reminded herself that Elizabeth's wedding came first. Once she'd had her special day, however she wanted it to be, then Mary could focus on her own. Right now, she was enjoying just being engaged to Bill.

"I couldn't eat one more bite," she said, finally setting down her fork.

He ate the last bite of his fish. "I won't insist on dessert this time."

The waiter came to the table right on cue. "Is there anything else I can get for you?"

"Just the check, please," Bill said.

"Yes, sir."

The waiter took the bill from his book and set it on the table. Then, looking faintly embarrassed, he added something else.

"The lady in the corner asked me to give this to you for her."

It was a business card with the phone number circled and CALL ME WHEN YOU'VE GOT A FREE EVENING! written across it in bold letters. Bill glanced in the direction the waiter indicated. Mary didn't have to. It was from that redhead, she was sure. What nerve the woman had.

Bill gave Mary a sly wink, and then gave the waiter his credit card. When the waiter came back and gave him a pen to sign for the meal, he did so. Then he used the pen to jot something down on the business card. When he was through he handed it back to the waiter with a little extra in cash.

"See the lady gets the card, will you?"

"Yes, sir. Thank you. I hope you both have a good evening."

"Thanks."

Bill stood up and helped Mary with her coat as she stood. Then they walked past the table in the corner and out of the restaurant.

"What did you write on the card?" she asked, pulling her collar tighter around her neck.

He chuckled and put his arm around her, blocking the bitter night wind. "I just put 'My evenings are booked for the rest of my life. Thanks anyway.'" He pulled her suddenly into his arms. "Oh, you don't know how nice it is to be able to say that, especially when you're the one I'll be spending my evenings with. I don't know anything about that woman, and I sure don't know why she decided to pick on me."

"She knows a good catch when she sees one." Mary leaned up to kiss his cheek and then shivered. "You're cold. Come on."

They scurried to the car and got inside. It didn't take long to get back home.

"Would you like to come in for a while?" she asked when he took her to the door.

"I left the engine running. We're going to be out late tomorrow night, so I'd better get going now."

He wrapped her in his arms, and she felt warm from head to toe. Then he kissed her and she felt even warmer.

"Talk to you tomorrow," she murmured, keeping her eyes closed for one last long moment.

"Tomorrow," he breathed against her cheek, and then, touching his lips once more to hers, he sprinted to his car and drove away.

Mary was smiling when she let herself into the house. She heard somebody scrambling around upstairs, and then a door opened.

"Elizabeth?"

"No, Martha," Mary called up to her. "It's me."

"Oh, thank goodness."

Martha came partway down the stairs, looking flustered and covered with more than her share of bits of thread.

"Martha," Mary said, trying not to laugh. "What are you doing?"

"Can you keep a secret?"

"Sure. But—"

"I mean it. You can't tell anybody at all, and especially not Elizabeth."

Mary went to the foot of the stairs, shedding her coat as she went. "I promise. What's going on?"

"Come up." Martha waved her up impatiently. "Hurry."

Mary hurried.

"Did you pick out rings?" Martha asked before Mary got to her.

"Yes. They're being sized and everything, but I have pictures."

"Okay." Martha grabbed Mary's arm and hurried her toward her bedroom. "I'm dying to see, but it'll have to wait for when Elizabeth gets home. For now—"

She opened the door, pulled Mary inside, and shut it again. Mary was surprised to see Martha's usually neat bed covered with fabric and spools of threads and sewing supplies.

"What are you doing? You don't usually sew up here."

"I'm making this."

She held up a piece of a quilt block, and Mary recognized it as the very intricate double wedding ring pattern. The interlocking rings that gave the pattern its name were made up of very small pieces that had to be put together precisely in order for everything to match up right.

"You're not doing that by hand, are you?" Mary asked her.

Martha nodded. "I started it when Elizabeth got engaged, and I wanted to do it all by hand, piecing and quilting. But it's taken me much longer than I thought it would. She's going to get married in a couple of months, and I've been coming up here every spare minute I have trying to catch up."

Mary let out a long breath. "And all this time she's been afraid you're sick or something. I was a little worried too. It's not like you to go to bed early or be tired during the day."

"I haven't gone to bed early at all. I've just come up here after dinner so I could try to get more of this quilt pieced. And if I'm tired during the day, it's because I've been staying up late working on it."

"Maybe you'd better tell her what you've been doing," Mary suggested. "It would be better than making her worry about you."

"I told her not to worry. I told her she could look at the report from my last physical. It's really important to me to make this for her and to get it to her on time."

"But, Martha, hand quilting? I didn't know you could do that. And it's a really slow process. You know how Elizabeth's struggled to get the hang of it."

Martha sighed. "I know. And, to be honest, I've just about given up on that part of it. I guess I could hand quilt it once the top is ready, but I probably wouldn't be very happy with the results. Rachel said she and her friends would be happy to quilt it as a present for Elizabeth."

Mary clasped her hands together. Rachel and the other Amish ladies were experts at hand quilting.

"Oh, that would be wonderful. They do a beautiful job."

"Of course, they couldn't work on it on Thursdays when they meet at the shop, but Rachel said they could arrange to meet privately at a different time, so Elizabeth wouldn't know."

"Right," Mary said, "but please let them do it. With a whole group of them working, they ought to be able to finish it up before the wedding." She thought for a moment. "On the other hand, why couldn't they work on it on Thursdays in the shop? Elizabeth wouldn't have to know it's for her. They could just say someone asked them to quilt it. A lot of their work is by commission."

"That wouldn't work. That wouldn't work at all."

"But why not? Elizabeth wouldn't think anything of it. Lots of people make wedding ring quilts. Just because she's getting married, that doesn't mean she'll assume it's for her."

"She'll assume about this one." Martha held up one of the blocks she was working on. "What do you see?"

Mary looked, puzzled for a moment, and then realization dawned. "Oh, those are scraps from Mama's things."

Martha nodded. "When we cleared out her closets and drawers last summer, I found several things that were in such bad condition we couldn't even donate them. But they had parts where the fabric was still good. I cut off the buttons for the button jar and cut out the best parts of the fabric to save."

"Good idea."

"Then Elizabeth and John got engaged, and I was trying to think of something special to do for them, and I thought this was perfect, especially in the double wedding ring pattern."

"It is," Mary said, admiring the beautiful way Martha had put together the different colors and patterns, and how each of them was a memory of Mama. "But how in the world did you think you could get this done by the time Elizabeth and John get married?"

Martha sighed. "I was overly optimistic?"

Mary hugged her. "Maybe a little bit. But it's a wonderful idea. Hey, why don't you ask Rachel if she and the other ladies would help you with the piecing too? If each one of them did a few blocks, it would come together really quickly, wouldn't it?"

Martha shook her head. "Then it really wouldn't be something I made her, would it? I guess I can consider farming out the actual quilting, but I want to put together the top for Elizabeth. Myself. You understand, right?"

"I do. Really. But if you can't—"

Mary broke off as the front door opened and closed. She and Martha froze where they were, looking guiltily at each other.

"That has to be Elizabeth," Martha whispered, "but she usually says something when she comes in."

"I'll go see," Mary said. "You'd better get all this put away."

Martha began gathering up her quilt blocks and sewing supplies.

Mary went to the top of the stairs. "Is that you, Lizzie?"

"Yes."

That was Elizabeth's voice, but it sounded strained, almost choked.

Mary hurried down the stairs and found Elizabeth still at the front door, taking off her coat and gloves. She wasn't crying, but she looked as if she might have been. Her face was pale despite the redness the winter weather had put into her nose and cheeks.

"Elizabeth? What is it?"

Elizabeth gave her an unconvincing smile. "Tina hates me."

CHAPTER SEVEN

W hat?" Mary gasped.

"What's wrong?" Martha asked as she hurried down to them.

Elizabeth just stared at her sisters, for a moment too stunned to say anything. Then she finally let herself sink onto the couch. Martha and Mary sat down beside her.

"Tell us," Martha urged.

Elizabeth squeezed her eyes shut. She'd promised herself she wasn't going to cry over this, but she wasn't quite sure she was going to be able to keep that promise.

Mary put an arm around her shoulders. "What happened? I can't believe Tina would say something like that. I know you two haven't had a chance to spend a huge amount of time together, but you have spent some time together, and she seems to really like you. She seems happy for you and John."

"Tina wouldn't say something like what?" Martha asked.

Elizabeth looked up at the ceiling, still blinking back tears. "She didn't actually say she hated me."

"You mean she said something ugly to you?" Martha asked, looking indignant.

"No," Elizabeth said. "She didn't say anything to me about it at all. She just pretended everything was the same as usual. I guess she's disliked me all along."

"What happened?" Mary pressed. "Why in the world would you think that?"

Elizabeth rubbed her eyes. "I don't know how the three of us are supposed to manage living together once John and I get married. I realize she's in her senior year of high school and she'll be going off to college in the fall, but our home will still be her home until she's ready to go out on her own. I wouldn't have said yes to John's proposal if I thought it would be a problem for Tina. I really thought she and I got along well. She's always been so sweet."

"Elizabeth," Martha said firmly, "tell us what happened."

"John and I were sitting in the living room having some coffee after dinner. We had been talking about what dates might be good for our wedding and what all we might want to do for a honeymoon. John said he'd been looking at some cruises that we might like, and he went to get his laptop to show me some of the websites he found."

Mary looked at Elizabeth expectantly. "And?"

"While he was gone, I heard Tina come in the back door. I waited, thinking she would come into the living room, but she didn't. I could hear her talking to somebody." Elizabeth put her head in her hands, unable to keep the hurtful scene from playing again and again in her mind.

"Everything was fine until she showed up."

Tina's voice was low and angry. Elizabeth knew she should say something or at least make some noise to let Tina know she was there, but she sat frozen where she was.

"Does she really think she can take her place? After all this time? I'd rather not have anybody at all."

There was a pause before Tina spoke again.

"No, I can't talk to him about it. He's already made up his mind, and there's nothing we can do. It's done. Ugh, I hate this."

There was another pause.

"Yeah. Okay. I'm home, so I'd better do the rest of the stuff I need to do. Talk to you later."

Elizabeth heard the refrigerator door open and close, and then Tina came in, her auburn hair in its usual messy bun and a soda can in hand.

"Oh, hi," she said, smiling. "I didn't know you were here."

Elizabeth forced a pleasant expression, wondering how Tina managed to look so casual and comfortable at such a moment. "Your dad said you had to go study with a friend and invited me to have dinner with him. I hope you don't mind."

"No, that's great." Tina sank into the armchair next to the couch. "I didn't want Dad to have to eat by himself, and you're going to be around all the time pretty soon, right?"

"Pretty soon."

"Pretty soon what?" John asked as he came back into the room with his laptop.

"Pretty soon Elizabeth is going to be here all the time," Tina said. She took a generous swig of her soda. "So I figure she ought to come over whenever she wants."

John beamed at her and then sat down beside Elizabeth once more. "We were talking about honeymoon possibilities," he told Tina.

"Oh yeah? You should go someplace different," she suggested eagerly. "Like South Africa."

John laughed. "I'm not sure we want to go quite that far. What do you think, honey?"

"Somehow," Elizabeth told her sisters, "I managed to keep up the pleasant small talk after that until I had a chance to say good night." She put her hands over her eyes. "What am I going to do?"

"Are you sure you heard her right?" Martha asked. "If you were in the other room—"

"I heard her. Every word."

"Maybe you should have said something right then," Mary said. "She's basically had her dad to herself the past few years. Well, she and her brother. It's got to be hard for her with everything changing so quickly."

"I expect there to be a few bumps in the road," Elizabeth said. "We're all going to have to make some adjustments. But I thought she liked me. She must have been pretending all this time."

"Why would she do that?" Mary asked. "She hasn't seemed that way to me."

"I don't know," Elizabeth said. "She loves her dad. Maybe she doesn't want to get in his way, no matter how upset she is about this for herself. How could I have been so mistaken about her?"

"That's what I'd like to know." Martha slipped her hand into Elizabeth's. "Maybe you should just ask her about it."

"I don't know. I don't think I can. And I don't want John to find out. I don't want to put him into a position where he feels like he has to choose between her and me. Maybe she feels the same way. Maybe she's just trying to get along until she goes off to college. But that's a terrible way for her to have to live. Even when she's not living with us, I want her to feel comfortable at home. I don't want her to feel like I'm trying to take her mother's place or trying to spoil things for her. What did I do wrong?"

"I don't think you did anything wrong," Martha told her. "She's trying to adjust to all the changes in her life, not just with you and her dad, but with school and trying to figure out what she's going to do with her life and how to be an adult. It's hard at that age."

Mary nodded. "And maybe she was just blowing off steam with whichever friend she had on the phone. It could be she was overwhelmed by everything that's happening in her life right then and she took it out on you. Maybe it didn't have anything to do with you at all."

"Maybe," Elizabeth said, not at all convinced. "What am I going to do?"

"Right this minute?" Martha asked her. "You're going to do nothing. I'm going to bring you some tea, and we're going to talk about the rings Mary and Bill picked out, and you're going to calm down. It won't get any worse if you step back a little bit and look at things unemotionally."

"Okay." Elizabeth took three deep, slow breaths. "Okay. You're right. I need to not overreact." She smiled at Mary. "And maybe she was just having a bad day. Everybody does, right?"

"Of course." Mary hugged her. "And I don't know who wouldn't like you in the first place."

"Unless you know of something you need to apologize to her for," Martha said, "then let it go for now. If there's really something bothering her, you'll be able to tell. Then you can talk to her about it."

"That's what's so hard about this," Elizabeth said. "I don't know of anything. We've gotten along great so far. John says she's happy that we're getting married, that she didn't like the thought of leaving him all alone once she goes to school. And maybe I won't be able to tell if something's bothering her next time I see her. I haven't been able to tell up till now. I still wouldn't know if I hadn't overheard her on the phone."

Martha went into the kitchen and got tea for all three of them. By then, Elizabeth was much calmer.

"I'm sorry, both of you," she said, taking a warm, soothing sip. "I spoiled all the fun about Mary's rings."

"I don't have anything to show you yet," Mary said, "but we took pictures of what we picked."

Elizabeth was relieved to be able to think about something besides what Tina had said, and for a few minutes she was swept up in Mary's excitement. But when they finished talking and told each other good night, Elizabeth looked at her own engagement ring and wondered again. What was she going to do about Tina?

Mary woke up the next morning tired after a restless night's sleep. Elizabeth was upset about John's daughter. Martha was worried about getting her quilt made in time for Elizabeth's wedding. Mary was worried about them and herself, though she couldn't quite pin down the exact reason for that last part.

She was excited about her beautiful engagement ring and very much looking forward to when she and Bill would be married. She was enjoying the time they had together until then, but there was still that tiny bit of doubt that nagged at her when she wasn't careful to keep it at bay.

That red-haired woman at the restaurant last night shouldn't have bothered her in the least, but she still did. Bill hadn't been interested in her. Mary knew him well enough to see that he was only annoyed and embarrassed by her overtures.

"I'm not going to let that woman, some strange woman we'll never see again, spoil one of the best times of my life," she told herself sternly. She turned to Tinkerbelle, who was still lounging in the bedding. "Come on, Tink. We're going to have a good day today."

Evidently, Martha had the same resolution. When Mary came downstairs, Martha already had pancakes on the griddle and crisp bacon to go with it. And she had squeezed some fresh orange juice.

"You look cheery this morning," Mary observed as she sat at the table.

Martha dished up pancakes and bacon for her and brought her a glass of juice. "I thought I'd better," she said conspiratorially. "Elizabeth's got enough on her mind without worrying about me too."

"Did you get any more done on it?" Mary didn't dare say what *it* was.

"Some. I'll talk to Rachel about the other part today if I get a chance to go over there."

Obviously Martha didn't want to mention any specifics either. Just in case.

There was melted butter and hot syrup already on the table, and Mary applied it to her pancakes liberally.

"You think of everything."

"We always liked it when Mama did that," Martha said. "I thought this might be a good morning for a little comfort food. For all of us."

Mary almost protested that she didn't need any comforting just now, thank you very much, but maybe Martha was more perceptive than she gave her credit for. Besides, the pancakes were amazing.

"Martha?" she asked once she'd had a few bites.

"Hmm?" Martha said, turning over a trio of perfectly browned circles.

"Did you ever worry about Chuck?"

"Worry about him? I guess so, off and on. Why?"

"I don't mean worry about him being sick or something, but worry about him, I don't know, losing interest or maybe not liking you as much as he did before you were married."

Martha slipped the pancakes off the griddle and onto a plate. "You're not worried about Bill, are you?"

"No. Mostly about me. I mean, what if we get married, and it changes everything? It did with me and Brian."

"I thought you weren't going to let Brian spoil what you have now," Martha said as she poured out more pancake batter, making the griddle sizzle again.

"I'm not. But things have to change when you're put in a new situation like Bill will be. He's been a bachelor for a long time. He's pretty much done whatever he wants, whenever he wants. That's going to change when there's two of us to consider. What if living with me isn't anything like he thinks it will be?"

Martha smiled. "It's going to be different. But different isn't always bad. I was worried about that when Chuck and I got married. It's been so long ago now, I hadn't really thought about it, but it was quite a change. And, yes, it was an adjustment. You've been married. You know."

"I know I felt more and more like I was in Brian's way. Like I couldn't do anything right. Like he was sorry he settled for me."

Martha's expression turned serious. "If Bill makes you feel that way, then you shouldn't marry him."

"No, he doesn't. He doesn't at all."

"But?"

Mary sighed. "I don't know. I just don't want to mess this up, and I'm trying to make sure I don't."

"Neither of you is going to do everything right. The point is that you are committed to each other, and that means working things out when you come to them. You're willing to do that, aren't you?"

Mary nodded.

"And don't you think Bill is also?"

Mary smiled and ate more of her pancakes. He was exactly that kind of man.

"Thanks, Martha."

Martha took the pancakes off the griddle and poured more batter. "For?"

"For making me say what I already know." Mary frowned at the full plate Martha put at Elizabeth's place. "Where is she?"

"She ought to be down."

"Sorry," Elizabeth said, hurrying into the kitchen as she buttoned the sleeves on her blouse. "I overslept." She noticed the breakfast at her place. "This is a treat. Thanks, Martha."

"I was telling Mary we could all use a little comfort food today. Did you sleep all right?"

"Okay," Elizabeth said. "I woke up around three and didn't go to sleep until after five. Then when my alarm went off, I was sleeping so hard, it took me a while to get moving. But I'm okay."

"Good. Do you and John have any plans for tonight? I know Mary and Bill are going out."

"Is tonight the concert?" Elizabeth asked Mary.

"I'm looking forward to it, though I almost wish we were just staying home. We've been going out a lot recently, and I know we won't always be doing that much. We're going to have to get used to just hanging out together."

Martha sat at the table with her own plate and glass. "I think you'll find that gets to be the best part."

"I hope so."

Mary ate a piece of Martha's perfectly cooked bacon. Maybe that was what worried her about getting married again. Would they be happy during those times when not much was happening? When it was just the everyday grind of life? But she knew herself so much better now than she had when she'd eloped with Brian. And she knew Bill so much better than she had known Brian. And, surely, she had made enough mistakes the first time around to at least not repeat those particular ones. How many more could there be?

She smiled to herself and then had a sudden thought. Maybe she could help both of her sisters at the same time. "Martha?"

"Hmm?"

"I know you're supposed to work at the shop today, but could I work for you?"

One of Martha's dark eyebrows went up. "I guess. Why?"

"I just think I ought to keep myself busy for a while. It'll do me good. You can make it up to me sometime or other. Besides, we close early today, so it won't be all that much of a workday anyway."

"Okay."

"What about me?" Elizabeth asked. "Maybe I'd like a day off too."

"No," Mary said with a cheeky grin. "You need to keep yourself busy too. Besides, if Verity and Katura come back in I want you to be able to talk about quilting with them and give me a chance to get better acquainted with Katura."

"I doubt they'll be back in the shop today. Not after they were already in yesterday."

"But if they are, we'll be ready for them."

Elizabeth laughed. "All right. We'll be on the lookout for them."

The three of them ate in companionable silence for a few minutes more, and then Mary looked at her watch.

"We'd better get going," she said to Elizabeth. "It's almost time to open up. Thanks for breakfast, Martha. It was wonderful."

"Thanks for the day off," Martha said, giving her a knowing little nod when Elizabeth wasn't looking.

Good. Martha would have most of the day to work on the quilt without Elizabeth worrying about something being wrong with her. Maybe Martha would even have time to go talk to Rachel about the quilting. If anybody could get it done in time, it would be Rachel and her friends.

CHAPTER EIGHT

The three sisters cleaned up the kitchen together, and then Mary and Elizabeth put on their coats and walked out to the shop.

It turned out to be a slow morning. Verity and Katura didn't come in. Neither did Dan Bontrager. Mary and Elizabeth talked about their upcoming weddings and where they might like to honeymoon. Rachel Fischer came in after lunch with some of her hand-quilted items for sale. Mary's favorite was a quilted vest with the traditional bright solid colors on a black background.

"That's so cute," she said, inspecting it more closely.

As always, the handwork on it was flawless, the stitches small and even.

"Very pretty," Elizabeth said.

"You should make one for yourself," Rachel told her. "Have you been keeping up with your hand quilting?"

Elizabeth winced. "Not really. There's been a lot going on."

"The wedding," Rachel said, a knowing look in her dark eyes. "I know you both have many things to decide. Just remember the marriage is more important than the wedding."

"True," said Elizabeth, "and there's so much more to consider than just the bride and groom."

"Families marry families," Rachel said. "They all must take each other into consideration."

"That's what makes it so hard sometimes."

"You know," Mary said brightly, "Martha would love to see that vest. You ought to go show it to her before we put it out for sale. I'd hate for it to be gone before she gets a chance."

"Do you think so?" Rachel caught Mary's purposeful glance and reclaimed the vest. "I will go see her."

"I'd like to make something like that," Elizabeth said as she watched Rachel leave. "Maybe some sewing would be good for my nerves."

"I don't think I could sit and do exactly the same thing for hours at a time," Mary said, "but a lot of people find it relaxing."

"I just haven't had the time lately. I feel like I ought to be figuring things out about my wedding so you can start planning yours."

"Like Rachel said, the marriage is more important than the wedding," Mary reminded her. "And Bill and I aren't going to rush. We'll get married at just the right time." She smiled. "Whenever that is."

"I know John and I don't want to wait too long to get married, even if that means we have something very simple as far as the ceremony and reception go."

"Nothing wrong with that."

They both looked over at the door when it opened, letting in a whoosh of frosty air. A young man in a wool cap and a leather jacket came inside.

"I think it's getting colder out there," he said with a grin.

"Feels like it," Mary said. "Come on in and get warm."

"I think I will," he said, pulling off his cap to display a shock of thick sandy hair. "Thanks a lot."

Elizabeth smiled at him. "I'm Elizabeth Classen, and this is my sister Mary."

"Hi. My name's Wes Rhys."

"It's nice to meet you, Wes," Mary said. "Is there anything in particular we can help you find?"

"Actually, I'm looking for someone. A friend of mine."

Mary gestured for him to come closer to the counter. "Oh yes? We have people come through here all the time. Not as many this time of year, but still a fair number. Did your friend come here to visit, or to live?"

"I'm not really sure. I know she was in Bird-in-Hand recently, but I can't be sure she's still here. I figured this would be a good place to check. I mean, I guess a lot of people come in here. If they're not Amish, I mean."

"We have Amish and *Englisch* customers," Mary said. "We try to have something for everybody."

"English?" He pulled off his gloves. "Like from England?"

"You've never been around the Amish before, have you?" Mary said.

"No, I guess not. Not till now anyway, but she was raised around them. All I really know is they don't drive cars or use electricity and phones and stuff."

"That's a simple way of putting it. The Amish generally use the word *Englisch* to describe anyone who's not Amish."

"Okay, then I'm Englisch. And I guess the girl I'm looking for is Englisch too."

"Does she know you're looking for her?"

Wes shrugged. "No, I don't think so. And maybe she doesn't exactly want me to find her right now."

Mary glanced at her sister. A young guy looking for a girl who didn't want to be found?

"Is this somebody you're related to?" she asked.

"No. Just a friend. She's got short blond hair. Kind of curly. Big blue eyes. Not as tall as me."

"About your age?" Mary guessed he was around twenty.

He nodded. "Have you seen anybody like that in here in the last couple of days?"

"We did have some tourists come through," Elizabeth said. "I don't remember anyone like that though."

"Me neither," Mary said. "She didn't tell you where she was going?"

He shrugged. "No. I've been kind of worried about her and thought I'd better make sure she's okay. You know how it is."

Mary raised her eyebrows, waiting for him to go on.

"I mean, you know..." He shrugged again.

"And you're sure she was in Bird-in-Hand recently?" Elizabeth asked him.

"Yeah. In the last couple of days."

"How do you know that? Did she tell you she was here?"

"Well, not exactly, but I figured it out."

Mary studied him for a moment. "I'm sorry, but we haven't seen anybody like that."

"I'm not a stalker or anything," he said quickly. "I just want to be sure she's okay."

"Is she in trouble or something?" Elizabeth asked. "My fiancé is a policeman, and you could—"

"No." He gave her a half smile. "It's not anything like that. I mean, I talked to her yesterday. She's all right. I just wanted to check on her."

"Does she know you're here?"

He shook his head guiltily.

"Why don't you call her and tell her? Maybe she'll meet you somewhere or tell you where she's staying."

"Yeah. Yeah, maybe." He didn't look as if he thought that was going to happen. "But you haven't seen anybody new around or anything? I mean, somebody Englisch, like I said. Maybe somebody who came in to use the phone?"

Mary shook her head, but she made a mental note to ask Martha about that. "Do you want to leave a message for her in case she does come in?"

"Yeah," he said eagerly. "Sure."

Mary got a notepad and pen. "And what was your name again?"

"Wes Rhys. That's r-h-y-s."

"And what message would you like to leave?"

"Uh, just say that I'm worried about her and want to hear from her."

Mary jotted that down. "And her name?"

He froze for a moment. "Uh, maybe I shouldn't be giving that out. She might not like it."

"That makes it kind of hard for us to know who to give your message to. But she can call you, right?"

"Yeah, sure. She just—I guess she doesn't have her own phone with her right now."

Because she didn't want him to call her or know where she was? Mary thought it was fairly likely.

"Even if she's in Bird-in-Hand," Elizabeth said gently, "that doesn't mean she'll necessarily come into our place."

"If she does *and* we realize it's her," Mary added, "the most we could do is give her your message and say you'd like her to call. That doesn't mean she will. And that's *if* she comes here in the first place." She gave him a wry smile. "This kind of thing isn't exactly in our line of business."

"Yeah, I know." There was pleading in his hazel eyes now. "It's just that I care a lot about her, and I want to make sure she's all right."

"We'll keep your message," Mary said, slipping it into the cash drawer. "That's about all we can promise at this point."

"Well, it's better than what I have now, which is basically nothing, so thank you." He nodded at Elizabeth. "Thank you both."

"Are you sure you shouldn't talk to the police about this?" Elizabeth asked, concern in her expression.

"No, no, it's nothing like that. She hasn't been kidnapped or anything. I did talk to her, and she says she's fine."

"Maybe you should speak to her parents. Don't they know where she is?"

Wes shook his head. "Her dad died a couple of years ago, and her mom remarried right after. She and my friend don't really stay in touch."

"She doesn't talk to her mom?" Mary asked.

"She's on her own. Has been since she got out of school. I was hoping she and I might…" His face turned a little red. "I thought if she and I got married, I could take care of her and everything."

He seemed terribly earnest, but he also seemed young for marriage. The Amish usually married young, but they had a lot of support from their families and the community at large. It seemed the girl he liked had no family to speak of. Did he?

Mary nodded. "And what do your parents think of that?"

He shrugged. "Dad thinks we ought to think very hard about it before we do something like that. So does Mom."

"Do they know you're looking for her?"

"Not really. I mean, I haven't lived at home since I finished college. That was right before Christmas."

Either he finished unusually early, or he looked young for his age. Maybe it was a little of both.

"I've got a decent job. It's a start, anyway." He looked suddenly embarrassed. "I guess you don't need to hear my whole life history, right? I just said all that so you'd know I'm not just being crazy or something. She and I would be all right if she'd just let me help her."

"But you think she's doing all right?" Elizabeth asked. "She's safe where she is?"

Wes nodded.

"And she can get in touch with you if she wants to."

Again he nodded, this time reluctantly. "Yeah."

"Then maybe you'd better leave it at that for now," Mary suggested. "If she's grown up enough to be on her own, then she's grown up enough to know whether or not she wants to be with you."

"But she wants to be with me!"

Mary looked at him questioningly.

He clenched his jaw. "She does. She just has…something going on right now, and she thinks it's better if I stay out of it."

Mary winced inwardly. She hated it, but her first thought was that this was about an unexpected pregnancy. She prayed she was wrong.

"Is there someone else you could talk to about this?" she asked. "A pastor or someone who could counsel you? She's not in trouble, is she?"

"No." He frowned at her. "What? No. If you think she's going to have a baby or something, you're totally wrong. It's nothing like that." His cheeks flushed pink. "We haven't—we haven't been together like that."

"Okay, okay," Mary said. "You don't have to explain anything to us. We're just trying to help."

He ducked his head. "I know. I'm sorry. You've been very nice to talk to me. I'm sorry there's not much I can tell you. I don't have much to go on. I just know she's been here, and I need to see her if I can."

Mary hesitated. Maybe it wasn't her place, but it had to be said.

"If she's not being held against her will or anything like that, if she's come here because she wants to be here, then maybe you just have to let her go. People sometimes change their minds about what they want and who they want. Maybe she decided she's not ready to get married yet. It's a very serious step to take." She nodded toward Elizabeth. "My sister and I both got engaged recently, so we know."

Wes gaped at both of them, and Mary laughed.

"Yes, even old ladies get married sometimes."

His color deepened. "I didn't—I mean, sure. Um…"

"We'll keep your number," Elizabeth said, her expression kind. "It seems like a long shot, but if we see your friend, we'll let her know you want to hear from her."

"Okay," he said meekly. "Thank you. Um, is it okay if I come back later maybe? Just to check?"

"Sure," Mary said. "You're welcome anytime."

He gave them a little wave and then left the store.

Rachel came back in just as he was leaving, the quilted vest over her arm.

"I brought this back for you to sell," she said, handing it to Elizabeth. "Martha thinks that if you sell this one quickly I should make more in a variety of sizes."

"That would be great. I'm sure they'd be very popular, especially when it gets closer to tourist season." Elizabeth gave her a warm smile. "Of course, your quilts always sell well here too. I know a whole quilt's a bigger job than a vest, but next time you make one for sale, we'd love to have it."

"I will remember," Rachel assured her, "but we are about to start one that is a rush order, so we will be busy with that for a little while."

"A rush order?"

Rachel gave Mary a subtle glance. "I believe it is for a gift and must be completed quickly."

"Will you be able to finish it in time?" Elizabeth asked.

"Gott helping us, we will."

"You should charge extra if people expect you to do rush a job."

Rachel's serene smile didn't change. "Oh, we will be pleased to do it, as we hope the one who is given the quilt is pleased with it and happy to sleep under it."

"Someday when I have time," Elizabeth said, "I'm going to quilt one too. Once I've practiced more, of course."

"You will be there soon," Rachel assured her. "Now I must go along home. I left bread in the oven with my children to watch it. They do not always keep their eyes and their minds on what I ask of them."

Elizabeth grinned.

"I worry about the children these days," Rachel said, shaking her head. "We try to raise them in the right way, but still they stray. My oldest daughter told me she saw one of the neighbor girls in the store buying hair dye. Why would any young girl wish to change the hair that Gott gave her?"

"Maybe she was buying it for someone else," Elizabeth suggested. "Maybe an Englisch friend."

"That could be so," Rachel said, still looking perplexed. "Well, we can only raise them up the best we are able and pray Gott to make up our lack."

"Very true. Thanks for bringing the vest. I'm sure it'll go quickly. See you soon."

"Bye," Mary added.

"Oh," Rachel said before she got to the door, "and Martha says for Mary to please come in when she can for lunch. It is ready."

Assuring them she would visit again before long, she left the shop.

"Is that okay with you?" Mary asked Elizabeth when she was gone.

"Go ahead. We're not busy. I'm going to start adding these new things of Rachel's to our inventory and pricing them."

"Be back soon."

Mary put on her coat and hurried into the house.

"Mary?" she heard from the kitchen as soon as she stepped inside.

"Yeah, it's me. Elizabeth's still in the shop. It's okay."

The smell of Martha's chicken casserole filled the house.

"Come on and eat," Martha called.

She already had plates and cups on the table along with butter and a loaf of fresh bread, and she was taking the casserole out of the oven.

"I don't know how you do it," Mary said, washing her hands at the kitchen sink and then sitting down. "I mean, I don't know how you do it on a regular basis anyway, but working on the quilt every minute you can, I'm surprised you didn't just whip something up out of a can or something."

Martha set the casserole on the hot pad in the middle of the table and took her own seat. "Well, don't say anything, but before I started on the quilt, I thought I might need some extra time, so when you and Elizabeth weren't home one day, I spent the whole time making and freezing a bunch of casseroles and soups and other things I can just thaw out and heat up later."

"Oh, good idea." Mary helped herself to some of the casserole and a slice of bread. "As long as Elizabeth doesn't find out."

"I nearly got caught last night when I lost track of the time. I should have already had something in the oven before you two came in. But she's got a lot on her mind. I doubt she's going to suddenly decide to go out to the garage and snoop in the big freezer. If she does, I'll just tell her I knew that with her wedding and yours coming up, I figured I'd need the extra time. It's certainly true."

Mary scooped up a steaming forkful of chicken and vegetables and blew on it to cool it. "I guess you and Rachel talked about the quilt."

"Yeah. Oh, do you want coffee?"

"Yes, please."

Martha got up to get them each a cup. "Anyway, thanks for sending Rachel by. She's been really great about the quilt. She says she's pretty sure they can get it quilted before Elizabeth's wedding as long as it's still a few weeks away and as long as I can get the top to her quickly."

"And?"

"And what?"

"Do you think you can get it to her quickly?"

"I'm trying."

Martha brought their cups to the table.

"Thanks," Mary said, taking a quick sip. "That's good. And, frozen or not, this casserole is delicious."

"I'm glad you like it." Martha looked thoughtful for a moment. "Rachel offered to help me with the piecing too."

"Maybe you should take her up on it. If you want to be done in time."

Martha shook her head. "Maybe it's silly, but I want to make this for Elizabeth. With my own hands, you know?"

"I understand. Really, I do. You just have to decide which is more important to you. Doing it all yourself or having it done in time for the wedding."

Martha laughed. "I want both."

"I know."

"I'll just have to keep working at it. Thanks for helping me out where you can."

"Well, I'm not a quilter, but you have a flock of those who'd help you if you wanted. Just let me know what I can do as you go along."

"You've been great about giving me time to work on it without Elizabeth noticing." Martha took a thoughtful bite of her food. "Has she said anything else about Tina?"

"Not to me. I think she's still trying to figure out what to do. I know she doesn't want to hurt Tina or John over this."

"It's going to be pretty miserable for all of them if Tina's really unhappy about the marriage."

"John didn't call her this morning," Mary said, only now realizing it. "He usually does, doesn't he?"

"Not every morning, I don't think, and his not calling doesn't necessarily mean anything. She's already upset about her pictures anyway."

"Her pictures?" Mary asked. "You mean the ones I took to Cindy?"

"Yeah. Elizabeth says they're not on her computer any-more. She doesn't know if she hit the wrong key and deleted them or if the computer ate them for some reason. I told her not to worry, that they're still on your flash drive, and that's safe at Cindy's, but she's still a little upset over it."

"I'm sure it's this thing with Tina. As far as I can tell from what Elizabeth says, John doesn't even realize how Tina feels." Mary sighed and speared a piece of chicken with her fork. "But I guess neither of us can fix it for her."

"I'm sure she'll work it out." Martha took another bite.

"We had an interesting visitor this morning, right after Rachel came to see you."

"Oh, really?"

Mary told her sister about Wes Rhys.

"I don't know how he thought we were going to recognize the girl he was looking for if he wouldn't even tell us her name."

"Did he show you a picture?" Martha asked.

"He was so secretive about the whole thing, I didn't even ask him. I figured if he wanted us to see one, he would have shown us. I think she may just be trying to get away from him. He seems like a nice boy, just a little lovesick. But who knows what he's really like or what he really wants."

"At least he says she's not in danger. That's good to know."

"But why doesn't she go home or at least tell him where she is if she's not trying to get away from him?"

Martha shrugged. "Why did she call him if she is?"

"Good question."

"Could he have tracked her cell phone?"

Mary frowned. "I guess it's possible, but would somebody like him have the ability? I guess there are all kinds of hackers out there. And if so, couldn't he have just called her back instead of coming here looking for her in person?"

"You'd think so."

"I don't remember any young blue-eyed blonds being in the shop yesterday except for Verity Shetler, and we know her." Mary shook her head. "I guess I should mind my own business, but it's hard to know when to get involved and when to stay out of it. I mean, like that woman who was killed in Portland by her married boyfriend, that mob guy, Carlisle."

"I read about that," Martha said quietly.

"Maybe if someone had helped her at some point, she wouldn't be dead. I mean, the article said he'd put her in the hospital a couple of times before when they'd had a fight."

"But she kept going back to him. I guess she thought the money and the high life were worth it."

"Maybe. But it seems to me that so many of these situations could end up at least not as bad if friends and family spoke up when something was turning bad and not just look the other way." Mary took the last bite of her lunch and then finished her coffee. "I'd better get back to the shop now," she said, standing. "Elizabeth will be getting hungry."

"Do you want me to go out for a while?" Martha asked.

"Of course not! You've got serious work to do, and we close early today. I'll see you later on."

Mary hurried back to the shop and sent Elizabeth home for lunch. She wasn't gone very long, and Mary wondered with an inward chuckle if Martha hadn't hurried her up so she could clean up the kitchen and get back to her sewing.

The afternoon was busier than the morning had been, and Mary was glad that it went quickly.

"You ought to have plenty of time to get ready for your concert tonight," Elizabeth said when they had a minute to talk.

"Yeah." Mary was rearranging a set of dishes that one of their customers had examined. "That's why we picked a Tuesday to go, but we got those tickets weeks ago. I didn't realize how busy things would be just now." She blew an unruly strand of hair out of her face. "I'd almost rather just have a quiet evening at home."

"Nobody says you have to go."

"It would be a waste of the tickets, and Bill would be disappointed."

"You two have had a lot to do lately, but I doubt it's going to be that way every single night."

"No, probably not. What about you and John? Do you have any plans this week? Have you talked to him about—"

Elizabeth stopped short when the door opened and two teenaged girls came in.

"Tina."

CHAPTER NINE

Hi, Elizabeth," Tina said, bringing the other girl, a petite brunette, up to the counter with her. "This is Cassie. She's in my theater group."

Elizabeth wasn't exactly sure why Tina would choose to come here after what she'd said, especially with one of her friends, but she smiled at both girls. "Hello, Cassie. Welcome to Secondhand Blessings. Tina, you remember my sister Mary."

Tina gave Mary a pleasant nod. "Hi. I remember meeting you and Martha."

"There was so much going on at the engagement party, I'm surprised you remember either of us at all," Mary said. "Today Martha gets to work at home instead of out here. It's good to finally have a real conversation with you, and I'm glad to meet your friend too."

"You're going to marry Tina's dad?" Cassie asked Elizabeth.

Elizabeth nodded, taking a quick glance at Tina to see if there was anything in her expression that might give away her thoughts.

Tina shrugged. "I think Dad needs somebody to take care of him when I go to college."

That was hardly an overwhelming vote of confidence.

"You have a great dad," Mary said cheerfully. "Martha and I are really glad he's going to be part of our family. And we're looking forward to getting to know you and your brother too."

"It'll be nice," Tina said.

Elizabeth cringed inwardly. Tina was being polite, but she didn't exactly sound thrilled with the prospect. She managed to smile again, but her smile felt forced.

"I'm sure you girls didn't come just to chat with us, did you?"

"We came to see your vintage clothes," Cassie said eagerly. "Tina says you have some great stuff."

"Sure," Mary said. "Right over here." She walked the girls over to the clothing section. "You have a look and let us know if you find something you're interested in or if you have any questions. Feel free to try on anything you'd like. The changing room is over there."

Mary came over to Elizabeth, a placid expression on her face. "She seems all right," she said, keeping her voice very low. "Maybe you should just talk to her about what you overheard."

"I don't know." Elizabeth busied herself tidying up a display of costume jewelry, keeping her back to the girls. "I don't want to bring up a family matter in front of her friend."

"No, not in front of her friend," Mary said. "Maybe you can call her up in a little while and ask her when you two could have a talk. Or maybe you could meet her at a coffee shop or something."

"I don't know. I'm afraid to bring it up. I mean, what if we talk and she admits she doesn't want her dad to marry me? Then what do I do? Break up with John? Postpone the wedding until we work things out? Can something like this *be* worked out?"

"You're marrying John, not his kids."

"But that's not entirely true. I'm going to be part of the family. I don't want to make either of the kids miserable."

"John must have talked to them about this before he proposed to you," Mary said. "Didn't he?"

Elizabeth nodded. "He said they were fine with it, that they want him to be happy, but evidently Tina doesn't really feel that way."

"Okay, for the moment, say that's true. Do you think she talked to John about it?"

"No." Elizabeth forced herself to not look over her shoulder at the girls as they chatted over the clothing they were going through. "I think if she had, he would have discussed it with me."

"All right. So, if she hasn't talked to him about it, don't you think that means she thinks who he marries is his decision to make?"

"Yeah. Maybe."

"And that she thinks it's better for him if she doesn't cause problems?"

"But that's so terrible." Elizabeth sorted through the jewelry again, making more of a mess of it than it had been before she started. "I don't want her to be unhappy at home. I don't want her to feel like I'm an intruder. I've thought and thought, and I can't figure out what I could have done to upset her."

"It doesn't have to have been something you did in particular. And it's not like you know each other all that well yet.

Maybe if you can spend some more time together, you'll find you like each other better than you think."

"But I like her." Elizabeth bit her lip, afraid she'd spoken too loudly. "I like her a lot. She's smart and talented and self-sufficient. I understand why John is so proud of her. And we've had fun when we've spent time together. I mean, the three of us have gone to the movies and to dinner. We even baked cookies together. She and I went to lunch not too long ago. She seemed to enjoy it."

"Wasn't she the one who asked you to go?"

Elizabeth nodded.

"Why would she?" Mary asked. "Unless she liked being around you."

"I don't know. Maybe John suggested it. Maybe he wanted the two of us to get to know each other better."

"And did you get to know each other better?"

"I thought we did, but now I don't feel like I know her at all."

"Lizzie."

"The worst part is not knowing how to handle it. Or if I should do anything at all. You know what they say. Least said, soonest mended."

"*They* aren't always right, you know. Whoever *they* are."

"And suppose I talk to her, and she tells me everything is fine and she's happy John and I are getting married even though that's not how she feels? Or, worse, what if she says she hates the idea of John marrying me? Then what do I do? I can't tell John that if she doesn't want him to know, and I'm sure it would hurt him if I did. He's told me more than once how happy he is that Tina and I get along so well."

"Shouldn't he know, though, if that's the case?"

"And do what?" Elizabeth asked, nearly in tears. "Break off the engagement? Or tell his daughter her feelings don't matter?"

"First, you ought to catch your breath for a minute. It's probably best if you don't get into it right here and now."

Mary didn't look toward the clothing section, but Elizabeth knew she was reminding her that the girls were just out of earshot.

"Okay," Elizabeth said, swiping one hand across her eyes. "Okay. Um, what about your date tonight? We could talk about that." She glanced at her watch. "It's a quarter till two."

"I have some things to do before I get ready to go out," Mary said, "but I'll have plenty of time."

Elizabeth went over to where Tina was rummaging through the clothes rack. "Did Cassie find something to try on?"

Tina nodded and smiled, evidently wanting to make an effort too. "One of those flapper dresses from the 1920s."

"Oh, that one is great. It's not really from the '20s. As far as we can tell, it was made in the late '60s, probably for a Halloween costume or something. Not in perfect shape but a really great find. And I'm sure it can be fixed up."

Again, Tina nodded. "I guess you're about to close."

Elizabeth wondered if she had overheard some of what she and Mary had said or was just aware they closed at two. It was hard to tell.

"Not for a few more minutes," she said, trying to keep the uncertainty she was feeling out of her expression, trying not to show the awkwardness she was feeling. "Tuesdays are the only day we close early. But take all the time you need. Did you find anything you liked?"

"Not really."

Cassie came out of the dressing room wearing the beaded red satin dress. "What do you think?" She turned around, letting them see it from all sides. "Is it too long for me?"

Mary came over to them and looked her over thoughtfully. "It's a little big on you in general, but I think it could be taken in without much trouble. The beading might make it hard to shorten though."

"What do you think, Tina?" Cassie asked. "It's really cute."

"It is cute," Tina said, "and it would be great for the show, but she's right about it being hard to take up for you." She looked faintly disgusted. "I'm sure Jasmine would know just how to fix it."

Cassie rolled her eyes. "She probably would, but hey, if that would get me the perfect dress..."

"Why don't you take it," Elizabeth offered. "If you can't make it work, just bring it back, and no harm done."

She looked hopefully at Tina, but Tina was inspecting the beaded hem of the dress.

"Could we?" Cassie asked. "We'll be careful with it, I promise, and bring it right back if we can't fix it."

"That sounds fine," Elizabeth assured her. "Did you say you were going to use it for one of your productions?"

Cassie nodded.

"Then why don't you consider it our contribution?"

Cassie's eyes lit. "Really?"

"Just let us know when you're putting on your show so we can come see it."

"Oh, thank you!"

Elizabeth looked at Tina, hoping she would be pleased too, but her expression didn't change.

"Yeah," she said quietly. "Thanks." Then she looked at her phone. "We'd better go, Cass. They're about to close."

"Just a second—I can wear the dress home." Cassie went to the changing area, grabbed her things, and headed for the door with Tina. "Thanks again," Cassie said as they left the shop.

"Come back anytime," Mary called after them, and then she turned to Elizabeth. "Oh, Elizabeth, do you think she overheard anything?"

"I don't know."

"I don't think she could have," Mary said, not looking at all certain. "She probably only noticed that you were looking at your watch."

"Maybe. But you know how it is. Even if you can't hear what someone is saying, you can usually tell whether the conversation is light or tense. We shouldn't have talked about Tina or John or anything like that while she was here. Oh, what a stupid thing to do. If she didn't like me before, she must really love me now."

"Don't blow things out of proportion."

Elizabeth exhaled slowly. "All right. I'm just going to stop for a minute and catch my breath. I don't have to fix this problem right this minute."

"That's right."

Just then Elizabeth's phone rang, and she answered.

"John." She forced a smile, hoping it would show in her voice. "Hi. What's going on?"

"Busy as usual, but just routine stuff. I couldn't take a break this morning, but I didn't want you to close for the day before I got a chance to say hi."

"Hi yourself," she said, feeling better simply hearing the warmth in his voice.

Mary gave her a wink. "Locking up," she mouthed, and then she went over to the door, leaving Elizabeth alone with her call.

"What have you been up to?" John asked. "Have you had a lot of business?"

"We haven't been all that busy," Elizabeth told him, "but we did have an interesting visitor."

She told him about Wes Rhys and his puzzling request. "He didn't want to contact the police about it, and from what I can tell, it's not a criminal matter. It doesn't sound like he thinks she's in danger."

"But he didn't want to call her himself?"

"Evidently not. Is there something I should do? What would you do?"

"Nothing," John said. "You don't know anything about the girl. All he's wanting you to do is ask her to call him if she comes by, which doesn't seem very likely in the first place. If she does show up and is bothered by him, I can give him an official talk that ought to make him think twice about following her around when she doesn't want him to."

"Thanks. That makes me feel better, though I'd be surprised if he came back."

"He might not. Did you have a good day otherwise?"

"Tina came by," Elizabeth said, hoping that, if for some reason Tina had talked to him about their upcoming marriage, he might think this was the perfect opportunity to talk about it.

"That's great."

"She and one of her theater friends came to find a costume for the production they're putting on."

"Did they find something?"

"Yeah. A cute little red flapper dress. It's pretty big for her friend. Cassie, is it?"

"Yeah, Cassie. They've gotten to be good friends since they're both in this show. They might even end up going to the same college."

"It's always nice to know somebody from the start," Elizabeth said. "I'm sure it must be hard for Tina right now with all the changes she's dealing with."

"She's a trouper," John said. "Whatever comes up, she deals with it. No complaints."

Obviously, Tina hadn't talked to her father. Elizabeth sighed.

"Everything okay?" he asked.

"Oh, sure."

"You sound a little down."

"I've just got a lot on my mind," she said, and that was true enough.

"You're closing up, right? How about I stop by for a cup of coffee and to see my best girl for a minute?"

"Can you?"

Maybe she wasn't ready to talk to him about Tina, but it sure would be good to see him, even for only a few minutes.

"Why not? I haven't taken lunch yet. I can come by there for a little while and then grab a burger or something afterward."

"I could fix you something," she offered. "Or, even better, I could heat you up some of the chicken casserole Martha fixed us for lunch."

"I wouldn't say no to that. That is, if you don't think your sisters will mind."

"We'd love to see you."

"Okay. Let me check in and tell dispatch I'm taking Seven, and then I'll come by."

"Great." By this time, Elizabeth knew that a Code Seven meant an officer was taking his meal break. "I'll see you soon."

By the time Elizabeth ended the call, Mary had already locked up for the day.

"Ready to go to the house?"

"Yeah," Elizabeth said. "John's going to come over for a little while, just for a quick visit."

"Are you going to talk to him?" Mary asked. "About Tina?"

"No. He won't be staying long, and he's in the middle of his workday. If I decide to bring it up, I want it to be when we really have time to talk and when he has time to think about the situation."

"That's probably best. Make sure you give yourself that space too."

"I definitely need to remember that."

But she didn't know, when it came right down to it, whether she would be able to tell him at all.

CHAPTER TEN

T hat was fabulous," Mary said as she and Bill drove back from the concert. "I was surprised when they did that medley of TV show theme songs after playing all those beautiful classical pieces, but it was really fun. Whoever arranged them knows what he's doing."

"I liked that part too," Bill said. "We'll have to go again sometime. After we're married." He grinned at her. "I'm still pretty amazed you said yes."

"You didn't think I'd say anything else, did you?"

"I hoped not, but you don't know what it's like having to jump right out there and ask and risk getting turned down. Besides, I've seen those 'proposal fail' videos on the internet. Guys don't always guess right about what the gal's thinking."

She put her arm through his, wishing she could snuggle closer to him. "Well, this gal was thinking that she'd much rather spend the rest of her life with you than anybody else."

He pulled his arm closer to his side, pressing her arm as he did. "I love you lots, Mary."

It was just a quiet statement, and he didn't even look at her, but it brought sudden stinging tears to her eyes and made her throat tighten. How did she ever get to be so blessed?

"I love you too, Bill," she said when she could trust her voice, and then she laughed softly. "You know, for a long time I thought I'd never get married again, but now I can't imagine being without you."

"You don't have to be. You're going to be stuck with me for good once you say 'I do.'"

She sighed. "I don't want to pressure Elizabeth, but I wish she'd make some plans for what she wants to do so you and I can do some planning too."

"Now, don't rush her. It's not like she's thinking of sometime next year, you know. Aren't they talking about getting married in the next couple of months? Or has that changed?"

"No, as far as I know, that's still the plan. But they haven't set a date or decided on what kind of reception they want to have or anything."

"We'll have our turn," he assured her. "It won't be long. Unless you'd rather wait awhile. I mean, we've only been engaged for a couple of days."

"Do you want to wait?" she asked, somehow disappointed at the thought.

"We can go to the justice of the peace tomorrow if you want," he said, squeezing her arm against him again.

She laughed again. "Sometimes I think that's not a bad idea, but I guess we'd better let Elizabeth have her wedding first."

"I told you already," he said. "However you want it is fine with me. I'm more interested in the marriage than the wedding."

"Rachel told Elizabeth and me something like that this morning. 'The marriage is more important than the wedding.'"

"And it lasts longer. Most of the time anyway."

He turned onto Ronks Road. They were nearly home.

"I hope you'll be patient with me, Mary," he said after a moment. "I've been a bachelor for a long time. I'm pretty set in my ways. But I'll try not to be, best I can."

"I had to make some adjustments when I moved back home," she admitted, "but we managed to work things out."

He pulled up in front of the house and turned off the engine. "We're here." Still with her arm captured in his, he leaned over and gave her a sweet kiss on the lips.

"Do you want to come in for a while?" she asked. "I'm sure Martha and Elizabeth would like to hear how the concert was."

He glanced at his watch. "You'd better tell them about it. I have to get going early in the morning. If I finish the job I'm working on ahead of schedule, I'll get a nice bonus. That could come in handy when it's time for a certain honeymoon I'm thinking of."

They got out of the car, and she slipped her arms around his neck and kissed him again.

"It won't be too much longer."

He hugged her close and then, taking her hand, walked her to the door. "I'll call you tomorrow."

He was halfway to his car when he suddenly turned and came back up the porch steps.

"I forgot to tell you. I saw Eli Bontrager today."

She huddled in her coat, turning a little to have her back to the icy wind. "You did? Was Dan with him?"

Bill shook his head. "It was at the hardware store. He was buying some pretty hefty hinges. Looked like they were for a gate or something big. Anyway, I asked him where his brother was. He said Dan hadn't been by much except for a couple of meals and going to church with him and Jedidiah."

Mary frowned. "Did he say what Dan was doing? I thought that, besides the funeral, he came here specifically to spend time with his father and brother and try to patch up their relationship."

"That's what I thought too. Eli said Dan helped him around the farm for a while the Saturday after the funeral, but that was all."

"Did Eli say how they're getting along?"

"He didn't seem very happy, to tell the truth," Bill said. "He told me their father was glad to see Dan back at the farm again, glad to see him working the place and going to Sunday service with them. Sounds like he was ready to let bygones be bygones even if Dan didn't join the church, but Dan hasn't been around much the past couple of days. I don't know what Eli expected of Dan, but obviously it wasn't this."

"The funeral's over, so if that's what he came for in the first place, why is he still in town?"

"He said when he was in your store that he wanted to buy something his father made, is that right?"

Mary nodded.

"Did you ever try asking Katura about Dan?"

"I ought to talk to Katura again. We never did really talk about her painting, and I think we could learn a lot from each other. And maybe I could get her to tell me a little about herself. I don't want to push her, but there's something about this whole thing that really doesn't seem right to me. Do you think there's a chance you could talk to Dan? Maybe if you see him out someplace you could just find out what his plans are, how things are going, just general stuff."

"Sure, if I can. I don't want to be obvious or anything. And if he really is up to something, he's not about to tell me about it."

"I know," Mary said, "but sometimes just a little thing here and there, like Eli saying he wasn't spending much time around the farm, adds up to something important."

He chuckled and wrapped her in his arms, warming her in the cold night. "I'll do what I can. For now, have a good night's sleep. I'll call you in the morning."

He stole one last kiss, hurried out to his car, and drove away.

The shop was busy again the next morning. Mary and Elizabeth didn't have much time to talk, and when there was a brief lull and they took a break, Mary managed to spill coffee on the front of her shirt. With a sigh, she told Elizabeth she'd be right back and went to the house to put on something clean and rinse out the coffee before it stained.

There were only a few customers in the shop when she got back, one of them a tall Amish woman who looked to be in her fifties. She wore a heavy wool cloak, a long dress of dark gray, and a neat kapp on her iron-gray hair. She looked up when Mary came in.

"Mary." Elizabeth waved her over and then turned to the woman. "This is my sister Mary. Mary, this is Sarah Miller. She's come here from Elizabethtown."

Mary gave her a welcoming smile. "It's good to meet you. Is there something you're looking for in particular?"

"Ja," Sarah said. "As I told your sister, I am looking for my niece. She has disappeared."

"Your niece?" Mary asked with an incredulous glance at Elizabeth. Two missing persons in such a short time?

"Ja," Sarah said, her gray eyes anxious. "Her name is Anna Nussbaum. She is the child of my sister and her husband."

Knowing the Amish in general didn't approve of having their photographs taken, Mary asked for a description instead.

"She is young, not yet twenty, with blue eyes and fair hair." The woman looked as if she might cry. "She cut her hair very short when she went away. Now she is ashamed to come back. To come home."

"This must be very upsetting for you," Elizabeth said. "Please, tell us how we can help you."

Sarah clasped her hands together. "Have you seen anyone who looks like her? She may be using another name. She may be dressed as Englisch or Amish, I am not sure."

"Did her parents send you to look for her?"

Sarah shook her head. "They were very upset with her. They told her they have no daughter. But they are sorry now to have been so harsh with her, that they did not see how much she had been hurt. They have forgiven her and want her back. If I can find her and bring her home, they will be very happy. My sister has been so upset by this."

"I'm sure," Mary said. "But why do you think your niece would be here?"

Sarah looked down at her folded hands. "There was some-one...seen here who might know where she is."

It had to be Wes Rhys. He had said the girl was Englisch, but this woman said she might be dressed as Englisch. He had said the friend he was looking for was a young woman with blue eyes and short blond hair. He hadn't said why she didn't want to go home. It would be more than a coincidence if he and this woman now weren't talking about the same girl.

"What happened?" Mary asked. "Why did she leave home?"

"It was very bad," Sarah said, still not lifting her eyes. "She worked in a store, a small grocery. It is run by people of our faith, so we all thought Anna would do well there. We thought she would be safe. Then this man came into the store, an Englischer, and began talking to her. After a time, he convinced her that he loved her and that she should run away with him to be married."

Mary felt a pang in her heart, pitying the girl, knowing how likely it was that she would have had to choose either her love or her family and faith.

"But he was not a good man," Sarah said. "He only used our poor Anna and did not marry her. And after a while, it was such a short time, he tired of her and left her on her own. It was then that she tried to come home to her parents, but they were still angry, still hurt that she would do so unwise a thing. That was when they told her they had no daughter, and she went away again."

"I'm so sorry," Elizabeth said softly.

"I cannot tell you how much it has grieved them since," Sarah told them. "If they could take back the words, I know they would. My sister's husband has been ill, and she must care for him, so they could not come to find Anna. I was hoping I could do something, but it is very hard to find someone who does not wish to be found."

"Do you have some reason to think she might be in Bird-in-Hand?" Mary asked.

"It is more of a hope than a reason, but it is the only hope I have. The man may have come here to try to find her. I do not know why he would come here or how he knows, but it may be that he has heard from her."

"And you think he or she might have come in here, into our shop?"

"I am not sure. I am asking everywhere I am able. But have you seen a girl like the one I have described? Someone new in Bird-in-Hand?"

Elizabeth shook her head. "We know almost everyone, and we haven't seen anyone who could be Anna. I'm sorry. You don't have any clues where in town she might be?"

"There is not very much more I can tell you."

Mary glanced at Elizabeth, not sure whether or not they should mention Wes Rhys at this point. He may not be the man Sarah was looking for, though parts of their stories were very similar. He certainly didn't seem the love 'em and leave 'em type. But maybe Anna's family didn't know the whole story yet.

"I'm not sure how we can help you," Mary said cautiously. "Is there somewhere we could reach you if we hear or see something?"

"I am staying with friends for now, but if I cannot find her, I will come see you again." Sarah straightened her kapp.

"Thank you for speaking with me. I am sorry I cannot tell you more, but I will be back to see if you have heard anything or seen anyone who could be our Anna."

With that, she pulled her cloak closed at her throat and went out into the brisk wind.

"So what do we do now?" Elizabeth asked.

"Good question." Mary sank into a chair. "I'm not sure if we should mention Wes Rhys coming here or not. He may have nothing to do with this Anna."

"They both gave the same description of the girl they're looking for," Elizabeth reminded her.

"I know. But there are a lot of young women who are blond and blue-eyed. And Wes didn't strike me as the type who'd do what Sarah said this man did. If they are looking for the same girl, I hope it's a misunderstanding all the way around, and they can work it out."

"That would be good," Elizabeth said, looking unconvinced.

Mary wasn't convinced either.

CHAPTER ELEVEN

Martha sighed as she threaded her needle. She knew she should have bought more thread before now, but she had thought she had an extra spool somewhere. Evidently, she didn't. Of course, in all probability, she'd find that extra spool as soon as she bought more.

She considered stopping work for the day. It was getting late already. But then again, she needed every minute she could scrape together if she was going to get this done and over to Rachel to quilt as soon as possible. Rachel had come by earlier in the day, when Mary and Elizabeth were still working at the shop, to check on Martha's progress and gently remind her that she and her quilters would need as much time as possible to get the quilting done before Elizabeth's wedding. Well, there was nothing for it but an evening run to the store.

She hurried down the stairs, meaning to slip past Elizabeth in the living room and go out back to let Mary know where she was heading. She knew Mary was feeding Wynken, Blynken, and Nod, their pygmy goats.

"Martha?"

Elizabeth's voice stopped her in her tracks.

"Yes?" Martha answered, trying her best to keep the frustration and hurriedness out of her voice.

"What's wrong?"

Martha drew a deep breath and went into the living room, feeling the valuable time ticking away.

"What do you mean?" she asked lightly. "Nothing's wrong. I thought of something I need at the store, and I figured I'd better hurry before everything closes."

"Is it that urgent?" Elizabeth asked, looking at her skeptically.

"Not urgent, I suppose. I just thought I'd go while I was thinking of it."

Elizabeth shook her head. "You're not fooling me. Maybe you're not sick or anything, but there's something going on. Look at yourself. You never go out looking that way."

Martha hadn't thought to look in a mirror before she'd stormed downstairs, but she knew her hair was probably a rat's nest. And as harried as she was feeling, she probably looked as if a pack of dogs was after her. Worst of all, her rumpled navy blouse was covered in traces of yellow chalk from her marking pencil, and cream-colored quilting thread. She'd probably have enough thread to finish the quilt if she could join all those pieces together.

"Please," Elizabeth said, "tell me what's going on."

Martha stood there for a moment, ready to deny every-thing, and then went over to her sister.

"It was supposed to be a surprise," she said with a sigh.

"A surprise? For what?"

"For your wedding."

Elizabeth looked baffled for a moment, and then she stood up, smiling. "You're sewing something," she said as she picked a particularly noticeable thread off Martha's blouse.

Martha nodded. "I wanted it to be something special, and I wanted to make it myself. By hand."

"That's so sweet, but you didn't have to—"

"I did. I really wanted to. I still want to. But it's not done yet, and I'm running out of time."

"Why? We haven't even set the date yet."

"I know, but what I'm doing is only the start of the present. The rest of it is going to take a while too, and I'm afraid it's just not going to happen, and then I won't have anything to give you and John."

Elizabeth put an arm around her. "You know you don't have to give us anything."

"I know, but this is important to me. As soon as you got engaged, I knew this is what I had to do for you. For a lot of reasons." She pushed a lock of messy hair behind her ear. "I knew when I started on this it would be hard to get it done in time for your wedding, but I thought I could do it."

"So you've been staying up late and getting up early and grabbing whatever time you could so you could work on it, right?"

Martha nodded.

"At least that much sounds like you."

"You didn't really think I was sick or something, did you?" Martha asked, regretting the worry she must have caused Elizabeth on top of everything else she was dealing with right now.

"I wasn't sure. I never thought it was something you were doing for me."

"I was trying to anyway. Now all I'm going to have for your wedding is a box of bits and pieces."

"That would be all right, you know," Elizabeth assured her. "I'm planning on being married to John for a very long time. It will still be a wedding present whether you give it to us next month or next year or five years down the road."

"I hope it won't be that late!"

"I'm sure it won't be," Elizabeth said, "and I'm sure it will be wonderful, whatever it is."

Martha considered for a moment, and then she let the whole weight of her self-imposed deadline roll off her shoulders.

"Do you want to see it so far?" she asked with a conspiratorial grin.

"Oooh, could I?"

"You can't mention it to John," Martha said with a shake of her finger. "Somebody's got to be surprised. And it's mostly for you anyway."

Elizabeth put one hand over her heart. "I promise I won't tell."

"Okay, stay here for just a minute."

Martha went back up the stairs and into her room to tidy up the mess she'd made and arrange things as attractively as she could. That done, she went downstairs to get Elizabeth.

"Can I get Mary?" Elizabeth asked. "Or has she already seen it?"

"She's seen part of it, but not what I've done all laid out together."

"Seen what?" Mary asked, coming inside.

"Martha's surprise."

"She told you about it?"

Elizabeth nodded eagerly. "I don't know what it is yet, but she's about to let me see."

"Well, good," Mary said. "Now she can quit killing herself trying to get it done in time."

"Okay, okay," Martha called. "Do you two want to come see or not?"

"Coming," Elizabeth said, and she hurried upstairs with Mary right behind her.

Martha led them to her closed door and put her hand on the doorknob. "Ready?"

"I can't stand the suspense," Elizabeth said.

"Okay, close your eyes. And no peeking."

"I promise."

Elizabeth closed her eyes, and Mary took her arm.

"Open the door," Mary said eagerly. "I'll lead her in."

Martha pushed the door open and went to stand at the head of her bed, waiting until Elizabeth reached the foot of it.

"That's going to be so wonderful," Mary said.

"Come on, you two," Elizabeth said. "Let me have a look too!"

Martha chuckled. Somehow this was as satisfying as presenting her gift to Elizabeth and John completely finished and beautifully wrapped.

"Go ahead and look, Elizabeth."

"Oh," Elizabeth breathed out. "Oh, Martha. Look at that."

Martha had arranged the finished quilt blocks on the bed the way they would be when they were eventually sewn to each other, so the interlocking rings of colorful fabric pieces fit together. She'd been pleased to realize when she laid them out that she'd already made enough to cover at least the top of the bed.

"There's a lot more to be done," she explained, "but at least you can see what it's going to look like."

Elizabeth leaned down to look closer. "Is it okay if I pick one up?"

"Sure. Go ahead."

Elizabeth and Mary each picked up a block.

"It's amazing that you're doing all of this by hand," Mary said, showing Elizabeth the block she held. "You sew just like Mama did, doesn't she, Lizzie?"

Elizabeth didn't answer her. She was looking at the block she had picked up, touching a sunny yellow piece with little daisies scattered on it.

"That was Mama's," she said softly, and when she looked up, there was the shine of tears in her eyes. She ran her finger over another little piece, an olive green stripe, and then a pink dotted Swiss and a navy print with tiny cherries all over it. "These are all from Mama's clothes."

Martha felt a sudden stinging in her own eyes. "To tell the truth, I was thinking of making myself a quilt out of the scraps from Mama's things, just as a keepsake, and I still might do that. There'll be plenty left over. But I wanted to do this for you, Lizzie. I'm so happy for you and John, and I couldn't think of anything I could do that would show that more than this."

"And you're doing it all by hand?"

Martha nodded. Then she swiftly wiped her eyes and smiled. "But that's not the best part. I was going to hand quilt it for you too, but I realized already there was no way I could get that done in time, so Rachel and the rest of her quilting friends are going to quilt it for you. As their present to you."

"I—" Elizabeth shook her head. "I don't even know what to say."

"How about thank you?" Mary said, hugging her.

Elizabeth laughed. "Oh, definitely." She pulled Martha into their hug. "Thank you. This is so amazing. It's such a wonderful idea, and you're doing a beautiful job."

"You don't mind too much if you don't get it in time for your wedding?" Martha asked, wondering now why she had let this become so stressful for her.

"I don't mind at all. Just knowing you're making it for us is the most wonderful present of all." Again, Elizabeth examined the block she held. "I don't know how you came up with this, Martha, but it's amazing. And, now that I know about it, maybe Rachel and her friends will let me watch sometimes while they quilt it. I'm still working on my own hand quilting, and maybe I'll learn something from them."

Mary clasped her hands. "You could quilt some of it yourself!"

"Oh, no. I'm not about to ruin my heirloom quilt by quilting on it myself. Maybe someday I'll feel like I'm accomplished enough for that, but not yet."

The three of them stood for a moment, admiring the finished blocks.

"However it gets done," Mary said, "it's going to be wonderful. I can't wait to see it finished."

"I've got to get it over to Rachel before long though, whether or not I get it done in time for it to be quilted before the wedding. I don't like making her wait. She came over today to ask how it was going."

"She didn't say anything else about who her daughter saw buying hair dye, did she?" Mary asked.

Martha shrugged and shook her head. "No. Why? Did she say something about someone buying hair dye? Is that bothering her?"

"No. It's just not very usual for an Amish girl."

"No, it's not," Martha said thoughtfully. "But somebody at the Shetlers' has some."

Elizabeth's eyebrows went up.

"How do you know that?" Mary asked.

"When I went to use the bathroom there the day of the funeral, my knee caught on the cabinet door under the sink. It was open just a little, and when I checked why it wouldn't close, I found a package of hair dye in the way. I thought it was odd, but I figured it was none of my business."

"That would be very unusual," Elizabeth said, "but maybe it belonged to somebody staying with them."

"I thought they were all Amish," Martha said.

"Who knows? Maybe Iris is trying to cover her gray or something."

"This was dark, not blond."

Mary bit her lip. "Oh."

"What?"

"I've just been thinking about everything, about Sarah and Wes both looking for a blue-eyed blond. What if Katura's the one they're looking for?"

"You're not serious," Martha said.

"Why not?"

"Katura's not missing. Anna Nussbaum is and, maybe, Wes's girlfriend is too. Maybe it's not a stretch to think they're the same blue-eyed blond, but why throw Katura into the mix?"

"It's easy enough for somebody to dye her hair and get contacts, isn't it?" Mary asked. "Katura is Amish. Anna is Amish. Wes says his friend was raised around the Amish. Why couldn't they all be the same girl? If she got in trouble with her parents because of her boyfriend, maybe the two of them ran off together. And then, like her aunt says, the boy dumped her and she's afraid to go home."

"But why should she disguise herself?" Martha asked. "Just dyeing her hair and wearing contacts isn't going to fool someone who really knows her."

"I don't know. It's all crazy, if you ask me."

"It's not like there's something criminal going on," Elizabeth said. "If Anna doesn't want her family to know where she is, then she has that right."

"But it sounds to me like Anna doesn't even know her aunt is looking for her," Martha said. "If she is Katura, then she's been here for three months. If she left home because she thought her parents didn't want her around, why would she try to hide?"

Mary huffed. "You're right. That doesn't make much sense. I tell you what, though, I can at least try to find out if she's the one dyeing her hair."

"How are you going to do that?" Elizabeth asked her.

"I'm going to ask Rachel."

"I don't know about that. I know Rachel mentioned what her daughter saw, but that was only in a general way. It doesn't mean she's going to name names."

"Maybe she'll tell me if I tell her I actually need to know."

"But you can't tell her why. What if you're wrong about Katura? You can't tell people a story like that if you're only guessing."

"Maybe if I tell her who I think it is, she'll tell me if I'm right."

Elizabeth and Martha looked at each other, clearly not convinced.

"It wouldn't hurt to try," Mary said. "If I mention what Sarah said and Katura isn't her niece, Anna, then no harm done. She'll just look at me like I've lost my mind and go on with whatever she's doing."

"And if she is Anna?" Martha asked.

"Then maybe she'll realize that her family wants her back and go home. I'm going to see what I can find out."

"Why are you so worried about Katura anyway?"

"I don't know," Mary admitted, "but Dan makes me wonder. Bill called me earlier. He said he was getting gas this morning and went inside the store to pay and get some coffee while he was there. He was already in there when Dan showed up, so he got out of line and went down the candy aisle until Dan got in line too. Then Bill got in line behind him, and they talked for a minute."

"And?" Elizabeth asked.

"And nothing. Bill tried making small talk to see what he could find out. Dan wouldn't say where he lived except 'out of state.' He wouldn't say what he did except he works 'downtown.' Bill said he ended up telling Dan a lot more about himself than Dan told him. What's that about?"

"Dan and Bill haven't spent time together in years," Martha said. "And, really, how much of a conversation could it have been if they were just in a checkout line at the gas station?"

"I don't know," Mary said. "It makes me wonder, that's all. So I'm going to talk to Rachel for a minute. I'll be right back."

Martha looked over at Elizabeth with a smiling shake of her head, and they watched their youngest sister hurry out of the room and down the stairs.

CHAPTER TWELVE

Not waiting for any more objections from her sisters, Mary grabbed her coat and drove the short way to Rachel's house. She found Rachel coming out her front door.

"Rachel!" Mary called to her, waving as she got out of the car. "No little ones with you today?"

"No, they are finishing preparations for dinner," Rachel said. "I will not be long away. I am only taking some soup over to Fern Huyard. She is not feeling well."

"I'm sorry to hear that. I hope it's nothing to be worried about."

"Oh, no. A cold, she says, but I told her she should stay in bed until she is well. Especially in this weather."

"Good. I'm glad you told her that. What kind of soup?"

"Chicken," Rachel said with a pleased smile.

"Oh, delicious."

Rachel's chicken soup was very tasty.

"I won't keep you but a second," Mary promised, "but I'm hoping you can help me."

"Of course. If I can."

"You mentioned the other day that one of your girls saw another girl buying hair dye."

"Ja," Rachel said. "It is not something that is good for a young Amish girl to do."

"I know you don't like gossip," Mary said, "but would you tell me who the girl was?"

"No," Rachel said decidedly. "I am sorry, but I should not have mentioned it in the first place. It is not my business to speak of what someone else does or does not do."

"Please understand. I'm not asking you out of idle curiosity, and I promise I won't spread the story around. But I would like to know, because it might be important to someone. It's a serious matter, and because I don't want to gossip either, I can't tell you anything more than that."

Rachel clutched the steaming covered bowl she was carrying and looked torn. "I am not sure it would be right."

"Please. I realize it doesn't make sense right now," Mary said. "I might be totally on the wrong track, and I may never be able to tell you what this is about, but please tell me."

"I am not certain that would be right. How can this information help you?"

"I'm afraid I can't tell you that right now."

A hard gust of wind hit them both just then, and Rachel clutched her soup closer to herself. "It is getting cold. I really should go."

"I know. I'm sorry. If I tell you who I think it is, will you tell me?"

"I would rather you not say. This is a serious matter?"

"I don't know. I am hoping to help someone."

Rachel considered for a moment. "And knowing this would truly help?"

"I don't know. I wish I did. I think it will, but I won't know that until I find out if what I think is really true."

"And knowing about the dye will help you find out?"

"It might help me know who to ask for more information."

Rachel glanced toward her buggy.

"I'm sorry," Mary said, trying not to sound too disappointed. "I know you're cold and the soup's getting that way. You'd better go."

"I really do need to go, Mary. But I promise I will think on what you have asked me. I know you would not ask it just for gossip's sake."

"Thank you, Rachel. If you want to talk, just drop by when you're through at Fern's. Oh, and Martha just told Elizabeth about her double wedding ring quilt, so we don't have to keep it secret anymore."

Rachel looked relieved. "That is good. She was pleased?"

"Oh, very much. And we're all looking forward to seeing it once it's quilted."

"We will work very hard on it," Rachel assured her. "We will do our best work for our dear friend's wedding."

Mary gave her a quick hug. "I know it'll be beautiful. Come by if you want to. We're all home."

"Yes, of course. I will."

Mary smiled. "You'd better hurry now."

Rachel did just that, and Mary drove back to the house. When she entered the kitchen, she found Martha and Elizabeth sitting at the table, talking and drinking hot chocolate.

"There's more cocoa on the stove," Martha said.

"What did Rachel say?" Elizabeth asked, almost at the same time.

"She didn't want to tell me," Mary said. She got herself a cup of hot chocolate and warmed her hands on it. "She was on her way to Fern Huyard's house. I really couldn't give her much information about why I wanted to know, because if it's nothing to do with Katura, then it doesn't matter."

"True."

"Well, you tried," Elizabeth said. "But even if Katura bought that dye, that doesn't prove she's Anna, you know."

"I know. But if I knew she bought it, then maybe I could let her know that Sarah had been here and that Anna's family wants her back. What would that hurt?"

"Nothing, I suppose. But it's a moot point anyway."

"Unless Rachel changes her mind."

Martha's eyebrows went up. "Do you think she will?"

"She said she would think about it. I guess we'll see."

Rachel came by before they'd finished their hot chocolate.

"Come sit down," Mary said, bringing her into the kitchen. "Would you like some hot cocoa to warm you up?"

"Oh, no, no," Rachel said as she sat down. "I can stay only a moment. My children will be wondering where I have gone." She smiled at Elizabeth. "But I heard you are going to have a very special gift for your wedding, and I had to come tell you how excited I am for you."

Elizabeth's face lit up. "Isn't it wonderful? I bet you already know all about it though."

"Ja," Rachel admitted, her smile widening.

"Martha told me you and the rest of the group will be quilting it." Elizabeth shook her head. "It's really too much for all of you to do that. I know what quilting like that costs."

"The cost is not important," Rachel told her firmly. "We do it because of our love for you. Because the work of the hand is the work of the heart."

Elizabeth's smile trembled a little bit, and she blinked hard. "I don't even know what to say. To you or to Martha. It's something that I will always treasure."

"You know we all wish you every happiness in your marriage with John." Her expression turning more solemn, Rachel turned to Mary. "I have thought about what you asked me earlier. It is something your sisters already know about?"

Mary nodded.

"Is there nothing more you could tell me about why you would like to know about this dye that was bought? It seems so unimportant a thing except maybe for the one who bought it."

"No, I really can't, but I promise I'm not being nosy. It would help to know."

"Oh, Mary, I should not—"

"Was it Katura Stolfuz?"

Rachel shook her head. "No, it was not Katura."

"Oh." Mary let her shoulders slump. "All right then. If it wasn't Katura, it doesn't matter who it was. Please don't tell anyone I mentioned her. I was wrong."

Rachel clasped her hands together, looking undecided.

"Maybe you are not so wrong," she said after a moment. "Katura did not buy the dye, but perhaps it was bought for her. If that is the case, then it may be that whatever help you think she needs is still needed."

"What do you mean?" Elizabeth asked.

"If it was bought for her," Mary said, her mind racing, "then who else would have done it but Verity?"

Rachel nodded reluctantly. "It could be, as I told my daughter, that it was bought not for any prideful cause, but for some reason we do not know. It is not for any of us to judge in such a matter. Gott knows the heart. If Verity bought it for a godly reason, and Katura wants it for such a purpose, then I say it is good."

Mary took Rachel's hand in both of her own. "Thank you for telling us. I know you'll keep this to yourself."

"Of course."

"And, again, I don't know if it really has anything to do with anything, but it might be important. If it is, you've helped do something good. If not, then there won't be any harm done. I can't tell you any more than that."

"I do not need to know any more than that. You will know what to say and what not to say." Rachel stood up. "Now I really must go home. Martha, you will bring us the quilt top as quickly as you are able?"

"Yes," Martha said. "Quick as I can."

"Are you sure we cannot help you with that as well?"

"No. Thank you, but I really want to do the top by myself."

"Very well then. The three of you stay warm. I will see you soon."

Mary walked her to the door and, with one more good night, watched her walk to her buggy.

"Now what?" Elizabeth asked when Mary came back to the table.

"Now I'll go talk to Katura."

"Right now?"

Mary huffed. "No, not right now. Tomorrow will be soon enough, but at least now I have a reason to go talk to her."

"You're not going to go over there and accuse her of dyeing her hair, are you?" Martha asked.

"Of course not. And Verity buying the dye doesn't prove anything by any means. But I can still see what I can find out."

CHAPTER THIRTEEN

As soon as the store closed the next day, Mary drove over to the Shetler farm. She pulled up to the house as Iris was stepping off her front porch with a galvanized pail.

"Oh, Mary. Hello." She came over to the car as Mary got out. "How are you today?"

"I'm fine. I thought I'd come see Katura for a few minutes if that's all right."

Iris's forehead puckered. "Is something wrong?"

"Oh, no. Not at all. Verity was asking about the quilting group Rachel Fischer has at our store. I was reminded of it because they met today. They always meet on Thursdays, and I thought I'd see if the girls were interested in coming next week. And I wanted to see if Katura was still interested in painting with me."

Iris smiled. "I think it would be good for both of them. You know, Katura does not go out very much, and I think, within reason, that she ought to. You go on inside. She is in the kitchen. I must take this oil out to the barn. One of our cows has the bloat, and Verity and I must dose her."

"Thanks."

"I will send Verity in when we are through," Iris added.

"Oh, no hurry. I can give Katura the information, and she can tell Verity."

"Very good. Mervin and our boys are in the shed sharpening tools, so they will not bother you."

"No bother. I won't be long. You and Verity take your time."

Mary hurried into the house and went straight to the kitchen. Katura was standing at the counter cutting up vegetables and humming. The tune was familiar, though Mary couldn't quite place it. She waited a second, hoping Katura would turn around, and then she came a step closer.

"Katura?"

Katura gasped, and the knife she'd been using clattered into the dish. She whirled around, clutching the edge of the countertop. Then she exhaled and grabbed a dish towel to wipe her hands.

"Oh, Mary. I am sorry. I did not see you."

"I didn't mean to sneak up on you. Iris said it was all right for me to come in and see you."

"You came to see why I have not made plans with you about the painting. I am very sorry. It seems that each time I think I will have a chance to come see you, I have something else that must be done."

"I realize that. And there's no hurry. You're always welcome, and I'm very interested in learning some of your techniques."

"Thank you." Katura ducked her head. "I—I am not sure I will be able to come. There are many things to do here on the farm. Iris will want me to—"

"She thinks you ought to get out a little more," Mary said with an encouraging smile.

"I will think on it." Katura wiped her hands again. "Is there something I can get for you? Some coffee?"

"I'd like that. If you'll stop and have some with me."

"The vegetables—"

"A minute or two won't hurt, will it?" Mary sat on the bench before the long table and patted the space beside her. "I don't think Iris expects you to work every minute of every day, does she?"

Katura's cheeks turned pink. "Iris is very kind, and she asks very little of me. I am grateful to her. More than I can say."

"She wants the best for you, I'm sure."

"Ja. I know she does."

Katura got them each a cup of coffee and sat down across the table from Mary rather than next to her.

"Anyway, you're welcome to come to the quilting circle. It meets at our store on Thursday mornings. If you and Verity are interested in learning, Rachel Fischer is an excellent teacher."

"I have seen some of her quilts. They are well made."

"I've never really been a needleworker, but my sisters are. They say it's very relaxing, and they enjoy doing something creative when they have time."

"It would take a long while to learn though, I am afraid."

"It does take a while," Mary admitted. "Elizabeth struggled with hand quilting until she got the hang of it. She still isn't as good as Rachel, of course, but she's improving all the time. You never know unless you try."

"I may not always be here."

Mary kept any sign of surprise out of her expression. "Oh? I thought you liked it here with the Shetlers."

"I do, very much, but who can say what may happen in the time to come? We cannot say what the good Gott might will tomorrow or even in the next hour."

"True."

Mary stirred her coffee even though she hadn't added anything to it, giving herself a moment to choose exactly the right words. Katura took a sip of her own, looking as if she wanted to slip out of the room.

"I have a confession to make," Mary said finally, trying not to stare too much at Katura's dark hair or look too searchingly into her dark eyes for the telltale rims of contacts.

Katura pulled back a little. "A confession?"

"I didn't come here just to ask you about painting with me or tell you about the quilting circle."

"No?"

"No. I've been worried about you."

"But why?" Katura asked. "Have I done something wrong?"

"No. No, of course not. It's just that when you were in the store the other day, I noticed you and Dan Bontrager having a disagreement."

"We were only talking," Katura said breathily. "Why should it worry you?"

"I realize it's none of my business, but you didn't seem to be very happy about what he was saying. And I thought at the gathering the other day after Bertha's funeral that you looked uncomfortable when he was talking to you. If he is bothering you—"

"No, he is not bothering me. We were only talking. We were only—" Katura coughed and took a wheezing breath. "I'm sorry."

"Are you all right?" Mary asked. She knew stress could bring on an asthma attack.

Katura took two deep breaths and then nodded. "I am fine. Perhaps I should return to my work. Iris will be in soon, and she will want to start preparing the evening meal. I want to have the vegetables ready for the casserole we are making."

"I'd be happy to help." Mary stood and went to the counter. "It always seems more fun to do chores if someone's doing them with you, don't you think?"

Katura smiled then, relaxing slightly. "That is what Verity always says, even if we are scrubbing pots or mending clothes."

"And it's true, isn't it?"

"Ja. It has been good to be here. I will miss all the family."

Maybe the idea that Katura was Anna Nussbaum wasn't such a far-fetched one after all. Had Sarah talked to her? Or had Wes finally found her and convinced her to run away with him again?

Mary placed a nearby cutting board on the counter in front of her, took a knife from the block, and started cutting up a carrot. Katura picked up the potato she had dropped and continued slicing it.

"Do you know Sarah Miller?" Mary asked after a minute or two.

Katura thought for a moment. "No. Who is she?"

"She came into our shop yesterday. She was looking for her niece, Anna Nussbaum."

Mary glanced at the girl from the corner of her eye, but Katura's expression didn't change. She was concentrating on her work.

"I do not know her. There was no Sarah Miller in Wrightsville, and I have not met one here."

Wrightsville wasn't too far from Bird-in-Hand.

"Is that where you came from when you came here?" Mary asked.

"No, but I lived there when I was young," Katura said. "I have no family there anymore."

Katura put the pieces of potato into a dish and picked up a large onion.

Mary started slicing another carrot. "I felt sorry for this Sarah Miller. She didn't give any details, of course, but she said her niece Anna had left her parents because she fell in love, and then the man abandoned her. Anna's parents were angry at first, but now they want her to come home. They're worried about her and want her back."

"I am sorry for them," Katura said with no change in her expression. "And for her *aenti*. I hope she finds her. Maybe this Anna will not want to go back, but she should be happy to know that she is wanted at home."

"Maybe you have seen her," Mary said, letting slices of carrot fall into the dish with the rest of the cut-up vegetables.

"It may be, but I do not see many people here on the farm."

"She may not have called herself Anna. Her aunt says she is young, not yet twenty, and has blue eyes and short blond hair."

Katura fumbled with the onion, left it only halfway done, and picked up another potato.

"And this aenti knows she is here? In Bird-in-Hand?"

"She thinks she is, but she's not sure. She said Anna's parents want her to know how much they love her. She wants to take her home to them."

Katura was holding tightly to the potato, her eyes fixed on it and her breath coming a little faster. "As I said, I do not see many people here on the farm."

"Oh, I know. But I thought it was sad to think of her being alone somewhere with her family missing her like that. Sarah wants very much to find her niece and bring her home. She sounded as if she was planning to stay in the area until she found her. If I happened to see Anna, I would want to tell her her aunt is looking for her."

"Ja. Of course." Something in Katura's face changed. She looked like she was going to be sick. "She should know someone has come for her."

Katura started wheezing. She put her knife down and fumbled in the pocket of her skirt to get her inhaler. Once she had shaken it well, she took a few deep, slow breaths and then seemed calmer.

Mary touched her arm. "Are you all right?"

"Ja." Katura nodded, still breathing rather quickly. "It is passing. I do not know when I will have an attack."

"I'm sorry. I didn't mean to upset you."

"No, it is not that. This is nothing. Very mild. They come when they come. There is no reason to them."

Mary brought Katura's coffee cup to her. "Does drinking something warm help?"

"Ja." Katura took a sip and then winced. "But this is not very warm now."

She dumped the coffee into the sink and poured herself a fresh cup. Then she did the same with Mary's and handed it back to her, not meeting her eyes.

"You should sit and drink that. You did not come here to work, I know."

"I came here to see you," Mary said, drinking but still standing at the counter. "I wanted to make sure you're all right."

"I am well." Katura went back to work on the onion she had half finished. "But it would be better if I finished my work before Iris and Verity come in from the barn. They will wonder what I have done all afternoon."

"You can tell them it was my fault. I kept you talking all this time."

"It was good of you to come, but you do not need to worry for me. And I do not know this Anna Nussbaum you ask about. If I do meet her, I will tell her it is good to be at home with those who love her."

She looked a little wistful.

"I know I would be lonely without my family," Mary said. "I have kids and a grandson, and even though I stay in touch with them, I miss them very much."

Katura smiled faintly. "I am sure you do. For me, there is no one anymore. Not now. That is why I am here. But Gott has given me the Shetlers, so I have a home for now. Later, only He knows."

Verity and Iris came in before Mary could reply to that.

"Mary, it is good to see you," Verity said, her blue eyes bright. "Maam said you had come to visit."

"I wanted to tell you and Katura about when the quilting circle meets, since Elizabeth couldn't remember whether or not she had mentioned it. It's every Thursday morning at ten o'clock at the shop. I hope you two will come. And if Katura doesn't want to try quilting, that might be a good time for us to paint, if I'm not working that morning."

Katura smiled a little at that.

"Do you quilt?" Verity asked Mary.

"No. It's not really my thing, but my sisters do. I keep thinking I'll give it a try, but I've never gotten around to it."

"It was nice of you to come by," Iris said. "And if my girls will finish with the vegetables, I might be able to finish preparing for dinner."

Katura gave Verity a guilty glance, and they both started cutting up vegetables.

"Will you eat with us, Mary?" Iris asked.

"Thank you," Mary said, "but I'd better not. I need to get home."

"You will come again, I hope," Iris said. "We would love to see you and your sisters."

"You come see us too. Anytime."

Mary was puzzled as she drove home, not sure what to make of the conversation she'd had with Katura. Suppose her hair was dyed. Suppose she wore dark contacts. That was possible, certainly. Was she truly shy, or was she hiding something?

She talked it over with her sisters that night at dinner.

"You couldn't tell whether or not she had on contacts?" Elizabeth asked as they ate creamy potato soup and Martha's fresh bread.

"I tried to see if there were any lines around the irises of her eyes. A couple of times, I thought there were, but I didn't want to stare too obviously, and Katura would never look at me directly for very long."

"She is very shy," Martha said.

"She seems to be," Mary considered, "but I'm still puzzled. When I told her about Sarah Miller, she didn't react at all. If she is her aunt, surely I would have seen something in her expression, but she really looked like she'd never heard of her."

"And when you mentioned Anna Nussbaum?" Elizabeth asked.

"The same. No reaction at all. She was polite and seemed a little sorry for her being away from home, but that was all. But then she had that asthma attack, and it made me wonder if she was upset by what I'd said. She claimed it was nothing, but it could have been from stress, don't you think?"

Elizabeth thought for a moment. "But you say she didn't have any reaction when you mentioned Sarah and Anna?"

"None that I could tell."

"Do you remember what you were saying when she had her attack?"

Mary frowned for a moment, thinking. "I was telling her what Sarah had said about her niece and what the girl looked like."

"That's all?"

"I told her Sarah wanted to find Anna and was going to stay in the area looking for her. Her face changed then, and I remember her saying, 'She should know someone has come for her.' I thought it was a little odd, but maybe it's only a particularly Amish way of putting things, you know? She didn't say Anna should know her family was looking for her but that she should know someone had come for her."

"Did you tell her about Wes?" Martha asked. She went to the counter, took some cookies out of the cookie jar, and arranged them on a plate.

Mary shook her head. "I'm still not sure about him or if I want her to know he's here."

"Maybe she ought to know and be the one to decide what to do about him," Elizabeth said.

"I don't know. Sarah seemed to think Anna's boyfriend, whoever he is, hurt her and then abandoned her. In that case, I don't know if I want to be the one to bring them together again."

"That's if Wes is looking for the same girl."

Mary put her elbows on the table and her hands over her eyes. "I know. I know. And I know it's really none of my business, but I thought Katura should know."

"If she's not Anna, then no harm done," Martha said. She brought the cookies to the table and sat down again. "If she is, now she knows her family wants her back. What she does with that information is up to her."

"And Wes?"

"She knows how to get in touch with him if she wants to. She's done it before."

Mary took a deep breath. "You're right. I'm not going to worry about this anymore."

"Good," Elizabeth said. "We've all got plenty of things to see to that really are our business."

"True."

She finished her soup and helped herself to a cookie as Martha and Elizabeth started talking about the wedding quilt. She had done what she could to help Katura. Why did she feel like she had just stirred up a hornet's nest?

CHAPTER FOURTEEN

There weren't many customers in the shop the next day, though Cindy Martin had come by about eleven to drop off the flash drive with Elizabeth's pictures on it. Mary had put it into her coat pocket so she could give it back to Elizabeth that afternoon after work. An hour or so later, when Martha had gone into the house to get a quick lunch, Mary was surprised to see Wes Rhys come back into the store.

"Hello," she said, careful to keep her expression cordial and businesslike. "Is there something I can help you with today?"

"I don't know." He came up to the counter and took off his knitted cap. "I haven't talked to anybody who knows anything about my friend. This is the only place I know for sure she's been recently."

"You know for sure?" she asked, warily. "How do you know for sure?"

"I told you, she called me from here."

Mary gave him a dubious look. "I know Bird-in-Hand is small, but it's not that small. Just because she called from this area doesn't mean—"

"No, I don't mean she called from Bird-in-Hand," he said. "I mean she called from here on Monday. From this store."

"Really?"

"Yeah. The number was on my caller ID, and I looked it up online. That's why I came here in the first place."

She thought for a minute, frowning. There was still something about his voice that tickled her memory. What was it? It suddenly struck her.

"Who's Ken?"

His face turned white. "What do you mean?"

"Who's Ken?" she pressed. "I've been trying to remember where I've heard your voice before, and I just did. You called me on Saturday asking for Ken and then said you had a wrong number. That was you, wasn't it?"

"N-no. My friend called me from here. I never called here myself. I swear."

"Maybe not, but you called my cell phone. I'm sure it was you." She grabbed her purse from behind the counter, got her cell phone, and checked her call history. "You called on Saturday. Then you called again on Sunday night. I know that's a Portland area code. Aren't you from Portland?"

"No!" he insisted, clearly trying to sound indignant.

"Okay," she said, and she touched the icon to redial the number. After a moment, his coat pocket started ringing.

Red-faced, he reached into his pocket, and the sound stopped.

"I think that's your phone," she told him, keeping her tone very mild.

He took a couple of hard breaths and didn't say anything.

"Who's Ken?" she asked again.

"I can't tell you," he said, his voice very low. "It's a big mess. My friend didn't do anything wrong," he added, suddenly urgent, "but she's got to keep out of sight for a while."

"Don't you think her family wants her to come home?" Mary said. "I'm sure they must be worried about her."

"Her family? She doesn't have any real family. I told you already that her father's dead and her mom's got a new husband and a bunch of kids."

Mary gave him a stern look. "I want to know how you knew to call my cell number. Okay, maybe your friend called you from here. Maybe she used the landline when we were taking care of other customers. That wouldn't be too hard to do. But how could you possibly know my cell number? It's not listed anywhere."

"I—I told you. It was only a wrong number. I misdialed."

She tilted her head. "I might not be an expert on statistics, but I'm pretty sure that the probability of you accidentally calling my cell phone right before your friend called you on my store phone is right at zero."

He bit his lip.

"I want to know how you got my cell phone number. Did you know your friend was here then?"

Surely he hadn't been randomly calling Bird-In-Hand telephone numbers.

"No," he said, looking down at his snow boots. "She called me."

"On my phone?"

"If you say so. I didn't know whose it was. I didn't recognize the number, but I picked up anyway. It was her."

"What did she say?"

"She wouldn't tell me where she was," he admitted. "All she said was that she missed me, that she was okay, and that she didn't want me to worry about her."

He looked very young right then. Mary wanted to tell him that everything would be all right, but she couldn't. She couldn't help him. All she could do was try to get him to be honest with her. He had sounded sincere when he said this girl had no family, but Mary still couldn't believe that his and Sarah's coming here, both of them looking for a girl with blue eyes and short, blond hair, was mere coincidence.

"Listen, Wes." Mary kept her voice gentle, but she made it firm too. "Do you love this girl?"

His face reddened, and he shrugged. "Yeah."

"Then don't you want what's best for her?"

"Sure I do. That's why I'm here."

"I might never see her or meet her," Mary said. "But if I do, I'll try to do what's best for her. And that's what I think you should do."

"I am," he insisted. "Like I said, she's got something going on, but I don't want her going through it alone. I want to at least make sure she's all right."

"She'd be all right if she was at home with her folks, don't you think?"

"I told you," he said, huffing in exasperation. "Her dad's dead. Her mom's got other things to do. She doesn't have anybody else. Nobody but me."

"Her aunt is looking for her too," Mary told him. "She says her parents have forgiven her and want her to come home." Mary put her hand on his shoulder. "Maybe they have the wrong impression of you. The best way to prove to them that you really care about Anna is to try to get her to go back to them."

He recoiled. "Anna? Who's Anna?"

"Anna Nussbaum. Her aunt, Sarah Miller, has been looking for her. I know Amish parents can be strict, but that's only to protect their children. If you can help her aunt find her and get her home, maybe Anna's parents will be more open to you two seeing each other."

He shook his head furiously. "She doesn't have an aunt. I don't know what you're talking about. I don't know anybody named Anna Nussbaum."

Mary pressed her lips into a tight line. "You said your friend is Amish."

"No, I said she'd grown up with the Amish. They were her neighbors, not her family. She was never a member of their church or raised that way. They were only her friends. I think you have her and this other girl mixed up. I'm sorry. I wish this was as easy as getting K—" He caught himself. "I wish it was as easy as getting my friend to go home again. It's just not." He jammed his cap back onto his head. "I don't know what else to tell you. She's not Amish, she's not Anna Nussbaum, and she doesn't have an aunt or a family to go back to."

Mary studied him for another moment. Either he was an incredible actor, or this was the most unlikely coincidence ever. Could there possibly be two girls and two separate disappearances?

He swiped his hand over his mouth and then composed himself. "You have my number in your phone. I'm sorry I can't tell you how she might have come to use it, but that's honestly all I know about it."

"No, it's all right," she said. "It wasn't really a problem, but I'd like to know how she got ahold of it and how she got it back to me without anybody noticing."

"She didn't say anything about that, but I'm glad you got it back. I'm sure she didn't mean any harm."

"What do you think happened to her own phone?" Mary asked him.

"I'm not sure. I'm guessing she either got rid of it so nobody could track her with it, or she has it locked up somewhere safe. Probably back in Por—"

She laughed a little. "In Portland?"

He nodded guiltily. "Yeah. But that's the other thing. If she was Amish like that aunt person says, then she wouldn't even have a phone."

"Or maybe that's why she had to use mine."

"Look," he said, "I don't know who this other girl is. I don't know her. I hope her aunt finds her and she gets to go back home, but she's got nothing to do with me or my friend."

"All right. All right. If that's the case, okay. I still haven't seen anybody like either of you describe."

"Like I said, you have my number in your phone. If you do see her, please ask her to call me." He started digging in the front pocket of his jeans. "I can leave you some money to pay for her using your store phone."

"No, that's all right. The phone isn't a problem. But I hope you're being straight with me."

"I am. I promise." He winced. "As much as I can be. There's a lot I can't tell you. A lot I don't even know. But I swear I only want to help her and make sure she's all right."

"Are you sure the police can't help? If you're worried—"

"She wouldn't want anything like that. Listen, just do me a favor, if you see somebody like her, tell her to call Wes. She knows the number."

"Okay," Mary said finally.

He thanked her then and left, and Mary knew she had to have an honest talk with Katura. She would tell her what had been going on, about Sarah's and Wes's inquiries, and then she'd offer her help. That was all she could do.

CHAPTER FIFTEEN

M ary could hardly wait until they closed the shop for the day. She hurried through dinner and then told her sisters she was going to see Katura. Martha wanted to go along so she could stop at the store afterwards, and Mary decided that agreeing with her would be the quickest way to get going.

"Are you sure this is a good idea?" Martha asked, not for the first time.

"If Katura is somehow involved with Sarah or Wes or both, she ought to know they've been asking about her. If I'm way off base with this whole thing, no harm done."

Verity opened the door when Mary knocked.

"Oh hello, Mary. Hello, Martha. Will you come in?"

She stepped back, and Mary and Martha entered the warm house. Iris was sitting at a large table in the living room cutting out black fabric for a dress.

"Come and sit down with us," she said, smiling. "There is coffee and snitz pie. I had to hide it from my boys, but they are out in the barn now, tending our sick cow, and it is safe to bring it out again."

Mary and Martha looked at each other and grinned.

"We'd love to have some," Mary said.

"Good." Iris waved toward the long bench across the table from her. "Sit down. Verity, please bring the coffee and pie."

"Ja, Maam."

"It is good to see you both," Iris said as Verity hurried to the kitchen. "You can see I am making a new dress. This one is for Verity."

Martha examined the fabric. "That's very nice. It should wear well too."

"I thought so," Iris said, looking pleased.

"We came to see Katura," Mary said, deciding it was best to get right to the matter at hand. "We were hoping to talk to her if we could. Is she out in the barn?"

Verity came in with coffee cups and slices of pie on small plates. She glanced at her mother.

"Katura has left," Iris said. "We are sorry to be without her, but she has had to go."

"Left?" Mary and Martha said at once.

"Where'd she go?" Mary asked. "When will she be back?"

"She left this morning. We cannot say where she is going or if she will come back," Iris said, through tight lips. "But we wish her well and pray Gott's blessing on her as she goes from us. She will be greatly missed."

"She will," Verity added, setting down the plates and cups in front of Mary and Martha. "We pray Gott will watch over her and keep her safe."

Martha looked at Mary questioningly and then at Iris. "She just left? I'm sorry we didn't get a chance to say goodbye."

"It was very sudden," Iris said. "It was a personal matter."

"Did something happen? Is she all right?"

Iris nodded. "You must not worry for her. There has been a difficult matter she has been dealing with, but she has gone to see to it. It is good for her to do it, and we are happy it will soon be over. She is very young to be in such a situation."

"But did—"

Iris put a calming hand on Mary's arm. "Truly, we cannot say more. Where she has gone and why is her own affair."

"No, I wasn't going to ask that. As long as she left because she wanted to, then that's all right. I was wondering, though, if someone came to get her."

Iris frowned. "Came to get her?"

"There was a woman named Sarah Miller, an Amish woman, who has been looking for her niece, Anna Nussbaum. And there is a young Englischer, Wes Rhys, who is looking for his girlfriend. Neither of them came here?"

"Not that I have seen. Verity, have you seen either of these people?"

"No, Maam," Verity said. "I have not seen them or heard of them before now. Do they know Katura?"

Mary let out a slow breath. "I don't know. I don't think so. They both describe a girl who doesn't look like Katura except for being around twenty. I was only wondering if one of them had come here to see if she was who they were looking for and if she had gone with them."

"No," Iris said. "She did not go with anyone like that."

"Did she have any visitors at all?" Mary asked. "Did anyone come looking for her?"

"We have had our neighbors come to call," Verity said, "but no one we do not know and trust. I do not think Katura would want you to worry for her, and this is a private matter for her. I am sure you understand."

"Of course we do," Martha said, giving Mary a "let it go" look. "We were just surprised that Katura left so suddenly. If you hear from her, please let her know we asked about her and hope everything is all right."

After that they had their pie and coffee and talked about Elizabeth's wedding and Mary's engagement and the dress Iris was making. As they were leaving, Iris asked them to pray for Katura.

"I believe things with her will be well, but there is never harm in prayer."

Mary assured her they would remember Katura in their prayers and then followed Martha out to the car.

"I didn't expect that," she said as they drove away. "Where could Katura have gone?"

"You've got to let it go," Martha said. "It's a personal matter."

"Yeah, yeah, I know." Mary exhaled loudly. "Maybe I've blown this all out of proportion. I'm still worried about her."

"Why'd you tell them about Wes and Sarah Miller? Katura's not who they're looking for."

"I was wondering if either of them had been by there asking questions. I don't know what's going on with Katura, but she's always seemed a little jumpy to me. I was wondering if something like having someone come by asking questions could have scared her off."

"But why would it?"

"I don't know." Mary thought for a moment. "One thing we could do is find out if Dan is still in town. If he is, then he probably doesn't have anything to do with this."

Martha gave an exasperated sigh. "It sounds to me like there's nothing for anybody to have anything to do with in the first place. Katura left because she wanted to leave. This Anna Nussbaum seems to be in the middle of a family matter. Maybe Sarah and Wes are looking for the same person. It seems fairly likely that they are, but we can't be sure of that. Wes says he doesn't know anybody called Anna Nussbaum, and his friend doesn't have an aunt."

"He could be lying because he wants Anna to stay with him and not go back to her family," Mary said. "But Anna, if that's the same girl, doesn't seem to want to go with him or anybody else."

"But his friend did call him and let him know she was all right," Martha reminded her. "She had to have known he'd be able to find out at least the area where she was if she called on a landline."

"Well, I feel sorry for Sarah. She seems very upset about her niece, and it's got to be hard for an Amish woman to come to a strange town alone looking for someone."

"You'd think she'd be asking the Amish around here, not us."

"I suppose she has," Mary said. "And, since everybody Amish knows practically everybody else who's Amish in the area, it would be the best place to start. But if she's already asked them, she'd have to start asking the Englisch too, wouldn't she?" She leaned her elbow against the armrest and her chin on her hand. "I think we should go see if Dan's still in town."

Martha glanced over at her. "What?"

"Just to make sure. It won't hurt anything to ask."

"Mary." There was more than a little exasperation in Martha's voice now. "Exactly what are we supposed to tell him if he is? We had to come by to check on you, Dan, because we're pretty sure you're some kind of predator?"

"Of course not."

"Maybe we should think this out a little. Maybe it would be better to have one of the guys talk to him. Bill would be a good choice. He knows the family better than we do."

"Okay, maybe you're right. He'd probably be less obvious than one of us asking Dan questions out of the blue."

"I still need to stop at the store and get the thread I need."

"No problem."

"It shouldn't take long. Anything you need? Do we need anything at the house?"

"Get some glass cleaner, if you would," Mary said, remembering they were almost out. "And Tink would like a bag of her treats. She ate the last one yesterday."

"Glass cleaner and doggie treats," Martha said. "Got it."

It wasn't far to the store, and Mary found a parking place close to the front door.

"Want to come in?" Martha asked.

Mary shook her head. "I think I'm going to just sit here and try to think. There's got to be something that would explain all of this, don't you think so?"

"There might be," Martha said, getting her purse from the floorboard. "And there might not be. Keep the doors locked, and I'll be right back."

Martha strode quickly through the store, wondering why it always seemed as if no matter what items she needed, they were as far away from the entrance and as far away from each other as possible. She found the glass cleaner and the thread she needed, and then she headed over to the pet section. As she passed the pharmacy, she wondered if they were low on any of their regular medical supplies at home—aspirin, Band-aids, hydrogen peroxide. That's when she noticed the man standing at the counter talking to the pharmacist. It was Dan Bontrager.

Had he seen her? She stood where she was for a moment as if she were studying the variety of antibacterial soaps on the endcap of the aisle. Then she slipped over to where the pain relievers were shelved, grabbed a bottle of aspirin, and pretended to read the ingredients, gradually moving closer to the counter as she did. She could hear the pharmacist clearly now.

"Has the patient used this before?" he asked.

"Yeah," Dan said. "Several years now."

"All right." The pharmacist rang up the purchase and handed Dan the bag. "Make sure she shakes the inhaler ten to fifteen times before using it."

She? Martha thought, moving slightly closer.

"I'll do that," Dan told the pharmacist, stuffing the bag into his coat pocket. "Thanks."

Before he could come her way, Martha put down the aspirin bottle and hurried into the pet section.

As soon as Martha got out and shut the car door behind her, Mary pushed the button and heard the satisfying snap of all the door locks clicking into place. Then she turned the heat down a couple of notches, not sure if she was actually too warm or was only feeling generally uncomfortable. If she hadn't seen how nervous Katura was around Dan after Bertha's funeral, if they hadn't been arguing in the store the other day, maybe she wouldn't be worried about Katura at all. She closed her eyes.

"God, be with her," she prayed. "Wherever she is, keep her safe, and show us if there's anything we can do to help her."

She prayed for Anna Nussbaum too, and for Wes's friend. She never had found out who Ken was. Maybe she'd get a chance to talk to Wes again. Of course, she could simply call him, but—

She snapped her eyes open at the urgent tapping on the car window. It was Martha. She had a plastic bag in her hand.

Mary unlocked the door.

"You'll never guess," Martha said, sliding into the passenger seat. "You'll never guess who I saw in the store."

"Who?"

"Dan Bontrager."

"You're kidding me."

Martha's cheeks were especially pink as she told Mary what had just happened, but whether that was from the cold or from excitement, Mary wasn't sure.

"He didn't see you?"

"No, and that's all I heard," Martha said. "But that inhaler wasn't for Dan. The pharmacist said 'she' should make sure to shake the inhaler before using it. Who's 'she'? Not his father or brother."

"A lot of people need them," Mary said, her pulse beating a little faster as she drove out of the parking lot. "Katura uses one. I know, I know, that doesn't mean Dan knows where she is

or was picking that one up for her, but isn't it a little strange
that he picked up an inhaler? I mean, just now? Right after
Katura left Bird-in-Hand?"

"This could be nothing," Martha said, "but I have to agree
with you. How do we check it out?"

"Maybe the pharmacist just made a mistake that I overheard, and it really was for Dan. Eli would know if Dan needed
an inhaler himself, wouldn't he?"

"He might. I don't get the impression that they've been
especially close recently, but Dan has visited him and Jedidiah.
Dan's done at least a little bit of work on their farm. If he regularly needs an inhaler, then they might have noticed while he
was there."

Mary gave her sister a hopeful smile. "We could ask,
couldn't we?"

"We can't just go over there and knock on the door and ask
if Dan uses an inhaler. It would be better if Jedidiah or Eli happened to come into the store or something and then we could
strike up a conversation."

"They don't come in very often," Mary said, "especially
Jedidiah. And if something is going on with Katura, we'd better find out sooner than later." She thought for a moment. "I
wish Ruby was still alive. It would be easy to go over there and
take some of your fresh bread and visit."

"I did make some only this morning."

"Your bread is delicious," Mary said eagerly, "and I don't
suppose Eli and Jedidiah make their own, so they'd probably
appreciate some that didn't come from the store. And, of
course, if we were to take some by, because we know Dan is

visiting and everything, it would be the most natural thing in the world, wouldn't it?"

"We're not exactly close friends," Martha reminded her.

"But they do come into the store. Dan and Eli were in just the other day. Mama and Daddy knew their family for years. We would only be being neighborly, wouldn't we?"

"And if Dan shows up?"

Mary winced. She hadn't thought of that.

"I don't know. Eli says Dan hasn't been around much. That's part of what makes all this feel so off to me. Why is Dan here if he's not spending time with them?"

"Okay, suppose we go visiting for a few minutes," Martha said. "Is that going to prove anything?"

"I don't know. Probably not. But maybe it'll tell us whether or not we need to be worried. I hope Katura is fine, like Iris and Verity said. But if I have all these questions about what's going on and something bad happens to her, I'm going to be very upset with myself if I didn't at least try to help."

"I'd feel bad too," Martha admitted. "And it won't hurt to be neighborly."

They went back to the house, dropped off the things Martha had bought, and picked up a loaf of fresh bread. Then they drove over to the Bontrager farm.

It wasn't a large place, but it was well kept. The house was small, painted white of course, and set on a hill overlooking the snowy pastureland. There were tire-tread marks among the buggy wheel and horse hoof marks on the road that led up to it, but there was no car out front now.

"Unless he's pulled around back for some reason," Mary said, "Dan's not here."

"Maybe that's for the best." Martha got the bread and her purse and got out of the car. "Now, we're not staying long, right?"

Mary got out too. "Right. Just long enough to visit and talk to Jedidiah and Eli."

"And not be obvious."

"And not be obvious," Mary agreed. "Come on."

CHAPTER SIXTEEN

Mary and Martha walked up to the Bontrager house and knocked on the door. It was Eli who answered.

"Mary. Martha." He looked faintly puzzled, but he gave them his usual shy nod. "Will you come in? Daed is in the barn if it is him you came to see."

"Hello, Eli," Mary said as she and Martha went inside. "We really just came by to drop off some of Martha's fresh bread. We thought that, since Dan is visiting you, you all might enjoy it."

"That is kind of you. Will you sit down? Daed prefers tea to coffee, but I would be happy to bring you either if you would like."

"Thank you," Martha said. "It is pretty cold out there. Some tea would be very welcome."

She handed him the bread, and he sniffed deeply of it.

A rare smile spread over his face. "This is like Maam used to make for us. It has been a long time, but I remember. It was very good."

He went to get the tea, and Mary gave Martha a nod. So far, so good.

"We must buy our bread," he said when he came back, bringing them each a steaming cup. "I suppose I might learn to make it myself, but there is always so much to do on the farm, the buying is easier."

"I'm sure it is," Martha said. "But if you'd like, I could put in an extra loaf once in a while for you and Jedidiah. Our parents and your grandparents were good friends. We ought to be better friends too."

"Ja, I would like that. You two and Elizabeth, you are all well?"

"Very well, thank you," Mary said. "I thought we'd be seeing more of you and Dan at the store since he's been here. Isn't he still helping you out at the farm?"

Eli didn't exactly frown, but he looked as if he wanted to. "I thought that is what he came here for and to spend some time with Daed. It is a very good thing to speak of wanting to become close once more to family, and it is another thing to take the time to actually do it. Daed thought that, since he stayed longer than Bertha Shetler's funeral, he came to see us, but for days we have not seen him."

He was as close to being angry as Mary had ever seen him.

"Do you think he'll go back to..." She gave him a slight smile. "I don't even know where he lives."

"Portland," Eli said.

Portland? That's where Wes said he was from.

"Oregon?" she asked, not letting her bewilderment show on her face.

"Maine. He works somewhere in the downtown area. I know it is far, but if Daed was important to him, he would at least visit with him while he is here."

"Maybe Dan's sick or something," Martha suggested.

"Sick? Dan?" Eli scoffed. "He is always well."

"Not even any little things he deals with?" Mary asked. "Allergies? Asthma? Something like that?"

Eli looked faintly disgusted. "Never. We were cleaning out a shed near our barn, and it was full of dust and everything else that had settled there since the harvest. He was not bothered by it, and I was coughing and sneezing from the dust. It seemed hardly fair."

"But it didn't cause you any real problems, did it?"

"Oh, no. Daed and I are long used to such things and used to breathing the clean, open air."

Martha gave him a commiserating smile, clearly avoiding looking at Mary. "At least Dan was helping."

"That was on Saturday. We have hardly heard from him since."

"I'm surprised he's not staying with you," Mary said.

"He said it is best he stays at Muhlenberg's. He said that way we need not bother about him. Perhaps it is he who does not wish to bother about us." Eli pressed his lips into a thin line. "Daed does not ask that he come back to live or that he become a member of our church, but since Dan is here, Daed would like to see him. He does not complain, but I can tell it is painful for him."

"I'm sure it must be." Mary sighed. "Maybe he's struggling with what he ought to say to your father or feeling like he can never make things right with him. Or with you."

"I suppose that could be," Eli said, but he didn't much look convinced. "Still, you did not come to hear our troubles. Would you like me to call Daed in from the barn? He is tending to one of our cows who has a new calf. The birth was very difficult…."

Mary listened to him describing what had happened with the calf and cow, hardly thinking of what he was saying, instead turning over in her mind what he had said about Dan being so healthy. So, who was the "she" the inhaler was for? The only one Mary could think of was Katura.

Where had Katura gone and why? Verity and Iris said she'd "gone away." She hadn't been taken away. She had gone away. Did Dan have anything to do with that? Where was she staying now, and if that inhaler was for her, why hadn't she gotten it herself?

Martha glanced at Mary and then nodded at Eli. "It's too bad Dan wasn't here to help you during the birth."

Eli shrugged. "He has lived in the city many years now. I would not expect he would be very much help in such things."

"He probably remembers what he used to do when you two were growing up."

"If he were to stay long enough perhaps."

"I know he came here for the funeral," Mary said. "We all loved Bertha Shetler, but I didn't know he was that close to her family. Of course, I wasn't here when he left home eight years ago. Were they close then?"

"Ja, some. Bertha was good to everyone, almost a mother. She was fond of Dan. He sometimes would send a letter to Daed, asking after him and me, and I believe there were times he would write to Bertha as well."

"That was good of him. I know Bertha must have been pleased. Do you think he'll stay in touch with the family now that she's gone?"

"I do not know. It does not seem very likely, but perhaps."

"He was talking to Katura last time they were both in our shop."

Eli wrinkled his forehead. "Katura?"

"He hasn't mentioned anything to you about her?"

"No. Why should he? She is not Bertha's family."

"That's true. It's only that he seems…concerned about her."

"It is hard to tell what he might be thinking." Eli stroked his chin. "He has been away from here for a long time. But Katura is a good, quiet girl, and she is with a good family. They will watch after her."

"Katura left there," Mary said. "Hadn't you heard?"

"Has she returned to her own family?"

"Verity didn't say. She only said that she had gone."

"Then I suppose she is well seen to."

They chatted a while longer about the farm and mutual friends. Eli thanked them again for the bread, and walked them to the front porch. Mary could hardly wait to get into the car.

"See?" she said as she pulled away from the house. "Dan has no reason to need an inhaler."

"That we know of," Martha reminded her. "But yeah, it does seem unusual. Who would he have bought it for? Eli doesn't need it. Neither does Jedidiah. Who would he be getting this inhaler for?"

"That brings us back to why he's still here if he's not visiting family or anybody else. It's not like he'd be interested in the Amish tourist sites or anything like that."

Martha chuckled. "Probably not."

Elizabeth was waiting for them in the kitchen when they got back home.

"Where have you two been?" she asked. "I saw what you got at the store. Or I should say that Tinkerbelle found the treats you bought. I managed to save most of them."

"Tink," Mary scolded, hands on hips.

Tinkerbelle ducked her head and looked up apologetically.

"Anyway," Mary said, "Martha went into the store to buy some things, and she saw Dan Bontrager buying an inhaler."

"And?" Elizabeth asked, clearly not seeing the importance of the discovery.

Mary and Martha told Elizabeth about Katura's sudden departure from the Shetler household and about their visit to the Bontragers'.

"We went over to see Eli to try to find out if Dan had any reason to need an inhaler himself," Mary said. "Eli says Dan's never had asthma."

"Maybe it's a recent thing," Elizabeth said. "Something Eli doesn't know about."

"It would have to have happened since Saturday. Eli said he and Dan were cleaning out a shed at their farm, and none of the dust and debris bothered Dan then."

"So he picked it up for someone else. What difference does it make?"

"Who would he have picked it up for?"

"Well, I don't know. You're not saying it's for Katura, are you? That's a little bit of a stretch, isn't it?"

"I'm not saying I know anything for sure," Mary said. "But don't you think it's a little odd that Katura uses an inhaler and that Dan got one that wasn't for him right after she disappeared?"

"But you told me Verity and Iris said Katura left. Dan didn't come get her."

"But how did she go?" Mary asked. "Where did she go? *Why* did she go? I wish we knew more than we do."

"You know what Iris said," Martha reminded her. "Katura always was a quiet girl and very private. And I'm sure they wouldn't gossip about something she didn't want everybody to know. She wanted to leave, so she did." She picked up her purchases from the counter where Elizabeth had placed them. "I'm headed upstairs to get some sewing in."

Elizabeth sank into a kitchen chair. "If Dan kidnapped her or something crazy like that, why would he still be here? Maybe we're all getting a little obsessive about girls going missing, with Sarah looking for her niece and that boy, Wes, looking for his girlfriend."

Mary sat down next to her. "I'm glad Katura isn't a blue-eyed blond. That would really complicate matters."

Elizabeth chuckled.

"It still bothers me," Mary continued. "What if Katura is in some kind of trouble? I'm worried about her."

"Are you saying this based solely on Martha seeing Dan pick up that inhaler?"

"Not solely. I've been uncomfortable since I saw him arguing with Katrina at the shop."

Elizabeth gave her a look. "Even before that, am I right?"

Mary nodded sheepishly. "Right after Bertha's funeral. I could tell she was uncomfortable around him, more uncomfortable than she usually is, I mean. He had to have said or done something that made her want to stay away from him."

"Do you know for sure that they hadn't met before the funeral?"

Mary considered for a moment. "I guess I don't know that for certain, no, but when would he have met her? He was long gone from Bird-in-Hand before she came here. And he asked who she was at the funeral."

Elizabeth tossed her head. "Well, that could have been a good bit of acting, maybe."

"Do you think John could do something? I don't mean arrest Dan or bring him in for questioning or anything, but maybe just ask around or talk to him. Find out more about what he's been doing in Bird-in-Hand. I don't know, look in his room at Muhlenberg's."

"You know he couldn't conduct a search without a warrant."

"I don't mean search," Mary said. "I mean go talk to him and look around a little bit and see if anything looks out of place. He's a policeman. He should know something to do."

"I guess I could ask him," Elizabeth said reluctantly, "but I don't think he has enough probable cause to do anything but chat with Dan. Maybe he can visit Iris and Verity too. Just to make sure Katura's all right."

"Please ask him. I'd feel so much better."

Elizabeth stood. "Do you want to contact him about this? You're the one who talked to Eli and to Wes and to Sarah. Did Sarah tell you where she was staying or give you any way to get in touch with her?"

"No. She said she'd be back to see if we'd heard anything about her niece, that's all. Do you think I'm overreacting about all this?"

"Actually, you've got me worried too. There's something going on, and the police are the best ones to check it out. I'll call John."

When she got John on the phone, Elizabeth told him what she and Mary had been talking about, and then she gave her phone to Mary.

"Hi, John," Mary said. "I'm sorry to bother you, but I'm really concerned about Katura."

"It's no bother," he said. "Sometimes it's hard to know when to involve the police. Sometimes it's a little scary, even if the officer is about to be your brother-in-law."

"That does make it a little easier," she admitted, feeling not quite as tense.

She told him everything she had found out about Wes and Sarah and Dan and about Martha seeing Dan picking up an inhaler at the drugstore.

"I can't help feeling like all of this is connected, but I can't figure out how."

"I'll admit, it does seem like there have been a lot of unusual things happening that don't have any satisfactory explanations. Of course, all of it could be absolutely harmless. Merely normal people going about their own business. But put together…"

"Put together," she said, "it doesn't sound harmless or normal."

"No. And you say the Shetlers aren't worried about Katura?"

"They say it's good that she's gone. It felt to me like they weren't very happy about her going. I couldn't tell if they simply didn't want her to go or if they were worried about where she was going."

"But Dan didn't have anything to do with her leaving? He didn't come see her or anything?"

"Verity and Iris say nobody came to see her."

"Based on what you've told me, Mary, I don't know if there's much I can do, but I can check it out. And the Shetlers didn't tell you where Katura was going?"

"No. They said what they've said about her since she came here, that she had some difficult things she was dealing with, and she didn't want to talk about it. I couldn't very well demand that they tell me anything."

"You don't think they could be up to something, do you? I realize they're your friends, but I have to consider all the possibilities."

"Oh no. We've known the Shetlers for as long as I can remember. Mama and Daddy knew them when they were young."

"But you've known the Bontragers too, haven't you?" John asked.

"That's true, at least my parents knew Jedidiah's folks, and we know him and Eli, but Dan's been away for eight years, and I never really knew him at all."

"Well, I'll do a little asking around. If anything seems to be out of place, then we can open a real investigation. How would that be?"

Mary smiled even though she knew he couldn't see it. "That would make me feel so much better. To be honest, that woman in Portland, the one in the Carlisle case, has been on my mind. I still can't help thinking that if someone had tried to help her, she might not be dead right now. I'd feel awful if there was something serious going on with Katura, and I did nothing."

"I understand," John said.

"Thank you. Will you let me know what you find out?"

"If I find anything worth knowing and it doesn't break protocol, I will."

"Great. Here, I'll let you talk to Elizabeth again."

"Thanks for looking into this for us," Elizabeth said. She listened for a few seconds, and then she suddenly looked troubled. "No. Thanks, but maybe next time. It's late." Again she listened. "Love you too. Talk to you soon."

"What was that about?" Mary asked her.

"Oh, he asked if I wanted to come watch a movie with them. He said Tina was making popcorn."

"Didn't you want to go?"

"I couldn't. Not as long as she feels like I'm intruding."

"You can't keep avoiding the issue," Mary told her. "I know it's hard, but if you go on the way you are, you're only going to make it worse. At least talk to John about it. You love him. Doesn't he deserve that much from you?"

"He does. I know. And I'm going to talk to him about it. I just have to figure out what to say."

CHAPTER SEVENTEEN

Saturdays were usually busy at Secondhand Blessings, and Elizabeth managed to keep her upcoming conversation with John at the back of her mind most of the time. Still, in between customers, it nagged at her. She loved John. She didn't want to lose him. But she reminded herself firmly that if their relationship wasn't strong enough to withstand a few bumps in the road, it would be better to know that now than after they were married.

She felt her heart sink when she heard John's ringtone coming from her phone. Every time he called, it reminded her that she was going to have to talk to him about the situation with Tina, and every time she couldn't seem to scrape up the courage to do it. She kept waiting for a better time, and it was becoming obvious that that better time was never going to come.

She picked up the phone. "John. Hi."

"Hi, honey."

There was a grimness to his voice that she rarely heard. Had Tina talked to him?

"What's going on?" she asked, trying to keep her voice neutral. "Is everything all right?"

"Yeah. Is Mary with you?"

"She's right here."

Mary looked over at her, one eyebrow raised.

"Good," John said. "Can you put me on SPEAKER? You both need to hear this."

"Okay," she said, glad there were no customers in the shop at the moment. "Hold on."

At least he wasn't calling to talk about Tina.

Elizabeth took the phone away from her mouth. "Mary? John wants us both to hear something."

"Okay." Mary came over and stood beside the counter. "Did he say what?"

"Not yet." Elizabeth switched the phone to SPEAKER and then set it down between herself and Mary. "John?"

"Right here," John said. "Can you both hear me?"

"I can," Mary told him. "Hi."

"Hi, Mary. Elizabeth?"

"I'm right here."

"Great. I just wanted to tell you both what I found out when I went to talk to Dan."

Mary's eyes widened.

"Okay," Elizabeth said.

"It's really important that you listen to me," John said. "Is Martha there too?"

"She's in the house," Mary said. "Do you want me to go get her?"

"No, that's all right. But I want you to relay this to her next time you see her. Make sure, all right?"

"We'll make sure," Elizabeth told him. "What did you find out?"

"I did a little checking on Dan before I talked to him, and then I went to see him. I can't tell you what we talked about, so please don't ask me, but the department is aware of what's going on. It's nothing you need to worry about."

"But Katura—" Mary began.

"We're in control of the situation, all right? That's all I can tell you. But don't worry about it anymore."

"Okay," Elizabeth said, looking sternly at Mary.

Mary gave her a frustrated huff.

"Mary?" Elizabeth pressed.

Mary scowled. "Okay."

"I'm sorry I can't tell you anything else right now," John said, his tone a little softer now. "If I can tell you anything later, I promise I will. Just let us see to it, all right?"

"We will," Elizabeth said. "And thank you for checking into it for us, whatever's going on."

"No problem. That's what we're here for." He paused for a second. "Thanks for listening, Mary."

"Sure," Mary said, clearly disappointed.

"Can you take me off SPEAKER now, hon?" John asked.

"Sure." Elizabeth picked up the phone again and returned it to its regular setting. "Done."

"I'm going to finish unpacking the crockery we just got," Mary said, and she went into the back room.

"What else is going on?" Elizabeth asked John when she was gone. "Are you having a good day?"

"I've had better."

"Is something wrong?"

That miserable sinking feeling struck her again. She was going to have to talk to him, and the sooner the better. She couldn't keep living with this hanging over her head.

"Not really wrong," he said. "I was wondering if you could come by for a while."

"Okay," she said. "Do you mean right away or later on?"

"Oh, it's not urgent," he assured her, "but I'd like it to be today, if that's all right with you."

"Today's all right. As soon as we close and have dinner, I can come over."

"That would be good. I'll be expecting you."

"Only you?" she asked. "No Tina?"

"No Tina. She's over at a friend's. I thought it might be a good opportunity for us to talk about things."

Elizabeth felt her heartbeat speed up. "Things?"

"Yeah. If you don't mind."

"Is there something you had in mind?"

"Actually, there is. Maybe it's nothing, but I figure it's good to find out for sure. If it's not nothing, then I'd like to see what we can do to make it better."

Elizabeth felt like someone had dropped a lead weight into her stomach. This was about Tina, she was sure it was. Well, it was time to get it resolved somehow.

"Do you want to tell me what this is about?" she asked, hoping and not hoping it was what she thought it was.

"Just come over, all right? We'll talk about it. We'll work it out."

He didn't sound so much optimistic as determined. He had to be wondering what he was going to do if she and Tina couldn't find a way to coexist. At least, if this was about Tina, she didn't have to worry about him finding out. That damage was already done.

"Please, God," she prayed once she'd ended the call, "help us all know what to do. Help me mend things with Tina somehow. Help me know how to love her no matter how she feels about me."

It didn't take long for her to get over to John's house once the shop was closed for the day. As he had told her, Tina wasn't there.

"She and her friend Cassie are learning lines together tonight," he said. "Evidently their new drama teacher is a real stickler."

"Is she?" Elizabeth took the cup of coffee he offered her and sat next to him on the couch. "But that's good, isn't it? Making all the actors give their best?"

"Tina doesn't mind working hard. She wants to improve every time she goes on stage. The problem is that this teacher, her name's Jasmine, wants them to do everything exactly by the book. She won't let them add their own creativity to their roles."

"I guess that's understandable," Elizabeth said. "She has to make a coherent whole out of what all the different players are doing."

"Sure. I know that has to be taken into consideration, but I don't think Tina wants to do anything way out there. Their last teacher encouraged them to see what each of them could add to his interpretation, and then he'd explain to them why that did or didn't work for the production they were putting on at the time. Tina loved that. She felt like she really learned a lot. Now she feels like she's only reading lines."

"I'm sorry," Elizabeth said. "I can see how a good instructor makes a big difference in a subject that has so much to do with creativity."

John grinned. "I told her she could at least learn to get along with someone like Jasmine, because if she ends up going into acting, she's going to run into directors she doesn't get along with. Probably more of those than the ones she loves working with."

"I guess we all need to know how to get along in difficult situations," Elizabeth said, giving him the perfect opening.

He took it.

"That's kind of what I wanted us to talk about."

She took a sip of her coffee, waiting for him to go on.

"I could tell Tina's been upset for the past few days," he said, the words almost tentative. "She didn't want to talk about it at all. She even said at first that there was nothing the matter. But today she came home really unhappy. At first I thought it was because she was frustrated with her drama teacher, but then she admitted there was something else."

Here it came. Maybe she had told him why she didn't like her prospective stepmother. That would be a place to start working things out. Unless Tina's real objection wasn't actually to Elizabeth but to the idea of her father remarrying at all.

Elizabeth braced herself. "What did she say?"

"Ever since you came to dinner the other day, she thinks she's done something or said something that's made you not like her anymore."

Elizabeth gaped at him. "What?"

"She's been trying to figure out how to talk to you about it. She wants to apologize for whatever it is, but she doesn't know what she did or what to say to make it right. What upsets her most is that it might come between you and me. She really doesn't want that to happen." He took Elizabeth's hand. "I don't either."

"I—I don't know what to say."

How could Tina put this on her?

John held on more tightly. "Is there anything she's done or said that's made you mad at her?"

"Not mad, no. And it wasn't something meant for my ears, but I couldn't help feeling awkward about it. That doesn't mean I don't like Tina. To tell the truth, I thought we were getting along great."

"I did too," John said. "What happened?"

"I don't know. When she came in the other day, when you went to get your laptop, I heard her on her phone. It might have been to Cassie. I'm not sure. But Tina told her that I was spoiling everything, and she didn't know why I had to be around all the time." Tears sprang to Elizabeth's eyes, and she blinked them back. "I'm sorry. I don't want to overreact, but it really surprised me. I had thought we were getting along great. Then I didn't know how to act when I was around her, knowing how much she wished I'd go away."

"Oh, honey, why didn't you tell me about it?"

"I didn't want to cause problems between the two of you. To be honest, I didn't know what to say. If you didn't know how she felt, and she didn't want to tell you about it, then I didn't want to bring it up and spoil everything."

"She's never said anything to me about not liking you. Quite the opposite, in fact. She hasn't said anything about us getting married except that she's glad I found someone so she can go off to school without feeling like I'd be alone all the time."

"She loves you. She wants you to be happy. I'm sure of that. She wants you to have what you want even if it's not what she wants."

He picked up his mug, staring into it for a moment before he took a drink. "Even when she told me she was upset this afternoon, she didn't say she didn't like you. She said you didn't like her."

"But that's not true," Elizabeth told him. "That's not at all true. Maybe I should have told her right away that I overheard what she said. I wasn't brave enough to do it. I thought it would blow over, but it seems that things have only gotten worse."

"Maybe all three of us should have a talk."

Elizabeth took a deep breath. "Maybe we should."

"She's been over at Cassie's for a couple of hours already. That ought to be enough practice for today. I'm going to ask her to come home, okay?"

Elizabeth wasn't at all sure it was okay, but maybe it was the best thing to do. "Okay."

It took Tina only a few minutes to get home once John called her. As she had the last time Elizabeth was there, she came in the back door in the middle of a phone call.

"I'm here now," she said. "I'd better go and get it over with."

CHAPTER EIGHTEEN

A moment later Tina came into the living room, her auburn hair in its usual messy bun and her brown eyes wide and uncertain.

"Hi," she said, looking from her father to Elizabeth and back again. "Um, here I am."

"Why don't you sit down for a minute," John said.

Tina sat in the chair across from them.

"Elizabeth and I were talking about what you and I discussed this afternoon," John said.

Tina looked down at her lap. "Okay."

"Tina," Elizabeth said gently, "I'm sorry if I've made you think I don't like you. That's not at all true. I think you're smart and funny and very, very talented. You're a hard worker, and you want to do what's right no matter what. I'm proud to know I'm going to get to be part of your family, and I'm looking forward to us being good friends."

Tina looked up, and there was only hurt in her eyes. "But you've been acting like you don't want to be around me. Like I make you uncomfortable." She leaned forward in her chair, suddenly earnest. "Whatever I did to make you mad, I'm sorry. I'm really sorry."

"I'm not mad, but I am confused," Elizabeth admitted. "I thought we were getting along great. I didn't realize that you felt like I was trying to take your mother's place. I promise I'm not. I'm not trying to be pushy or get between you and your dad. I'm sorry I've made you feel that way, and I want to work it out with you."

Tina frowned and put her head a little to one side. "What are you talking about?"

"Elizabeth heard what you said on the phone the last time she came over," John told her.

"What I said? I didn't say that. I'd never say that to anybody."

"But I heard you," Elizabeth said. "And I understand those feelings. I know it would have been hard for me and my sisters if one of our parents had remarried. I'm not at all saying you don't get to feel whatever it is you feel. I really want to work things out with you."

"But that's not what I feel," Tina said, clearly baffled. "I'm glad you and Dad are getting married. I told him that. Mom's been gone a long time. Dad shouldn't have to be alone."

"But you said—"

John held up both hands. "Wait. Wait. What exactly did you say, Tina?"

"I don't remember. When was that? Monday? Tuesday?"

"Monday," Elizabeth said. "You came in the back door, still on your phone, and then got yourself a soda and came in here. We were talking about honeymoon destinations."

"Oh yeah. I'd been over at Cassie's again." Tina thought for a moment. "We were working on blocking at her house, and then she called me on the way home to remind me of something our teacher said about—oh." She put one hand over her mouth. "Oh, now I remember."

"Tell us," John said.

"I was mad, because of the way Jasmine said we had to do a certain bit of business. We wanted to try something else, something our other teacher would have let us do, and I was mad about her ruining everything. Oh, Elizabeth, I'm so sorry." Tina reached across and covered Elizabeth's hand with her own. "It wasn't about you. It had nothing to do with you."

"But you said something about your dad already having made his mind up. That wasn't about me?"

"No, it wasn't about Dad," Tina insisted. "Cassie was wondering if we could talk to the principal about assigning our old teacher to our class again. I told her he'd already made up his mind about it, and there wasn't anything we could do. It wasn't about Dad or you."

"I shouldn't have jumped to conclusions or been listening in," Elizabeth admitted, relief flooding through her. "My mother always told me that eavesdroppers never hear anything good." She laughed a little. "And I had to make everything worse by acting uncomfortable around you, didn't I?"

"I thought I'd done something wrong," Tina said, ducking her head. "I thought I'd ruined everything for Dad."

"I wish both of you had just told me what you were dealing with," John said, "then neither of you would have had to worry. We're going to have to figure out how to make this work over the next few months, so I hope we'll start off by learning to talk things out."

"I think neither of us wanted to worry you," Elizabeth told him.

"She's right, Dad." Tina squeezed Elizabeth's hand once more. "And I know you weren't listening in. I knew you were here that night. I saw your car outside." She shrugged a little sheepishly. "I guess I spend a lot of time in theater making sure my voice carries. I don't exactly need to use that skill in my everyday life. Even when I'm throwing a minor tantrum."

She and Elizabeth exchanged a grin.

"Are we all okay now?" John asked, a twinkle in his eye.

"Yeah, Dad." Tina got up and kissed his cheek. "I feel a lot better. And, really and truly, I'm glad you two are getting married." She gave Elizabeth a quick hug. "I really am."

"I'm glad too," Elizabeth told her. "And I think we're going to get along fine."

"Anyway, I'd better go now. I have a ton of homework."

"Okay," John said. "I'll talk to you in a little bit. Don't stay up all night. Church tomorrow."

"Yeah, okay." Tina gave them a little wave and went to her room.

Elizabeth slumped back against the couch and let out her breath. "I'm so glad that wasn't serious."

"Me too." John pulled her close. "Next time something's bothering you, come talk to me about it, all right? Your problems are my problems, and we'll figure them out together."

"Even if one of the kids hates me?"

"Even then," he said, and then leaned over to kiss her. "Like that's ever going to happen."

Mary sat in the living room with Tinkerbelle curled up at her feet, Butterscotch asleep in her lap, and Pal sprawled out beside her. It was sweet, but it made it hard for her to use her laptop very efficiently. Martha had already observed that that was most likely the cat's plan from the beginning.

"I'm going over to Rachel's for a few minutes," Martha said, laying down her sewing. "She told me a while ago how much easier it is to do hand quilting on quilts that have their seams pressed a certain way. Or, actually, she was talking about how nice it is when they're not pressed a certain way."

Mary looked up from the honeymoon destination website she was scrolling through. "It makes a difference?"

"I don't think it's as important for machine quilters, but hand quilters usually like to have as few layers as possible to sew through. Of course, with quilting, there are usually as many opinions on everything as there are quilters, but the only opinion that matters in this case is Rachel's. Before I put the blocks together for the wedding ring quilt, I want to know how she'd like it done."

"Good idea. Tell her I said hi."

"Okay. I probably won't be long, but I have a few other questions to ask her too. Some of the fabrics I'm trying to use, a few of the ones from Mama's dresses, don't want to play nicely with others. I don't know if I should use some kind of stabilizer and, if I do, how that will affect Rachel's quilting. I figure I ought to ask her about that too."

Mary grinned. "You might be a while. That's okay. Bill's working a little late tonight, trying to finish up a job, so I'm going to stay here and dream of tropical beaches. Or scenic mountain views. Or maybe historic old-world sites. We'll see."

"You have fun then," Martha said. "I'll be back."

Once she was gone, Mary got out a notepad and started writing down honeymoon ideas she wanted to discuss with Bill. She wasn't set on any of them yet, but this would be a place to start. She had almost filled the page and was about to fix herself a cup of tea when there was a knock at the front door.

She put down her pad, unable to keep from smiling. Bill hadn't said he might come by tonight and, even though it was dark now, that wouldn't keep him from doing the indoor finishing work he had planned for this evening, but it would be nice to see him anyway. And she had found so many great places they could go after they were married. She'd love to talk about them. Oh, who was she kidding? It didn't matter what they talked about. She just wanted to be with him.

"Coming," she called as she headed toward the door.

When she opened it, she saw Sarah Miller standing on the other side. Mary was too surprised to be disappointed.

"Sarah. Hello. Is there something I can do for you?"

"I am very sorry to bother you. I know this is your home and not a public place, but I was wondering if I might speak to you for a few moments. Please."

"Sure. Come in and get warm. I was about to make myself some tea. Would you like some?"

"It would be very welcome on a cold night. Thank you."

Mary offered her a place on the couch and then got their drinks.

"Now," she said, sitting beside Sarah, "how can I help? I'm afraid I haven't had any news about your niece. I hate to disappoint you, but we really aren't the ones you should talk to about someone who's missing. The police—"

"Oh, no, no," Sarah said, looking mortified. "Anna is not a criminal. She has done nothing against the law."

"I realize that. But if the police can help you find her—"

"But they will not," Sarah insisted. "They will say she is an adult and may go where she will. Unless we can say we know some crime has been done, they will not help."

"No, I suppose not. You're right. So what did you come to talk about?"

"I cannot be certain yet, but I may have heard of someone here who knows where Anna is. Or at least he may know something that will help me to find her."

"That's good news. Who is it?"

"I am not entirely sure, you understand," Sarah said earnestly. "It is only a name I have heard before, and I heard it again today when I was having my supper. It is not an uncommon name, I suppose, but to hear it here and now, when I think my Anna must be nearby, I cannot help but wonder."

"Did you talk to the people who mentioned it? To ask where this person is?"

"No. I was so startled by what they said, for a moment I could not think. And then they had gone." Sarah wrung her hands helplessly. "I know it was foolish of me to not speak up at once, but I am so worried for Anna I do not know what I am doing most of the time."

"It's all right," Mary soothed. "I know you're worried. I'll help you if I can, but I really don't know anything. I haven't heard anything that would be any use to you. I have tried to find out if Anna might be here, but I haven't had any success."

"But I have heard the name of the man," Sarah said, leaning forward. "The man who took our Anna away and then so cruelly abandoned her. Would he have come here of all places if he did not also think she might be here?"

"Why would he be looking for her? If he abandoned her, why would he care where she was?"

"Oh, I do not know." Sarah sounded on the verge of tears. "Who can say what such a man might do?" She lowered her voice. "I have not said this to you before, but he was cruel to her. He would not allow her to see her family. He would not allow her to have friends. It could be he needs to have someone he feels he can control. There are such men."

"I'm sorry to say there are. But are you sure of this?"

If Wes Rhys was the mysterious boyfriend, Mary couldn't quite picture him as the type who would treat a woman in the way Sarah had described. But appearances were often deceiving.

"And when Anna finally broke free of him and tried to come home," Sarah said, "her parents would not allow it. You can see how hard that must have been for her."

Mary almost felt like crying herself. "They must feel terrible about that now."

"Ja, it is very bad for them. They want more than anything to have Anna home again. If my brother were not so very sick right now, he would have come himself. But as it is, there is no one but me to look for her and beg her to come back."

Mary frowned. "I thought you were Anna's mother's sister."

"Oh, ja," Sarah said quickly. "I meant to say my brother-in-law. He and my sister have been married so very long, it feels as if he is my brother." She laughed faintly. "You must not listen to me sometimes. I am so worried these days, I do not know what I say half of the time."

Mary patted her arm. "I understand. It's all right. But this man who Anna was with, are you sure he's the one whose name you heard?"

"No. No, I am still not certain of anything. But if I knew where he was, and if he is the man she was with, perhaps I could tell him to leave Anna alone. None of us in the family have met him or spoken to him. He should know that Anna is not alone and helpless."

"Yes, he should. But how will this help you to find Anna?"

"Why is he here if he is not looking for her?"

"I suppose that could be true," Mary said, taking a drink of her tea and hardly tasting it. "He could be looking the same as you are."

"And he might know something," Sarah pressed.

"If he did, would he tell you?"

"Maybe he would not. But maybe I could tell where he goes. What he does. Maybe I could tell him I will go to the police if he does not tell me what he knows or what he has heard about Anna."

Again Mary frowned. "I thought the police wouldn't do anything about this."

"Oh, they will not, but he may not know that. And if his conscience is guilty, and it well should be, it may be enough to tell him they will."

"Maybe," Mary said.

Sarah took a quick breath. "His name is Daniel Bontrager."

For an instant, Mary was stunned. "Are—are you sure?"

"I have told you, I am not sure of anything, but it is a name I have heard, and I know the man has come here. I must speak to him."

"But Dan—"

"You know him, I see." Sarah grabbed Mary's hands. "Oh, please, tell me where he is. I only wish to speak to him."

Mary hesitated, but only for a moment. Sarah couldn't have just happened to pull the name Daniel Bontrager out of thin air. If Dan had something to do with what had happened to Anna Nussbaum, especially if Katura really was Anna, then maybe Sarah could talk to him. Maybe she could let him know that Anna wasn't alone in the world, and she wasn't dependent on him. Maybe just knowing Anna had a family that wanted her home would make him let go of her for good.

"He's staying at Muhlenberg's. It's a bed-and-breakfast."

"Ja. I know of it. Thank you. I will go see him." She squeezed Mary's hands and then released them as she stood, her eyes bright with tears. "Thank you."

"Can I give you a ride over there?" Mary asked, standing too.

"Oh, no. Thank you. I have someone who will take me. She stopped to visit a friend on the next road. It is no trouble for her to drive me."

"All right," Mary said, wondering, if Sarah was so upset, why her friend hadn't come with her to talk to Mary. "Is there anything else I can do to help?"

"No, I do not think so. You have been very kind. I pray this will soon be all over, and Anna will have no more worries."

"Good. I hope everything works out well."

Sarah smiled hopefully and opened the front door. The wind caught under her kapp, pulling it up a little and tugging her hair up over one ear. She quickly patted it back into place and hurried away.

Mary shut the door. Then she locked it. Then she turned out the living room lights and peered out the front window and watched Sarah walk very fast down the road. She had pierced ears. Or at least she had one ear pierced. Mary's fears were confirmed when she saw Sarah get into a car a little way down the road and drive away.

Amish women did not have their ears pierced. And Amish women certainly didn't drive cars.

Mary quickly grabbed her coat, left the house, and got into her own car. She didn't have time to leave a note for Martha, but she didn't expect to be gone long. She was only going to see if Sarah went directly to Muhlenberg's. Whatever was going on, was Sarah in on it with Dan? If Mary saw them together, then she'd tell John about it. She didn't know what the police had against Dan. John had only said they were aware of the situation and that they had it under control. But, she told herself, they didn't know about Sarah. How did she fit in?

Careful not to get too close, Mary followed Sarah's car to Muhlenberg's, stayed back as Sarah parked and went inside, and then pulled into the lot and parked between two cars where she had a good view of the hotel's front door. She wasn't interfering, she told herself, remembering John's warning. She was only watching. If Sarah and Dan left the building, either together or separately, she'd see where they went. That was all.

She sat there in the dark silence, not sure how long she should wait. Her conscience nagged at her, but she quieted it with promises that she was only an observer. Dan and Sarah wouldn't even know she was out here. There was no risk.

Her conscience nagged again, and she got out her phone.

"John, it's Mary," she said before he could even say hello. "Look, I probably shouldn't have, I know, but Sarah Miller came over tonight, asking more about Anna Nussbaum and then about Dan. I told her he was here at Muhlenberg's and then I realized she couldn't be who she says she is."

"Mary, what—?"

"I'll give you the reasons later, but she's gone in there to talk to Dan. I don't know if the two of them are in some scheme together or what. I don't feel right about it. I was going to follow Sarah and see where she went, but maybe you should get someone else to do that. Someone from the police."

"Listen to me, Mary. This is very serious. Katura is Kennedy Sherman. She's the eyewitness in the Carlisle case. Dan's the policeman they sent to keep her safe until she can testify. That's why I wanted you to stay out of it. You shouldn't be there.

You shouldn't be there at all. I'm heading your way right now. Are you where you can be seen?"

"No, I don't think so," Mary said. "Just where I can watch the front door and Sarah's car."

"Okay, stay where you are, and stay out of sight. I'm coming."

He hung up, and Mary sat unmoving where she was. She wouldn't get into the middle of anything between Sarah and Dan. She only wanted to make sure Sarah didn't leave before John got here. And if she did?

She'd have to follow Sarah so she could tell John where she went.

She had done little more than put down her phone when the B and B's front door opened, and Sarah came out. Katura was with her, the two of them walking very close together. Sarah's arm was around Katura's shoulders, and her other hand was firmly in the pocket of her coat. What was Katura doing here? Had Dan brought her here to hide? And had Sarah somehow gotten her away from him?

As they came closer to the street, Mary could see their faces more clearly. Sarah's face was hard, unyielding. In Katura's face, there was only terror. She wasn't struggling, but she wasn't going willingly either. Then Mary realized why Sarah was walking so close to Katura and why her free hand was in her coat pocket. That way no one but Katura would know that she had a gun.

CHAPTER NINETEEN

Sarah and Katura were nearly at the car now, one Sarah had rented, judging by the stickers on it. In a few seconds more, they would drive away. Mary couldn't let Sarah take Katura away somewhere. She had to stop them, or at least stall them until John got here.

She quietly opened her door and got out of the car. *Don't let her know you know something's wrong,* she told herself firmly. *Stall her for a minute. All you have to do is keep her here till John shows up.*

She closed the door as silently as she could and walked toward Muhlenberg's. Then, a sudden idea struck her. She concealed herself behind a tree, quickly snapped a picture of Sarah and Katura, and texted it to herself and to Elizabeth. Then she slipped her phone back into her purse and walked casually toward Muhlenberg's.

"Oh, Sarah," she said when Sarah caught sight of her. "I'm glad I caught up with you. I wanted to make sure you got over here all right."

"It is very good of you," Sarah said stiffly, still trying to pretend she was Amish. "But, ja, I have found my niece, my Anna."

"This is Anna?" Mary asked as Katura looked at her pleadingly. "I thought you said she was blond."

"She has dyed her hair, but it will grow out before very long. We must go now. We thank you for your help."

"You'll need a ride," Mary said as they moved again toward the car. "If you like, I could take you somewhere. To the bus station? Or would you like me to call you a taxi?"

"No," Sarah said. "I—I am expecting my friend to return. She had to put gas in the car, but she will be back. She will take us. You have been very kind, but we really must go."

"You're welcome, of course. I'm glad everything's all right." She smiled at Katura. "Are you doing okay now, Anna?"

"She is fine," Sarah said, tightening her hold on the girl. "Ja, Anna?"

Katura nodded jerkily, unconvincingly. She looked worn out, even sick, and her breath was coming more and more quickly.

"And, truly," Sarah added, "we have to go now."

Mary swallowed hard, not knowing what else to do to stall them, afraid to do anything more and equally afraid that Sarah would get away with Katura if she didn't.

"I hate to leave you standing here in the cold. Are you sure I can't take you anywhere? It's no trouble."

"No. We thank you."

Sarah stepped off the curb, pulling Katura with her.

"No," the girl gasped, suddenly digging in her heels. "Mary, help me. Please."

"Come along now, Anna," Sarah said. "We do not have time for—"

"Stop," Mary said, fighting to keep out of her voice the sheer terror she was feeling. "Just listen to me."

"I've done all the listening I'm going to do," Sarah said, her accent suddenly gone and her gray eyes cold as steel. "I don't have time to fool with you right now, but I have a gun and it's pointed at the girl." She pushed the gun closer to Katura, pulling her coat more tightly around her body as she did. "Do I have to use it right here?"

"You work for Anderson Carlisle, don't you?" Mary asked. She took a step closer to them. "And that's Kennedy Sherman, right?"

"You stay where you are," Sarah said. "I don't want to make a scene, so you get back into your car and go home and keep quiet about what you've seen, and you'll be okay."

"You let her go, and then you can leave."

"Or I can simply shoot you both. That would be easier, wouldn't it?"

Mary's stomach turned over, but she refused to let that show in her face. "My sister is engaged to a policeman. He's already on the way here. If you shoot us, he'll be after you in a heartbeat."

"It's a risk I'm willing to take," Sarah said coolly.

"I took a picture of you just now," Mary told her. "I texted it to someone who will know who's responsible if anything happens to me or to Kennedy. Do you really want to give your life to save Carlisle's?"

Sarah hesitated.

"And killing us won't save your boss anyway," Mary added, remembering what she had in her pocket and thinking furiously as she spoke. "Because I have something that's going to convict him with or without the witness."

Sarah narrowed her eyes. "And what is that?"

Not quite knowing how she managed to keep calm, Mary pulled out the flash drive she had meant to give to Elizabeth. "This."

"And what exactly is that?" Sarah demanded.

"That wedding ring your boss lost, the one that will nail him on the murder charge. It's in a locker at the bus station, and the location of the key is on this flash drive," she said, the story spilling out of her almost on its own. "Like I said, even without the eyewitness, this will be enough to convict him, especially with the other evidence against him. Kennedy picked it up at the murder scene. Carlisle's ring with his girlfriend's blood on it. He's not going to be able to get around that, eyewitness or not. Now, you let Kennedy go, and I'll give you this. Even exchange."

"Mary, please," Katura pleaded.

Mary stepped off the curb and held the little plastic rectangle out, angling her arm more to the side than toward Sarah, but letting her get a good look at it.

"How do I know that's what's on there?" Sarah asked.

"You don't," Mary told her. "But Kennedy was the one who saw the murder. She was at the scene. Do you know for certain she didn't grab that ring and put it away somewhere as a bargaining tool in case Carlisle sent someone after her?"

Sarah jostled the girl's arm. "Is that what you did?"

Katura lifted her chin, her lips trembling. "I'm not telling you anything."

Mary silently blessed her for saying exactly the right thing.

Sarah looked at Mary again, unconvinced. "And you just happened to have that in your pocket when you came here?"

"I came to bring it to Dan Bontrager. I realized I was wrong about him and that he was working on this case. I knew he would know what to do about the ring. And I came to warn him about you."

"How do I know you don't have copies of that somewhere?" Sarah asked Mary.

"I do," Mary said. "And if anything happens to me or her, it goes right away to the police."

"Do you think I'm a fool? You said the police are already on their way."

"You're right. If you want a chance to get out of here, you'd better get going. You can take this, get the information about the locker, and get the ring before the police have time to get there first."

Sarah pulled the gun out of her pocket. "What's to keep me from killing you both and taking the drive right now?"

"Nothing," Mary told her, holding the drive out above the opening in the curb, "but if you shoot, this goes right into the storm drain, and your boss gets a murder conviction."

Sarah stared at her.

"You're wasting time," Mary said.

For the longest time, Sarah didn't move. Then, at the sound of a police siren in the distance, she pushed Katura toward Mary.

"Okay. Give it to me. I have to get out of here."

She grabbed the flash drive, ran to her car, and peeled off, tires squealing.

Katura clung to Mary, sobbing and gasping.

"Thank you. Oh, thank you."

She fumbled in her pocket until she found her inhaler, shook it rapidly, and then took several very deep breaths. Mary hugged her close until she calmed enough to talk again.

"I was so scared. I know she was going to— She was going to—"

She burst into tears once more, and Mary let her cry.

"It's all right," Mary soothed, feeling a little shaky herself. "The police will be here in a minute." She handed Katura some tissues from her purse. "I called them when Sarah went into the hotel."

Katura removed the dark contact from her right eye and then her left, revealing the natural blue. Then she unpinned her kapp and the knot of dark hair at the back of her head, hurled everything to the ground, and ran her hands through her curls.

"I am so. Tired. Of this."

"It's all right," Mary murmured.

"I don't want to be ungrateful," Katura—Kennedy—said. "Verity and Iris and all the Shetlers were so kind to me, but I can't live their way. I can't keep being who I'm not."

"It's all right," Mary repeated gently, pressing more tissues into her hand. "They understand that, I'm sure."

"I just want to go home," Kennedy sobbed. "I want this to be over."

"It is over. You're all right. The police will be here any minute now."

"It's not over." Kennedy pushed herself away from Mary, scrubbing her tear-swollen face with the heels of her hands. "It won't ever be over. Even if Carlisle is convicted, he'll be after me. He'll send somebody to get rid of me. I'll have to hide for the rest of my life."

Before Mary could respond, they heard the siren, and then John pulled up in his squad car and jumped out. Elizabeth pulled up behind him.

"Are you all right?" he asked, looking first at Mary and then at Kennedy. "Both of you?"

They nodded.

Elizabeth came over to them, a mixture of anger and relief on her face. "What do you think you were doing, Mary?"

"I couldn't let Sarah take Katura, I mean Kennedy, away." Mary caught a shaky breath and gave her sister a tight hug. "Don't ever let me do anything like that again."

"I didn't let you do it in the first place," Elizabeth said. "Thank God you're all right."

John gently took Kennedy's arm and sat her down in the back seat of his car with her feet still on the ground.

"You're Kennedy Sherman, right?"

Kennedy nodded, trembling.

"Where's Dan? How'd Sarah get you out of there?"

"Dan—" Kennedy hiccupped. "Dan went to get some prednisone for me. I guess the stress really made my asthma flare up, and he had to either leave me to go get it or take me to the hospital. He told me to keep the door locked and not let anybody know I was in there, but I thought he had come back, so I opened the door. I was scared to be there by myself. I wanted him to be there with me."

"Is he up there now?" John asked. "Did Sarah do something to him?"

Kennedy shook her head. "He isn't there. You know he's a cop, right?"

John nodded. "I figured he wanted to get you out of the Shetler house and keep a closer watch on you when Sarah showed up."

"What about Sarah?" Kennedy asked him. "She took off with that evidence Mary gave him."

"Evidence?" John looked at Mary. "What evidence could you have possibly had in this case?"

Mary winced. "I gave her a flash drive in exchange for her letting Kennedy go."

"We've already got officers on her tail," John assured her. "She won't have it long. But what was on it? And why did you have it?"

"I told her it had the location of Carlisle's wedding ring, the one everybody's been looking for. I convinced her it was more important than any testimony Kennedy could give. Sarah decided they could always send someone later to get rid of Kennedy, but that little bit of evidence would still convict him."

"How in the world did you get ahold of that? Was it yours, Kennedy?"

Kennedy shook her head. "I never heard of anything like that before. I don't know where it came from."

"As far as I know," Mary said, "there isn't any such thing."

John gaped at her. "What?"

"I made it up. I read that his wedding ring was missing when he was arrested, and he hasn't been able to account for it. I figured it was something he'd want to have back, and something that could definitely place him at the scene of the murder. It was the only thing I knew to do. And I had a flash drive in my pocket."

Elizabeth put both hands up to her mouth, obviously realizing which flash drive that must have been.

"But what was really on it?" John pressed.

Mary looked guiltily at her sister. "It was the flash drive with your pictures on it. Elizabeth wanted me to make a scrapbook with them. I got the flash drive back from Cindy yesterday. I was going to give it back to Elizabeth, and I forgot it was in my pocket."

"Oh, Mary," Elizabeth breathed. "Those were the only copies I had. I told you."

"No, no!" Mary said, giving her a reassuring hug. "It's okay. Really. Cindy will still have them on her computer. She still has a lot of work to do with them."

"Mary." Elizabeth shook her head at her. "I don't even know what to say, except I'm glad you still have our pictures." She smiled then and returned Mary's hug. "And I'm more glad you're both okay."

"That was some quick thinking, Mary," John said, "but you should never have put yourself or Kennedy at risk like that. That was very dangerous."

Mary ducked her head. "I know. I'm sorry. I couldn't let Sarah disappear with Kennedy. I was afraid we'd never see her again."

John's stern expression softened a little. "I understand, but next time leave it to the professionals, okay?"

"All right."

"How on earth did you get mixed up in all this?" Elizabeth asked Kennedy.

Kennedy managed a ghost of a smile. "I lived in the same apartment building as Niki Holder, who, it turns out, was Mr. Carlisle's girlfriend. I didn't know much about her, only enough to say hi, but I was coming home that night pretty late, and I heard the shots, and then I saw Mr. Carlisle run out of her apartment. He left the door open, so I went in and I saw... Well, I saw everything. So I went to the police."

"He didn't try to shoot you too?" John asked, eyes narrowed.

"He never saw me, but his people found out about me later, so the police in Portland thought I'd better hide out somewhere until they could get him tried and convicted. Dan found out I had been raised not far from here, and since he was raised here too, he thought this would be a good place for me to disappear."

Another squad car pulled up then, and Officers Martinez and Stahl got out. John quickly briefed them on the situation and sent them in to secure Dan's room. Then he started getting more information from Kennedy and from Mary and Elizabeth. A couple of minutes later, Dan pulled up to them and rolled down his window.

"What happened? What's going on?"

"You should have let us know what you needed at the store," John said, going over to him. "We could have helped you out. You wouldn't have had to leave Kennedy alone."

"I should have. Hang on." He parked his car behind John's and then came over to them, his expression grim. "But it doesn't matter now. It's all over. The trial doesn't matter anymore."

Kennedy looked up at him.

"What do you mean?" John asked.

"Carlisle is dead."

Kennedy caught her breath and put one hand over her mouth. "Dead?"

"Yeah. Take these."

Dan handed her a bottle of pills, and Kennedy obediently took two.

"I just got a call from my boss back in Portland," Dan said. "He wanted me to know that Carlisle hanged himself in his cell tonight."

Kennedy leaned over and buried her face in her arms.

"But why?" Mary asked, hardly believing it. "He was so determined to get away with that murder. Why would he have gone to all the trouble of trying to kill Kennedy if he didn't want to live in the first place?"

"He did want to live," Dan said. "My boss is pretty sure that suicide was arranged for him. Maybe by another prisoner. Maybe a guard. Maybe a little of both."

"Why?"

"Paid off, of course."

"By who?" John asked.

Dan shrugged. "Rival boss. Right-hand man who wants to move up a notch. Who knows? The department is looking into it. I have my own theory."

"Which is?"

"Did you ever hear who Mrs. Carlisle is?"

"I did," Mary said. "I read an article about her. Her father was a mob boss twenty or thirty years ago."

"She'd certainly have connections," Elizabeth said.

"She's the one I'd put my money on," Dan said. "From what we've found out, this affair with Niki wasn't his first rodeo. Maybe Mrs. Carlisle didn't care too much as long as it wasn't common knowledge, but it had to sting to have it plastered all over the papers, rubbed in her face more or less. This mess could have been the last straw. We don't know anything for sure yet, but that's my bet."

Once more, tears filled Kennedy's blue eyes. "Then it really is over."

"I think so," Dan said gently. "There's no reason for anyone to be after you now. Not for anything. You can go back to Portland."

"You can go back to Wes," Elizabeth said, smiling at the girl. "If you want."

Kennedy caught her breath. "You know about Wes?"

"He came looking for you at the shop."

"Wes is here?" Kennedy's eyes brightened. "In Bird-in-Hand?"

Mary nodded. "He's been really worried about you."

Kennedy wiped her eyes, smiling. "I know. And I hated leaving him the way I did. I wasn't supposed to let anybody know where I was, but I couldn't just leave him hanging all this time."

"That's what we were arguing about that day in your store," Dan said. "I caught her using your shop phone while Verity distracted Elizabeth."

Kennedy blushed faintly. "I…care about Wes a lot."

"Are you feeling up to giving a statement now?" Dan asked her. "Or would you rather wait? I know you weren't feeling too good a little while ago."

"I feel better now, just knowing all this is done. I think I'd rather take care of things tonight."

"Maybe while we're taking you into the station to get squared away, you can give Wes a call, and he can meet you there."

Kennedy looked over at John hopefully.

"Sure. You can use my phone," John said, clearly unable to keep his expression quite as stern as it had been. "That shouldn't be a problem." He turned to Mary. "You'll have to come give at least a preliminary statement too, before you can go home."

"I'm coming too," Elizabeth said. "And I'm calling Martha. We'll meet you there."

"I'd better let Bill know," Mary said, looking at her phone. "He's already left a couple of messages for me. Probably asking where I am. I guess I'd better face the music right away."

"I think you're going to get the whole orchestra this time," Elizabeth said with a shake of her head.

Mary steeled herself and called Bill.

CHAPTER TWENTY

Elizabeth had insisted on driving Mary to the police station, and Mary was glad she did. She was feeling a little shaky now that everything was over. Bill was waiting for them when they got there. So was Wes.

"Ken!" Wes called, jumping up from his chair.

Kennedy ran to him. "Wes. I'm so glad you're here."

She threw herself into his arms, and he hugged her tightly.

Bill hurried over to Mary. "Are you sure you're all right, honey?"

She was happy to feel his arms around her too. "I'm fine, like I said." She pushed a lock of hair back from his forehead. "I know you were worried."

"I'm just glad I didn't know what you were up to till it was all over."

"Me too," Martha said. She stood there with her hands on her hips, but she gave Mary an enormous hug anyway. "Are you sure you're all right?"

Mary nodded guiltily.

Martha grabbed her by the shoulders. "Never do anything like that again," she said, and then she hugged Mary again. "Oh, Mary."

"Come on," John said, putting his arm around Elizabeth. "Let's get this taken care of so we can all go home."

Dan and John got the information they needed as quickly as possible, but it still felt like it took forever.

"If we need anything else," Dan said at last, "we'll be in touch. Kennedy, do you think the Shetlers will let you stay with them for another day or two? Until we can arrange for you and Wes to get home? It might be a little less intimidating than staying in a hotel room by yourself."

"I'm not sure," she said, glancing at Wes, who hadn't let go of her hand since he'd seen her. "Do you think they'd let him come too?"

"I think they'd understand why you'd want him to be around," Mary said. "And I know all their visitors have gone back home now. They should have an extra room where Wes could spend a night or two."

"Do you want me to go there with you?" Dan asked them. "Put in a good word and everything?"

Kennedy glanced at Wes and then shook her head. "Wes can take me. Verity and Iris knew about me all along. They already know about him."

"Really?" Wes asked, looking pleased.

"Really. They'll be glad to meet you." Kennedy turned to Dan. "I've been meaning to tell you thank you for putting me with the Shetlers. They've been wonderful, especially Verity."

Mary grinned. "I was starting to wonder why she was always running interference for you. Now it makes sense."

"She can be pretty sly when she wants to be. The only way I got to call Wes from your shop was by having her distract Elizabeth with all her quilting talk so I could use your store phone. I don't know how the Amish stand it. I was about to go crazy without mine."

"If you want to thank the Shetlers," Dan said, "you should start with Bertha. I contacted her right off when I knew we needed someplace safe for you to stay until the trial."

Mary and Elizabeth both looked at him in surprise.

"Bertha was your contact?" Mary asked.

"Not my contact per se," Dan said. "But everybody knew the kind of person she was. I figured if we were going to hide Kennedy out in Amish country, Bertha'd be the right person to ask for help, and she was. She said to bring Kennedy right over. Didn't even bat an eyelash."

Kennedy smiled sadly. "I wasn't pretending when I said I missed her after the funeral. Thank you for bringing me to her and her family, Dan. I guess I won't be seeing you anymore."

"Some, probably," he said. "You'll have to testify against Sarah, aka Kathy Damon, for kidnapping and whatever else we've got on her."

"Did they find her yet?"

"Yeah," John said. "One of our officers picked her up a few minutes after she left you. She had asked around town enough to hear about the girl who came to work for the Shetlers three months ago, about the time Kennedy Sherman disappeared. But when she got over there, still pretending to be looking for her wayward niece, she found out Kennedy was gone. Her last hope was to find where Dan was hiding her."

"I'm glad they caught her," Mary said, feeling more than a little righteous indignation.

"She's probably being booked right now."

Kennedy clung closer to Wes. "Thank God."

"There are still some things to wind up on the case," Dan said, "some information you'll have to give, that sort of thing. But yeah, I won't be trying to look after you anymore."

Kennedy's face turned a little pink. "I'm sorry I messed up so many things and didn't always do what you told me to."

"Didn't always?" he asked, one eyebrow raised. "Or didn't ever?"

She leaned up and gave him a kiss on the cheek. "Thank you."

"I'm sorry we won't have a chance to get to know you," Mary said. "The real you."

"I'm sorry I couldn't confide in you." Kennedy gave her a hug. "And I'm sorry I stole your phone."

"Borrowed," Mary reminded her. "How did you do that anyway?"

"I took it out of your purse when you left it with everybody else's purses and coats in the back room at Verity's. I tried a couple of other ones, but theirs were locked. Yours wasn't."

Martha gave Mary a reproving look.

"But how did you get it back to me?" Mary asked. "It wasn't in the back room when Bill and I came back over to look for it."

"No, but I slipped it back into your purse when you were searching."

Mary shook her head. "And here I was sure Dan had put it back when he and Eli were at the store the next day. And that was because I could tell he was up to something."

"I'll have to work harder on my undercoverness," Dan told her. "But yeah, you should protect your valuables and your information from now on."

"I will," Mary said, "but there was no harm done, and maybe all of this worked out for the best after all. At least Kennedy doesn't have to pretend anymore."

"Thank goodness," Kennedy breathed.

Wes took Kennedy's hand again. "Are you ready? We've got a lot of catching up to do." He ruffled her dark hair. "Looks good, by the way."

She laughed, and they walked away together.

"I guess you'll be going back to Portland too," Mary said to Dan.

"Not for a while yet," he told her. "I wasn't lying when I said I want to patch things up with Daed and Eli. Now that this case has been taken care of more or less, I think I'll stick around for a few days and relax."

"Jedidiah and Eli will like that," Elizabeth said. "And the rest of us will enjoy getting to know you better."

"Now that we don't have to wonder what you're up to," Mary added.

Dan glanced at his watch. "It's late. I'll go see them tomorrow. Now that I can tell them what my real life is like, things might be a little more comfortable between us. I don't know if Daed will ever approve of me, but maybe we can get along better."

"I hope so," Mary said.

Dan shook John's hand. "Thanks for your help, Officer. If we can ever do the same for you in Portland, let me know."

"Thanks. We'll make sure and give you a call if we're planning a visit."

"Ladies," Dan said, and with a wave, he was gone too.

"I guess that leaves us," John said. "Are you sure all of you are all right now?"

"Sure." Elizabeth kissed his cheek. "We're fine."

"Can I drive you back to your car?" Bill asked Mary. "There are a couple of things we need to discuss."

Mary was pretty sure he was going to tell her how foolish she'd been to risk her life and Kennedy's with her impetuous actions.

"I'll see you later," Elizabeth said.

"Okay, Mary?" Bill asked.

Well, he had every right to be upset with her.

"Sure," Mary said. "I'll see you at home in a little while, Lizzie."

"See you later, Elizabeth," Bill said, and then he shook John's hand. "John."

"See you, Bill," John said. "Mary, you be careful."

"I will," she said, and she walked with Bill out to his car.

Before they got far from the police station, Mary and Bill agreed they would stop at his house for a while. They needed to talk for longer than the short time it would take to get to Muhlenberg's. He assured her he'd come pick her up for church in the morning, and they'd go get her car afterward.

Now, Bill unlocked his front door and ushered her into his living room. She loved his house, a hundred-year-old craftsman-style home, as solid and dependable as he was. But tonight it was a little chilly.

"Have a seat, honey," he said. "I'll start a fire."

He already had the wood laid out. All it needed was a few pieces of newspaper to get it going.

She settled herself on one end of the old sofa that sat under the front window, suddenly tired. John was right. What she had done was reckless. How she'd had the courage to do it, she didn't quite know now, but she was glad, thank God, that everything had worked out despite her impetuousness. On the drive to his house, Bill had listened quietly to her description of what had happened from the time Sarah had showed up at her front door until Mary called him to ask him to come to the police station. All he had said was that he didn't know what he would have done if something had happened to her.

"I'm sorry," she said again now.

He was kneeling by the fire, using the iron poker to push the logs around, encouraging them to catch fire. He looked at her, eyebrows raised.

"I'm sorry I didn't think before I tried to stop Sarah. Or Kathy or whatever her name is. I couldn't let her take Katura—Kennedy—away like that."

He put the poker back into the stand, dusted off his hands, and came and sat beside her. "I know you thought you had to do what you did, and it turned out okay, but maybe you could leave the heroics to the police from now on, okay?"

She smiled a little. "I promise I'll try to keep that in mind from now on."

"I'm just glad I wasn't there for that part of it. I probably would have carried you off bodily before you stepped out where she could see you."

"I don't know." She slipped her arm through his. "You might have tried to jump out and wrestle that gun away from her so you could save Katura yourself."

He chuckled. "I don't know if you think I'm really brave or really stupid."

"I think you'd try to help somebody who was in trouble if you could."

"How about we both leave situations involving armed criminals to the police from now on? Deal?"

"Deal. I'm glad this is over. I'm glad Katura—Kennedy—can go back to Portland. And I hope things work out with her and Wes. He's young, but he seems like a really good man who genuinely cares for her."

"He did come all this way to make sure she was okay. Now that all the excitement is over, they have to figure out if they enjoy being together during the not-so-interesting times."

"Like sitting on the couch together at the end of a long day?" she asked mischievously.

"Exactly like that." He put his arm around her and pulled her a little closer. "I can't think of anywhere I'd rather be."

"Me neither. I'll be glad when I won't have to go home at the end of the day. I feel so good just like this."

She looked into his warm brown eyes until he finally smiled.

"What?"

She shook her head. "I don't want this to change. I want to feel like this for the rest of my life."

"Everything changes," he told her gently. "We'll change too, as time goes on. Think how much we've changed since you first came back to Bird-in-Hand. You didn't think of me as anything but an old friend. That was nice, but now is better. Once we're married, it'll be even better still. I love you, and I don't want you to doubt that. Not ever. You're not going to do something or say something that's going to suddenly make me change my mind."

She laughed softly and looked down. Was that what she'd been worrying about all along? Maybe it was, and he'd never done anything to deserve that from her.

"I know," she said. "I know the kind of man you are, and I know I can trust you. Maybe there are a few little bits of self-doubt and uncertainty I have to get rid of. I might not get rid of them all right away, but I'm going to try as hard as I can."

"Good. Things aren't ever going to be perfect, you know, but whatever happens, we'll handle it together, whatever it is."

"We will." She cupped his face with her palm. "And I'm not going to waste my time worrying what might happen instead of enjoying what is happening."

He brought her hand to his lips and then let it go. "Warmer now?" he asked, since the fire was finally blazing.

She nodded. "I wish it wasn't too late for coffee, but I don't need to be up all night. We've got church tomorrow."

"How about some hot chocolate then? That'll warm you up without keeping you awake."

"That would be perfect. Do you want me to make it?"

"No. You take it easy." He gave her a quick kiss on the cheek and stood. "It won't take me a minute, and you need to relax for a while."

She knew she couldn't stay long, but it was nice to be in Bill's cozy living room in front of his cozy fire. They hadn't decided where they were going to live once they got married, but this was a possibility. It was comfortable and familiar and welcoming, just like Bill.

She was glad she had decided to come here instead of going straight home. She really hadn't thought it through before she tried to stop Sarah. Looking back at that whole situation now left her more than a little shaky. She needed to spend a little quiet time with Bill until she felt calmer. Until she felt safe. She hadn't told him that, but he seemed to know it anyway.

She almost dozed off watching the hypnotic dance of the flames in the fireplace, and she jumped when he came back into the room.

"Did I startle you?"

"Some," she admitted. "I was daydreaming. Thinking about how nice it is just being with you."

He was carrying a tray that had two heavy mugs on it and a little wrapped package between them. He set it down on the coffee table and sat beside her again.

"What's that?" she asked.

"Hot chocolate. I know you've seen something like it before."

She tried not to smile. "Smart aleck. I mean the package."

"Oh." He shrugged nonchalantly. "It's a package."

"No kidding. I never would have guessed."

He handed her one of the mugs and took the other for himself, and she didn't ask any other questions. She was almost certain she knew what was in it. Almost.

"Did you finish early?" she asked, pretending the package wasn't there.

"Early?"

"The job you were working on. The one you're supposed to get a bonus for if you get finished ahead of time."

"Oh yeah. I guess with everything that's been going on, I forgot to tell you about that. And yes, I finished today, and the clients were so pleased they gave me a little more of a bonus than they promised in the first place. So we've got to talk about where we want to go on our honeymoon. This little windfall won't pay for the whole thing by any means, but it'll sure help."

"Part of that depends on when we get married," she reminded him, after taking a sip of her hot chocolate. "Summer destinations wouldn't be the same as the fall ones or even the winter ones."

"We're not going to wait that long, are we?"

"I hope not, but we still need to see what Elizabeth wants to do. I can't imagine she and John would wait any longer than May to get married. Maybe March or April. That's not so far away."

"No, not so far."

She took another sip of her drink. "This is good. Exactly what I wanted. Thank you."

He put his arm around her again. "I'm glad you like it."

He drank some of his own hot chocolate and didn't say anything else, and Mary didn't look at the package again. It was a little large to be what she suspected it might be. Not really large, but not as small as a box with an engagement ring might be or even a box with an engagement ring and two wedding rings. What exactly was in that package? She was determined not to ask.

Finally, he set his mug back on the tray. "I suppose you know that's for you."

In spite of her determination to play it cool, she felt a frisson of excitement run through her body. "I thought it might be."

She set her half-full mug down next to his empty one, and he picked up the package in both hands.

"I know I asked you to marry me kind of suddenly, but that doesn't mean I haven't been thinking about it for a very long time. Only I wasn't sure you were ready to get married again. Especially to me."

"You're the only one I would have even considered," she said.

"I didn't quite know what to do to show you that I was serious about you." He turned the package in his hands as he spoke. "I wanted to give you something that nobody else could. Something that would be special to us both."

She looked at him questioningly. It didn't sound like he was talking about their rings. Yes, those were special to them both, but they weren't unique.

"Something especially for you," he said, giving her the package at last.

He watched her as she opened it, as if he wasn't quite sure what she would think of the contents. She didn't have a clue what to expect. What had he—

"Oh," she breathed once it was unwrapped. "Oh, it's beautiful."

It was a small wooden box, not much bigger than her two hands cupped together. It was carved from pieces of light, medium, and dark exotic woods, the inlaid pieces delicately set together like interlocking puzzle parts or the precisely cut pieces of Martha's intricate wedding ring quilt. The wood was highly polished, shining like dark glass, and Mary was sure the hinges were real gold.

"Bill, it's amazing. Did you make it?"

He nodded. "You probably don't recognize them, but remember last summer when we went to that lumber yard? You wanted me to distract the manager so you could do some sleuthing without him noticing, and I ended up buying some pieces of the exotic woods he had out in his warehouse."

"I thought you bought that so he wouldn't be suspicious about your going out to the warehouse."

"I could have told him I didn't see what I wanted right then. But I knew I wanted a special box to put your ring in."

"Bill," she said, cupping his cheek again. "You mean you were thinking about proposing even back then?"

"Longer than that," he admitted, "but yeah."

"It's so beautiful."

"Go ahead and open it," he urged.

Her heart beating a little faster, she lifted the lid. There, resting on a piece of black velvet, was her engagement ring along with the two wedding rings they had chosen. Before she could say anything, he took the box from her, set it on the coffee table, and then got down on one knee.

"Mary Frances Classen Baxter," he said huskily, taking the engagement ring from the box, "I love you. Will you marry me?"

"Yes," she breathed, tears of joy pooling in her eyes. "Oh yes!"

He took her left hand and slid the ring onto her finger, the elegant circle formed by two slender golden bands twined together with a clear, brilliant diamond nestled between them, and then he took her into his arms, holding her close as he gave her a warm, tender kiss.

"Oh Bill, I love you."

He kissed her again and then pulled back a little so he could look at the ring. "Do you like it?"

"It's perfect. It fits just right. It's beautiful. Thank you."

"It looks beautiful on you, honey. Now, you need to take care of this for now." He handed her the larger of the two gold bands that were still in the box. "And I'll look after yours until it's time."

"We'd better try them on first to make sure they fit."

She took off her engagement ring and let him put the wedding ring on her finger. She put his wedding ring on him. They both fit perfectly.

"Three for three," he said, holding out his hand to look at his new ring. "What do you think?"

"It looks great. Did they get the inscriptions right?"

He took his ring off and handed it to her. She took off her own and inspected both of them. Their initials were engraved inside. In his were the words *Grow old along with me*. And in hers, *The best is yet to be*.

They were perfect.

"I didn't know you were picking them up today," she said, giving her wedding ring back to him and putting his in the box he had made.

"They called me this afternoon. I picked them up right after I finished work."

"I'm sorry. If I had known, I would have been with you and not chasing after Sarah."

He hugged her close again. "Maybe that was for the best, but I'm so glad you're all right. I couldn't stand losing you."

She stayed there, warm in his arms, until he finally pulled back from her.

"I guess I'd better take you home now. Your sisters will be wondering if we've eloped."

He stood, bringing her to her feet with him, and she snuggled against him.

"Maybe that wouldn't be such a bad idea."

He chuckled and kissed her on the nose. "You say the word, babe. I'm there."

"Better not," she said, and then she gave him a wry grin. "But maybe I'll change my mind if Elizabeth doesn't start getting her plans together."

He drove her home, walked her to the door, and left her with a kiss that warmed her to her toes. It was going to be good being married to him, knowing how well they complemented each other, knowing theirs was truly that friendship set on fire she'd always heard of.

She watched as he drove away. Her eyes brimmed with happy tears at the thought of the ring he was keeping for her until they were finally married, and the words inscribed in it filled her heart.

The best is yet to be.

A NOTE FROM THE AUTHOR

Dear Reader,

In this book, I wanted to give the ever-competent and efficient Martha a task that she couldn't possibly finish as quickly as she wanted to. So, of course, I had to have her make (or at least try to make) a beautiful and complicated double wedding ring quilt for Elizabeth's wedding present.

I think every serious quilter I know has this pattern on her to-do list. I don't know that many who have actually done one though. And yes, I'd love to give this a try too. Like most tasks, I believe it's simply a matter of time and patience (both of which are in short supply at my house), of gathering up the right materials, taking a deep breath, and plunging right in.

Of course, like Martha, I have to confess to giving more than one person a wrapped box containing a stack of fabrics, a pattern, and a promise that the contents will, before too much longer, actually be a quilt. Fortunately, these gifts have been received with grace and humor and understanding. And yes, I have actually finished these promised quilts and given them to the patient and much-appreciated people they were meant for.

And, of course, a quilt lasts far beyond the one day—birthday, wedding day, Christmas celebration, or whatever else—that it's meant to commemorate. Just like the love and thought that are put into it.

Many blessings!

DeAnna

ABOUT THE AUTHOR

The author of twenty-three traditionally published books and with more to come, DeAnna Julie Dodson has always been an avid reader and a lover of storytelling, whether on the page, the screen, or the stage. This, along with her keen interest in history and her Christian faith, shows in her tales of love, forgiveness, and triumph over adversity. A fifth-generation Texan, she makes her home north of Dallas with three spoiled cats and, when not writing, spends her free time quilting, cross-stitching, and watching NHL hockey. Her first novels were a trilogy of medieval romances (*In Honor Bound, By Love Redeemed,* and *To Grace Surrendered*) for Crossway Books, and she has since written a number of contemporary mysteries for Annie's Fiction and for Guideposts, and has more in the works. Also, as Julianna Deering, she writes the Drew Farthering mysteries set in 1930s England. The series debuted from Bethany House with *Rules of Murder* and is followed by *Death by the Book, Murder at the Mikado, Dressed for Death, Murder on the Moor,* and *Death at Thorburn Hall.* She is represented by Wendy Lawton of the Books & Such Literary Agency.

MORE TO THE STORY

Amish Funerals

A mish funerals typically take place three days after some- one's death. A funeral director will usually embalm the body of the deceased, but then the body is returned to the family home so friends and relatives can visit to comfort the grieving and pay respects to the dead. The coffin is usually handmade and very plain. Often the deceased, male or female, is dressed in white, and married women are often laid out in the same white aprons they wore the day they were married.

The funeral service itself reflects the plain way the Amish live. No one brings flowers. People speak of their respect and love for the deceased without praising him or her. They do not have eulogies, and they speak a hymn rather than sing it. The one-and-a-half- to two-hour service, usually held at the home of the deceased, reflects trust in the will of God and acknowledges that death is a part of life. It serves as a reminder that we will all one day stand before God. Though the Amish do not typically believe they can be assured of salvation in this life, they have, as they call it, a living hope that God, in His grace and mercy, will extend salvation to them.

When the service is over, loved ones file past the casket, and then the casket is closed, loaded onto a hearse wagon, and taken to the cemetery. The mourners follow in their own buggies, which have been numbered in order of priority: earlier numbers are close relatives, and later numbers are friends and neighbors.

The Amish are typically buried in Amish church-district cemeteries where the graves are dug and filled in by hand and marked with tombstones that are very simple and very much like the others in the same cemetery, emphasizing the equality of all people.

Afterward, the people who were at the funeral and other friends and family usually gather to eat and remember the deceased, sometimes as many as three to five hundred people. As with any funeral, the people talk and visit and comfort the bereaved. In memory of the dead, an Amish woman may dress all in black for a period of time that is dependent on how close she was to the deceased.

With the Amish, as with all Christians, a funeral is a time to reflect on the brevity of life and to trust in and be comforted by the goodness and providence of God.

FRESH FROM MARTHA'S KITCHEN

Funeral Pie (Raisin Pie)

Because raisins are a year-round staple in Amish kitchens, it's only natural that raisin pie would be a go-to dish to take to a family in the community that suffered the sudden loss of a loved one, earning it the nickname of "funeral pie." This recipe uses simple ingredients and is easy to make even for a happy occasion.

Ingredients:

2 9-inch pie shell pastries

1¾ cups water

½ cup white sugar

3 tablespoons all-purpose
   flour

¼ teaspoon salt

½ teaspoon vanilla extract

1 tablespoon butter

1 tablespoon lemon juice

2 cups raisins

Directions:

Preheat oven to 450 degrees.

   Combine water, sugar, flour, salt, vanilla, butter, and lemon juice in a saucepan. Mix and then add raisins. Simmer for 10 minutes over low heat and stir frequently.

Line a 9-inch pie pan with one pastry. Pour in raisin mixture. Cover the pan with the second pastry, seal the edges, and make sure to cut steam vents in the top crust.

Bake 15 minutes at 450 and then lower the temperature to 350 degrees and bake 25 to 30 minutes more.

Serves 8!

Read on for a sneak peek of another exciting book
in the Mysteries of Lancaster County series!

A Missing Memory
by Kathleen Y'Barbo

Martha Classen Watts stepped behind the counter and smiled. This felt just as natural as if she were standing in her kitchen at home.

Only she wasn't.

And a dozen sets of eyes were watching her closely. Well, at least a half dozen were.

Of the remaining six who had signed up for the twice-weekly Cooking with Martha class at the Lancaster Senior Center beginning on the first Tuesday in March, five were alternating between checking their phones and looking like they were bored out of their minds.

The twelfth member of the cooking class was a wiry fellow in jeans and a Boston Marathon sweatshirt who hadn't bothered to hide his preference for a nap over a cooking class. He'd taken the cookbook she'd provided as an incentive to try the recipes at home and was using it as a headrest.

At the moment, he was also snoring.

The woman beside him was a petite firecracker of a lady with white hair perfectly coiffed in an elegant French twist and bright blue eyes that appeared to miss nothing as she scribbled notes on a legal pad. Without looking away from Martha's presentation, she poked her noisy neighbor with one pink-painted nail. He snorted twice and sat bolt upright.

Only then did she spare him a frown before she quickly returned her attention to Martha's demonstration of how to roll out and prepare fresh pasta. When it came time to ask for a volunteer to help with the process, the little lady in the back of the room immediately raised her hand.

"What is your name?" Martha asked when the woman arrived at her side.

"Lucille Ransome Hill," she said, "but I prefer to be called Lucy."

"All right, Lucy," Martha said. "I'm going to have you mix a batch of pasta. Do you remember how I showed the class to do that?"

"Absolutely I do." Lucy made a well in the center of the flour that Martha had poured onto the counter and began to crack eggs into it. "You made it look so easy. Just..."

She stopped speaking, her hands frozen in midair. On her face was an expression of distress.

"What is it?" Martha asked.

No response. It was as if she'd been frozen in time.

"Lucy?"

At the sound of her name, Lucy jolted out of whatever had held her captive and returned to her work making the pasta. "Where was I?"

"You were showing us how to mix the flour and eggs."

"Yes, of course." A broad smile tilted her lips. "Yes, indeed. So, just like Martha taught us," she said to the class, "this is how easy it all goes together."

Alyssa Benedetto, the director of Shady Grove Assisted Living Care Home, slipped into the back of the room and offered Martha a smile. When Alyssa mentioned two Sundays ago at church that the Lancaster Senior Center was looking for teachers for their spring continuing education class series, Martha had offered to pray for the right people to step up.

To that, her friend had immediately said, "I think I'm looking at the right person. Please teach a cooking class. It's only for six weeks, and the people are so sweet and appreciative. You'll love it. I promise."

Martha had said no, but somehow that no had become a yes and here she was, standing in front of the class watching Lucy Hill make pasta. "Are you sure you haven't done this before?" she asked her prize student as Lucy's nimble fingers made quick work of the task.

"Never," Lucy told her, "but I certainly plan to make this again, although a certain Mr. McMartin will likely not be treated to it. Unless he somehow learns to pay attention instead of napping." Lucy paused to give the man a pointed stare. "Naps are for old people, Mason."

"Hey now, doll," Mr. McMartin said. "I've been paying close attention. You make that pasta look good."

Lucy gave Martha a what-am-I-going-to-do-with-him look then went back to her work. Martha shrugged and shifted her attention to the back of the room, where she returned the care home director's smile.

Once the pasta was mixed, rolled out, and cut, Martha and Lucy made short work of boiling it—just two or three minutes was all they needed—and then readying the samples for the students who had remained awake all the way to the end of the presentation.

"Thursday we will be making cheesecake," Martha announced. "Have a great day, and I hope to see you Thursday afternoon."

While the students swarmed Lucy to get their portions of pasta, Alyssa made her way to Martha. "Well?" she asked. "Was I wrong? Do you love it?"

"Love it?" Martha repeated as Lucy jabbed Mr. McMartin with her finger when he tried to grab a second serving of pasta. "I'm not ready to go with love just yet." She grinned. "Like? Definitely. And it has been fun. Lucy is a delight."

"She is," Alyssa agreed. "It's hard to believe she's eighty-four."

Martha's mouth dropped open. "You're joking."

"No, I'm serious. Lucy can run circles around the rest of us, for sure." She paused. "I worry about her, though. Some days it just seems like..." Alyssa shrugged. "Well, never mind. Lucy has lived a long and eventful life. Believe it or not, she flew military planes during the Cold War. It was all very classified, and she says she can't talk about it."

Martha tried to imagine the little lady in the cockpit of an airplane and just couldn't manage it. She seemed too tiny, too ladylike.

"That's impressive," Martha said. "And no, I can't imagine it."

Alyssa's smile faded. "She can have her moments, and no one would blame her."

"Moments?" Martha asked. "As in freezing and forgetting what she's doing?"

"So you saw it," Alyssa said. "Yes, in a manner of speaking. Sometimes she's lost for a minute of two. Other times she stays lost for hours. I can't say anything further about her medical issues, but suffice it to say that I do worry, especially since she has no close family." She paused. "None other than the Cousin Cartel."

"The Cousin Cartel?" Martha frowned. "What in the world is that?"

A look of distaste came over her friend's face. "Distant cousins, from what I understand. Lucy calls them the Cousin Cartel because they've banded together to try and tell her what's best for her. They've even threatened to go to court and get a guardianship declared so they can make decisions for her. As you can imagine, Lucy doesn't like them much."

"No, I would assume not." She glanced over at Lucy, who appeared to be taking great joy in her role as queen bee of the kitchen. "Watching her now, I can't believe anyone could convince a judge that she needs help caring for herself. She's the life of the party over there."

"Well, she's old enough that there might be some merit in what they're saying. But I don't think the talk of guardianship is exclusively about Lucy needing help caring for herself."

"So she's rich?" Martha asked.

"In secrets, yes."

Martha raised her eyebrows. "What does that mean?"

"Her husband was famous for his contributions to science, especially during those contentious years with Russia in the 1970s," Alyssa said. "Lucy is the keeper of those secrets."

"All done." The object of their discussion appeared beside them. "Thank you for a wonderful lesson," she said to Martha. "You've made my day, and I cannot wait for Thursday."

"Thank you, Lucy." Martha looked at Alyssa as the older woman walked away. "Okay, I love it."

Alyssa jingled a set of keys. "My driver is out sick today, so I'm the chauffeur. Otherwise I'd invite you for coffee. Maybe Thursday?"

"It's a deal."

Those who had come in with Alyssa followed her out while the others wandered away or left on their own. Martha turned her attention to washing the dishes and found Lucy at her side.

"Need some help?"

"Aren't you going to miss your ride if you stay and help me?"

There was that twinkle in her blue eyes again. "I just might," she said, "but it would serve Mason right to have to ride back without me." She paused to reach for the pink gloves lying on the counter. "And it gives me an opportunity to speak to you privately when you take me back to Shady Grove."

Martha shook her head. "I don't know, Lucy. Shouldn't you at least let Alyssa know I'm taking you home?"

Lucy shrugged, put on the gloves, and reached into the soapy water. "I already did. Now, what do you know about our conflicts with Russia during the Cold War and the years following?"

"I only know what I've read. I understand you flew military planes."

Lucy snorted. "Flew them, fixed them, and even invented a thing or two that made them fly better, faster, and with more efficiency, although most of that was done unofficially and out of the country, mostly in England."

Martha took a dripping mixing bowl from her. "That's pretty impressive, Lucy. How did you come to do this?"

"That's easy," Lucy said. "I loved a man who loved to fly. So there I was. I'm a quick learner." She paused. "And when my brain is working right, I have a photographic memory. That can be helpful when you've got to learn things quickly and remember them without panicking."

"Indeed," Martha said.

"Have you ever heard of the gray lady?"

"No." Martha put the dried bowl into the cupboard below the sink then straightened. "What is that?"

Lucy opened her mouth to speak and then froze, her pink gloves dripping with dishwater. A moment later she shrugged.

"Lucy?" Martha prompted. "You were going to tell me about the gray lady?"

Those beautiful blue eyes clouded with confusion. "Who is she?"

A NOTE FROM THE EDITORS

We hope you enjoyed this volume of the Mysteries of Lancaster County series, created by the Books and Inspirational Media Division of Guideposts. We are a nonprofit organization that touches millions of lives every day through products and services that inspire, encourage, help you grow in your faith, and celebrate God's love in every aspect of your daily life.

Thank you for making a difference with your purchase of this book, which helps fund our many outreach programs to military personnel, prisons, hospitals, nursing homes, and educational institutions. To learn more, visit GuidepostsFoundation.org.

We also maintain many useful and uplifting online resources. Visit Guideposts.org to read true stories of hope and inspiration, access OurPrayer network, sign up for free news-letters, download free e-books, join our Facebook community, and follow our stimulating blogs.

To learn about other Guideposts publications, including the bestselling devotional *Daily Guideposts*, go to ShopGuideposts. org, call (800) 932-2145, or write to Guideposts, PO Box 5815, Harlan, Iowa 51593.

Find more inspiring fiction in these best-loved Guideposts series!

Secrets of Wayfarers Inn
Fall back in history with three retired schoolteachers who find themselves owners of an old warehouse-turned-inn that is filled with hidden passages, buried secrets and stunning surprises that will set them on a course to puzzling mysteries from the Underground Railroad.

Sugarcreek Amish Mysteries
Be intrigued by the suspense and joyful "aha" moments in these delightful stories. Each book in the series brings together two women of vastly different backgrounds and traditions, who realize there's much more to the "simple life" than meets the eye.

Mysteries of Martha's Vineyard
Come to the shores of this quaint and historic island and dig into a cozy mystery. When a recent widow inherits a lighthouse just off the coast of Massachusetts, she finds exciting adventures, new friends, and renewed hope.

Patchwork Mysteries
Discover that life's little mysteries often have a common thread in a series where every novel contains an intriguing mystery centered around a quilt located in a beautiful New England town.

Mysteries of Silver Peak
Escape to the historic mining town of Silver Peak, Colorado, and discover how one woman's love of antiques helps her solve mysteries buried deep in the town's checkered past.

To learn more about these books, visit Guideposts.org/Shop

Sign up for the
Guideposts Fiction Newsletter
and stay up to date on the books you love!

You'll get sneak peeks of new releases, recommendations from other Guideposts readers, and special offers just for you . . .
and it's FREE!

Just go to Guideposts.org/Newsletters today to sign up.

Guideposts.

Visit Guideposts.org/Shop or call (800) 932-2145

HE

D1255391

H   EN

SHADOW

BOOKS BY CARLA KOVACH

HER

HIDDEN

SHADOW

CARLA KOVACH

bookouture

Published by Bookouture in 2023

An imprint of Storyfire Ltd.
Carmelite House
50 Victoria Embankment
London EC4Y 0DZ

www.bookouture.com

ISBN: 978-1-83790-310-8
eBook ISBN: 978-1-83790-309-2

To those who battle with past trauma on a regular basis and to those who take the time to listen and be there for them.

PROLOGUE

Eight years ago

I turn in bed and pull the sheet over me. The air is sticky and the nights have been unbearably humid. A slight breeze catches my face, drying the droplets of perspiration on my forehead. Slowly, slowly, I feel sleep taking hold. Deeper and deeper I drift, until I'm dreaming of our wedding. My mind is filled with images of me in the fifties-inspired dress that I've chosen, vintage and fluffy skirted, all in an off-white. I want to be a bride. I want to be her bride and I want babies. She's kind, loving, everything I always wanted in a partner, and I know she'll stick with me through sickness and in health until the end of time. We have everything; perfect well-paid jobs and lots of friends. I love my life.

A slight cracking noise sets me on alert. I know it's not her, she's in New York on business. Thanks to that noise I'm awake again. I don't sleep well when she's away. Knowing that it's just the breeze or the joists helps a little. The house is old and sometimes it sounds like the floorboards are alive. I hear another crack so I hold my breath and listen, but the blood rushing through my body is whooshing in my ears as my heart pumps hard, and I can't hear. I try to reassure myself that it's nothing. It's the house and it's a noise I've heard many times before, so why am I scared?

Swallowing, I pull back the sheet and adjust my cotton pyjama shorts. If I don't check the house and all the locks, I will never get back to sleep. Maybe I should turn the light on. My index finger hovers over the switch. If there is someone there, the light will tell them that I'm awake and which room I'm in. My vision is nicely adjusted to the dark, so I move my finger away from the switch. If there is someone out there... damn, I'm already thinking like there is an intruder. It's the floorboards and I'm simply fulfilling my need to check. To be fair, I do this at least twice a week. It's becoming an unhealthy routine.

A tapping sound comes from the stair area, echoing throughout the building. That's not right. The house doesn't make that noise. A flash of panic makes me gasp for breath. I need to call the police. Someone really is out there. It's not my imagination this time. Our house is being burgled or worse, maybe I'm about to be attacked. I begin to creep back towards the bed and feel along my bedside cabinet for my phone. It's not there. I left it there. Panic rises as I get down on all fours and trace the carpet with my shaky fingers, then they move under the bed. My phone has gone.

A crash behind my door stops me dead. I don't know what to do, where to hide. I lie on the floor and try to slide under the bed but there are too many boxes, and I can't fit under. The wardrobe – I could hide in it, or I could shift the chest of drawers in front of the door.

I've left it too late. The door handle comes down as the intruder stands just metres away from me, his own breaths coming thick and fast behind the partially opened door.

As I stand, I wonder if I can escape out of the window. Tears force their way out and begin to slip down my cheeks. I'm too high up. If I jump, I'll break my ankles and then the intruder has me regardless, or they might leave me in pain to die. The door creaks open and all I see is a dark figure standing at the entrance to my bedroom. The door bangs against the wardrobe as his heavy steps enters my space. I gasp for breath and my vision is prickling.

'Please don't hurt me. Take what you want. My car keys are in the kitchen. Take it. There's money in my bag.' I hold my breath, in the hope that he leaves.

He takes another step closer, and I feel sick, or I fear I might faint. It's as if the world is spinning and I can't control it. He makes no effort to leave the room and head downstairs for my car keys and that tells me one thing. He wants me.

I go to scream but I know it's useless because we don't have neighbours. We decided to live in the country where we wouldn't be bothered by other people and their noise but right now, I wish I could bang on a wall or shout out the window at someone walking a dog or coming back from the pub.

A light almost blinds me. My phone flashes with a message and he's holding it. I glance at my intruder, and I see his dark head to toe clothing and a slit where his eyes are.

I scream and beg as he drops my phone and drives his heel into it. That's when I see him pulling something light coloured and patterned from his pocket. Its length tells me it's a scarf and it's familiar. It's my scarf, the one that my wife-to-be bought me. I'd left it on the coat hook downstairs. I know he's come to kill me.

Standing, I charge towards him, knowing all I have is the fight in me. He hasn't said a word. He doesn't want to talk, and I sense that he's enjoying my fear. As I make contact, it's like hitting steel. I bounce back onto the carpet. From the floor, I kick hard aiming for his crotch, and he screams. I struggle to my feet, knowing I have a moment to get away. Before he has a chance to react, I hit out again, catching his nose. I dart past him and down the stairs but he's upon me before I know it and the dull thud to my head tells me it's game over. Dazed, I slip to the cool, tiled floor, my long spiky earring bouncing away from me. I feel the silkiness of the scarf as he snakes it around my neck. Drops of his blood slip down my arm. If only I'd hit him harder. I don't want to die. I'm not ready. Tears fill my eyes as I gasp for breath. All I can think of is the wedding I'd never have, the babies I'd never hold and my wonderful partner. It was going to be me and her forever. I'd found my happy ending. In my mind, I tell her that I love her, and I hope she knows.

It's over. I'm over.

ONE

LAUREN

Sunday, 29 January

'Here's to the best fiancé ever,' Lauren shouted over the din as they clinked glasses in a roar of cheers. This was her sixth mojito, or was it her seventh? She'd lost count. Maybe it was the eighth. A slice of lime fell out of her glass and landed on her red-hot cheek as she downed the drink. All that dancing had made her face glow a prickly red. It had been such a long time since she'd been out with her friends but nights like this were precious. She bit her bottom lip, still reeling that Tiffany had decided to cry off, citing that she felt like she was coming down with a cold. It wasn't the first time Tiff had let them down, but Lauren wasn't going to let her absence ruin a night of celebration. 'Bunch in ladies.' Maxine and Dee huddled close as Lauren held out her phone and pouted. She hit the photo button and with a swift edit to reduce the redness, followed by a filter that livened up her inebriated face, she WhatsApped it straight to Robbie.

'Congratulations to our friend, Lauren.' Maxine held up her near-empty glass.

Robbie had finally proposed after five years together and Lauren had accepted. Married life was about to begin, and she couldn't wait for all the happy years to come.

Her mother didn't like him, but then she didn't like any of her boyfriends. At the end of the day, she knew exactly what she was doing. *When you know, you know.* She was a firm believer in that.

'That smile you're wearing is the smile of a super-happy woman.' Maxine nudged her.

'I've found the one I want to spend the rest of my life with. When I'm not with him, my heart aches. I've never known anything like it, Max.' What on earth was she saying? She needed to save soppy talk like that for her bestie, Sienna, not her work pals who were single and treated her to a succession of comedic talks about dates gone wrong. She'd never live that statement down when she was back on the make-up counter on Monday. They did all like to take the pee. Thinking about Sienna, she was disappointed that she had let her down too, but she did have a valid excuse, not like Tiffany.

Max looked at her with glassy eyes and laughed. 'I can see where the passion comes from. I'd do him.'

'Control yourself, girl.' Dee giggled as she elbowed Max in the side.

It was okay, Max hadn't registered the soppy drunken talk so maybe Lauren wouldn't be ribbed at work on Monday. Lauren pulled up the photo she'd just taken and smiled as Max and Dee laughed. She'd remember this night for the rest of her life. She clicked the Instagram app and stared wide-eyed at the three hundred comments congratulating her on their engagement. All she'd posted was a picture of her hand wearing that gorgeous diamond. 'Wow, I've never felt so popular.'

'What?' Maxine scrunched her brows.

Lauren clocked the time on her phone. It was almost two in the morning. No wonder Robbie hadn't seen her photo, he'd be fast asleep. She couldn't wait to get back home. She was going to sneak in, undress and snuggle up to him in bed because the next day she was going to desert him again for a spa day with Sienna, where she'd finally get to celebrate with her best friend. 'Taxi will be outside in fifteen minutes.' She hadn't left anything to chance knowing that all the taxi ranks around the centre of Birmingham would probably be empty on a Saturday night, the taxis all taken by revellers.

As they staggered out into the chilly January air, Lauren breathed out a plume of white steam. While waiting, the three women huddled together in their tiny dresses. Heels like towers threatening to break their ankles should they slip on the icy pavement. How she wished she'd brought a coat now. Maxine held her leopard print cape open for the three of them to bunch under and that's how they waited until the taxi turned up, the same driver that had picked them all up from Lauren's earlier.

'Thank goodness.' Lauren hurried into the front seat and the others struggled with their seat belts in the back. Before long, they were on the road back to Cleevesford. As she began to feel her numb fingers again, the motorway streetlights sent her eyelids drooping. She yawned and glanced back. Maxine's head lay on Dee's shoulder, and she snorted before dribbling. Both were out cold. In about fifteen minutes after the other two had been dropped off, she'd be safely home and tucked up, warming her cold feet on Robbie.

Streetlights came and streetlights went. The car got warmer and warmer, and the soothing music blended with the sound of the heater, lulling her into slumber. So warm, so comfortable. She smiled as she imagined how she'd look in her white dress on the big day. They planned to marry the following June. It would be warm and there would be bridesmaids in soft mint-green taffeta dresses, like little garden fairies. Then, the man of her dreams would be waiting for her, ring in hand as her mother begrudgingly gave her away. Her mum would come round to the wedding by then and they'd all be happy. Sienna would be her chief bridesmaid. The gorgeous best friend who she'd known since nursery school.

'Miss, miss?'

She prised her sticky eyes open and cleared her sandpaper throat. The mojitos weren't sitting well. Acid stung her gullet. Where were Max and Dee? 'What?'

The taxi driver undid his seat belt and came around to her side where he opened the door. 'You're home. I dropped your friends off first. You've been asleep since we hit the motorway.'

He leaned in and began to pull her under the arms. She batted him away. How dare he lay his filthy hands on her. She was drunk, vulnerable. 'Get off me,' she yelled. 'I can get up on my own.' Had she paid him? She pursed her lips as she thought. Yes, she'd paid for the return journey up front.

He stepped back. 'Okay, lady, I was just trying to help. Maybe you should take your shoes off.'

He was right. She slipped off her red pointed stilettos and struggled out of the car. The cold bit at her bare shoulders and her teeth began to chatter. 'Thank you. I'm okay now.'

'Just to be clear, I was only trying to help you out the car.' The taxi driver's dark-eyed stare made her look away.

'Yes, of course.' She couldn't believe she'd fallen asleep and not said goodbye to her friends. Or worse, she couldn't believe she'd slept while alone in a stranger's car. Anything could have happened. Why didn't her friends wake her up? The driver stared. 'I'm okay now. Thank you.' She stood on the pavement, almost sobering up on the spot as the cold penetrated her bare feet. She watched as the man got back into his car and drove a little way down the road, before pulling up just ahead. His car lit up as he held his phone to his ear. It was okay, he was just talking on the phone not stalking her. All was fine. They'd had a great night out and she was now going to bed.

Giggling, she began to hum a song by Rihanna that she'd been dancing to earlier that night as she fumbled in her tiny bag for her keys. Out spilled the tissues. Her favourite lipstick shattered on the pavement, and she was sure she dropped a five-pound note. Never mind. She'd come and gather her stuff up in the morning, or maybe Robbie would help her look for everything. With trembling fingers, she eventually managed to get the key in the lock and turn it.

Creeping into the hallway, she listened for any sign of life but not a sound could be heard. She popped her keys in the fruit bowl on the console table and dropped her shoes with a clunk onto the floor. As silently as she could, she crept to their bedroom and cautiously nudged the door open. In pitch darkness, she fumbled around, removing her dress and lifting the quilt up on her side. She sunk into their luxurious mattress. She edged her toes over to Robbie's side where her foot met his leg. He was stone cold. Reaching out, she pressed her finger into wetness. Jolting up, she reached for her lamp and fought to find the switch. As light filled the room, she struggled to breathe as she took in the bloody body of her best friend, Sienna. Her dark, blood-soaked hair sprawled out on Robbie's pillow.

As she went to scream, she heard a bang coming from the living room. Her heart began to thump, and a faintness came over her as she gasped for breath. Where was Robbie and who was outside her bedroom door? Without another thought, she screamed as loud as she could and pressed nine-nine-nine on her phone before the intruder entered.

TWO

'No.' Gina pulled her naked body away from DCI Chris Briggs's warmth as she reached for her buzzing phone.

He rubbed his eyes and rolled onto his back, dragging the quilt from her. 'What time is it?'

'Shh.' She answered the call and gestured for him to stay silent. Whoever was calling from the station couldn't know that her DCI was currently in her bed, and he knew the drill. He smiled and stroked her back as she waited for the caller to speak.

'DI Harte?'

'Yep.' She rolled over onto her side. His hand reached her buttock. She playfully slapped it away.

'We had a call come in just after three a.m. Murder of a young woman. The address is 29 Bell Road. Four uniformed officers are currently in attendance, and you are listed as being on call tonight. We'll keep trying DS Driscoll. Forensics are on their way and the rest of your team will be informed.'

Gina leaned back against her pillow. 'I'm leaving in a minute.' She ended the call.

'Who was it?'

'Dispatch. Murder on Bell Road.' She leaned down and kissed him on the lips, her chin brushing against the stubble that he'd shave before going into the station.

He ran one of his large hands through his hair and sat up. Gina's cat, Ebony, jumped on the bed. 'I'll feed her, get up and head to the station. As soon as you've weighed up the scene, call me.' He called the cat and left the bedroom.

'Will do.' Hurrying to the bathroom, she got cleaned up and left. She didn't know if she could trust him totally after all they'd been through, but she needed his warmth and closeness. When someone knew a person as well as he knew her, it was impossible to let go, and she did love him, even though they almost parted for good not so long ago. A flash of insecurity made her shudder.

Twenty minutes later, she pulled up on the road behind the blue light vehicles. Two police cars, an ambulance and a forensics van had already arrived at the scene. She spotted Crime Scene Manager Bernard Small's tall gangly frame dressed in a crime scene suit. He hunched over as he pulled his forensics toolkit from the van. Three assistants followed him, carrying camera bags and various bits of equipment. A uniformed officer was tying the outer cordon around a final lamppost, blocking off the whole cul-de-sac. PC Smith stood guard with his clipboard ready to manage anyone entering the scene.

DS Jacob Driscoll pulled up a little further down the road in his dark saloon car. He hurried toward her, and she stepped out of her car to meet him. 'Morning, guv,' he said. She brushed down her black coat, removing the cat hairs, then she quickly dragged her long brown hair into a bobble. Jacob smoothed his short back and sides down with his hands.

'Morning, Jacob. Best get to it.' She stopped walking as she reached PC Smith. 'Fill us in.'

'Alright, guv.' The uniformed officer rubbed his gloved hands together. 'The person who found the victim, Lauren Cross, called us at five past three. She reported an intruder and the murder of her best friend. Her partner, Robbie Shields, is nowhere to be seen and was meant to be home. When she called she thought the murderer was in her home, so we rushed a police car over. Since arriving, officers have searched the rooms for the intruder but found no one. When we went in the bedroom we found Lauren Cross sitting on the bed crying, and the body of her friend lying in the bed. One officer immediately checked the victim for a pulse but there was no sign of life, in fact he said the body was cold. Another officer led Miss Cross out of the house and into the ambulance where she is about to be taken to hospital. She's drunk, in shock, and was screaming and trying to fight us off. The paramedic offered her something to calm her down which she took, so I think she's slightly sedated.'

'Do we know the victim's name?'

'Sienna Moorcroft.'

Jacob stepped forward. 'Is there anything else you can tell us yet?'

PC Smith shook his head. 'No, that's it for now. Bernard is in the bedroom processing the scene.'

Gina nodded. She took the pen and clipboard, filling out the crime scene log. She stepped under the cordon, grabbed two crime scene suits packs, passing one to Jacob and opening one for herself. By the time they reached the front door, they'd both togged up, put their boot covers, face masks and gloves on, ready to check out the scene. She glanced down at the shattered lipstick and crumpled tissues next to the step.

A crime scene assistant rushed past them. Gina didn't recognise her. 'Is Jennifer working the scene?' Gina asked Jacob as she wondered if his fiancée would be there.

'No, guv. She's not on tonight.'

Gina called out to the CSI. 'Are we able to speak to Bernard yet?'

The assistant nodded. 'Yes, I'll just get him for you.' She hurried in, leaving them standing on the stepping plates at the doorstep.

Moments later, Bernard arrived at the door and pulled his face mask down under his chin, allowing a bit of grey beard to escape. His head almost touched the doorframe as he blocked out the light from the hallway.

'Can you tell us anything yet?' Gina knew forensics had barely touched the scene, but she remained hopeful.

'I've been here half an hour. I have a scene that has been contaminated by several officers and a homeowner who got into bed with the victim, but we have managed to get the stepping plates down and it is a roomy bungalow. You can enter but stay on those plates and stay by the entrance to each room. Come through.' He returned his mask to his mouth.

Gina stepped in first and Jacob stayed close behind, their shoes clopping on the plates with each step. The door to the right led to a spacious lounge and dining area. Straight ahead the door to the kitchen was open, but they followed Bernard to the left, past a large bathroom and then she stopped as they watched the assistants marking out evidence and taking photos and video. Gina struggled to swallow as her gaze reached the victim. Her delicate features pale in death and her dark hair splayed out on the pillow. Jacob looked away and held a hand over his mouth. 'You okay?'

He nodded and took a step back.

'Look, if you're not feeling so good, step out. I'll be okay here.'

'Thanks, guv.' He left the room.

Bernard cleared his throat and continued talking. 'As you can see, the victim has been stabbed in the upper arm, but this injury did not cause her death. She was stabbed first, then see that thin scarf on the floor, looking at the blood pattern on it and the ligature marks around the victim's neck, she was then strangled with it. We've placed bags over her hands to preserve any evidence under her nails.'

Gina glanced at the beautiful scarf, dotted with blue flowers. 'She's dressed.' The victim wore a little black dress that reached just above her knee.

'Yes, she is. Her dress hasn't been tampered with.'

'Any signs of sexual assault?'

'We know she's recently had sex but there is no sign of force that we can see. We have noted that she wasn't wearing any underpants and there are none on the floor or in the bed.'

'Have we found the weapon that was used to stab her with?'

'No, not yet.'

'We need to check the whole perimeter of the bungalow, the garden and the bins as soon as we're able to disturb the scene.' She hoped they'd be able to do a thorough search soon.

'I'll let you know when.' Bernard nodded to the CSI as she photographed the scarf.

'There's another dress there.' She pointed to another little black dress on the carpet.

'Yes, the woman who left in the ambulance had nothing but a blanket wrapped around her.'

'So, it could be her dress. Do we know how the murderer got in?'

Bernard swallowed. 'There are no signs of forced entry.'

Gina exhaled. 'So, the murderer lives here or was let in and there is no sign of the other homeowner.'

'I'm really sorry, but I'm going to have to ask you to wait outside as I don't want to delay getting samples collected and sent to the lab. We need to take all we can from the body in situ. Sorry as I know you need to be here too, but as soon as everything's done, we can hand the scene over to you. I'll be as fast as I can, I promise.'

'Of course. Any clue as to the time of death?'

'Looking at the state of the body and the progression of rigor mortis, I'd say between four and eight hours.'

Gina did a quick reccy in her head. 'So, she was murdered between eight yesterday evening and midnight?'

'Say between seven yesterday evening and one in the morning. Just to be sure.'

'Thank you.'

'I'll call you straight away if I find anything that will help. The post-mortem will take place either Monday morning or afternoon. I'll email the details to you.'

Gina had a final glance of the pretty young woman. She took in the petechiae – the telltale red speckles in the whites of Sienna's eyes caused by strangulation. The raw indentation that the scarf had left on her neck was covered in scratch marks where the woman had desperately clawed at her own flesh while trying to escape her attacker. Gina imagined her struggling and finally giving up as she succumbed to death, unable to find the strength to fight any longer as the blood vessels in her eyes burst. She wondered if Sienna could have fought her attacker off had she not been stabbed first.

'Bernard?' A crime scene assistant walked in. 'An officer has found something in the hedge that runs alongside the side of the building. I've placed a marker down and it's ready to photograph.'

'What is it?' He held his creaking back as he stood tall.

'A nail file covered in blood.'

Gina needed to speak to Lauren Cross and find out more about Sienna. As she left and met Jacob on the doorstep, she removed her crime scene clothing and placed it in the bag next to PC Smith as he logged them out. 'Where's the ambulance?' Speaking to Lauren was now her priority.

'It'll be heading to Cleevesford General, guv.' PC Smith lowered the clipboard.

Damn. It looked like they'd now have to go to the hospital. Jacob stared into the crowd that had begun to form and she followed his gaze. Lines of worry deepened on his forehead. 'Do you see anything?'

He shook his head.

'Are you okay?'

He blew out a breath. 'Yes, I'm fine. I just feel a bit icky, sorry.' He raised his eyebrows.

Gina stared into the crowd, wondering if their murderer was watching on. A woman waved. 'Are you detectives?' she called out, in a Geordie accent.

Gina hurried over. She was almost covered with a huge blanket-like coat. 'Yes, I'm DI Harte, this is DS Driscoll.'

'I woke up when Lauren came home. I heard a car engine humming, so I looked out of the window.'

'Did you see anything out of the ordinary?'

'Yes, and it gave me the right chills.'

THREE

'May we come in?' Gina waited with Jacob outside the woman's front door. She looked back, it was almost directly opposite Lauren Cross's bungalow.

The woman threw her coat over the banister and nodded, allowing Gina and Jacob to follow her through to the kitchen where the smell of pizza hung in the air. The worktop was littered with empty sweet and crisp wrappers. 'Try to keep it down if you can. I have two kids in bed.'

Gina smiled and waited by the worktop. 'Of course. Could we take your name, please?'

'It's Kimmy. Kimmy Lloyd. What's been happening over there? I saw Lauren head off in an ambulance.'

'I'm sad to say we're investigating a murder. I can't say any more at the moment.'

'No way.' The woman shivered and placed her hands into the pockets of her sweater.

'Can you tell me what you saw tonight?'

The woman paused as if reflecting on the enormity of the crime. 'Right, sorry. I saw something strange when Lauren got dropped off in a taxi. The driver walked around the car. He opened the passenger door, so I nudged the window open a little. That's when I heard Lauren shouting at him, telling him not to touch her. Anyway, I recognised the car as I'd pulled up with a takeaway earlier that night. It was the same car that picked her up.'

Jacob finished writing a few notes.

'What time did Lauren get picked up?' Gina asked.

'Around nine. I don't know the exact time. Three women got into the car. One was Lauren and there were another two. They were all dressed up. I waved and said alright before grabbing my pizza and going. It's when she got dropped off that has me worried.'

'What time was this?'

'Around three. I noticed the driver leering at Lauren so when I heard her shout get off me at him, I was on high alert. I watched her leave the taxi to make sure she was okay. I'm sure she said something like, "you can go now". Maybe not exactly like that, but he was staring at her in a weird way. Anyway, I grabbed my dressing gown, thinking I might have to go down and help her if he got any creepier but then he left. Well, I say he left.'

'Are you saying that he didn't leave?'

The woman nodded. 'That's exactly what I'm saying. He drove a little way down the road and pulled up on the pavement. I saw his phone light up as he watched Lauren in his rearview mirror. As I said, creepy. I was quite relieved when he left and then when I saw you lot show up. The blue light brigade. Before he left, he did something strange.'

Gina waited for Jacob to catch up. 'What was that?'

'He turned the engine off, got out of the car and went up to the bungalow. It just looked like he was creeping around. I couldn't see much as the hedge covered him, but I thought he could be snooping around. I swear he looked like he was up to no good. Would you like a drink?'

Jacob shook his head.

'No, thank you,' Gina replied. She'd have loved a coffee, but time was against them. 'Did you see the driver at any other time yesterday evening?'

'I wasn't looking for him. I was watching a film with my kids, then I went to bed. I only saw her leave and come back, nothing in between.'

'Can you describe him?'

'It was dark, and he wasn't exactly under my nose but I'll do my best. White. Taller than Lauren in her heels, but not by much. He was wearing a bomber jacket and he had thin legs, I mean sparrow thin. Tight jeans. Dark hair. That's all I saw.'

Gina was quite impressed by how much Kimmy had remembered. 'Did you catch the make of his car, or did you see any signage that might tell us who he works for?'

'No signage but it was a saloon. It looked shiny and was either navy blue or black.'

'Do you have a doorbell camera?'

'No, wish I did but I never have any spare pennies with my two.'

'Mummy.' Gina heard the tiny voice coming from the landing.

'Damn, looks like the youngest has woken.' The woman walked to the kitchen door. 'I'll be up in a minute, kiddo. Wait in bed.'

'Is there anything else you can add?'

'No, sorry. That really is it. Just that he was a bit creepy, and she was telling him not to touch her.' The woman paused. 'Is Lauren alright? I don't really know her well, but she seems nice. She always says hello if I see her but generally, she keeps herself to herself.'

Gina nodded. 'We hope so. Can you tell us who she lives with?'

'Oh yes, Robbie, the charmer.'

'Robbie the charmer?'

'Yes, he's always flashing smiles and saying good morning. He's a lovely guy. Always available to help the residents with building flat-pack or carrying a bit of furniture.'

Gina had no information at all on Robbie Shields, except that he was living with Lauren. 'How was their relationship?'

'Beautiful. They were always hand in hand, had these sneaky kisses when they thought no one was looking.'

'Did you see anyone else visit the house today?'

The woman shook her head. 'I only saw Lauren and two other women getting into the taxi. Contrary to what you might think, I don't spy on my neighbours. I just happened to be awake in the early hours this morning.'

'Well, thank you so much for your time. An officer will see you shortly to take a formal statement. In the meantime, if you think of anything else, please call me straight away.' Gina passed the woman one of her cards.

'Oh, there is one other thing, and I don't like to gossip but knowing that a murder has been committed, I think I should tell you.'

'Please, go on. It can sometimes be the smallest of things that can help a case.'

She bit her bottom lip and proceeded to speak. 'It was over a week ago. I saw Lauren at the end of the street, and she was walking away from a man. It was evening as it was dark but I don't know what time. Before eight, though. He grabbed her arm, and she shook him off. She then pushed him with both hands on his chest. I don't know what had been going on or who he was, but she was angry. Before you ask, I couldn't describe him, he was too far away. I recognised Lauren from her outline. She often wears mid-length coats and heeled boots. Her hair is always up in a knot on the top of her head. I know it wasn't Robbie as he'd just gone into their bungalow. Who has been murdered? Is Robbie okay?'

'It's not Mr Shields.' Gina did love a nosy neighbour. As for suspects, they had a suspicious taxi driver, Robbie Shields himself and the man Lauren was seen arguing with. 'Can you remember the day?'

'No, it wasn't a weekend so maybe it was last Friday, or Thursday.'

'Who does the black VW Passat on the drive belong to?'

'That's easy. It's Robbie's as Lauren doesn't drive. I assume she can't drive because I've never seen her behind the wheel.'

A picture was forming in Gina's mind. A dead woman in Lauren and Robbie's bed. She'd recently had what appeared on the surface to be consensual intercourse and now Lauren's partner was missing. Right now, charming Robbie Shields was at the top of her list, and she needed all resources ploughed into finding him fast.

Another possibility whirred through Gina's mind. Lauren Cross left her bungalow around nine yesterday evening. That gave Lauren opportunity, given that the time of death was between seven and one in the morning. She needed to speak to Lauren and her two friends, now.

FOUR

TIFFANY

Thoughts muddled through Tiffany's head, like it had been stuffed with cotton wool. A hazy memory came back to her from the night before or was it a dream? She'd argued with Lauren, but the words were jumbled and made no sense. She'd only had one glass of wine last night or was it two? Her intolerance to just about everything was getting worse by the minute. Chocolate upset her stomach. Fragrances made her nauseous and even the wrong type of lighting sent her giddy. She wasn't right and unless she wanted to give up all hope of getting her life back, she had to figure out what was wrong and get better. That was easier said than done when her doctor had all but accused her of being a hypochondriac.

Tiffany went to reach for her glass of water, the one always left by her bedside, but it wasn't there. Her head thumped like never before, another symptom that had fuelled her anxiety. She heard her husband mutter as he plumped his pillow up. 'What time is it?' He always had his phone next to his bedside, which meant he was the one who always knew what time it was.

'Go back to sleep. It's Sunday and it's still dark. We said we were having a lie-in.' Kieron pulled more quilt over his side.

She let out a deep breath and rubbed her eyes, staring into the darkness of their bedroom. Guilt ate away at her from the inside. Lauren had wanted to celebrate her engagement last night but as usual, Tiffany hadn't felt well. No one understood what being constantly ill was like, and it wasn't the first time that the others had judged her. She'd overheard Maxine and Dee joking about her being ill yet again when Lauren called her from the club. No one understood. The headaches, the fatigue, the nausea – they were all real. She was ill and the worse thing about it was, she had no diagnosis. Doctors blamed it all on her past, referred to her symptoms as psychological and offered her cognitive behavioural therapy and a concoction of pills for depression and anxiety. One even told her to start exercising. She didn't have the energy for that. Her little job at the beauty outlet wiped her out. She didn't want to sit and think or sit and talk. She wanted tests and lots of them, maybe a full body CT scan or more bloods. Tears began to fall down her cold cheeks.

'Are you crying?'

She went to speak but a loud sob came out. It's amazing how the middle of the night always made these thoughts and feelings worse.

Kieron sat up and switched the lamp on. He grabbed a pile of quilt and snuggled her in it before hugging her closely. 'What is it, love?'

'Lauren hates me.'

He stroked her hair and passed her a tissue. 'Lauren does not hate you. She was just a bit tipsy. I'm sure she'll apologise in the morning.'

'Max and Dee think I'm pretending to be ill.'

He squeezed her. 'I'm sorry, love. Some people just don't understand but I'm sure Lauren does and she will come round.'

'I don't have any friends. Everyone's abandoned me, or they

do eventually. They don't know what to say, what to do, how to be around me. Lauren's right to be pissed off at me for not going. I let her down like I let everyone down.'

He pulled a stray hair from the corner of her mouth. 'You did not. You're ill and we're going to get to the bottom of what's wrong even if we have to go private.'

She knew she'd never be able to afford to go private. She cleaned the department store for two hours a day and after that, she had to go home and sleep for four. Kieron pulled double shifts at the factory to keep a roof over their heads. There was no spare money for private medical care. Her heart rate began to pick up just thinking about the arguments she'd had with her doctor. She knew the professionals missed things all the time. There was always a scare story in the news, telling of someone who'd died because they had to wait forever to get tests, or they'd had the wrong tests. The thumping headaches, the brain fog – maybe it was a brain tumour or early-onset dementia. She had a distant uncle who had Parkinson's. Maybe it was that. She sometimes felt a bit jittery, especially in her more hyper insomniac moments. She blew her nose.

'It's all going to be okay. I'm going to get a weekend job and we'll soon have the extra cash. We'll get it sorted; I promise.'

She cleared her throat. 'I'm going to get a drink. Do you want one?'

'I'm good. Here, I'll get it. You keep snuggled and get warm. Or do you want a tea or hot chocolate?'

'Just water. Love you,' she said as she kissed Kieron. He really was her everything. She had no idea what she'd do without him. She listened as he ran the tap. Moments later, he was back with the water. As she took huge gulps, her dry throat enjoyed the instant relief. Maybe it was time to cut out the wine completely and practice a little more self-care. It wasn't a cure, but it would be a start and it would stop the doctor bringing her moderate drinking into every conversation about her health.

She never had more than two glasses and he always spoke to her like she was an alcoholic. Shifting in bed, she felt something gritty on her foot. She reached down and picked a speck of gravel from between her toes.

Kieron smiled at her. 'Better, now can we get some sleep?'

She reached for her neck, tracing where the scarf had cut off her breath. The harder she tried not to think of that night – the one that turned her into a wreck – the more she couldn't get it out of her head. That was the start of her pain and all it did was get worse.

Kieron reached for her hand. 'I should never have left you alone that night.'

She shook her head. 'It's not your fault. You can't be with me every second of the day.'

'But I didn't need to go to that stag do. I didn't even want to go.'

She realised then that he too was living with the guilt of what happened. They'd gone from lovers to carer and victim overnight. 'It's all in the past now.' She lay down and Kieron spooned her as he soothingly stroked her hair. Only in his arms did she feel safe. 'Did I sleepwalk and go outside last night?'

He kissed the back of her head. 'I found you out the front, standing on the pavement. We fell asleep on the settee and when I woke up you were gone. It's my fault, I forgot to double lock the door. Can't believe I was so slack after all that's happened.'

'I don't know what I'd do without you.' She shook her head. 'Thank you for being you and looking after me.'

'Always. Now let's get some sleep or we're both going to be shattered all day.'

He reached over and turned the light off. As she inhaled and exhaled, her arms and legs felt like lead. The police had never found the man who came into their home and tried to strangle her with her own scarf. He was still out there. She often wondered if he came back, or if he watched her. That's why her body was failing. Trauma had taken its toll. That's why she was ill, and it was the reason she let people down. While he was out there, identity unknown, she would remain his prisoner.

FIVE

Gina passed Jacob a machine coffee and grabbed her own, then they headed to the ward where Lauren Cross had been admitted. She sipped the hot liquid, hoping that the caffeine would work its way through her body rapidly. 'You haven't said a word since we got here.'

Jacob swigged his drink as their steps echoed through the wide corridor. A nurse pushed a patient in a bed past them but there were no visitors around with it being only five thirty in the morning. 'I'm just tired, guv.'

She arched her brows. She'd seen Jacob tired on many occasions, but tiredness had never rendered him that speechless. 'Are you and Jennifer okay?'

'Yes, couldn't be better.'

'How's Thumper?'

'Oh, you know. He's just being a rabbit as usual. Keeps trying to mate with the footstool but I guess that'll pass.'

'I was thinking about this case,' she said. 'It's screaming affair. Lauren Cross's friend comes over all dressed up as soon as Lauren goes out. They have sex, then what goes wrong?'

Jacob coughed. 'Sorry, wrong way.' He held his coffee up.

Gina continued. 'The victim, Sienna Moorcroft, was stabbed first. Then we have the taxi driver. Why did he park up, go to the bungalow and then walk back to the car? It's far from straightforward.' She stopped. 'Here we go. Ward sixteen.' She entered first, holding the door open for Jacob. They reached an inner door with an intercom and threw their empty coffee cups in the bin.

Gina buzzed and a nurse finished tapping words onto a keyboard before he let her in. 'How can I help you? Visiting for this ward isn't until ten in the morning.'

'I'm DI Harte, this is DS Driscoll.' They held their identification up. 'Are we able to speak to Lauren Cross?'

The man headed behind the counter and checked his computer screen. 'Ah, yes. From what I can see, she's a bit calmer now. Follow me and we'll check with the patient, see if she's up to talking. A police officer came in with her, but he just asked where the vending machines and toilets are.'

The nurse knocked and entered the tiny room. 'Miss Cross, there's two police detectives to see you.' He opened the door, allowing Gina and Jacob into the room. 'I'll be back at the nurses' station if you need me.'

'Thank you,' Gina said as she stepped towards the woman's bed. 'Hello, Lauren. Is it okay to call you Lauren?'

The young woman sat up and nodded, her eyes panda-like from all the smudged make-up and her foundation had smeared on the crisp white hospital sheet. She rubbed her nose and moved her straggly blonde to brown ombré coloured hair from her face.

'It must have been such a shock, seeing what you saw.' Gina sat on the plastic chair next to Lauren's bed and Jacob took his notepad out and remained by the door.

'I... I was in bed with her. I didn't know and I had her blood on me...' The woman hiccupped and released a little cry.

'I know this is hard, but we need to ask you a few questions.

We would really like to find out who did this. Are you okay to speak?'

Lauren adjusted her hospital gown and nodded. 'Yes.'

'Can you tell me what happened in your own words?'

'Sienna is my best friend and by best friend, I mean we went to school together and she was like the sister I never had.' Lauren paused. 'I came home and got into bed in the dark. I thought Robbie was in bed but when I moved to be closer to him, I felt wetness and she was so cold. I didn't know it was her at that point. Then I heard some noise coming from the living room, and I thought the killer was in my home. I've never been so scared in my whole life.' Lauren's teeth chattered and Gina could see her fingers trembling as she gripped the edge of the sheets too tightly.

'Where was Robbie? You live with Robbie Shields, don't you?'

'Yes, and I don't know. I thought he was at home. He said he was staying in all night while I was out. Did he come home? Can I see him? I need to see him.'

Gina swallowed. 'We don't know where he is, and we need to find him. Do you know where he might go? Does he have parents close by, or any friends he might be with?'

She shook her head. 'No, he should have been at home. His car was on the drive.'

'Would he have walked?'

'No, Robbie never walks anywhere. Something's happened to him.' She gasped for a breath and sobbed. Gina passed her the box of tissues that were on the bedside cabinet.

'Can you tell me about earlier in the evening, just before you left to go out? Was Robbie at home then?'

She sniffed and cleared her throat. 'He stayed in the bedroom, watching TV. My friends turned up as we were all going from my place. We had a couple of drinks in the kitchen and got into a taxi about nine.'

'Which taxi firm did you use?'

She shrugged. 'I don't know. Robbie booked it for me. He was going to drive us, but he said he fancied a drink instead and he would never drive after a drink.'

Great, Gina couldn't even ask Robbie about the taxi. 'How did he seem when you left him?'

She shrugged. 'I don't know. Normal, I guess. I went into the bedroom; gave him a kiss goodbye and he seemed fine. He told me to have a good time and that he'd see me later.'

Gina needed to know more about the taxi driver. 'Tell me what happened next. How was your journey?'

'Okay. We got there with no problems.'

'Did the driver speak to you?'

She nodded. 'He asked where we were going and if it was a special occasion. He said we all looked lovely and made small talk.'

'Who else was with you?'

'Dee and Maxine. I work with them at Hoopers. It's a beauty outlet on the retail park. It's a department store type shop. We all work different departments.' Lauren stared into her hands.

Gina made a mental note to ask Lauren's friends if they'd seen Robbie, given that he was already in bed, and she wondered if Sienna was already dead at this point. Had Sienna come over to see Robbie, thinking that Lauren had already left and had Lauren attacked her with the nail file? And what happened after? She shook that thought away for the time being. There were too many variables to make such a deduction and with Robbie Shields missing, she couldn't ask him about the evening either. She glanced at Jacob and noticed that he was biting his bottom lip. 'How did your night go? Did you call Robbie from the club?'

'No, I didn't call him. I don't have to check in with him.'

'I wasn't suggesting that you did.' For a moment Lauren

looked annoyed. 'I'm just trying to establish what happened,' Gina added.

'We all danced and drank a lot. It was a good night until I got home.'

'A neighbour says that you told the taxi driver to get off you, do you remember?'

Lauren shrugged. 'Sort of. It's all a bit hazy. I fell asleep in the taxi and when I woke up, Dee and Maxine had already been dropped off, so it was just me in the car. I think he was trying to pull me out and I got angry with him for leaning into the passenger side to drag me. It doesn't matter because I left him and went into the house.'

'Your neighbour said the taxi driver pulled up a little way down the road.'

A confused look washed over Lauren's face. She scrunched her nose. 'I can't properly remember. Maybe he did. I went in and I didn't think any more of it.'

'She said that he got out of the taxi, went up your path and was there for a short while. He then left. Do you know why he might have gone back to your bungalow?'

Lauren stared. 'Do you think he did this? Do you think he could have dropped us off and then went back to my home and...' Lauren took a succession of deep breaths and placed a hand over her heart. 'Why was Sienna in my bed?' More tears began to flow. 'I can't think,' she wailed.

'Could Sienna and Robbie have been in a relationship?'

Lauren frantically shook her head. 'She would never do that to me. She was my best friend in the whole world and Robbie loves me. We're getting married.' Her brows furrowed and she sobbed. 'It's obvious though, isn't it? He must have been sleeping with her.' Lauren gripped the sheet and let out a long painful cry into the fibres.

Gina felt her pain. An affair between Robbie and Sienna was looking likely. Maybe Robbie had invited Sienna over to call it off and then, Sienna had threatened to tell Lauren and then bam – he killed her and now he was on the run. The motive could be that simple. 'Could I take your friends' details? We'll need to speak to Maxine and Dee.'

Lauren lay down in the bed and sobbed like a child. She had lost her dreams and her best friend. 'I don't have my phone. Their details are in my phone.'

'We're really sorry, it's more than likely been booked into evidence if it was found at the scene.'

'Can someone call my mum? Her number is listed under Mum?'

'Of course. Is there anyone else you want us to contact?'

'No. I just want my mum.'

'Again, I'm really sorry for what you've been through. An officer will arrive shortly to take a formal statement. If, in the meantime, you think of anything that might help us to catch Sienna's killer, please ask a nurse to call us straight away. I just need to ask, were you arguing with someone at the end of your street on the nineteenth or twentieth of January, evening time?'

'Who said I was?'

'A witness.'

'A drunken guy nearly fell on me, that was all. I'd just got off the bus and I think he was attempting to run towards it. He crashed into me and I was angry. It was nothing. The guy could barely stand.'

Gina waited for Jacob to catch up. 'When you're discharged, where will you go?'

'Can I go home?'

Gina felt her stomach knot. 'I'm sorry again. Forensics are there and it's an active crime scene. I'll let you know as soon as we're finished but it could be several days. Also, for your own safety, I'd rather you didn't stay there for now. Is there anyone you can stay with?'

'I'll have to stay with my mum. Please call her. Tell her I

need her. I'll need someone to pick me up from here. My passcode is Lauren 1 2 3 4,' Lauren said, her voice getting hoarse.

That was one less phone for Garth in tech to crack. 'I'll go to the station now and do that right away. You shouldn't be alone at a time like this.' Lauren looked almost child-like as she turned to lie in the foetal position. Gina wished she could stay with the young woman until her mother arrived, but she was expected at the station. She'd need to get back and go through Lauren's phone. Maybe Lauren took photos while out, or sent messages back and forth to Robbie Shields. Gina spotted a uniformed officer peering through the little glass square in the door. He nodded. At least someone would be there if Lauren thought of anything else to tell them. In the meantime, they'd have to put out a missing person notice for Robbie Shields. Right now, he was their prime suspect and she wanted him in an interview room. Her phone beeped and a message popped up from Briggs.

Can you head back to the station now? We need an urgent briefing. It has been confirmed that the nail file was used to stab Sienna Moorcroft and we have two phones. One belonging to Sienna and one belonging to Lauren. Garth in tech is just about to crack them.

SIX

Gina headed straight to her office, grabbing her suit jacket and a couple of painkillers. After being woken from such a deep sleep, she was cursing the pulsating ache in her head. She swallowed the pills down swiftly as she entered the hustle and bustle of the incident room. DC Harry O'Connor sat at the back of the room eating a doorstop sandwich, the strip light reflection shining on his smooth head. DC Paula Wyre removed her thick coat and drank from her water bottle, her black hair pulled in a tight bun. That's when she spotted PC Jhanvi Kapoor, smiling.

Briggs cleared his throat. 'Right, today was going to be a day of big announcements and celebrations, but all those celebrations are now on hold. I'll say what I have to say quickly, and we can all go down the pub and do this properly when things calm down a bit around here. After successfully impressing in interview, PC Kapoor has been admitted onto the Initial Crime Investigators Development Programme. She will be working with the team as a trainee DC. Congratulations, Jhanvi!'

A small round of applause filled the air and Briggs continued. 'That leaves us with a gap. Having specified PCs on the team has proven to be invaluable. Jhanvi Kapoor had given us a lot of support and we need another PC to take her place, so let's also welcome PC Shafiq Ahmed. He will be assisting us along-side PC Smith who is currently still at the murder scene.'

Another round of applause filled the room. PC Ahmed stood and uncomfortably half waved. 'Thank you for having me. I'm excited to be a part of this team.' He swiftly sat back in his chair as if nervously trying to get out of the limelight.

Gina knew of Jhanvi's new position, but she hadn't said a word to anyone else.

'Let's waste no more time. Like I said, once things settle we'll celebrate properly. On to the case. Gina, can you fill us in on what you know, then we'll go over what's in Lauren Cross's and Sienna Moorcroft's phones. Trainee DC Kapoor, can you take the pen and jot everything down on the board?'

Jhanvi stood, a full smile on her face as she began heading up the board. Her smart black trousers and white shirt looked brand new out of the shop.

Gina headed to the front of the room. 'Jacob and I have visited the scene and the hospital. On the surface, it looks like Sienna Moorcroft had been having an affair with Robbie Shields. Lauren Cross came home after a night out, got into bed and found she was lying next to her dead friend. Bernard is managing the crime scene. He said that Sienna had recently had sexual intercourse, but there were no signs of force. Robbie's phone hasn't been found at the scene. Sienna had been stabbed and then strangled with a scarf. She died as a result of the strangulation. While we were there, a nail file was found outside and there was blood on it. These are all preliminary findings, so we need to wait for Bernard and his team to arrange the post-mortem and lab work. As for Lauren, she's currently in ward sixteen at Cleevesford General and has been treated for shock. When Jacob and I saw her, she looked distressed.'

Briggs took a sip of coffee and put his cup on a desk. 'The main suspect is Robbie Shields?'

Gina nodded. 'Yes. We don't know where he is at present. We also need to speak to the taxi driver who dropped Lauren home. We spoke to a neighbour, and she overheard Lauren telling the taxi driver to get off her. I asked Lauren about this, and she didn't seem overly concerned about him, but the neighbour said that the driver parked up and walked back to Lauren's bungalow once she was inside. He spent a short while in her front garden then came back out. Why was he loitering there?'

Gina waited for Jhanvi to make a note about the taxi driver on the board before continuing.

'One of the neighbours said that she saw Lauren arguing with a man on the previous Thursday or Friday at the end of the street. When we asked Lauren about this she claimed that a drunken man walked into her and she pushed him off.'

Briggs interjected. 'Any confirmation on the time of death?'

'As usual, it's approximate. Between seven p.m. and one a.m. Lauren didn't leave the bungalow until nine which means that she too had opportunity. We can't rule her out. As a theory, maybe she suspected that Sienna was having an affair with Robbie. Maybe she called that taxi herself for nine and told Robbie that she was originally going out at seven. I'm just theorising, but if Lauren had suspected that Sienna was sleeping with her fiancé, maybe she set up some scenario where Robbie thought she was going out earlier and Sienna turned up. Maybe after watching her fiancé having sex with her friend, she plunged the nail file into her friend's upper arm? Maybe Sienna fought her, so Lauren grabbed a scarf, managed to wrestle it around her neck and kill her. I can't think of the logistics in full, like where was Robbie when this was happening, but we can't completely rule Lauren out as the opportunity is there. The friends are key in getting to the bottom of this one. When did the two women arrive at the bungalow, and could Lauren have been present when Sienna was murdered? We need her friends' details from her phone.'

Briggs thanked her for updating them. 'Right, I agree that we need Robbie Shields found. I'm going to issue a press release this morning making an appeal for him. Someone must have seen him.'

'He left his car behind, sir, and Lauren did say that he never walked anywhere. We need to find out if Sienna had a car. Maybe he took her car and absconded after killing Sienna. There's a couple of initial theories to consider for now, but as always, we follow the evidence as it comes in.' Gina sat and took a cup of coffee from the centre of the table.

'Have we contacted Sienna Moorcroft's next of kin?' Briggs looked around the room.

DC O'Connor scratched his head. 'We have her address, but no one has been to visit as yet. Her parents live in Sheffield.'

'Right, Gina, you're senior investigating officer. I'm going to head to my office to prepare a statement as the press are already gathering.'

She stood and nodded. 'We need to contact Sheffield police and ask someone to break the bad news. Jacob and I will head to Sienna Moorcroft's address, see if anyone else lives there with her. O'Connor, would you contact Sheffield police? It's not going to take long for this news to break so her parents need to know first.'

'I'm on it.' He left the table.

'Jhanvi, will you work closely with O'Connor for now? He'll help you record everything for your portfolio.'

'I'd love to.' Jhanvi passed the pen to DC Wyre and headed out of the room with O'Connor.

Gina glanced at the board. 'We need to add Lauren Cross's two friends to the board. All I have so far are the names Dee and Maxine. Who here has been liaising with Garth in tech?'

Wyre transferred her weight from one foot to the other. 'O'Connor and I have been.'

'Can we start with Lauren's phone. What did you find?'

'She communicates mostly through Instagram and Whats-App. She has a popular TikTok account where she does make-up tutorials. She does have contacts named Dee and Max in her phone and we have their numbers. There was a flurry of messages in a WhatsApp group in the run up to their night out. Nothing stands out in the content, but there is another person in the group, a woman called Tiffany who was also invited out last night but said she couldn't go. We can see that Tiffany made a phone call to Lauren at eight forty-five last night. It lasted about three minutes.'

Gina pointed to the board and scrunched her brow. 'Okay, so we have another in this equation. Tiffany was meant to go but didn't. She's definitely someone we need to check out too.'

Wyre replied, 'Oh, the WhatsApp group is called Hooper Girls.'

Gina nodded. 'Colleagues. They must all work at Hoopers. All three need to be interviewed. I want to know if Maxine or Dee saw Robbie when they turned up at the bungalow and how everything seemed. We also need to know why Tiffany didn't go and where she was last night.'

'Lauren made one more phone call, guv. She called a taxi firm at seven.' Wyre made a note on the board.

Gina paused to digest that statement. 'Hm. I'll take the details of the firm. If you could email them to me, that would be great.' She shook her head. 'Why did Lauren tell us that Robbie booked the taxi when the call was made from her phone?' She really needed to speak to the friends. 'Wyre, can you and PC Ahmed go through the phone in more depth with tech and also find Lauren's mother's number? Let her know that her daughter is in hospital. Can we move on to Sienna's phone?'

'Yes, guv.' Wyre grabbed a pile of printouts from the main table. 'She has a Facebook, Instagram, email and WhatsApp accounts but she doesn't post much on social media. She has a collection of really explicit messages on her phone. It looks like she's been sexting someone since Christmas, but when we delve into who it could be the phone isn't registered and it doesn't appear to be in use now. Her texts and call register only go back to Christmas. She either wiped her phone back to factory settings or got a new phone.'

'Were there any messages that relate to what she had planned for yesterday?'

Wyre nodded. 'There is one message from the unregistered phone, and it says, "I can't wait to see you again." That was at five in the afternoon. She replies with an emoji of an aubergine and a peach before saying that she couldn't wait to see him again. That was at eight.'

'So, she was alive at eight unless the killer sent that reply.' Gina knew that was a possibility. 'Were there any messages between Sienna and Lauren?'

Wyre nodded. 'They were meant to be going out today and they had planned to meet at Cleevesford Manor for a spa day. Sienna mentions that she was going to drive, and that she would pick Lauren up at ten in the morning.'

'So, Sienna does drive. Jacob?' He flinched as he dragged his gaze from the table to her. 'We're heading to Sienna's.'

O'Connor walked back in with Jhanvi. 'An officer is on their way to break the news to Sienna's parents. I told them it was urgent, and they said the address was almost on their doorstep.'

Gina exhaled as she thought of the poor parents who were about to receive the news of their daughter's murder. 'Thank you.' She buttoned up her coat. 'Wyre, will you please call Maxine, Dee and Tiffany? We need their full details and tell them that one of us will be visiting them sometime today. O'Connor and Jhanvi, can you get everything loaded onto the system and orchestrate the door-to-doors on Bell Road. I know officers have started speaking to Lauren's neighbours, but we need all that information collated. See if anyone has CCTV too. Oh, we need the registration of Sienna's car, then we can flag that up.' O'Connor nodded and Gina smiled at Jacob. 'We best head straight to Sienna's. If she lives with someone, maybe they can shed some light on who she was texting and seeing. The most logical explanation right now is that it was Robbie, but we need that confirmed. In the meantime, if Robbie turns up, call me straight away.'

SEVEN

Gina pulled up as Jacob stared out the passenger window. First light was breaking through the grey clouds and the hint of frost had melted. She reached behind and grabbed her bag off the back seat. A message flashed up. 'Sienna's parents have been informed of her murder.' Jacob grabbed his pen and popped it in the top of his suit jacket. 'Jacob, you know you can always talk to me if there's something on your mind.'

He smiled, opened his jacket and checked that his notepad was in there. 'I'm okay, honest.'

'You're not. How long have we been working together?'

'Can't remember, guv. Far too long,' he joked.

She could tell he was using humour to mask whatever was going on. 'Which is why I can tell something's up.'

He opened the car door. 'Haven't we got an interview to do?'

It was obvious that Jacob didn't want to speak to her about his problems. She did suspect something was going on at home. Maybe he and Jennifer had been arguing. 'What number is it again?'

'Twenty-three. Looks like the house on the end.' Jacob

began walking across the green, treading on damp grass. Gina opted for taking the pavement. When they finally reached the end of the terrace, she glanced up at the characterless red-brick house with its dilapidated porch and steamed up windows, and she thought of Sienna, the woman who would never be coming home again. As she knocked, the glass in the door rattled. 'I wonder if she lives alone.'

A bang followed the clunking of locks, then a rotund, middle-aged woman answered with a piece of toast dangling from her mouth. She removed it and stared at them for a couple of seconds. 'Hello.'

'I'm DI Harte, this is DS Driscoll. May we come in?'

'I ain't done anything. What Minty said wasn't true. I don't even like garden ornaments so why would I nick them?'

Gina took a deep breath. 'We're from major crimes. Does Sienna Moorcroft live with you?'

The woman threw her toast on the grass out the front and reluctantly opened the door. Gina stepped into the dark hallway first, then they all went into the living room. The curtains were still closed, and a rerun of *Friends* played. The woman grabbed the remote and turned the TV off. ''Av a seat. What's this about Sienna? She doesn't get into trouble. Anyway, she's not here so you might have to come back later, or maybe try calling her.'

There was no good time to spill the news of Sienna's murder. 'I'm afraid we have some bad news.'

'What?'

'I'm really sorry to tell you that Sienna's body was found in the early hours. Is there anyone we can call? Someone who can be with you?'

The woman went to speak but remained open-mouthed.

'Are you and Sienna friends?'

'Yes, well I'm her landlady, but we really get on. She's been living with me for three years and we've become close. How...'

Gina swallowed. 'I'm afraid Sienna has been murdered.'

The woman swallowed then coughed, almost choking on her own saliva as she collapsed into an armchair.

Jacob stepped forward. 'Erm, would you like me to make you a drink?'

She shook her head and cleared her throat. 'No... thank you.'

Gina sat in the armchair opposite the woman and leaned forward, waiting for the news to sink in. 'Could I take your name, please?'

'Patsy Griffin. I can't believe it, seriously.' The woman tugged at a dark strand of hair that was grey at the root. 'Was it him?'

'Him.' Gina waited for Patsy to elaborate. Maybe she knew of Sienna's relationship with Robbie.

'Smarmy-looking charmer, goes by the name of Gerard.'

Gina glanced at Jacob who was scribbling a note of the name.

'Can you tell me about Gerard?'

'That man is a nasty piece of work. She's been seeing... had been seeing him for a few months. He kept pressuring her to move in and she tried living with him for a couple of weeks, but he's as jealous as they get. He was also trying to get her to part with her money too. Sienna had been saving for a house deposit and she had about thirty thousand pounds. Anyway, as soon as she moved in, he wouldn't let her go anywhere apart from work, so she escaped and came back here. After she left, she had to get a new phone number because he kept ringing non-stop.'

'When was this?'

'About a month ago. She left him mid-December. I could tell though when they first started dating that he was no good, but she was taken in by his charm. I saw the change in her though. She stopped being her bubbly self and began dressing differently. He didn't like her wearing make-up.'

This had opened the investigation up even more. Now they had a jealous ex to contend with. 'Do you have any more details on Gerard?'

'Yes. He's about five ten, blond, tanned and fake teeth. Not false, they're more like veneers.'

Gina had hoped for more. 'Do you have a surname or place of work?'

'No to the surname but I know she said he worked in the same line of business as she did. He worked in facilities management, and she did admin for the alarm company that they used.'

'Where did Sienna work?'

'Brunswick Security. She was trying to save a deposit for a house by living here. I'm sure her work would know who he was.'

That was another avenue they'd have to pursue. Gina's mind was full of further possibilities. Gerard could have been following her. She then pictured a man with veneers turning up at Robbie and Lauren's bungalow, catching Robbie and Sienna together before killing Sienna in a jealous rage. Gina bit her lip. If that was the case, where was Robbie and where was Sienna's car? 'What does Gerard drive?'

'A huge black saloon, a Merc, I think. But he's also turned up in a black four-by-four before.'

'What time did Sienna go out yesterday?'

'I'd say about four. She was all dressed up in this short black number, said she was meeting someone. She claimed she was going out with friends, but she didn't elaborate. In my heart, I just hoped it wasn't Gerard. I had a feeling she might have been seeing someone else, someone new but that's only a thought.'

'Did she leave in her car?'

The woman shook her head. 'She caught the bus because she said she'd be drinking later that night.'

'Where is her car?'

'It's the old blue Fiat parked on the road, the one with the cracked bumper.' That had blown out their theory of Robbie Shields taking Sienna's car to get away from the crime scene. She made a mental note to let the team know that they were no longer looking for Sienna's car in their search for Robbie as soon as she left.

'When was she expected back?'

'About midnight. When she didn't come home, I just thought she got lucky. I'm not her mother so I don't monitor her comings and goings. She's in her twenties. But I was a bit fed up she didn't call because, you know, I thought at the time she was taking advantage of my good nature. Now I know what happened, I feel awful to even think that. Poor Sienna. Have you told her parents? They moved to Sheffield a couple of years ago to be closer to his elderly mother.'

Gina nodded. 'Yes. What did you mean by taking advantage of your good nature?' That statement had confused her.

'Well, her daughter, Dora, is upstairs in bed. She's still sleeping.'

'Sienna has a daughter?'

'Yeah. She's four. I look after her a lot. She's a sweetheart.'

'Is her father around?'

'No, her dad was a soldier, died before she was born. He and Sienna had only been dating a couple of months when she fell pregnant, but they were happy. Problem was, he never came home. Died in Afghanistan. Dora has now lost both parents. What am I going to do? How do I tell her?'

Before Gina had the chance to say another word, Patsy's phone rang. 'It's Sienna's mother.' Gina nodded to Jacob. They went and stood in the hall while listening to Patsy offering her condolences and discussing the little one.

A girl began creeping down the stairs, a teddy dangling from her one hand. She rubbed her sleep-crusted eyes with the other. 'Who are you?'

'I'm Gina.' She smiled at the dot of a child. 'This is Jacob.'

She watched as Jacob interrupted Patsy by stepping back into the living room.

'Aunty Patsy,' Dora called out in her shrill voice.

Patsy ran from the living room and scooped the child up, tears rolling down her cheeks. She took Dora into the living room and began playing cartoons on the television. 'You watch these for a minute while I speak to our visitors in the kitchen.'

'Where's Mummy?'

A pause filled the hallway. 'Erm, look, it's Peppa Pig.' She closed the door. 'I can't do this. How do I tell Dora that her mother's dead? How?'

Gina didn't have the answer. There was never an easy way to break such tragic news.

'Please find Gerard. Find out who did this. I really do think there was someone else in the picture, another man. Maybe she confided in him.' Patsy sniffed and wiped her nose on the back of her hand.

'Ms Griffin, would you mind if we took a look at Sienna's room?'

The woman nodded. 'It's the first bedroom on the right. She shares it with her daughter.'

Jacob took a deep breath as they reached the landing. 'I'm not feeling too well, guv.'

Gina left him there and had a quick look through Sienna's paltry belongings. What she saw was a woman who'd been living frugally to save all her money to get on the housing ladder. Photos of her daughter were pinned all over a corkboard. Gina's eyes watered slightly. She took a deep breath and went back downstairs with Jacob.

'Once again, I'm so sorry for your loss. If you think of anything, however small it may seem, please call me.' She passed the woman a card.

A few minutes later, they were back at the car. Jacob leaned against the passenger door. 'Are you getting in?'

He held a hand up and ran to a nearby bush where he vomited. Walking back, he loosened his tie and got into the car.

As she started the engine up, he opened a packet of mints and began to suck on one. 'Jacob, please. I can tell you're not right. Are you ill?' Gina really didn't want to probe but she was sure she could see him shaking.

'Yes, I'm okay now. Better out than in as they say. I had a curry last night. Probably a bit of dodgy chicken or rice. All better now.'

She reversed out of the space. He was far from alright, and she knew it. She almost gasped inwardly as she thought of Sienna's relationship with Gerard, knowing how easy it was to feel like a prisoner in a possessive relationship. She tried to imagine his anger as Sienna cut him off by changing her phone number. Had he taken to physically stalking her instead? Her phone beeped and she saw Bernard's name pop up. 'Can you read that message?'

Jacob picked up her phone. 'We can search Lauren's house at lunchtime.'

'Great. Contact the incident room and arrange for a team to meet us there at noon. Ask Wyre to find out if Brunswick Security have an out of hours number. Being a firm in this line of business, I'm sure they will. We need to find Gerard. O'Connor and Kapoor can visit Dee's home, and we'll have just enough time to speak to Maxine. We need to know if either of them saw Sienna or Robbie.'

EIGHT

TIFFANY

'That was the police.' Tiffany placed her phone on their little bistro table in the kitchen.

'What did they want?' Kieron buttered a piece of toast and passed it to her, along with a cup of tea.

She shrugged. 'They need to speak to me about an incident. Maybe they've found the man who attacked me.' Her heart began to hum as she hoped they had. Finally, she might have some answers. Her mind whirred. 'If they've found him, I'll have to go to court, relive everything again. Maybe he's struck again and hurt someone else.'

Kieron finished buttering his toast and joined her at the table. 'Don't get your hopes up. We've been here before.'

Her shoulders dropped and she hunched forward. 'Maybe it's nothing to do with me. It could be something else.' She furrowed her brows as she tried to recall any of the previous evening. She remembered drinking a glass of red wine and then another before drifting off into the deepest of sleeps. The night before that, she'd barely slept. The jitteriness that worried her so much had plagued her all that night. She'd been convinced she had a neurological disorder. Then she had to get to work for seven in the morning. The day had seemed long so falling asleep on the settee after a couple of glasses of wine was expected. 'You fell asleep too, last night, in the living room?'

He nodded and tore the corner of the toast with his front teeth. 'I was so tired. I think all the overtime finally caught up.'

'Do you know how long I was outside for?'

He shook his head and chomped on the toast. 'No. I'm sure it wasn't long. It can't have been.'

'Maybe I did something. Damaged a car, shouted at someone...'

He sighed. 'Tiff, you're the loveliest person I know. I can't imagine you vandalising a car or being horrible to anyone. You can't have been out there that long. Seriously, don't worry about it.'

'But you can't be sure how long I was out there and you don't know what I was doing.'

He dropped his toast onto the plate with a deep sigh. 'Tiff, I love you to bits, in fact, I adore you. I'll say it again, you didn't do anything. Whatever the police want, it's not about you sleepwalking last night so don't let that worry you.'

He was right. She'd simply strolled out the front door in her sleep.

'Have you taken your pills?'

'Not yet.' She knew she had to take her diazepam, and something the doctor gave her for the aches and pains, then there were her vitamins. Without her vitamin D, she ached even worse. 'Can you pass me my pill box?'

He grabbed his glasses off the side and opened the medication cupboard, then he placed a pill box on the table.

She opened the Sunday compartment and tipped the tablets into her hand. She popped them into her mouth one by one and swallowed them down with cold coffee. 'Thanks.' She unlocked her phone and began scrolling through Facebook. Her jaw slackened until she was staring at the latest news with her mouth open. 'Kieron?'

'What?'

'I think I know why the police want to see me.'

He took the phone from her and read a post that someone had shared from the 'What's Up Cleevesford' Facebook group. 'This is only on the next street. Someone has died.'

'Kieron?' She swallowed. 'The bungalow in the photo belongs to Lauren. They say that someone has been killed.' She quickly typed in *Warwickshire Herald* and scrolled down their posts. 'It's not Lauren, thank goodness, but that is her bunga-low.' She remembered the argument they had last night on the phone and her heart sank. Maybe it was a blessing that she didn't go out with her colleagues. If she'd met up with Lauren at her bungalow, it might have been her body the police were dealing with today. A wave of panic flushed through her, and her fingers began to shake. 'What time did you find me outside last night?'

'I don't know. I think it was about nine, maybe ten. I can't remember, I'd been asleep myself.'

'Maybe I saw something or...' No, she had never been violent, never, not when she was awake. 'Could I have had something to do with it?'

He took the phone off her. 'No, definitely not. Stop thinking things like that. There's no way.'

She felt her eyes welling up. 'But that time. I...' She couldn't get her words out.

'It was nothing, okay. Repeat after me. It. Was. Nothing. Just a bit of a sleepwalk onto the pavement.'

She reluctantly repeated his words, but she couldn't avoid the fact that she had stabbed Kieron with a kebab skewer once while sleepwalking and still he would not believe she was capable of anything horrible. While asleep, she'd dreamed he was her attacker and she thought she was defending herself.

She hadn't meant to stab him. It still upset her to think back on how much he suffered with that wound. He'd refused to go to A&E, treating himself at home until the broken skin and flesh eventually started knitting together. He didn't want the police to ask questions and arrest her. She thought of the tiny round scar on his bicep, the one forever reminding them both of what she did.

He walked over to her side of the table. 'Come here.' He held her and kissed the blonde curls on the top of her head. Kieron might be convinced that she had nothing to do with the incident, but Tiffany wasn't. She sobbed into his arms as she imagined herself confessing to everything as soon as the police arrived. Her life as she knew it was over.

NINE

'Maxine Winterbourne?' Gina held up her identification. 'I'm DI Harte and this is DS Driscoll.' Gina glanced at Jacob. He still looked a little pale and he hadn't said much in the car. He forced a smile and they both stepped into the woman's hallway.

'Can you take your shoes off, please? Sorry, it was a huge mistake getting such light carpets.' Gina nodded and bent to remove her black ankle boots. A white Bichon Frise with a huge snowball-like head began licking her hand. She reached out and petted the dog while waiting for Jacob to do battle with his double-knotted laces.

'Tilly, kitchen,' Maxine ordered, and the dog obliged. Gina followed her through the white plush hallway with its sparkly silver mirrors, her feet sinking into the deep pile as they entered a cosy, but well accessorised lounge. She'd never seen so many cushions or throws.

'Take a seat.' Maxine swallowed. 'I've seen the news and they've just announced that it was Sienna who was murdered. I can't believe it.' She paused. 'I didn't know Sienna, but I've tried to call Lauren and I can't get through. Is she okay? I've been worried sick since your officer rang earlier.'

'We have her phone which is why you've been unable to get through. You can call the hospital and leave your number with a nurse. We need to ask you a few questions about last night.'

'Can I get you a drink? I've just boiled the kettle.'

Gina nodded and looked at Jacob. He really needed a drink. 'I'd love a coffee, thank you. Black, no sugar.'

Jacob cleared his throat. 'Just water, please.'

The woman left the room and the dog yapped as she entered the kitchen.

'Are you feeling okay now?' Gina asked.

He nodded.

She glanced at the shiny silver-framed photos on the mantelpiece. Maxine had been photographed with her arms around lots of people in social settings, but the centrepiece was reserved for her beloved dog.

Maxine hurried through the door carrying the drinks on a tray. Gina reached over and took her coffee. 'Thank you.' Jacob took a swig of the water and pulled out his notebook as Gina began. 'Can you talk me through yesterday?'

'Starting from when?'

'When you first heard from Lauren or arrived at her bungalow.'

'Okay, I was at Hoopers up until lunchtime, but Lauren had booked the day off. I work in the hair extension and wig department, she's normally on the make-up counter. I got home about two and I WhatsApped Lauren and the rest of the group to say how excited I was about the night we had planned. She replied with a photo, showing me a couple of her dresses. After that, I got ready, watched a bit of telly and left about eight. I caught the bus at the end of my road and got to Lauren's about eight twenty, maybe eight thirty. The taxi turned up at nine and we left. That was it really.'

Gina waited for Jacob to catch up. 'Did you see her partner, Robbie Shields?'

Maxine shook her head and began to fiddle with what looked like a honey-coloured hair extension. Her dark painted on brows made her forehead look pale. 'No, she said he was keeping out of our way. We went in the kitchen because she didn't want our giggling to disturb him, and she gave me a glass of wine. Dee arrived about five minutes later and she joined us in the kitchen. Lauren then said she was going to check on Robbie—'

'Check on Robbie?'

'Yes, she said he might want a glass of wine as we'd opened the bottle. There was a bit left, and she knew the taxi was due. She rejoined us and said he was watching TV in bed. He was meant to drive us to Birmingham, but she said he'd had a drink, so he called us a taxi instead. It wasn't like him to not come out and talk as he's normally very sociable and I wondered if he was a bit under the weather, but I wasn't worried.'

Robbie wasn't acting normally in the eyes of Maxine at this point. 'What was he usually like?'

'Smiley, he's a hugger. Talks a lot and is quite the joker. He likes to be centre stage, where all the action is. That's why I thought he might be ill.'

'Did you hear him at all in the other room?'

'What are you getting at?'

'Please, Miss Winterbourne, it's important that you answer as best you can.'

She pressed her lips together, thought for a few seconds and picked up a mug of coffee from the tray. 'No, I didn't see or hear any sign of him. Are you saying he wasn't really in?'

'No, I'm just trying to establish what you saw and heard. The questions are routine.'

'Right. Sorry.'

'Did anything else happen between waiting for the taxi and leaving?'

'Not really.' She took a sip of her steaming drink.

'Not really? Did something happen?'

Maxine looked through the gaps in her fringe and bit her bottom lip. 'Only that Lauren had an argument with Tiff over the phone, but I can't see why that matters.'

Gina glanced at the notes on her phone. 'Tiffany Crawford?'

'Yes, I think. I don't know her surname. She too works at Hoopers, as a cleaner. Mostly does mornings.'

'Are Lauren and Tiffany close?'

Maxine shook her head. 'Not really. Lauren feels a bit sorry for her as she doesn't get out much. Tiff's quite nervous and quiet. For whatever reason, I can't think why Lauren wanted her to come with us to the club as she's hardly the life and soul of anything. Tiff messaged to say she couldn't come, something about having a dicky stomach but we all thought that it was an excuse. That phone call was Lauren's last-ditch attempt to persuade Tiff to join us. I like Tiff but I also think she's a hypochondriac. She's always going on about her aches and pains, her IBS, her brain fog. Doctors find nothing wrong, and she thinks they're all ignoring her symptoms because they want her to die. It's all melodramatic.'

Gina knew she'd have to speak to Tiffany. Maybe there was another reason she cried off from their night out and the illness was a cover. 'How well do you know Sienna Moorcroft?'

'Not that well. Lauren talks about her a lot – only good things. They went to school together. She's popped into Hoopers to meet Lauren in her lunch break a couple of times, and I've said hello. She seemed really nice and chatty.'

'Did you see her yesterday?'

Maxine shook her head.

'Did Lauren mention her yesterday?'

'Only in passing. She said they were meant to be enjoying a spa day today and that her daughter was going with them too.' Maxine stared blankly into her cup. 'That poor little girl.'

She swallowed and fanned her watery eyes with her free hand.

'How come Sienna didn't go out last night, to celebrate Lauren's engagement?'

'Lauren said she couldn't get a babysitter. I wish she had come now and none of this would have happened.' She paused. 'I'm not stupid. This happened in Lauren's house while we were out, and I've just seen an appeal online to find Robbie. Did he do it?'

'I wish I had more answers. If you do see or hear from Mr Shields, please call us immediately.' Gina knew they had a number for the taxi company and that had led them to the name of a firm, but that business had about thirty drivers working for them. 'Can you describe the taxi driver who took you and dropped you off last night?'

'Oh him, yes. Skinny, dark jacket and brown hair. He had a very faint mole under his left eye. I kept catching him glaring down my top through the rear-view mirror. I couldn't wait to get out of that taxi.'

Gina wanted to say, *and you left Lauren on her own in the car with him*, but she bit her tongue. It was better to keep her onside. 'Who did he drop off first?'

'Dee, then me and then Lauren.' Maxine paused. 'Do you think he did it, while we were out? If he did, why was Sienna at Lauren's? Was Robbie having an affair?'

Gina knew the rumour mill would be in full action that very morning. Social media was full of speculation, and everyone would be on the lookout for Robbie. 'As I said, we're just trying to establish the facts and build a timeline. Is there anything else you can think of that might help?'

She blew out a breath. 'I think Robbie did it. He's a flirt and it wouldn't be the first time he's had a fling. I was happy about the engagement for Lauren, I really was, but I was only happy because she was happy. She can do much better than him. He slept with a woman while they were on holiday. I mean, who does that? I know it was a long time ago, but it was right under her nose, and she discovered them at it. Wait, I think I caught the taxi driver's name. I remember someone talking to him on the radio and they called him Ulrich. He had a slight accent too, maybe German.'

They had a name and that was a result. She quickly fired off a message, asking Wyre to call the taxi company and ask Ulrich to come to the station. Ulrich had a few questions to answer. A message from Bernard popped up.

You can now search Lauren Cross's bungalow. There's something here you need to see and it's hugely concerning. We've found more blood and it's not in the bedroom. Bernard.

TEN

All togged up in their crime scene suits, Gina and Jacob led the team into the hallway of Lauren Cross's and Robbie Shields's bungalow. As a newbie, trainee DC Kapoor stood proudly next to O'Connor, while several PCs awaited instruction. A couple of them gave her a congratulatory nod.

'O'Connor, can you and PC Ahmed start with the kitchen and the garden shed?'

'Yes, guv.'

'Kapoor, can you take two officers,' Gina pointed to two PCs, 'and please search the living room?' She glanced up at the loft hatch. 'And the loft too?' Kapoor nodded.

'Jacob and I will take the two bedrooms, the bathroom and the hallway. Call if you find anything that might lead us to Robbie Shields. Look through as much paperwork as you can. If he has a caravan, a boat, or even if he's recently bought a tent, I want to know.'

The team nodded and left to start searching their allocated rooms. The tall crime scene manager ambled in, his eyes looking dark underneath after a long night. 'Morning, Bernard.'

'It will be when I get out of here and have a shower and some breakfast. The body is at the morgue, and we have taken a lot of evidence to the lab. The samples will be analysed over the coming days and as I get results, I'll send them over to you.'

'Thank you. So where is this blood?' Gina asked.

'In the hall cupboard.'

'Let's take a look so you can head home and have that shower.'

Bernard led Gina and Jacob along the hallway. 'As you can see, there is a really old rusting slide-lock on the outside. That isn't too worrying as there is some shelving that is stacked high with bleach and household detergents. The lock was probably put there to keep kids away from the chemicals. What is worrying is this.' He opened the door. 'Look at the dinks and scratches in the wood. See that tin of paint, there?'

Gina nodded.

'It too is dinked, and the damage matches that on the wood. We have also found traces of fresh blood in here. Someone was recently locked in this cupboard and fought to get out. Of course, we know Sienna Moorcroft had a lot of wounds on her hands from fighting but we've yet to fully assess them. It could be that she was locked in this cupboard before she was stabbed and strangled. As I said, the samples have all gone to the lab so we should have some news soon.'

'Can you fast-track everything?' Gina knew the team was stretched but she had to ask.

'As you know, there's always a backlog at the lab and the staffing issues are affecting us all. We'll prioritise the blood and semen sample. Another thing, there are fingerprints on the paint can but they're partials. It looked like someone tried to clean them off but it's not perfect. It looks to be a rush job. I'll do my best to get through the workload swiftly.'

Gina smiled. 'Thank you.'

Bernard yawned. 'Right, I really have to go home now before I drop. Beauty sleep awaits me. I've just had a message from Jennifer. She's about to email you all the crime scene photos and the video from the office.'

'Thanks again. You get off, we'll speak soon.'

As Bernard left, Gina stared into the cupboard.

'There's a lot of damage to the door, guv.' Jacob used his torch to light up the tiny space and nudged in beside her for a look.

'Let's theorise that Lauren and her friends left in a taxi. Sienna turned up. They had sex and then something happened. Did possessive Gerard turn up and hurt Robbie? Or did Sienna offer Robbie an ultimatum to make a choice between her and Lauren? Or maybe she planned to tell Lauren about their affair. Had things got that tense, he locked her in the cupboard while thinking of what to do? Then he killed her and left without his car. Where the hell is he?'

She shivered as she thought of Sienna curled up next to the vacuum and mop, trapped in the cupboard. She imagined being in there herself, suffocated by the darkness and the not knowing what was going to happen next. A brief flashback to her dead ex-husband Terry locking her in the understairs cupboard for a whole day made her shudder. She thought he was going to leave her to die, and Sienna must have thought the same, which is why she had fought with her life to escape. 'She must have been absolutely terrified in there, knowing he was about to kill her.' Gina stepped back from the cupboard, wanting to unsee that small space.

Jacob led the way into the smaller bedroom at the back. He stepped in and Gina noted the empty desk in the corner and the dust marks outlining where a laptop had been. She knew that Bernard would have made sure that the computer reached the tech department and Garth, the tech assistant, was probably going through the files. Gina crouched down and flashed her phone torch underneath the grey sofa bed but there was nothing hidden there. With her gloved hands, she felt around all the crevices, searching for anything that could be hidden, while Jacob riffled through the desk drawers. His gloved fingers got tangled in string and paperclips. A few minutes later, they'd finished in that room. The bathroom also yielded nothing.

Gina stood outside the master bedroom, not wanting to push the door open. Only a few hours ago she'd seen Sienna Moorcroft's lifeless body in that bed.

'I don't want to go in either, guv.' Jacob looked away.

'It never gets any easier. Ever.' She pushed the door open and was instantly hit by the stench of stale body odour, urine and a nasty sweetness that she struggled to describe if anyone asked. The smell would remain for a long time even though the body had been removed. She knew that forensics had searched thoroughly for physical evidence but now it was time to delve a different way. 'I'll take the wardrobe; you take the drawers.'

'Okay.' Jacob passed the bed and headed to the chest of drawers under the window.

Gina welcomed the woody smell of the wardrobe. It wasn't enough to mask the scent of death, but it helped. She opened the first of three doors and all Lauren's clothes were neatly hung. Without wasting time, she had her hands in each of the pockets of the woman's high-end dresses and trousers. At the back of her mind, she wondered if there might also be some clue as to who Lauren was arguing with just over a week ago.

'You know Lauren claimed that the man she was arguing in the street with was just some drunken man who had bumped into her?'

'Yes,' he replied as he continued searching through Lauren's T-shirts.

'I'd like that confirmed. As far as Lauren's phone showed,

there were no messages or calls to any unidentifiable numbers on that Thursday or Friday and no suggestion that she was seeing anyone else. So, her explanation of it being a random encounter stacks up. But Lauren does have Snapchat on her phone. Any messages would have been long gone. That encounter is now niggling away in my brain.' Gina shook her head and wondered if she was wasting her time with that lead, especially as Robbie was out there somewhere and they had Sienna's ex, Gerard, and the taxi driver to consider.

She stepped across and opened the next door. All Robbie's shirts had been neatly hung up on the one side and all his trousers and jackets on the other. Once again, she fished through pockets and again, she found nothing of interest. That left one more part of the wardrobe to search. She opened the last door. It had been sectioned off into shelving. Several pairs of shoes were stacked up but right at the bottom were two metal file boxes, labelled up with Lauren and Robbie's names. Gina pulled Lauren's box out and placed it on the floor. After going through all her paperwork, she couldn't find anything relevant to the case. Kneeling, she dragged Robbie's box out next and removed all the folders. She pulled out a folder marked HMRC and flicked through it. He had an average job for a company and earned a good salary. It looked like he'd had the same job as an office manager for years. She flicked through the next file, and it was full of old bills and documents, including his birth certificate and passport. She randomly flicked through some of his bank statements and could see that he paid a large sum every month to his and Lauren's joint bank account. It was otherwise sparse. Gina guessed that the rest of their bills got taken from their joint account. There was only one regular payment going out and it was referenced as CM. This payment had got bigger and bigger over recent months.

As she reached in to pull the rest of the files out, the paper part of Robbie's driving licence had almost slipped out of its plastic sleeve. She pulled it out. As she unfolded it, a small photo fell to the carpet. Gina recognised the face in the photo instantly. She could feel a roughness on the back. Turning it over, she saw the writing that had almost been scratched through the paper and things began to make sense. *She deserves to know.*

'Jacob, you have to see this.' He dropped a pile of socks back into the drawer he was working through. She gave him the photo. 'Turn it over, read the words. And look at these.' She passed him the bank statements.

Her phone rang and she answered Briggs's call. 'Hello.'

'Gina, we have the address of the taxi driver. His name is Ulrich Fischer, and he lives close to where you are now. While you go and visit Mr Fischer, I'll prepare the team here. Robbie Shields's image has gone out on our social media and it's due to hit the local news this evening, so the lines will go ballistic later. He's without a doubt our prime suspect but we can't rest at that. In his absence we have to cover every angle. Hopefully someone will come forward and tell us where he is. He can't stay hidden forever, that's a fact. Another thing.'

'What is it?' Gina bit her dry bottom lip as he spoke.

'We've managed to look into Lauren Cross and Robbie Shields's recent bank transactions. There has been no money taken from his personal account, her personal account, or their joint account since last night. He's vanished and hasn't spent any money at all. We now have his car and we now know that he didn't take Sienna's car.'

'Maybe he's prepared for this scenario, sir.'

'Maybe. Let me know how it goes with the taxi driver. It could be that he saw Robbie Shields at the bungalow when he dropped Lauren off. I know Lauren claimed that she didn't see Robbie, but we need to check that out.'

'Jacob and I are on our way. If you could message me the address, that would be great. I'd also like to know why he parked down the road, then went up to the bungalow after dropping Lauren Cross off? Don't drivers normally just drop people off and go? I'll report back.' She bagged up the bank statements and the photo. 'And, sir, Robbie has the biggest motive ever to kill Sienna. It looks like he is Dora's father.'

ELEVEN

Gina buzzed Ulrich Fischer's bell and waited outside the tall block of flats. Jacob began biting the skin around his thumbnail as he gazed at his feet. 'Robbie Shields is Sienna's daughter's father. I know it's unconfirmed at the moment, but that would throw a different angle onto the whole case.'

Gina nodded. 'Yes, it's a completely different story to what Sienna's landlady told us about Dora's father being a soldier. If Sienna was telling everyone that story, it stands to reason that she'd have said the same to Lauren. Those payments going out of his account, referenced CM seems to suggest child mainte-nance. Again, it's also strengthening a motive for Lauren. If she knew that her best friend had her boyfriend's baby, who knows how she would have reacted. Maybe she found out somehow. I mean, how easy was it? All I did was go through his unlocked files and I found that photo. Lauren could have known for ages.' She pressed the buzzer again in the hope that the taxi driver was in. 'But we still need to find Robbie. As it stands, we know where Lauren is, and Robbie has absconded. I know who looks more suspicious right now.'

'What?' A man's voice boomed out from the speaker and his slight German accent told Gina it was probably Ulrich.

'DI Harte and DS Driscoll. We need to speak to you with regards to a serious incident.'

'I'm trying to sleep. Can you come back later?'

'Sorry, no. As I said it's serious and we need to talk to you now.'

The buzzer went and the door clicked. Gina pushed it open and started walking up the stairs until they reached the fourth floor, her calves burning as she stepped onto the landing. Her pulse banged away as she knocked on his door. The steps had done her in, but Jacob looked unaffected.

Ulrich opened the door and began to battle with a curtain before letting them into the dark hallway. Gina caught a hint of bacon in the air, probably the remnants of what he'd eaten after his shift. 'Come through. Excuse my mess, I wasn't expecting visitors.' He scratched his backside over the top of his pyjama shorts.

They entered his tiny, cluttered lounge. He removed a dirty plate from the arm of the sofa and took it into the kitchen. 'Have a seat,' he called out before re-entering the room. Gina and Jacob sat on the two-seater sofa, and he sat on a pull-out chair opposite them. 'So, what is it you want to know?'

Gina got her phone out and held out a photo of Lauren Cross that she'd taken from the woman's social media. 'Do you recognise this woman?'

He began playing with the mole under his eye as he gazed at it for a few seconds. 'Am I meant to?'

'You picked her up and dropped her off last night. Her name is Lauren Cross.'

'Yes, booking for Lauren.' His eyebrows furrowed as he looked again. 'Yes, although she looked different then with all her make-up on and her hair down.'

'Can you talk us through the pickup?'

He stared suspiciously at them for a few seconds. 'It was around nine in the evening. I pulled up at about five minutes early and rang the bell. She answered, telling me they'd be out soon so I waited in my car. She and two other women came out. The woman in the photo, Lauren, waved at her neighbour across the road who was holding a pizza. I only noticed that as I was hungry. They all got in and I dropped them off at Hurst Street in Birmingham. They were a little drunk and giggly on leaving. We arrived at about nine forty-five. The three women got out and headed into the club.'

Jacob noted down what the man had said.

Gina sat forward a little on the uncomfortable sofa. 'Can you remember what they talked about?'

'They were taking selfies and laughing. Lauren was talking about her engagement and showing them what I thought were pictures of wedding dresses. I gathered that's what the celebrations were about. I don't think much else was said. The other two women were being mean about another woman called Tiffany, I think.'

'Mean, in what way?'

'Lauren was upset that she wasn't with them and one of the others said she didn't like her much anyway and that she would have ruined the night, that she wasn't a fun person; things like that. Lauren jokingly told her to stop being mean. That was all really.'

Gina waited a bit longer than usual for Jacob to catch up. She noticed him scribble out a line and start again. 'Okay, let's move on to when you collected them from Hurst Street.'

'I was booked to pick them up at two fifteen and they were there waiting in the same spot where I dropped them off. They were really drunk; staggering and loud. Lauren got into the front seat and the other two got into the back. Not long after starting off, the two in the back fell asleep, then Lauren fell asleep too. I was quite grateful for that, and I hoped I'd get them home before one of them vomited in my car. I dropped the two in the back off first and Lauren last. She got out and I left. No one spoke on the way back so if something happened after that, I can't help.'

Gina knew that Kimmy the neighbour had told them another version of events, one that didn't match up to what Ulrich was telling them. 'There was a murder at Lauren Cross's house. You probably haven't heard it on the news if you've been asleep.'

'Shit. Was it her?' He ran his fingers through his dark greasy hair.

'A witness heard Lauren telling you not to touch her.'

He flung himself back in the chair. 'But I didn't hurt her. I was helping her out of my car. She was very drunk, and I couldn't leave her there all night and I had another job to go to. I just pulled her by the arms, that was all. I didn't hurt her.'

'The witness claimed that you waited around a little longer, and that you pulled up down the road.'

'Yes, I wanted to check my phone and I don't drive while looking at my phone. When I stopped, I noticed an umbrella in my car, so I got out and walked to her door. I thought I should ask if it was Lauren's before I drove off, only when I got to the door, I heard crying and thought, it's nothing to do with me. Instead of knocking, I took the umbrella and left. I don't think it was hers anyway. It's at the office in lost property. After that, I got a call to say my next job was cancelled. I drove back to the office and headed home.'

'Where were you between dropping Lauren and her friends off and picking them up?'

'Taxying people all over the place. It was Saturday night. I don't have enough time to stop for a piss on Saturday nights. I can't remember all my journeys but the taxi controller, Bert, has a record of them so you can check with him.'

Gina knew this was something that could easily be checked

so she waited for Jacob to add that to the list. She then selected a photo of Sienna Moorcroft and showed it to Ulrich. 'Do you recognise this woman?'

'No, she wasn't with them last night. I've never seen her.'

'Did you see anything suspicious at the bungalow when you dropped off or picked up Lauren?'

Ulrich pressed his lips together. 'I heard something, so I checked down the side of the bungalow after dropping her off. It was just before I heard the crying. I thought someone might be walking into the garden, but I didn't see anyone, so I thought that it was probably a fox. Do you think that's why she was crying because there was an intruder?'

Gina didn't know the answer to that. She wondered if someone had been in the house when Lauren had returned. Maybe Robbie had been making his escape out the back.

'Is she okay? You didn't answer my question.'

Gina nodded. 'Yes.'

He leaned back and exhaled. 'I'm sorry that something bad has happened but it was nothing to do with me. I'm glad Lauren is okay.'

'Just another question, who called and booked the taxi?'

'That I can help with. I was at the office when it came through. Bert has trouble hearing so he answers on loudspeaker. It was a man and he booked it for Lauren.'

So, Robbie had booked the taxi. Gina could conclude that he had used Lauren's phone. She was beginning to build a picture of last night. In her mind, she imagined Robbie wanting Lauren to go out because Sienna was coming over. If he had to take the three women to Birmingham, it would have eaten into his time, so he called them a taxi. He would have had the evening to himself to murder Sienna. Robbie fled the scene after Lauren returned. Maybe he was in the house, trying to work out what to do with the body. He panicked and fled. She thought back to the cupboard and imagined Sienna trapped and trying to escape, while she wondered if Robbie was going to kill her. Had she demanded more maintenance? She'd recently had sex and they had assumed it was with Robbie. She really needed the lab results on the semen and blood to come back fast.

'Is there anything else?' Ulrich stood.

Gina shook her head, knowing they would follow up with Bert the taxi office controller and if it turned out that Ulrich had lied, she'd be back. 'We will need you to come into the station to make a formal statement. It is a serious crime, so I'd be grateful if you came today.'

He nodded. 'I'll get dressed and go there right away. I want to help, and I should have knocked when I heard Lauren crying.'

As Gina and Jacob headed back to the car, Gina fired a message to Wyre, asking her to verify Ulrich's alibi. Another message popped up. It was from Kapoor.

Guv, the door-to-door officers have just spoken to Lauren Cross's next-door neighbour. He said his little girl claims to have seen a figure jumping over Lauren's fence and disappearing onto the path at the back. This was a short while after Lauren called the police. She doesn't have a description unfortunately as it was too dark. An officer is on their way to take a statement.

That message confirmed what Ulrich had just told them. Lauren had been in the bungalow crying at the time, so it had to be the murderer. Everything pointed to Robbie. And he was on the loose. Gina had to find him before someone else got hurt. He was now on the run and desperate, which made him dangerous.

TWELVE

NANCY

'Come on, my love. Let's get you into the car and away from this horrible place.' Nancy held her daughter's hand as she led her across the hospital car park.

'Thanks, Mum.' Lauren sat in her mother's tiny car and put her seat belt on. 'Can we stop off at a shop. I need some things. They won't let me back in the house. I don't even have my phone.'

'No need, Mum's thought of everything.' Nancy smiled sympathetically as she pulled away, taking her daughter away from the horror of everything that had happened. She was going to look after Lauren. Once they got back to her little house in the peaceful country setting, Lauren could rest while Nancy made her daughter's favourite dinner, lentil cottage pie. From the minute she set eyes on that man, she knew that Robbie was no good. She hadn't trusted him for a second. He was just like Lauren's other boyfriends. She remembered the loser that Lauren was set to marry a few years ago, just before she met Robbie – he was a loser too and he was definitely no good for her beautiful only daughter. Then there was that stupid boy at school, the one who thought he was going to be a footballer.

Lauren had been with that idiot for a whole six months. Nancy had been right. Footballer he was not. She'd seen him while out shopping, trailing around his four kids with a sweary woman. She placed a hand on her daughter's knee and patted it, knowing that from the moment she gave birth to Lauren, she'd only wanted the best for her. 'I'm going to look after you. We're going home.'

Lauren sighed. 'It's only going to be for a few days, then I'm going back to the bungalow.'

'Nonsense. How can you want to go back? Sienna was murdered in your bed. I'd be worried sick. And the memories. It will never be the same again, love.' Nancy swallowed. She couldn't bear to lose Lauren. 'What if Robbie comes back and kills you too? He's got nothing to lose now. He's done it once, might as well go down for two murders instead of one.'

Lauren began to sob. 'Where is he, Mum?'

'Hiding, that's where he is. But don't worry. The police will catch him, and they'll bang him up. He's a coward and that so-called friend of yours... and him. I never did like Sienna. I did try to warn you, but as usual you never listen. I wasn't lying when I said I saw them flirting and now you know.'

Lauren's choking sobs filled the car. 'How could I not see it? I should have listened to you, Mum.'

'You're just too trusting, my love. People take advantage of kind, beautiful souls like you. I've always had to look out for you. Remember your ex? If I hadn't have seen that text pop up on his phone from the other woman saying how much she enjoyed their night of passion together, you'd have married him. And then you went on to meet another cheat. Not only that, he's also a murderer. I want you to see that you're better than them. You're an amazing woman and—' Nancy felt her grip on the steering wheel tightening. No one messes with her daughter like Robbie did and gets away with it. Finally, Lauren had seen the man for what he was. 'I just hate seeing you get hurt like your dad hurt me. He was a cheater too. It's not always the act, it's the lies and the mind games. You know you're right and they make you doubt yourself and before long, you're losing your mind. I've been there. Maybe we're both the same. Maybe it's my fault. You're getting drawn to the same type of losers that I got drawn to all those years ago.'

Lauren blew her nose. 'It's not all about you, Mum.' She paused. 'I was so happy; so, so, happy and she ruined it.'

'They both ruined it.' Nancy swallowed. It was easy to blame a dead woman without knowing everything, but her daughter's so-called best friend had shattered Lauren's dreams and that was unforgivable. 'Come on. Everything will be alright. We'll be fine. They'll catch Robbie, charge him, and you can get on with your life.' She regretted that sentence as soon as it came out. It was ridiculous to think it would be as easy as that, if the past was anything to go by. Lauren pined for months over past break-ups and no doubt, this one would be ten times harder to handle. Why was she saying such ridiculous things? She was nervous, that's all. Nervous, worried and scared.

Lauren slapped a hand on the dashboard. 'How can you say that? As if it's easy. Yes, just catch him, bang him up and all will be fab – woohoo. Then Lauren will be happy. How can I ever be happy again? My fiancé killed my best friend, and they were both dirty rotten cheats. I'm sad, so bloody sad and I feel as though there is this huge hole in my heart because Sienna is dead, but I hate her too. I hate her,' Lauren yelled, as another flood of tears came forth. 'Robbie killed her, and I hate her, not him. Why do I feel like this?'

Nancy pulled up on her drive and glanced at the Malvern Hills beyond the cottage. 'I can't pretend to understand, but I love you and I'm here for you. It's me and you against the world, like it always has been.' Nancy leaned across and placed an arm over Lauren's shoulder. 'Come on, let's go in and get you out of those joggers they gave you at the hospital. You can borrow some of my clothes until we can get yours.'

Lauren shrugged her off and got out the car.

Nancy followed, knowing her daughter hated staying at her cottage and she'd hate wearing her clothes even more. Being so far from a bus stop or even a shop made Lauren feel penned in. It had been the same when she'd been growing up. Her daughter had always nagged her to move to the centre of Malvern or Worcester so she could 'have a life', but Nancy liked nature. She liked her home-grown veggie garden when she'd kept one. She now enjoyed watching the foxes and badgers at night and seeing the stars. Nancy unlocked the door and led the way. As she did, Fifi yapped at her ankles and jumped-up Lauren's lower legs. 'Shall I make us both a hot chocolate? I've got the stuff you like and there are sprinkles.' Nancy stroked the white terrier's head.

Lauren ignored her question. 'Have you still got your tablet or a laptop? I need to be able to message my friends and the police have my phone.'

'I'm so sorry, my love. You know me and technology. I have my phone but it's an old thing and doesn't even have the internet. I'll pop out in the morning and get you a cheap one. The police have the landline number and our address so if there is any news, they'll let us know.'

'I don't care about them. I want to call Max.'

'You can borrow my phone. Make as many calls as you like.' Nancy pulled her phone out of her bag and held it out.

'I don't know their numbers, that's why I need the internet, so that I can Facebook them.'

Nancy could help with that. 'I have the internet. I need it for Netflix.'

Lauren hit the wall. 'It's no use to me if I don't have a device to connect to it.'

'I'm sorry.' Nancy went to hug her daughter, but she

recoiled. 'I didn't know this was going to happen and I promise I'll get you a phone in the morning. Please try to rest. The doctor said you should take it easy today and I promised her I'd look after you. It's all been a huge shock. Let your mum look after you, please.'

Lauren left Nancy standing as she stomped up the stairs like she'd regularly done as a teen. Fifi followed her.

'Go away.' Lauren slammed her bedroom door, and the little dog came running back down. As it reached the bottom of the stairs, Nancy scooped the dog up in her arms and kissed its wiry-haired head. 'She didn't do it on purpose, Fifi. Your sister's just upset. Let's go and make some dinner.' She placed the dog on the floor and hurried into the kitchen. Her phone buzzed and another message popped up.

You revolting bitch. I hate you!

Yes, of course you do. She didn't care one bit about her horrible messenger. It wasn't the first or the last time she'd received messages like this, it came with the territory. Being part of a group that stopped traffic in the name of environmental protests, she often received abusive messages, which was why she'd bought a basic phone and come off social media, but she didn't want to burden Lauren with her problems. There was nothing else she could get rid of though, she needed to be able to message her fellow activists and remain a contact for any new recruits, so she deleted the message and grabbed her apron. It wasn't as if this person knew where she lived.

She would do everything it took to protect Lauren. It was time to chop some onions. Another message popped up.

Watch your back, bitch!

THIRTEEN

TIFFANY

Tiffany nervously bit the nail she'd managed to grow on her thumb. Kieron stopped stirring the bolognaise and walked over. 'Look, the police could come anytime, or it might even be tomorrow. You've got to stop worrying like this. You'll give yourself a heart attack. Have you still got palpitations?'

She nodded. He was right, her heart was banging so loud, if the police were here, they'd tell instantly that she was hiding something. She stood up from the table and walked over to the sink. It was starting to get dark and the little patch of grass outside was coated in a white frost carpet. The smell coming from the pan was turning her stomach. She didn't know if she'd be able to eat, at least not until the police had been. Why were they taking so long? She glanced at the clock and only another five minutes had passed since she'd last checked the time. The waiting was killing her. 'It's no good.' She opened the medication cupboard and pulled out her diazepam.

Kieron dropped the spoon in the bolognaise and took the packet from her. 'You had one at lunchtime.'

She snatched the blister pack from him and popped another pill out, swallowing it dry. 'I don't care, I need another.'

'You've had your dose for the day. You'll make yourself ill.' He left the food bubbling on the cooker and stormed off into the living room shouting, 'I'm doing everything I can to help you, to make you feel better. I'm working like a dog and saving up for tests and I don't know why when you're hell-bent on destroying yourself and I'm saying all this as someone who loves you.'

She turned the hob off and followed him. 'I'm sorry, it's just... I need them. I don't normally take more than I should. When the police have been I'll be better. My heart won't stop banging and it feels as though my veins are twitching, like they're alive and the jitteriness... it's like insects are under my skin. You don't understand. I don't need you turning against me. Please, Kieron. You're all I've got.'

He sighed and turned his back to her. 'Seeing you deteriorate like this hurts. I do everything I can to care for you and to look after you, and when I see you abusing yourself, it kills a part of me. Can't you see?' He turned around.

She could see. His eyes began to glass up as a few tears welled in the corners. He swiped them away. She'd hurt him. Reaching out, she went to stroke his arm, but he pulled it away. She stepped closer and touched him again. This time he didn't recoil, he wrapped his arms around her. 'I'm sorry, okay. I shouldn't have taken that pill. It won't happen again.'

She flinched and he dropped his arms as someone knocked on the door. Kieron left her standing in the middle of the room and then her heart began to bang even louder as she heard the detectives introducing themselves. She quickly plumped up the cushions on the settee and hoped that the detectives would not be able to tell that they were upset, but then again, what had happened at Lauren's bungalow was upsetting.

'This is DI Harte and DS Driscoll. They just want to ask you a couple of questions.' Kieron sat on the chair and the detectives both sat on the settee. 'Can I get either of you a drink?'

Both mumbled their nos. The female detective, DI Harte, sat on the edge of the settee. The male detective leaned back and opened a notepad. 'Can I just confirm your full name?' DI Harte said as she smiled at Tiffany.

'Err, Tiffany Crawford. Please call me Tiff.' Her banging heart was beginning to respond to the diazepam. She exhaled, relieved that she had regained some control over her stupid anxious body. An image of the meat skewer stuck in Kieron's flesh intruded on her thoughts. Not now. Why wouldn't they go away and leave her to get through the interview. It was as if her inner voice was torturing her. It was an accident. Kieron was right. Nothing more and nothing to worry about. It was a product of her trauma, and he was the only person in the world who understood her.

'Tiff, can you tell me how well you know Lauren Cross?' DI Harte tilted her head. She had a warmth about her, and Tiff felt that she should tell her what she knew.

'We work together at Hoopers. I clean, so I mainly see her in the mornings. I really like her, and we get on well. I saw her bungalow in the news. What happened?'

'We're investigating a murder. Lauren is okay but we're speaking to her friends and people who knew the couple.'

Tiffany felt the detective's gaze flitting from her face to her arms, as if she was searching for something. Was she a suspect? Tiffany tried to steady her trembling hands. 'Who was murdered?'

'A woman called Sienna Moorcroft. Do you know her?'

Tiffany shook her head. 'Lauren mentioned that she had a friend called Sienna. She said they've been friends for years.' Tiffany scrunched her brows. 'Why was Sienna at Lauren's place? From what I know, Sienna wasn't going out with Lauren last night. It was meant to be me, Maxine and Dee.'

The detective ignored her question. 'You and Lauren had

an argument last night, on the phone. Can you tell me what was said?'

Her banging heart was starting up again, and her fingers itched for another tablet. Why was the diazepam failing? They were meant to relax her muscles and calm her down. She was ill, seriously ill. 'It was nothing.' Her hands began to tremble uncontrollably, so she thrust them under her bottom and sat on them. 'She wanted me to go out with her to celebrate her engagement, but I didn't feel well. People don't understand, I get ill a lot and have to pull out of things last minute.'

'Sorry to hear that.' DI Harte pressed her lips together waiting for more.

'I'm hoping the doctors will run more tests. I get these piercing headaches; a really bad stomach and I either can't sleep all night or I sleep too much. Sorry, I don't want to bore you with my health worries. Last night, I felt really nauseous and lethargic, so I called her. She felt I'd let her down and accused me of making up an excuse not to go. That was it, really. Lauren isn't like that, though.'

'What do you mean?'

Tiffany didn't know how much she should say but someone had been murdered and she had to believe it wasn't her who had a part in it. Kieron stared at her, waiting for what she was about to say. 'It's the other two. They can be mean. I've heard them telling other people that I make it all up, about being ill, but I don't.' She couldn't hold back the tears that were bursting out. 'I feel terrible, every day, and no one cares. They laugh at me. Lauren is the only one at Hoopers who is nice to me, and I hate that I upset her by letting her down last night.'

The detective waited for her colleague to finish writing. 'Do you know her partner, Robbie Shields?'

Tiffany had seen the man on occasion. 'He drops her off at Hoopers sometimes, normally if it's raining or he starts work a little later. I can't say that I liked him.'

'What made you feel like that?'

Tiffany scratched her curls. 'He seemed a bit smarmy, called the women names like beautiful, and chick. He was a bit touchy-feely. When he spoke to Maxine or Dee, he'd touch their arms or wink. He'd try to catch people's eyes and maintain eye contact. I don't know, maybe it's me. Maybe he was just being friendly but men like that give me the creeps.' Her mind flashed back to the night of her attack, the scarf around her neck, tightening as she watched her life flash before her. She let out a gasp and held her neck.

'Tiff, are you okay?' DI Harte looked concerned.

Kieron stood and hurried over to her. 'I think my wife's had enough. As you can see, she's struggling. She didn't really know the victim and she was in with me all night.'

DI Harte swallowed. 'We're not accusing Tiff.'

'I'm sorry.' Tiffany felt the need to explain her behaviour, if not she'd look suspicious. 'Kieron is just trying to help. Knowing that someone was murdered so close by is terrifying the life out of me. I was attacked about four years ago. We didn't live in Cleevesford at the time. We lived in Webheath in Redditch. While Kieron was away on a stag do, someone broke into our house and tried to strangle me with my own scarf.' Tiffany paused and tried to fight back the tears.

The detective furrowed her brows. 'A scarf?' Right then, Tiffany knew there was a connection by the way the detectives were both looking at her. She nodded. 'I nearly died and my attacker has never been caught. Whenever I hear of anything like this, it floors me. I automatically think it's him and that he's coming back to finish the job.' Tears slipped down her cheeks. 'Is it him?'

'We are currently investigating several avenues. Who dealt with your attack?'

'Redditch police.'

The detective looked more alert than at any moment since

her arrival. Despite the detectives not answering her question, she knew there were similarities to her attack. It was pasted all over DI Harte's face. She walked out the room and sobbed in the kitchen wishing she could curl up into a ball and never go out again.

He was back and he was coming to kill her.

FOURTEEN

Jacob closed the passenger door and Gina turned the car lights on, clocking that night was now fast approaching and they were nowhere near finding Robbie Shields. She checked her phone and no further messages had come in. 'Jacob, can you please call the incident room. Tell them to check the system and pull up everything they can on the Tiffany Crawford attack. Two women, two strangulations, one survived, one was murdered. It may be just a coincidence, but I want her name up on the incident board. Also, can you find out if Sienna Moorcroft's parents have arrived yet. We need to speak to them?'

He nodded and pulled his phone out. She opened up her messages and emails, having a quick glance at the crime scene photos Bernard's team had emailed through. She then clicked onto Lauren's Instagram account. The last photo uploaded on her feed was of Lauren at the nightclub with Maxine and Dee. Three women, all made up and pouting for the camera while having a lovely night out. She scrolled to the photo underneath of Lauren and Robbie. Hundreds of people had offered their congratulations on hearing their engagement news which had been announced two weeks ago, but then the vitriol followed. Comments galore made by people speculating that it was Robbie who killed Sienna, accusing him, calling him names. Some people saying that he deserved to die. She went onto the *Warwickshire Herald* website and Robbie Shields's face filled the landing page. She hoped that someone would spot him and report him. Wherever he was, he couldn't hide from them forever.

Jacob finished on the phone. 'Mr and Mrs Moorcroft are staying at Cleevesford Manor.'

'Any news on Sienna's ex-boyfriend Gerard?'

'Not yet, guv. The team phoned Sienna's workplace, but with it being a Sunday, they've only managed to leave a message. The emergency number for the company takes the caller to a call centre, not directly to the company. They'll all be back in work again tomorrow, so we'll be able to speak to them then.'

After a short drive out of town, Gina pulled onto the tree-lined road that led to the huge manor house. She shivered as she remembered a particularly disturbing murder that had happened in this very building a few short years ago, but that was in the past now. They entered the beautifully lit up reception and headed over to the suited woman behind the counter. 'Hello, are you checking in?'

Gina cleared her throat. 'We're here to see two of your guests. Mr and Mrs Moorcroft.'

'I'll call them for you.' The woman relayed that the Moorcrofts had visitors. 'They'll be down in a few minutes. Please take a seat in the bar area.'

While they waited, Gina bought a couple of coffees, handing one to Jacob. It seemed like ages since they'd had a drink and her stomach was rumbling. She ate the mini cookie that had been placed on the saucer. Several minutes later, a puffy-eyed blonde woman in her fifties stepped out of the lift, followed by a tall white-haired man. Gina stood and respect-fully nodded. 'Mr and Mrs Moorcroft?'

'You must be the police.' Mrs Moorcroft twisted the round pendant on her necklace.

'I'm DI Harte, this is DS Driscoll. Can we get you a drink?' Gina could see that they had been through so much, she thought offering them a drink was the least she could do.

'We're fine, thank you.' They sat on the two chairs opposite.

Thankfully, soft music played, and the bar was otherwise empty. 'Are you okay talking here or would you like to come to the station, or maybe we could go to your room? I could even ask reception if they have a meeting room.'

Mrs Moorcroft shook her head. 'I just want to stay here. We've come from the station not long ago. I don't think I can bear to sit in another clinical room while I talk about my girl—' She burst into tears. Mr Moorcroft pulled out a bunch of balled up tissues and passed them to his wife.

'May I just say how sorry we are. This must have come as a terrible shock to yourselves and your granddaughter.' Gina hated this part of the job. Her own stomach knotted as she thought of her daughter Hannah. They weren't close but if anything like that happened to her, Gina would feel like her world had ended.

'We haven't told the little one yet. She thinks she's going on holiday to Sheffield. I don't know how we're going to tell her.' Mrs Moorcroft pulled her dusky-pink shawl over her shoulders and rubbed at what looked like a wine stain on her jeans.

'Sienna was our only child.' Mr Moorcroft placed a loving arm around his wife.

Gina could tell that he was forcing his emotion aside. The trembling of his lip and the shake of his hand told her how fragile he was. 'Can you tell me a little about Sienna?'

'She was wonderful and so lovely as a child.' Mrs Moorcroft sobbed and wiped her eyes. 'When we moved up to Sheffield to care for my mother-in-law, we really hoped she'd move too but she'd made a life here. She was saving for a house, for her and Dora, but I think she liked living with Patsy. Patsy helped her with the little one and I liked the thought of her being in the house with someone else. I thought she was safe, but then she met Gerard.'

'Can you tell me a little more about him?' Gina asked. She watched Jacob making notes, his fingers shaking a little. She knew he'd need to go home after this interview. He hadn't looked well all day.

'Horrible piece of work. But I didn't know that until after she moved out. Out of the blue, Sienna told me that she'd moved in with him. She hardly knew the bloke. Anyway, they split up after two weeks and she moved back in with Patsy.'

'What did Sienna tell you about Gerard?'

Mrs Moorcroft bit her bottom lip as she rolled up a damp tissue. 'Not much. After it had all happened, Patsy told me how jealous he was, how he accused her of being with someone else, how he wouldn't let her out of the house, and he'd started telling her what she was allowed to wear now that she lived with him. All the red flags were there, and Sienna saw it immediately. She said it happened fast and it was intense. He was even trying to get her to part with her savings. Sienna literally grabbed what she could and ran back to Patsy's. I can't believe she hid something like that from us. We could have helped. But we know it wasn't him, don't we. It had to be Robbie. He needs to pay, and he will never see Dora, ever.'

Gina wanted to get onto the subject of Sienna's daughter. 'You knew about Robbie and Sienna?'

Mrs Moorcroft nodded. 'Sienna said she'd never tell anyone else, that she and Robbie were handling things in their own way and that they had an arrangement. He paid her maintenance, not nearly enough in my opinion. It didn't even cover half of her preschool costs. I didn't agree with her decision, but I didn't want to fall out with her either. The last thing I wanted was to push her away, so we kept her secret too.'

'Can you tell us about Sienna and Robbie's relationship?'

'What relationship? It was one drunken night. Sienna had gone over to see Lauren while tipsy. Robbie had just got back from a session at the pub and apparently it just happened. Anyway, long story short, she kept the baby and neither of them wanted Lauren to find out, ever.'

Gina sighed, wondering how they thought they'd keep such a big secret. 'Did Sienna mention Robbie recently?'

'We spoke on the phone about twice a week. I got the feeling she was seeing someone because she seemed happy. I asked her about it, but she said she was just doing well and had started to look at houses. She sounded hopeful...' Mrs Moorcroft began to cry. 'How could he do this to us?'

Mr Moorcroft couldn't hold back his own tears any longer. 'You must get Robbie. God help me if I see that murdering bastard first.'

'Sorry to have to ask you this but who did Dora think was her father?' Gina wondered what Sienna had told her daughter. She thought of the words on the back of the photo. *She deserves to know.* They suggested that Sienna was no longer happy with their arrangement, that she didn't want to keep their well-guarded secret any longer. This would have blown his relationship with Lauren apart and ruined her friendship with Lauren.

'Sienna kept this silly pretence up, that Dora's father was a soldier who died while fighting in Afghanistan. I went with it because I had no choice. We argued about her decision but that didn't seem to make a difference.'

'Did she mention ever telling Dora the truth?'

'Not to me but I kept on at her to.' Mrs Moorcroft sniffed. 'We spoke about it just before Christmas and I pleaded with her to come clean so that Dora could know who her father was. That's why he killed her. He wanted to save himself. He got angry that my daughter was going to tell Lauren, so he killed her and now he's run away. There's something else, something that gives me the shivers.'

'What is it?'

'Sienna came up to visit for two days just before Christmas and we went out, as a family. We came back, drank a lot and we were having so much fun. The conversation turned serious, and she drunkenly joked that if she ever told anyone that Robbie was Dora's father, he'd kill her. Then she changed the subject. I asked her about what she'd just said, and she denied saying it which was really odd. But there it is. I know what I heard. That man said he was going to kill her. I know my daughter and she feared him.' She brought her hands up to her face and then banged them on the table. 'Why haven't you found him?' She banged the table again and again.

The man behind the bar glanced over and Mr Moorcroft grabbed his wife's flailing hands and drew her into his chest. 'Come on, love.'

Gina grabbed a card from her pocket and passed it to him. She needed to leave the couple alone for now. 'If you think of anything else that might help us, please call me, anytime. Again, we are so sorry for your loss.'

'She needs to lie down. Sorry, can we talk again another time.' Mr Moorcroft helped his crying wife up. 'Find Robbie. You don't need anything else from us. You have your answers.' He helped his wife towards the lift.

Gina took a deep breath and swallowed. That had been harder than she thought. It was time to go back to the station, catch up with the day's findings and get some rest, ready to go to Sienna's workplace first thing. She wanted to slam her own fists on the table. Why hadn't they found Robbie? It was infuriating.

'Guv, I feel bad. I need to leave.' Jacob closed his notepad and stood. He rubbed his eyes. 'I don't think I'm going to be able to come in tomorrow.'

She followed him outside. 'Is it something I can help you with?'

He went to open his mouth but closed it again and walked off. 'No, I just want to go home.' And that was it. Gina knew it was serious. His engagement had to be off.

She glanced at her phone and saw that Briggs had sent her a message.

Updates. There's pizza in the incident room. Sienna Moorcroft's post-mortem is taking place tomorrow afternoon. A witness has also come forward. He claims to have seen a woman standing at the end of Lauren and Robbie's road around the time of Sienna's murder. The description is vague but we're going to put out a call for information with the local media, requesting that she come forward as a witness. The description is odd, he said she was wearing pyjamas.

FIFTEEN

Monday, 30 January

'Nathan, hurry up. We're going to miss the bus if we don't get a move on.' Finn hated that Nathan always took so long. He'd been hauled into Mr Braithwaite's office so many times because Nathan always made him late and now his mum was on his back about it, not that he cared what his mum thought, but he could do without it. He also hated this shortcut which meant walking across a muddy football pitch and balancing on a log to cross a stream. He always ended up with a mucky trouser hem as they climbed the bank.

Nathan stopped to kick a can at the goal. 'Chill, Finn. It's not like they can kill you for being late. What are they going to do? Tell Mummy.'

Nathan was right and Finn was making himself look uncool. Stuff his mum and stuff Braithwaite. He stepped on the early morning grass. White frosty blades crunched beneath his every step. He glanced at the hedge, the very place his mum

would stand as he played football. She'd always embarrassingly
cheer him on as he kept missing the passes, not realising he'd get
a ribbing for it later in the changing rooms. Yes, his mum was
loud, too loud. He wished she'd just stay at home and leave him
to play football alone.

Finn glanced at his friend who was now dribbling with the
same can. It bounced off a solid tuft of mud and he managed to
kick it again. Nathan was right. There's nothing the school
would really do. It wasn't like they were bad kids. They never
got into fights, they did their homework, and they were polite.
Mr Braithwaite would call him in, he'd moan and tell his mum,
that's all. His mum would try to ground him, she'd fail because
Finn knew how to charm her. He'd make her a cup of tea and
say he was sorry.

He pulled his rucksack off his back and felt around the
creases as Nathan shouted goal and ran around in a huge circle.
The can had passed through the goalpost. Finn's fingers
brushed the cigarettes. He pulled them out and opened the
pack. There were two left, so they'd have to share one now and
that would leave another for tomorrow. He watched the roof of
their bus as it trundled towards the stop. They had no chance of
making it anyway and it was fifteen minutes until the next bus.
'Nath, shall we bunk?'

His friend hurried over, repositioning his rucksack and
ruffling his sweaty hair. 'Yeah, I don't like French anyway. Hate
it. My dad leaves for work in about half an hour. We can go to
mine and play Xbox when he's gone.'

They hurried back towards the stream, checking to see that
no one was watching them. Finn knew that a couple of his
mum's friends walked their dogs around this field, so they had to
go to the hideout. He grinned and held the cigarette packet up.
'Let's go to the lounge.' Finn led the way, running across the
grass and cutting through the hedgerow. The lounge was their
secret place. It was nothing more than a few stacked wooden

pallets that had been arranged in a circle, but it was hidden away, wedged into the tiniest space and surrounded by dense shrubs. It was so close to the road, as people passed by, no one knew they were there. Just as they slipped away, Finn saw one of his mum's friends walking her yapping dogs. 'That was close. Could do without Nell telling my mum I'd skipped school.'

As they jumped over a few ditches and pushed through the thick brambles, Finn could see the clearing. He threw his bag down and wiped a couple of pallets off with his arm. He pulled out a cigarette. Nathan passed him the lighter. 'You can go first.'

'Cool.' Finn took the lighter and popped the cigarette in his mouth. They'd been smoking for a while now, but only occasionally. Cigarettes were hard to come by, but they'd got lucky when a sixth former went into the shop for them last week. He lit the end and coughed a little as he drew inwards, then he passed it to Nathan.

'This is so much better than school.' Nathan shivered. 'It's bloody cold today.'

While Nathan enjoyed another puff of their cigarette, Finn stood and peered through the trees. Rush hour cars began to whizz past, and people walked like they were on a mission. He wasn't going to have a job that got him up at stupid-o-clock when he grew up. He was going to own a bar, or do something where he'd have to work at night, or work in a cinema. He liked films as much as he enjoyed gaming. Maybe he'd be a filmmaker, but he'd need money for that. He'd tried to make one with his phone but really he'd like to be able to edit on a computer. The one his mum let him use for homework kept freezing up on him and the software he needed was too expensive. He began to film the frosty branches. He'd be able to play about with the footage and post it to TikTok later. Something shiny caught his attention just as the emerging low winter sun poked through the gaps in the trees. He squinted and placed his phone back in his pocket. It was a fifty pence piece. A little further up was a pound coin. 'Nath, we'll stop at the shop on the way back, get some crisps.'

'Sounds good. Is that money?'

'Yes.' Finn walked over and picked up the coins. That's when he saw the wallet. 'Someone's lost this.' He held the folded black leather up.

'Well open it up.'

'Shouldn't we hand it in?' Finn prised it open and saw forty pounds and a driver's licence tucked into the compartments. He looked at the photo.

'No way.' Nathan passed the cigarette to Finn. 'Here finish this and we can go and buy some goodies and head back to mine. This money is ours now. Only idiots lose their wallets.'

'What if he was mugged?'

'Durr, and the mugger left his money and bank card? He's lost it and he's probably already ordered new cards. It's ours for the taking.' Nathan snatched it out of Finn's hands. He removed the money and dropped the wallet back on the earth below.

'Wait.' Finn edged forward and kicked the rug that had been pushed into the undergrowth and just as the end unrolled, an arm entangled in a piece of rope slipped out.

'What the—' Nathan stared, mouth ajar. Finn went to touch it and Nathan grabbed his arm. 'Don't go near it. We've got to get out of here, now.' Nathan began running back through the brambles.

'Wait, we can't. We need to call the police.'

'What do you mean, Finn? We can't be here. We have to go.'

Finn looked at the cigarette butt that Nathan had dropped. He picked it up and placed it in his pocket. He didn't know much but his mum always watched detective dramas. They'd touched the wallet. The police would find their fingerprints and they'd be in big trouble if they ran away. The ground had started to thaw, and their shoe prints were everywhere. He stared at the arm and wondered who was wrapped up in the rug. Was it a man, a woman? He swallowed. It hit him. Someone had been murdered and dumped. He couldn't run. He pulled his phone out ready to call the one person he could trust, and he hoped he wouldn't be in too much trouble. 'Nathan, come back. We can't run away from this. The police will find us.'

His friend had gone.

'Nathan!' he yelled in frustration. A crunching sound came from the other side of the bushes. He turned to catch whoever was watching but there was no one there. His heart juddered in his chest as he held his phone to his ear.

SIXTEEN

Gina yawned as she waited for DC Wyre to meet her outside the Brunswick Security offices. Jacob had called in as suspected and said he was poorly. She could at least vouch for him. He'd looked terrible the previous day. Whether he was having relationship problems or getting over food poisoning, she hoped he was okay. Maybe she'd send him a get well soon message later. She leaned against her car in the shiny new office park. The low sun reflected off the mirrored windows. However hard she tried to peer through the glass, she couldn't. A few minutes ago, several suited people turned up and flashed their passes at the sensor to get in. Some of them had clocked her presence but they'd been far too polite to ask who she was and why she'd parked in their company spaces.

Wyre pulled in and parked at the back of the car park. She stepped out and pulled her long black plait out of the back of her coat and headed over. 'Morning, guv. Did you manage to get some sleep?'

'Yes, thanks.' For once she had. Briggs had stayed over, and they'd brought the leftover pizza home to eat while they pored over the crime scene photos and videos. She didn't mention to Wyre that she'd had another slice for breakfast as she left the house. Her health-conscious colleague wouldn't approve. 'In the absence of Robbie, let's head in there and get all we can on Gerard.' She pressed the intercom and a woman's voice came through.

'Brunswick Security. Who are you here to see?'

'Police, it's DI Harte and DC Wyre. We need to speak to someone with regards to an incident.'

The door buzzed. Gina pushed it and they both entered the large reception, brightened up by a huge bunch of mixed flowers and a coffee machine. A red-haired woman in her twenties pushed the door and entered. 'I'm Carol. I just heard about Sienna this morning. The whole team know now, we're just... I don't know what we're doing. Her assistant is in tears and...' The woman sniffled a little. 'I couldn't help looking at the photo of her little girl on her desk... I have a little girl too.' The woman let out a sob.

'I'm really sorry for your loss, Carol.' Gina paused until Carol cleared her throat and stood back up straight. 'We need to speak to someone in the company, possibly Sienna's manager. Is her manager in?'

The woman nodded. 'Come through. We have a little staff lounge.' She led them through the various offices, passing the accounts and business management departments. Carol pointed to the door at the end. 'Just head through there and help yourself to a drink. There are cups and coffee pods. I'll go and get Pierre.'

As Carol left, Gina began making two drinks, knowing they might be left waiting for a short while. She passed one to Wyre and sat at one of the round tables. Wyre opened her notebook and made a note of the manager's first name. 'It's heartbreaking, guv. I can't stop thinking about little Dora.'

'Me neither. Jacob and I spoke to Sienna's parents last night and they hadn't told her yet.'

'Where would you start?'

Gina leaned back in a wooden chair and sipped the hot coffee. 'It's the post-mortem this afternoon. I spoke to O'Connor last night. He and Kapoor will be attending.'

'Is Jacob, okay? I've never known him be ill before.' Wyre placed her cup on the table.

'He had a bad stomach yesterday. I'm sure he just needs whatever's playing him up to work its way out of his system.' There was no way she'd mention her suspicions about him and Jennifer.

'Hello, I'm Pierre Fournier. I work with Sienna. Such terrible news. We can't believe what has happened,' he said in a light French accent as he joined them at the table. 'What is it you'd like to know?' The lines around his eyes told her he was maybe in his late fifties.

'Thank you for speaking with us. How closely do you work with Sienna?'

'Very closely. We shared an office; we chatted a lot and sometimes sat out here to have our lunch together. She was a lovely young woman, hardworking and ambitious.' He pressed his lips together and frowned.

'How did Sienna seem lately?'

'Happy, she was looking at houses. For ages, she's been saving for a deposit and at last, she had all the money. In all her breaks, she'd be on the search engines and looking. She'd turn her computer screen around excitedly and show me house after house. She couldn't wait to have her own place and she hoped to stay close to where she was living, wanting to stay near Patsy. Patsy would pop by now and again with some lunch for Sienna. I think she mothered Sienna a little and Sienna liked it.'

'Do you have a client called Gerard?'

He nodded. 'He works for a company that we service. Sienna dated him for a while, but it didn't work out.'

'What was their relationship like?'

He shrugged. 'I don't know really. She said he was nice but not her type, so she ended it. I think he called a few times for her, and she wouldn't take the calls. She did move in with him, but it was only for a couple of weeks, I think. She didn't say much else. I think he stopped calling her soon after and now one of his colleagues calls us when they need something. I think he got the hint.'

Gina knew that Sienna probably kept the details of her relationship to herself. 'How did she seem on Friday, that's if she was in work that day?'

'She was. I may be speaking out of turn here.' He paused.

'Whatever you know, it could be important to the case. Sienna has been murdered and we need to find the person who did it.' Gina wondered if what he had to say involved Robbie.

He closed his eyes. 'Hearing you say those words is hard.' He opened his eyes again. 'So far, I've had to keep it together for the staff, but I don't know how long I can.' He ran his fingers through his thin greying hair. 'I saw a few texts flash up on her phone. She would leave it on her desk all the time. It wasn't as if I was spying on her, they were right in front of me. I didn't mention that I'd seen them, I never would. I was happy for her, really, I was.'

'Happy for her.'

He nodded. 'They were of a sexual nature. She'd split up with Gerard and I thought it was nice she'd met someone else. I know she'd planned to see this person on Saturday and err, to do... you know.'

Gina nodded. She had seen the messages on Sienna's phone, and she knew they'd come from an unregistered phone that was now turned off. They had no way of tracing it. If it was

Robbie's phone, he could have easily taken it when he scarpered. She had been planning to meet someone on Saturday. She turned up at Robbie's place and she'd had sex. 'Thank you for that. It can sometimes be the small things that really help a case and if you remember anything else after we've left, please call me.' She passed him a card. 'Can I please have Gerard's contact details and full name.'

'Of course, I'll print out his company address and the phone number for you. He's based in Redditch, so it's not too far away. And likewise, if there is anything else you need to know, please call me.'

'Did she have any friends within the company, someone she may have confided in?'

'Carol. She and Carol also took breaks together quite often. I can send her in if you'd like to speak to her.'

'That would be much appreciated.'

Half an hour later, Gina had got no further information from Carol. She and Wyre stepped back out. Wyre flicked through her notes. 'Everything is pointing to Robbie Shields still.'

Gina had to agree. 'It is but we'll call in and get someone to contact Gerard Hale now we know where he is. We definitely can't rule him out just yet.'

Her phone rang. She snatched it out of her pocket. 'Sir.'

'Gina, we have another body. You're not going to believe this.'

'What? Who?'

'You need to get over to the Canford Road football field straight away. Park on the roadside and you will see the van. The body is in the land between the footpath and the field. It's a hedged off area full of trees and shrubs so it's challenging to get through. It's a bit of a nature area and not designed for walkers. The body was hidden just out of sight from the road. Forensics have been called so they should either be there or close behind you. Officers have cordoned off the area and the route the killer would have taken to dump the body, which is from the road, over the grass and through the hedge.'

'Do we know who it is?'

'It's Robbie Shields. He's been brutally murdered.'

SEVENTEEN

NANCY

'Did you sleep well, love?' She paused. 'Stupid question, especially as I heard you tossing and turning all night. I have home-made granola; would you like some?'

'No.' Lauren walked over to the counter and poured herself a coffee. 'I'm not hungry.'

'You have to eat, or you'll feel worse.'

'How the hell can I feel any worse, Mum?'

'Sorry, I should think before I speak.'

Lauren sat at the table and began to bite her nails. 'I've been watching the news. They still haven't caught him. They would have said if they had him, wouldn't they?'

'They'd have called.' Nancy was sure that the police would tell Lauren first if they had new information, at least she hoped they would. 'Did you get up in the night?'

Sighing, Lauren drank some of her coffee and rubbed her eyes. 'I couldn't stop thinking about what happened. It won't leave my head.' She hiccupped a sob. 'I got into bed with Sienna, and she was dead. I put my hand on her bleeding body and—' Tears spilled in abundance.

Nancy hurried over and hugged her daughter. She wished

the bad things had happened to her instead. What her daughter saw was as horrific as it got. Robbie would get what he deserved for all that he'd done. She knew that much.

'Every time I close my eyes, I can see her dead eyes. I can see the angry red marks around her neck.'

'It'll get easier, love.' There she went again. It wouldn't get easier. How does a person deal with being that close to a dead friend, even a deceitful dead friend?

The dog whined and placed its head against Lauren's leg. She leaned down and picked Fifi up. 'I'm sorry I shooed you away yesterday.' Lauren ruffled the dog's head and wiped the tears from her face. 'I will have some granola, Mum. I should eat. You're right.'

Nancy exhaled. Getting granola was something she could do, everything else was hard. She really didn't want to put her size sevens in it by saying the wrong thing. She'd just got her daughter back, the last thing she wanted was to lose her again. Robbie had come between them for too long. She'd never let a man do that to them again. She placed the nutty cereal in a bowl and poured a generous amount of oat milk over the top. 'Here you go. Get that down you. All we can do is take every day as it comes.'

Lauren placed Fifi on the floor and the dog began crunching on a bowl of kibble. 'Where did you go this morning?'

'Nowhere.'

'I heard your car pull away.'

'Oh that. I drove to the bottom of the hills to take Fifi for a walk.'

Lauren furrowed her brows as she ate a spoonful of cereal. 'You normally just go out your back gate.'

'I used to but now she likes other places. She gets bored. We have to change it up a bit, don't we, Fifi.' She reached down and disturbed her eating dog.

'Can we go and get a phone after breakfast?'

'Of course, love. As soon as you're dressed, we'll head to Tesco.'

The house phone rang. Nancy hurried into the tiny lounge and snatched it off the cradle. 'Hello.' Leaning on the mantelpiece, she waited for the caller to speak. As soon as the conversation was over, she ran back into the kitchen. 'We're going to have to stay in. The police are coming over. They want to speak to you.'

'What is it? Have they found him?'

'They said they couldn't say anything over the phone. They need to speak to you in person.' Nancy's mobile beeped. She read the message.

You filthy snake. I know what you did. Yes, I know! Watch your back, or better still don't – haha. Maybe I'll treat you like the snake that you are, catch you in a net and skin you while you scream.

Nancy deleted the message with shaky hands and placed the phone down.

'You okay, Mum?'

She pasted a fake smile on her face. 'Of course, love. Don't you worry about me. All is good here.' All was far from good but at least she was safe in her home. She glanced out the window at the hedges and rolling hills that stretched out forever. Was she safe? She stood up and locked the back door. 'There's been a lot of rural burglaries. If you let Fifi out, make sure you lock the door.' Better to be safe than sorry.

EIGHTEEN

Gina yawned as she and Wyre stepped out onto the road. She used her hands to shade her eyes from the sun while approaching the officer guarding the cordon. 'Morning.' She grabbed a forensics suit and began pulling it over her trousers and jumper while the PC filled the log out for her and Wyre.

'The crime scene team has just arrived,' the woman said as she adjusted her police hat. 'The manager said to follow the plates.'

'Thank you. Who found the victim?'

'Two thirteen-year-old lads. The mother of one called in to say her son had found the body but we're trying to locate the father of the other boy. They are heading to the station once he's been located. He works as a driver so it might take a short while.'

Gina lifted the cordon up and let Wyre go through first. Their boots clopped on the metal plates until they reached a dense hedge. Wyre pushed through first and Gina followed.

'Stay right there,' Bernard said as he stood in the middle of a tiny clearing that was surrounded by wooden pallets. Gina stopped. Two crime scene officers were attending to the surroundings, taking photos and bagging evidence. 'It's a bit tight here so I'll ask that you don't wander. If you remain on that spot, we're good. We haven't been here long and there isn't enough room to erect a tent. We know it's only a matter of time before the public start to realise something's going on, so I want the body dealt with swiftly.'

As Bernard muttered further instructions to his team, she noticed that Jennifer wasn't with them. That's when she knew that she'd been right. Jennifer and Jacob were having problems. Or maybe they'd both eaten the same thing. She shook those thoughts away. Whatever was wrong with her colleague was the least of her worries today when there was a body on the ground.

'That's blown our main theory out of the water.' Wyre rubbed her gloved hands together.

She was right unless Robbie had died by suicide. Wrapping himself in a rug? No, that was impossible. 'Do we know how he died?' she asked, hoping Bernard could now spare her a few moments. The sooner she got what she needed from him, the sooner she could head to see Lauren Cross and break the news. She also wanted to be the one who spoke to Gerard Hale. He'd just bumped up to prime position on their suspect list. If he knew that Sienna had been seeing Robbie, that might have fuelled a murderous act of revenge. He had motive, that was for sure.

'Again, he was injured. He wasn't stabbed like the last victim, but he was struck over the head with something jagged. At the moment, I'd go with a rock. This didn't kill him. He was strangled.'

'Just like Sienna was.' She glanced at the rope.

'Yes, a rope this time.'

Gina's chest began to flutter with nerves as she thought of what Tiffany Crawford had told her. She hoped the team had managed to pull up all the details of Tiffany's attack in readiness for her return to the station. A sense of uneasiness squirmed in the pit of her stomach. Three strangulations, two with scarves. One dating back a few years. The most recent only days apart. 'Do you have a rough time of death?'

'We have some decomposition of the internal organs. The body has come out of rigor mortis. I'll know more after the post-mortem, but I'd say he died a little after the last victim. I can't be too precise, but I can give an approximation of between one and four yesterday morning.'

She was thankful that he'd been found outside as she knew decomposition meant smell and she knew she'd struggle to deal with that right now. 'Can you tell us anything else about the body or the scene that might help us?'

'He has what appear to be splinters stuck in his fingertips and nails.' Bernard nodded as one of his team called him over.

Gina turned to Wyre. 'I'm thinking Robbie Shields was locked in that cupboard.' Bernard was heading back. 'Have we processed the blood and semen samples from the other scene as yet?'

'I'm sorry but we are doing our best. I have put a fast-track on it at the lab so hopefully it won't be long now.'

'Was he killed here?'

'I'm going with no,' Bernard replied. 'There's no way anyone could have rolled the body up in the rug like that, right here. There are no rug fibres caught in the wooden pallets and there just isn't the room. I'd say he was killed somewhere else, rolled up in the rug and dumped here from the roadside. There are some rug fibres and drag marks on the grass, leading from the road. Whoever brought him here came to a stop the other side of that shrub.' Bernard pointed to the bush. 'They parted the shrubbery and hoisted him through. It would have been a struggle but it is doable. Whoever did this would have been strong. It would have taken some effort to get the body here.'

'Paula, would you please make a note of the rug descrip-tion? We need to know if it belonged to Lauren and Robbie.

We're seeing Lauren next so we can ask the question.' While Wyre scribbled a few words down, she turned to address Bernard. 'Thank you. I don't want to keep you any longer. Is there anything missing?'

'Actually, there is something missing. He is wearing trainers, but he is only wearing one sock.'

She pondered that fact for a moment. 'Have you found any of his personal belongings or a phone?' She wondered if Bernard had come across the burner phone that had been used to message Sienna.

'No to the phone, but yes to a wallet. There is nothing in it but a bank card, a credit card and his driver's licence. That has already been bagged.'

'Thank you. You have my number should you find anything that might help us. I know DC O'Connor is attending this afternoon's post-mortem so hopefully there will be more information later.'

'I'll keep you posted.' Bernard turned back to his colleagues. The best thing Gina could do was get out of his way and let him get on with processing the scene. Once back on the path, she called the incident room. 'Sir, we need an officer to break the news to Robbie Shields's next of kin. I have a couple of witnesses to speak to before I can get to them. O'Connor is going to be tied up with the post-mortem and Wyre is with me. With Jacob out we're a bit thin on the ground.'

'Of course. I'll arrange that. PC Ahmed will be able to go.'

'Thank you.' She brought him up to date with the approximated time of death.

'Excuse me, DI Harte.' One of the crime scene assistants called her back over to the cordon.

Gina hurried towards her. 'Have you found something?'

'Yes, in the pocket of his jeans. It's a pair of women's under-wear, size twelve.' The woman held up the evidence bag. 'Obviously the underwear will need to go to the lab but Bernard thought we should share this information with you.'

Gina tried to picture Lauren Cross. She was thinner on the hips compared to Sienna, more like a size eight to ten but Sienna was curvier. 'Thank you. Please add them to the fast-track pile at the lab.' She wanted to know if they contained traces of semen and if that semen was Robbie's.

As they walked back to the car, Wyre stopped before getting in. 'That's complicated things. Have we got a murderer who collects trophies or one that likes to plant a trophy on the next victim?'

A rush of blood flooded Gina's head. 'Tiffany Crawford. We need the case details asap. If the scarf that was used to strangle her isn't in evidence, it might mean that the killer kept it. Sienna was strangled with a flower-printed scarf. Without having the lab work done, we worked on the theory that the scarf belonged to Lauren or Sienna. I'm worried for Tiffany, really worried.'

NINETEEN

Gina knocked on the cottage door, taking in the sideview of the Malvern Hills behind it. A dog yapped from behind the wood. While waiting next to Wyre as the person on the other side battled with the lock, she glanced at the tiny white building with its black-framed windows, criss-crossed with lead. The garden full of bare branched bushes and mulched up leaves looked like the perfect place for nature to thrive. The insect house stood empty on the fence.

The door was eventually opened, and a red-eyed Lauren answered. 'Sorry about the wait, I couldn't seem to get my mum's key in the lock properly. Everything here is so bloody broken. Have you found him?'

By him, Gina knew Lauren was referring to Robbie. The stiff door creaked as the young woman opened it wide to let them in. The dog barked from behind the living room door and the shower sounded like it was running upstairs. 'We have some news.'

'Fifi, shut up. Come through to the kitchen.'

They stepped into the cramped space. Gina took in the shelves full of ancient-looking casserole dishes and a mishmash of different cups and plates that had been haphazardly stacked.

'Have a seat. Do you want a drink? It will have to be with oat milk and chicory coffee. That's all my mum has.'

Gina shook her head. 'No, thank you. Is your mum in?'

'She's in the shower.'

'Would you like to take a seat?' Gina knew that the news she had to share would be a shock. She felt her eye twitch from tiredness, and she blinked it away.

Lauren sat on one of the wooden chairs and shifted her mum's pile of post out of the way. 'What's happened?'

Wyre remained quiet at the other end of the table.

'I'm sorry to have to tell you this but we found a body earlier today.' Gina had once suspected Lauren Cross, only a little, but the thought had niggled away at her. There was no way that Lauren could have killed Robbie. She had been at the club, in the taxi, or at the hospital at the time of his murder, giving her the perfect alibi.

Lauren swallowed and began playing with the ends of her clumped hair. 'Who is it?'

'We've confirmed that it's Robbie. Please accept our deepest condolences.'

Gina watched as tears welled up in Lauren's eyes. 'But, how?'

'We don't have all the details as yet, but his death is being treated as murder.'

Shaking her head, Lauren gasped for breath and closed her eyes. 'I don't understand. I thought... me and Mum thought that he'd killed Sienna.'

'As I said, we don't have all the details and we won't for a while, but forensics are working the scene as we speak. I know this is hard, but we need to ask you a couple of questions. It would really help us if you wouldn't mind.' Gina hoped Lauren was up to it. She had so much to ask, and she also had a lot to tell. She wondered if Lauren had known about Sienna having Robbie's baby. The woman was going to be devastated.

Tears slipped down her blotchy cheeks. 'I've lost everything and Robbie... I can't believe it. We were getting married. We were going to have children and spend our lives together and it's all gone, just like that. I just want to go back to last week.'

'It's a lot to process.'

Lauren walked over to her mum's fridge and pulled out an open bottle of what looked like home-made wine. With shaking hands, she poured a large measure into a tumbler. 'What do you need to know?'

Wyre pulled out her notebook and smiled sympathetically.

Gina exhaled. 'Do you own a mustard-coloured rug? A large one?'

Lauren's brows furrowed. 'There's one in the room we use as a study.'

Gina had searched that room and there hadn't been a rug in it or any outline of a removed rug, which means the killer must have brushed the carpet to cover their tracks. The blood in the cupboard must have been from Robbie's head. She pictured him being caught unaware by their attacker. Had he been bundled in there while the perp murdered Sienna? Maybe he then tried to claw at the door before banging at it with the tin of paint while he listened to her screaming for help. Had the killer then opened the door, struck him with the rock and then brought the rug close to the cupboard, ready to roll him up? They would have needed a vehicle to transport his body all the way to where they found it. Who was the woman in the pyjamas? 'Do you own a scarf with blue flowers on it?'

'You mean the one like Sienna's? I saw it on my bedroom floor when I err...' she paused and closed her eyes for a second, 'when I found Sienna's body in my bed.' Her brows furrowed.

'So that was Sienna's scarf?'

Lauren shrugged. 'It's not the type of thing she normally

wears. I've never seen her wearing that type of scarf but it's not mine so it must have been hers. I've never seen her wearing it before.'

Gina glanced at Wyre. They both knew that there was a huge possibility that the scarf at the bungalow had been the one that had been used to strangle Tiffany Crawford. 'How long have you known Tiffany Crawford?'

'I don't know. A year maybe, not much longer.'

'Had you ever met her before that?'

'No, definitely not. I know she lives on my estate, but I didn't know her before she started work at Hoopers. You don't think this has anything to do with Tiff? She's scared of her own shadow.'

Gina raised her brows and sat back. 'Definitely not. We are looking into a historical case at the moment, but I can't say anything as yet.'

'Something to do with Tiff?'

Gina had no intention of revealing too much so a change of subject was in order. 'I can only apologise that we've had to take your phone as evidence. I'll endeavour to get it back to you as soon as it's been processed.'

'I was going to ask about that. My mother virtually lives off-grid. I'm a bit cut off here.' Lauren began twiddling her fingers. 'Can I see Robbie's body? I know he was cheating on me, and I should be angry, but I want to say goodbye. I need to see him.'

'We'll call you when that's possible. It will probably be in a few days. Do you know anyone who might have wanted to hurt Sienna and Robbie?'

'No, they didn't even mix in the same circles or share friends. I can't think of anyone at all. I'm the only person who connects them and I didn't do it. I would never hurt anyone, not even if I was angry at them.'

Gina tilted her head and smiled sympathetically. 'If you do think of anything or anyone after we've gone, please call me.'

She swallowed, dreading what was coming next. 'There's something delicate I need to ask you.'

'I don't think things can get any worse for me right now.'

Gina wished that were the case. 'What did you know about Robbie and Sienna's relationship?'

Lauren shook her head and shrugged. 'Nothing until Saturday night, or maybe early Sunday morning, once I'd processed what had happened. I didn't think Robbie would ever cheat on me again.' She dabbed her tears on a tissue. 'He slept with someone while we were on holiday, and he begged me to give him another chance. I trusted him and I believed him. I guess I was a total fool.'

'There's something you should know.'

'What?'

'It looks like Robbie was paying child maintenance to Sienna and Sienna's mother confirmed that Robbie was Dora's father.'

Lauren shook her head. 'No, she slept with this man. He was a soldier and he got shot in Afghanistan.' A loud sob emerged from her mouth. 'It was all lies, wasn't it? How could I have been so stupid?'

Telling Lauren about Sienna's daughter had left Gina's heart banging. She felt the woman's anger, her loss, her sense of confusion. Within two days her whole world had fallen apart. All her dreams of an upcoming wedding, her new life – shattered.

Lauren's mother burst into the kitchen, towel wrapping up her hair, bathrobe tied up around her waist. 'What's going on?'

'He's dead. Robbie has been murdered and that's not all. He was Dora's father. They were lying to me for years, Mum.'

'I'm so sorry, love.' The woman drew her daughter in and stroked her hair like she was a little girl as Lauren cried into her chest. 'I think she needs a break. Sorry, I'm going to have to ask you to leave. Can we continue with this later?'

Gina stood and nodded. 'Again, we are so sorry for your loss and if you remember anything else, please call me.'

Nancy nodded. 'Thank you.'

Wyre finished noting down what was said and popped her notebook in her pocket. As they left the cottage, Gina glanced back, wondering how Lauren was going to get through the next few days. She pulled her phone from her pocket and saw that she had a message. It was Briggs asking her to call him as soon as she could.

She pressed his number.

'Gina, we have an update. We've found fibres of that rug in the boot of Robbie Shields's car. He was transported in his own car and then it must have been returned before Lauren Cross came back. We also have a witness. Someone else saw Robbie on the evening of Sienna's murder. They're out of the area now but they're coming into the station this afternoon.'

'A witness, that's great. I'll make sure we're back for that. Wyre and I are going to visit Gerard Hale's place of work next. As soon as we're finished there, we'll hurry back. We haven't called ahead so our visit will be a surprise. We need to catch him off guard, not give him a chance to think. It's all happening right now.'

'I won't hold you up then. Keep me updated if you find anything out.'

'Will do. Please send someone to Tiffany Crawford's to let her know that we'll be conducting drive-bys. For now, to be on the safe side, I want the cases linked until we've seen Tiffany Crawford's case file. Can you urgently get me the file?'

'I'll chase it up right now.'

TWENTY

TIFFANY

Another knock on the door sent Tiffany shaking. She kept her back against the kitchen wall in the hope that the caller wouldn't peer through the window. When the caller headed back down the path, she'd glance through the window and decide if it was safe to answer. Only then would she open the door. Over the sound of her heart pumping and the blood whooshing through her head, she heard crackling, like that of a police radio. It was the police again. It had to be. Could she even trust the police when she'd read that so many forces were being held up for not tackling misogyny and racism. Those in trusted positions were coming under scrutiny and being charged with the most heinous of crimes it made her skin crawl. Hell, her attacker could have been police for all she knew. No wonder everyone was scared. She was scared and she wasn't about to trust anyone.

Her fingers itched to answer the door but with Kieron being out at work, she didn't feel safe. She exhaled. Then again, if it was the police, they might have something important to tell her. Maybe she had to trust them. With shaky legs, she crept to the door, slid the chain across and opened it. 'Hello.'

'Mrs Crawford, I'm PC Smith and this is my colleague, PC Benton. May I speak to you for a moment?'

'Can I see your IDs?'

The officers held them up. She stared at each in turn, a man and a woman. 'I need to call the station to check. It's nothing personal but I'm on my own here. I've been watching the news and, frankly, I don't trust anyone, especially the police.'

'Of course,' he replied as he passed her a card. 'Call that number. If you need to google it, you'll see it's the number for the station at Cleevesford. We prefer that people check and we understand that you can never be too sure.' PC Smith smiled.

She closed the door, feeling slightly bad for checking on them especially as they seemed pleasant. Hands shaking, she pressed the numbers into her phone and waited for an answer. Within minutes the person on the other end of the line had confirmed that the officers were genuine. She then opened the internet on her phone and double-checked the number and it did belong to Cleevesford Police. She hurried back, her slippers slapping on the tiled hallway floor, and she opened the door. 'Come in.'

'Thank you.' The PCs removed their hats and followed her to the living room.

She gestured for them to sit. 'I only spoke to someone yesterday. Detective—' She grabbed the card off the table. 'This is her, DI Harte. She spoke to me about Lauren's friend's murder. I told her everything I know.'

'Yes, we have something we need to speak to you about, relating to the incident. Also, officers will be driving by your property throughout the day. We don't have a lot of information to share with, but we know you mentioned to DI Harte that you were attacked in the past.'

She felt her jaw begin to tremble. It was a related incident. She'd read the detective's expression correctly and now her attacker was back for her. 'He's coming for me. That's what you think, isn't it?'

'We're just being precautionary at this stage. There are similarities to your attack, and we want to make sure you're safe.'

'And how the hell are you going to keep me safe? He could smash his way in through the back. I'm on my own all day in this flat.' She now wished they lived on the top floor. She didn't want to move into a ground floor flat, but Kieron had insisted, saying he'd miss a garden when they moved. Her stomach spasmed and her head began to pound. It was the fear that had kept her awake all night. Hour upon hour, her heart had palpitated away only to leave her exhausted when Kieron's alarm went off. Still, she wasn't tired, and she doubted she'd ever have a good night's sleep again.

'We would like to fit a panic alarm in your flat. Would that be okay?' PC Smith leaned forward a little and linked his hands in front of him. 'We can also get someone to check your windows and doors, see if they're secure enough. Will you be in all day?'

She nodded.

'Are you okay, Mrs Crawford?' PC Benton asked, the officer's brows furrowed, a look of pity on her face.

'No.' Her voiced quivered. 'It's like it happened yesterday, the attack I mean. I have tried so hard to move on and I can't. No one understands what it's like, knowing that he's out there and he could come for me at any time. I'm scared to go out. I'm scared at work. When I see a man, it goes through my head – could it be him? Why didn't you catch him? Why did you lot fail me?' She couldn't hold back the tears any longer. The attack had caused her illnesses. It was the start of everything that had gone wrong in her life. She'd lost her career. She'd decided against having a family. She lived like a hermit, relying on Kieron to do almost everything for her and she hated what that evil man had turned her into.

PC Smith furrowed his brows. 'We're so sorry, Mrs Crawford.'

'Am I in danger? What do you really think?'

'The truth is, we don't know but we don't want to take any risks. I know DI Harte will want to speak to you again when we know a little more. Do you have anyone who can come and sit with you, or is there anywhere you'd rather stay for now?'

She shook her head. 'I'm not in touch with my family. We fell out years ago. I don't have anyone. Kieron is my absolute rock, but he has to work. He'll be back around teatime. I'll be okay.' She had no choice. 'I'll take the panic button, please, and thank you for the drive-bys.' She wasn't going to turn down their help, not until the local murderer was caught. For a moment, she dared to hope that he would be caught, and did turn out to be her attacker. She imagined stepping outside as the weight of her fear floated away. Then she swallowed. She still couldn't recall anything from the night of Sienna's murder, yet she was found outside, sleepwalking. A thought flashed through her mind. Bare feet stepping onto the kerb. She opened her mouth, wondering if she should say something. A sharp pain went through her lower stomach. Was it her IBS or maybe it was appendicitis, or something worse, much worse? Maybe a tumour. *Stop.* She had to stop doing this to herself, thinking the worst all the time was making her sicker.

'Is there something you want to tell us?' PC Smith shifted to the left slightly to stop himself sinking into PC Benton on the couch.

She closed her gaping mouth and shook her head vigorously. 'No. I was thinking, that's all. It's horrible knowing that someone was killed close by. It gives me the shivers. And she was killed in my friend's home.' She pulled her full-length cardigan across her chest. 'I'm not feeling well which is nothing new, but I think I might need to go to bed for a bit.' Her inner dialogue whispered in a menacing voice. *You did it. It had to be you. You attacked Kieron too.*

'Thank you for speaking with us.' They stood and PC Smith continued to speak. 'We'll see you later. Hope you're feeling a little better by then.'

She led them to the door and as soon as they left, she pulled the chain across and leaned against it, breathing rapidly until the dark speckles that plagued her vision subsided. She couldn't pass out, not now.

Kieron was right. She couldn't harm anyone, not intentionally, and she didn't go to Lauren's place while she was sleepwalking. Why would she kill Sienna? Then she answered it for herself. The voice was right. She'd stabbed Kieron because she thought he was her attacker. She'd been asleep and she hadn't known. She swallowed and almost slipped to the floor as the confusion dancing around her head became overwhelming. *Did I? Didn't I? Did I?* Those questions repeated in her head at a dizzying speed.

She shook the intrusive thoughts away and began pacing. That whole evening was a blank. She almost toppled as another image flashed through her mind. Metal piercing flesh. Blood. Shouting. She ran into her bedroom, jumped into her bed fully clothed. She dragged the duvet cover over her curls. The fear was real and it was justified.

'Go away,' she yelled as she gasped for breath. 'Leave me alone.'

TWENTY-ONE

Gina stuffed the rest of her chicken wrap into her mouth while Wyre finished her banana. That was all the fuel they'd get for a while. The chill in the air sent a little shiver across the back of her neck. She adjusted her woollen scarf, her fingers fiddling with a crease at the back. As she worked the knot out, she thought of Sienna and the terror she must have felt in her final moments. 'Time to check out what Gerard Hale has to say.' She stopped on the path. 'We know he was jealous. Sienna had left him. We know he didn't take it well if he kept trying to call her at work. Question is, had he known that she was having an affair with Robbie Shields, and did he kill them both?'

Wyre straightened her stiff white collar underneath her grey coat. 'With Robbie now a victim, he's definitely in the picture.'

Gina entered a showroom. Gas fires were displayed on every wall, some set back into cosy nook-style alcoves, setting the scene. Toasties was a huge company. Gina had spent a short while researching them at home last night. She knew they had shops in most major cities and a head office in Norway. She also knew that Gerard Hale looked after all the buildings. It was his job to make sure they were secure, fire safe and alarmed. That's where Sienna's company had come into it. They serviced and maintained all their systems in their shops and offices throughout the UK. 'Can you see a bell or an intercom?' They walked around, browsing for a door or a corridor.

'No, guv. I have no idea how we're meant to get anyone's attention.'

A camera housed in a corner whizzed around to face them. She smiled at it. 'I think they know we're here.'

Within seconds a woman with long red hair appeared through a hidden door that had blended in with the granite-coloured walls. 'Hello, welcome to Toasties. Apologies, our receptionist is having lunch. How can I help you?' She looked a little confused. 'This is an office. We have shops locally if you're looking to browse our fantastic fires.'

Gina held her ID up. 'I'm DI Harte, this is DC Wyre. We need to speak to Gerard Hale.'

'Gerard? I see.'

Gina glanced around. 'Sorry, may I take your name?' She needed to know who she was speaking to. Wyre flipped open her notebook and leaned on the counter.

'Saffi. I'm the area sales manager.'

'Is Mr Hale in today?'

She shook her head. 'No. He went on leave last Friday and isn't due back until next week. Is this to do with Sienna? I saw the news. We've talked about nothing else this morning.'

Gina nodded. 'We're investigating her murder. Did Mr Hale say he was going away or staying at home?'

She let out a smirk. 'What home?'

'What does that mean?'

'It means he lost his house just before Christmas and he's been staying in his static caravan, that's until that gets discovered as an asset. He's not even meant to stay there as the park doesn't open all year round. He leaves his car by the river and takes the walking trail in, so the site manager doesn't see him.'

From what Gina had heard, Sienna had been living with him and she had left him mid-December. He must have lost his home after that. 'Which caravan park is he staying at?'

'Honey Pots Park in Stratford but he might not be there at the moment. He said he was going on holiday. He mentioned going on a short break to Magaluf, only for a couple of days. I don't know whether he's gone yet or if he's going later this week. I didn't ask. Didn't want to know.'

Gina sensed that Saffi didn't like Gerard.

'I guess you're here because you want to speak to him and in his absence, you want to know more about him. I can help you.'

Perfect. That was just what Gina needed. They'd have to check out Honey Pots later. 'That would really help.' Gina gently gestured for Wyre to follow her towards the wall. 'Could you call in the information about Honey Pots Park? The sooner we can visit, the better.' They could bring him in for questioning if he wasn't yet in Magaluf. She checked her watch, knowing that she had a witness arriving at the station soon, as well as the boys who found Robbie Shields's body. On top of all that, O'Connor would want to speak to her about Sienna Moorcroft's post-mortem. Time was slipping through their fingers.

Gina pulled her own notebook out as her colleague stepped to one side to make the call. She headed back towards Saffi. 'Did Mr Hale mention Sienna Moorcroft?'

'Yes, he referred to her as his bird, which I felt was derogatory. Before he announced they were seeing each other, we wondered why he was always making excuses to go to Brunswick's and then we found out. He'd been taking her to lunch on the company card. It flagged up with accounts when they were doing his expenses. He said they were having meetings. Accounts thought that was odd as they wanted to keep our business, so they normally paid for entertainment. Anyway, he was treating Sienna to posh dinners on company money. He got a slap on the wrists and that was it, so we thought.'

'What happened after that?'

'He seemed to toe the line for a while and then he announced she was moving in with him. He had this nice little semi, three bedrooms and a long garden. He showed me pictures on his phone. I don't think Sienna was ready to move in with him.' She paused and began to play with a strand of hair.

'Why is that?'

'Because I heard him joking about it, saying he was working on her, persuading her. No one needs persuading if it's something they want to do. It came across like he was pressuring her. He would also call her every time he had a break. It seemed too full on and if she had a day off, I'd hear him asking her where she was and when she'd be home.'

'Was this when she moved in with him?'

Saffi shook her head. 'No, this was before. Anyway, she moved in with him and he started coming in late, saying that he needed to drop her off at work and then he'd leave early to pick her up. No one seemed to mind the hours he kept because he did a lot of work from home, but it was as if he wouldn't let her out of his sight. A few weeks into her living with him...' Saffi exhaled. 'This is horrible, but I'll say it as it is. I get the sense he's not quite right and I can't put my finger on what's wrong. He comes across as controlling. I think that's why she left him. It didn't take her long to find out.'

Wyre returned and took over the note-taking. Gina continued. 'And after that?'

'After she left, he came into work looking dishevelled but not upset. He was angry. If someone made the tiniest sound, he'd jump down their throats. It was like walking on eggshells. That's when things went downhill fast. We found out his house was being repossessed and that he'd accrued a lot of debt. He probably spent too much on Botox and his stupid teeth. I overheard a phone call he made to Sienna while she was at work, just after she left him.'

Gina held her breath in anticipation of what was coming next.

'He called her a slag and he used the f-word first. Then he used the c-word. I'm not saying it. It makes my teeth itch, but you know the one I mean. He said it was her fault he was losing everything. I think he was hoping that Sienna's savings were going to get him out of a hole. He did mention that she had some money in an ISA that she'd saved up for a house deposit. It wasn't just about the money though. While on the phone, he ranted about her sleeping with someone else. I don't know who the man was, but Gerard had seen her with him. I think he'd been following her otherwise how would he know these things? He seems the stalker type. He loves himself, he's a narcissist and he seem to worship every chauvinist, using a men's rights group as a front on the internet. He wears designer clothes that I know he couldn't afford on his salary and his teeth, the man is as vain as hell. But the way he spoke to her – I'll never forget that. He lost it on that call.'

There was a lot to process, and Gina knew that she had to get Hale to the station as soon as possible. He seemed to know that Sienna had moved on and he was angry. Sienna and Robbie had been murdered. Tiffany Crawford niggled at the back of Gina's mind. She still needed to work out if the cases were connected. 'Would you come into Cleevesford Police Station to give a statement after work?'

Saffi nodded. 'It's not ideal going on record as I have to work with the man, but yes. I'll do it for Sienna. There is one other thing, but I can't go on the record with it so stop writing in your pad.'

Wyre popped the notebook in her bag.

'He cornered me one day, in the stationery cupboard, way before he started seeing Sienna. I've never felt so scared. For weeks, he'd been asking me out for a drink, but I had no interest in him. I didn't even like him and I thought I'd conveyed that fact well but instead of deterring him, he saw me as more of a challenge. He forced me against the shelving, and I felt his erection through his trousers. He began slobbering on my neck and I don't know how but I managed to get him off me. The whole shelf came down in the struggle. As I reached for the door to let myself out, he grabbed me and he said if I told anyone he'd say that I'd been harassing him, sexually, and that he'd get me sacked.' The woman looked down at her shiny black heels.

'What he did to you was serious. Do you want to report it now?'

She shook her head. 'I hurt him. In the struggle, I managed to break one of his toes and he also said he'd then report me for attacking him because I brought the shelf down on him. Problem is, a few years ago I got into a fight. It was stupid really. I was drunk and I found out that my friend had slept with my then boyfriend. Cut a long story short, I punched her, got a caution, she forgave me and now we're friends again. I was nineteen and stupid but that gave me a history of violence. I've never hurt anyone before that or since. If I report him and he goes not guilty, I'll get torn apart. He will just say that I fancied him, he rejected me, and I attacked him. He said he'd tell everyone I was a crazy bitch. I only told you about what happened to me so that you knew the type of person you're dealing with. I hope it helps you, but I won't say any of that on record, ever. I think it shows that he was capable of hurting Sienna. You can get your notebook back out now.'

Gina suspected they had all they were going to get. They thanked Saffi and headed out, knowing that she'd be interviewed again later.

As they approached Gina's car, Wyre stopped. 'What did you make of that, guv?'

'I know we need to interview Gerard Hale. I can't believe

that Robbie Shields has gone from suspect to victim, and Tiffany Crawford is confusing me. I checked my messages. PC Smith has been to see her, and he's organised for some officers to go back and fit a panic button in her home. We need a deeper background check on Mr Hale. Did you manage to speak to someone at the station?'

Wyre nodded. 'O'Connor had just got back from the post-mortem, so he's checking out Honey Pots with PC Ahmed. They did say the witness has arrived and he wants to speak to us about seeing Robbie Shields on the night of Sienna's murder.'

She checked her watch. 'Let's get back. If he has something crucial to say, we'll be the first to hear it.'

TWENTY-TWO

Gina finished checking her emails then she sent a message to Jacob, asking him how he was feeling. She followed the link to Tiffany's file. There was a knock at her office door and Wyre peered through the gap. 'Cheesy twist? Mrs O sent these in, and she sends her best for the big case.'

Gina nodded. 'Yes, please.' She took the pastry from Wyre and bit into it. 'Wow, all butter, just what I needed. Take a seat. I'm just going through the Tiffany Crawford file.'

'I spoke to PC Smith, and he said that the panic alarm has been fitted in her flat. He noted how scared and nervous she seemed.'

Gina scanned the notes and interviews from the original case. 'I'm not surprised reading this.' She looked away from the screen and placed the half-eaten cheese twist on her desk.

'What is it?'

Shaking her head, Gina continued reading. 'It was a horrendous attack. Her husband was away with friends, so she was alone. Someone entered through an upstairs window that had a faulty catch. Her husband had left a set of wooden ladders outside, resting alongside the house after he'd been cleaning the windows. The perpetrator crept in. She awoke to see someone staring at her in the dark, wearing a balaclava. When she went to reach for her phone, it wasn't there, and she could only conclude that he'd already taken it. It was later found in the spare bedroom.' Gina bit the edge of her nail. Her heart began to thrum as she read on. Strangulation was one of her personal triggers. Her abusive dead ex-husband used to grip her by the neck until she went blue. She'd never felt happier to see anyone as dead as him after he'd tumbled down their stairs.

'And?'

Gina scrunched her brows as she continued. 'In the statement, she says she tried to talk to him, and she begged him to take anything he wanted from the house, but he then pinned her down. He stabbed her in the back of the neck with a spiky earring and she never knew why. The officers who took the original statement mentioned what a strange thing that was for her attacker to do. She tried to fight him off, but he sat on her and within seconds, he had a scarf wrapped around her neck and he pulled. She goes on to describe how she fought and eventually, she managed to punch him in the neck. It took his breath away. He stumbled out of the room and left through the front door. She describes how she watched him running off into the darkness and seconds later she heard a car pull away.'

'Where did she live at the time?'

Gina turned her screen around so that Wyre could see the details. 'Webheath, in Redditch.' She pulled up a map. 'Look at where she lived. This was her house.' Gina pointed. 'To the left is a road and I know this road leads to a maze of single track, country lanes. He knew how to avoid ANPR.' She knew that no vehicle of any relevance had been picked up by automatic number plate recognition. No one saw a car that shouldn't be parked up at the time and no one saw this man. 'All I can say was that the perp must have known the area well to avoid detection like he did.'

'What about the neighbours?' Wyre pulled her chair in closer.

Gina clicked on another file. 'No one reported seeing anything. At the time, Kieron Crawford mentioned an old boyfriend of Tiffany's, one who apparently didn't treat her that well, but the man had a concrete alibi. There were no other suspects, and the case remains unsolved. No notable forensics were found, suggesting that the perp was forensically aware. There were no fingerprints, but Tiffany did say he wore gloves. He left nothing, not a jot.' Gina opened the photo files. 'Look at this.'

Wyre stared wide-eyed. 'That's not the actual scarf used, is it?'

Gina read the notes underneath. 'No, it's an exact copy of the scarf that the attacker used to strangle her with. She'd bought it from Primark the week before and it was missing from the scene. He took it with him after he attacked her.'

'And it's the same scarf that was used to strangle Sienna Moorcroft.'

Gina nodded. 'It's identical and it's at least four years old. I doubt Primark still sell them now. He takes a trophy, then he uses it in his next attack. That's his personal signature. And look at this, the earring he stabbed her with didn't belong to Tiffany.'

Wyre blew out a breath. 'Do you think it was taken in a previous attack?'

Gina nodded. 'I suspect we have a serial strangler and he's escalated to murder. We need to share this with the team now, and then we need to look for any other similar unsolved crimes. To prove this theory right, we need to find an unsolved attack, involving strangulation, where an earring was taken. It's a long shot, I know. Our killer is getting more dangerous by the minute, and we need to stop him before he attacks again.'

TWENTY-THREE

After everyone had been updated in the incident room, Wyre followed Gina into interview room one. 'It's great that DCI Briggs has agreed to link Tiffany Crawford's attack to the murders of Sienna Moorcroft and Robbie Shields,' Wyre said as they walked.

'It is.' Gina opened the interview room door and smiled at the middle-aged man who was pulling at his long hair. He dropped a strand onto the floor before searching for another one with his tobacco-stained fingertips. 'Mr Sallis. Thank you for coming in,' Gina said as she and Wyre sat opposite him. She explained that they'd be taping the interview and Wyre started the tape rolling and made the introductions.

'I don't know if it's worth taping. It's just something small really. I caught the end of the news earlier. When I saw the appeal for that man, err Robbie something, I knew I had to call.' He dropped another hair on the floor.

News of Robbie Shields's murder hadn't broken yet, but she knew from the briefing that his brother, who was also his next-of-kin, had been contacted. 'I'm sorry to say that you may have been the last person to see Mr Shields alive.'

'You mean he's dead? I thought he was just missing.' He furrowed his brows and scratched his stubble. 'What do you need to know, and I'll do my best to help.'

Wyre opened the paper file and passed Gina his details. She quickly scanned the page, taking in all the key pieces of information. 'You work at Happy Drinker's Wine Shop, the one on the corner of Link Street. Is that correct?' Gina knew that Link Street was a short walk away from Robbie and Lauren's bungalow.

'Yes, I'm the manager and I was working there alone on Saturday night. I have passed the CCTV to one of your officers so you can get exact times. The footage is timestamped.'

'Thank you for that. That will help us a lot. Can you tell us what happened, from the moment you saw Mr Shields, until he left.'

The man nodded and pulled his chair closer to the table. 'I was sweeping up. We open until ten at night, but we don't get a lot of customers in that late. He came in around nine thirty. He grabbed a bottle of White Zinfandel and I remember him loitering, so I offered him some help. When he turned to face me, I thought he was going to pull a knife out because he just stared. It wouldn't be the first time that's happened. Robbers seem to think we have a ton of cash in the till, but the truth of it is we mostly take card payments. Anyway, at first, he looked like he was on something but then his demeanour mellowed, and I could see that he seemed upset, almost teary. I knew I'd misjudged him. I asked if he was okay, and he shrugged and slammed the wine on the counter. He said that his life was over.' The man paused.

'Did he leave then?' Gina wondered for a moment if he knew what lay ahead for him.

Mr Sallis shook his head. 'I tried to engage with him. My first thought was that he might be suicidal, and I wanted to make sure he was okay before he left. I told him that every problem could be solved, well I said something like that. I said that he shouldn't be too hard on himself. Really, I had no idea what to say. I sell wine. I'm not a therapist, but I did my best. He then looked at me, slammed a ten-pound note on the counter and hurried off. I found the whole encounter strange and I really worried that I'd said something wrong. When I went home, I told my wife and that night, I struggled to sleep because what he said played on my mind. There was something seriously wrong and now you tell me he's dead. He knew his life was over. He knew he was going to die.'

Gina mulled over the man's statement. Had Robbie Shields known what was going to happen to him or was he upset that Sienna was going to tell Lauren about their child? 'Did you see him leave?'

'Oh, yes, he headed left out of the shop, and he looked to be on foot. We only have two parking places outside, and neither were taken. He carried on walking all the way to the end of the road. If he came by car, he would have parked close by, and I'd have seen him get into a car.'

Gina visualised the wine shop and Robbie leaving. Robbie had taken the fastest route back home on foot.

'There is something else.' Mr Sallis nervously pulled another hair out.

'Was this after he came into your shop?'

The man nodded. 'I decided to close early. At about quarter to ten, I locked up, got into my car and started driving home. When I got to the end of the road, I saw him kicking a lamppost, so I pulled up at the junction and watched him. He smashed the wine against it and hurried off through the houses flinging his arms in the air, in a frustrated way. A part of me thought I should pull over, but I didn't. Now I wish I had. Did he die by suicide?'

Gina passed the notes back to Wyre to pop back into the file. 'No, please don't feel that you didn't do enough. It was kind of you to ask him how he was. Have you ever seen Mr Shields before?'

He shook his head. 'No. But I thought I recognised the woman, the other victim that was on the local news. I saw that report just before leaving to come here. Or maybe it wasn't her who I saw. My glance at the TV screen was brief. I didn't really catch the whole report as I was rushing out the door.'

Pulling a photo of Sienna from another file, she handed it to Mr Sallis and spoke for the tape. 'I'm handing Mr Sallis a photo of Sienna Moorcroft. Is this the woman you recognise? Take a long look.'

He took the photo and gazed at it for a few seconds. 'You know, I'm sure it is. Yes, it was her. I'm so sorry. I wished I'd seen the news report in full but then again, I'm here now so you can ask me about her too. She came into the shop earlier on the Saturday and I remember her buying a ready-mixed cocktail in a can and a small bottle of cola. Oh, and I think she bought crisps.'

'What time was this?'

'I can't remember. Sometime in the afternoon, maybe after five thirty. I'll check the CCTV later and send it to you.'

'What was she wearing?'

'A short black dress, no jacket. I kept thinking that she must be cold.'

'Was she wearing a scarf?'

He closed his eyes for a few seconds and tapped his fingers on the table before opening them again. 'No.'

Gina needed to rule out that the flowery scarf did belong to Sienna. 'Was she with anyone?'

'Well, I did get curious. She was all dressed up. It can get boring in the shop, so I do tend to people watch and make up little stories in my head about their lives. It passes the time. When she left the shop, she hurried across the road in her heels and got into the passenger side of a dark saloon car, which drove off a couple of minutes later.'

'Does your CCTV cover that area?'

'No. It only covers the inside of the shop and the pavement directly in front of it. The cameras used to capture the road and beyond, but the people living opposite complained about their privacy. It wasn't worth the hassle, so we had its line of sight adjusted.'

Flicking through the paperwork, she tried to find out what type of car Gerard Hale drove, but she didn't have that information to hand. She knew that Robbie Shields owned a black VW Passat so that put him in the picture. Then she remembered being told that Hale drove a black saloon and a black four-by-four. Gina wondered if one was a company car. She needed to check. 'Can you describe the driver?'

'No, but I did see a silhouette of them both. She leaned in and they kissed passionately, like a pair of teenagers. They were too far away for me to even begin to describe him, that's if it was a man; that would be me assuming. It could have been anyone.' He scrunched his brow. 'There was something else.'

'What is it?'

'There was an altercation after they kissed. I saw a hand come up. She then slapped her companion before he or she pulled away. They must have been arguing, at least I think that's what I saw. The driver sped off, literally burning rubber.'

'Is there anything else you can think of, about them, or the car?'

'The back bumper and the tyres were muddy. I don't know why I remembered that. Actually, yes, I do. My wife is always accusing me of being borderline obsessive about keeping our car clean.'

Gina thought back to Robbie Shields's car. She didn't remember it looking muddy, but she knew that Gerard Hale lived on a campsite and that he parked a little out of the way and walked to the caravan. She wondered how rural the surrounding roads were. She tried to picture the route in her head. There was a small ford on one road, a severely boggy ford.

TWENTY-FOUR

NANCY

Nancy passed Lauren a bowl of lentil soup on a tray. The air filled with the scent of cumin and garlic, and all the other lovely ingredients she'd added to make it as tasty and warming as possible. Her spice rack made all the difference.

'Thanks, Mum.' Lauren placed her new phone down after constantly tapping away on it for the last hour.

'How are you, love?' She sat on the pouffe, the one she normally put her feet on.

Lauren shrugged. 'I can't remember Max or Dee's numbers and I can't remember my logins for Facebook or Instagram. They don't use TikTok so I can't message them there either. I've just set up a new account and friend requested Maxine, but I look like a weird spammer.' Tears drizzled down Lauren's cheeks. 'I'm lost, so friggin' lost. I just want this nightmare to end.'

Nancy placed a loving hand on her daughter's arm. 'You've had a traumatic couple of days. The police are going to find whoever did this, I promise.'

Sobbing, Lauren placed the tray on the coffee table. 'But I'll still feel like this. I trusted Sienna and I was going to marry

Robbie. Why do I keep making the same stupid mistakes in life? Why do I trust all the wrong people?'

Nancy didn't have an answer to that. She'd tried her best to protect Lauren and could see through everyone who'd ever hurt her daughter but as usual, Lauren never listened to any of her concerns. Nancy daren't tell her that just now. It wasn't the right time and the last thing she needed was an argument. Instead, she grabbed a box of tissues and placed them on the sofa next to Lauren.

'What am I doing wrong? What did I do to deserve this?'

'It's not you, sweetheart. It's them.'

Lauren's phone flashed. She unplugged the charger and stared at it. 'It's Max, she's accepted me.' Lauren began typing away on the tiny phone.

'I'll leave you to it.' Nancy walked into the kitchen and poured herself a ladle of soup. Fifi ran into the kitchen and began to bark at the back door. She walked over and went to turn the key. The door hadn't been locked. She let the dog out and hurried back into the living room. 'Lauren, did you let Fifi out earlier and forget to lock the back door?'

She stopped typing. 'Err, maybe, I don't know. I don't think I'd have forgotten but maybe I did. Sorry, Mum. My mind's all over the place. If it's unlocked and you didn't leave it unlocked, it must have been me.'

Fingers shaking, Nancy clenched her fists by her side. 'You must be more careful, okay. You know what happened to Sienna and Robbie!'

'I said I was sorry. There's no need to shout, besides no one knows where you live. I don't even think Robbie could have got here without me directing him and none of my friends have been here. We're safe, Mum. Chill.'

Storming out, Nancy had to leave the room before she said any more. The last thing she would ever do was burden Lauren with her problems right now. The messages were getting to her and the person sending them knew full well she couldn't tell the police.

She hurried back to the kitchen and glanced out of the window. Fifi had gone. She opened the door and called the little dog, but she couldn't even hear Fifi's barks or snuffling in the undergrowth. She stepped out onto the cobbled path that led all the way to the back gate. She wished she had a security light right now. 'Fifi.' She held out her phone, torch shining ahead, lighting up the open gate. A gentle breeze sent a shiver across the back of her neck as the plastic covering over the garden furniture flapped in the breeze. 'Fifi.'

'Mum, the WiFi's down,' Lauren called.

She glanced back. Lauren hadn't even come into the kitchen to tell her that. She'd merely bellowed her words at the top of her voice in the hope that Nancy would hear. Nancy had locked the back gate earlier, she was sure, or was she? Yes, she was sure. Doubting herself wasn't helping the situation. The slide lock had been pulled across at lunchtime. Creeping forward, she held her breath. Out the back were acres of trees and uphill land. The quietness which was always most welcome now gave off threatening wilderness vibes. There were no other houses close by at the base of the Malvern Hills. The only way was up, through the dense woodland followed by hill upon hill. She heard rustling coming from the bushes ahead. 'Fifi, come out now. Bad girl. Mummy's not happy that you're making her do this.'

She knew coming out in her slippers had been a bad move. If she had to run wearing her flimsy open-backed footwear, she'd be falling all over the place or worse, they'd fall off and her feet would get slashed by all the twigs and stones below. The light from the torch on her phone wavered as she gripped the gadget in her shaking hand.

The phone beeped. She opened the message.

Scream Bitch. Scream!!!

She heard Fifi yelp and that was followed by her own whimper, as she dropped the phone and turned to run. That's when she tripped over her own feet, flew through the air and landed hard on a rock. A shadow of a person approached but she couldn't make out any features as she rubbed her throbbing elbow, then she screamed and screamed, knowing that she couldn't protect herself and that meant her daughter was in trouble too.

TWENTY-FIVE

'O'Connor, many thanks to you and Kapoor for being present at the post-mortem today. How did you get on?' Gina smiled at the trainee. She knew her first post-mortem would be a tough one.

'I kept my food down, guv. So, all is good.'

'Great to hear. Can you and PC Ahmed prep the team of officers together. We have a warrant and we're going to the caravan park tonight. If Gerard Hale is in the country, we will be bringing him in. I want his car located so we need to check the surrounding roads. Officially, he's not meant to be on the site until March, but we know he's staying there. Did you check if he had any other cars?' She'd come out of the interview and tasked O'Connor and Kapoor with that as soon as they arrived back.

Kapoor smiled and nodded. 'Certainly did, guv. Hale only owns his four-by-four, but his mother owns a Mercedes Saloon, which he's insured to drive.'

'That makes sense as Patsy Griffin, Sienna's landlady, mentioned that he drove a black saloon and a black four-by-four. Great work. We have two boys to interview. O'Connor can you and PC Smith interview Nathan. His father is with him and they're waiting in the family room?'

'Yes, guv.' O'Connor crunched on a cheese twist, then glugged from his water bottle.

'Wyre, you and I will speak to the other lad, Finn. Both boys are only thirteen and had been bunking off school. Treat them gently. It must have been a huge shock for them, finding a body. Are we all clear on what's happening next?'

There was a hum of yesses before everyone left the room. Briggs entered and raised his eyebrows at Gina. She knew he had something to say to her. 'I'll catch up with you in a minute,' Gina said.

'I'll go and prep Finlay Jones and his mother for interview. See you in five.' Wyre left them alone in the room.

'Is everything okay?'

'I'm not sure. I'm a bit worried about Jacob.' Briggs let out a deep breath.

'What's happened?'

He closed the doors for privacy and gently pulled her to the side. 'I've been speaking to Bernard, mostly about the case.'

'And?'

'Jennifer has been staying in his spare room. She moved out and left Jacob.'

'I knew it. He didn't seem right yesterday. I could see there was more going on than a dodgy takeaway.'

'Anyway, I've had an email from him, and he said he won't be in for the foreseeable and has requested urgent leave. He's popping by in the morning to grab some of his personal things.'

'What?' Gina knew a relationship breakdown wouldn't be easy on him. He doted on Jennifer. 'But he loves his job.'

Briggs shrugged.

'I need him.' Gina relied on Jacob for a lot. He was her right hand in every investigation. She needed him on the case they were working on, and she liked him, a lot.

'I guess we'll know more in the morning. Maybe you can speak to him?'

'Yes, definitely. I don't want to lose Jacob. I know he's upset, and he must feel lost without Jennifer, but he has to know we're more than just his colleagues. We're his friends. We're like family.' She puffed out a breath and placed her hands on her hips.

Briggs checked his watch. 'Look, we'll talk more about this later. It's getting on. Go and speak to the boy, hurry up at the caravan park and when you get home, I'll have a really nice dinner on the go. I'll head to mine in a bit, pick Jessie up and I'll go to yours, okay?'

She nodded, glad that he was bringing his dog as his dog-sitting neighbour was away for a week. 'Okay.' She turned and hurried out, heading to the interview room. She hated speaking to children in such rooms, but O'Connor was already interviewing the other boy in the family room. All she could do was try her best to put him at ease. As she entered, Wyre introduced them all for the tape and Gina opened the file on the desk. 'Ms Jones, thank you for waiting, and thank you too, Finlay. Is it okay if I call you Finlay?' She smiled at the boy.

'Finn. I hate Finlay.' His round face and button-shaped nose made him look like he was around ten years old.

'Finn it is. Can you talk me through your morning, from when you got to the field?'

He nodded and glanced up at his mother.

'Just tell them the truth, Finn. I won't be angry about anything.' She placed an arm around her son.

'I'm sorry, Mum. I know I should have been on the bus.'

The woman raised her eyebrows. 'We'll talk about that later.'

He looked up at Gina while picking at the thread on his jumper sleeve. 'Me and Nath were just playing about. We kicked a can on the field and thought we'd go and hang out and sit on the pallets. We go there a lot. When we got there, I saw the rug and thought it had just been dumped. People always dump old things there as it's close to the road. I kicked it and that's when I saw an arm slip out. I know I shouldn't have picked up the wallet, but I did. I picked it up before I knew someone was wrapped in that rug. Am I in trouble?'

'No, you're not in any trouble at all. Forensics know that you picked the wallet up.'

The boy began rooting in his pockets then he stood and began to dig deeper. 'There's a hole in my pocket.'

'What are you doing, Finn? We can worry about that later.'

'Got it.' Finn pulled out a fifty pence piece encrusted in mud and placed it on the table. 'I should have given this to the police lady earlier. Sorry.'

The boy's cheeks had reddened. Gina leaned forward a little and spoke in a gentle tone. 'For the tape, Finn Jones has placed a fifty pence coin encrusted with dried mud on the table. Did you find this at the scene?'

He nodded. 'There was a pound coin too, but it was smaller, so I've lost it through the hole. We just thought someone had lost a bit of change and we were going to spend it at the shop.'

'Well, thank you for giving it to us.' Gina placed a pair of latex gloves over her fingers. She took the coin and placed it in an evidence bag before passing it to Wyre to catalogue for the lab. Something told her that Finn was holding back, and it was about something bigger than a couple of coins. She knew that the officer who turned up on the scene reported the smell of cigarettes. Maybe that's why he was looking a little worried. 'You saw the rug and you kicked it, and then you saw the arm? Is that right?'

'Yes.'

'In your earlier statement, you said you heard something after that, something that scared you.'

He nodded. 'Nath had run off and I was on my own. He didn't go far, just away from the pallets. Behind me was a few bushes and trees and after that there is a road. I could just about see people passing by, but I heard someone lurking the other side. The bushes were too thick for me to see who it was but there was someone there. I stood on one side of the bushes and whoever was there, stood at the other side. I could hear them breathing. I didn't know what to do. That's when I called you, Mum. I asked them who they were then they ran away. I heard the branches crunching as they went. I really thought I was going to get hurt. Someone put that man there and all I could think of was, they were going to kill me.' His eyes looked a little wet. 'I'm scared, Mum.'

The woman leaned over and hugged her son.

A few minutes later, the interview was wrapped up. Finn had nothing more to tell them. She waved at Kapoor who was putting her stab vest on. 'We're ready to go, guv. We've informed the site owner and told him to stay in his house and not go anywhere near the caravan.'

'Great. If Hale is there, we'll have him in an interview room before we know it, but we need to be careful. If he is our murderer, he's killed twice and possibly attacked others. That makes him dangerous. Let's go.'

TWENTY-SIX

After an extensive search of the area, no one had seen Gerard Hale's four-by-four parked anywhere. Now it was time to close in on the caravan. Gina pulled up underneath a lamppost. She held up the map that Kapoor had printed off, using the light shining through the windscreen to read it. The owner had confirmed that Gerard and his mother jointly owned the caravan on plot fifty-six. She knew that she and Wyre were currently on the road at the back of the caravan. They'd have to jump over a tiny brook and stealthily head alongside the naked foliage, while uniform did their bit by surrounding the structure. 'You ready?'

'Ready as I'll ever be.' Wyre tapped her stab vest and stepped out of the car.

Gina followed her towards the brook. The sound of trickling water led the way. No torches. If Hale was there and he saw them coming before the officers were in place, he might run. They couldn't let him go. She stood on the bank of the brook. 'It's wider than I thought.'

Wyre took several steps back, sprinted, leaped and landed on the other side like an Olympian. Her fit colleague was always going to make it. 'It's not as hard as it looks. Come on, guv. You've got this.'

The last thing Gina wanted was to end up falling in freezing cold water on a chilly night when the night's work had only just started. She glanced ahead, taking in the light shuffling sounds of approaching officers on the other side of the water. She jogged backwards, took a deep breath and ran with all she had and as soon as she reached the edge, she leaped into the crisp air. As she landed on the other side, she missed her footing and slipped on the hard soil below. 'Ouch.'

'Damn, you okay?' Wyre hurried over and helped her up.

Gina laughed. 'Not as young and nimble as I used to be but, yes, I'm good. No broken bones.' She stood and stretched out her aching leg and side.

Wyre walked ahead. 'There's a light on in the caravan.'

She hurried over to Wyre and watched as uniform moved in closer. If Hale jumped out of any window, Gina knew they'd have him. There was no escape for Hale. Heart racing as adrenaline coursed through her body, Gina straightened her waterproof jacket and began walking slowly alongside Wyre to the front door.

The structure looked to be at least twenty-five metres long. An officer shone his torch in the direction of the beige-checked curtains. All of them were closed so no one could peer in. Decking surrounded the whole caravan with moss-smeared steps leading up to the only door. Gina squatted, flashing her torch to peer underneath the caravan but all she could see was a rusty old lawn mower. If he'd have darted out from there, he wouldn't have made it to the end of the cutesy little path or the washing line. She nodded to PC Ahmed. That was his cue to go. 'Police, open up. We have a warrant to enter,' he shouted, after banging several times on the door. He shook his head a few seconds later.

They were going to have to enter by force. She gave him the nod again.

'Mr Hale, we're coming in. Please stand back from the door.' With that PC Ahmed slammed the battering ram at the metal door and it instantly gave. Several uniformed officers entered and seconds later, PC Ahmed came back out. 'It's empty, guv, but you need to see the second bedroom.'

She sighed. They should have waited and scoped the place out covertly. At least they had officers discreetly parked up near the entrance. Hale would be picked up if he returned and he wouldn't even know they were in his van. She waited for the officers to come out before heading up the wooden steps then inside, with Wyre. Kapoor called all the officers over to discuss what would happen next.

Gina stood in the compact kitchen, snapped on a pair of latex gloves and turned right. She opened the door that led to a dark, woody-smelling corridor. The first door on the right led to a tiny bathroom. The sound of dripping came from inside the shower cubicle. She opened the door and saw that there was a leak. The dried-up flannel and dry towels told her that no one had showered recently. With each step they took, the floor creaked, like it might give.

She nudged open the far door and as expected, it led to the master bedroom. The bed was made, and the room smelled of lavender.

'This must be the second bedroom.' Wyre pointed to the last door.

Gina pressed the handle and pushed it open to reveal a tiny room containing two small single beds and overhead storage. That's when she saw the corkboard full of pinned pictures of Sienna and next to it was a small whiteboard. It had a list of locations written on it, mostly coffee shops and pubs. He'd also written down Lauren and Robbie's address. On one bed the quilt and undersheet was all disturbed, and a pile of clothes filled the one corner of the tiny room. 'We need those bagged up in a minute. If he killed Sienna and Robbie, they might be teeming with forensic evidence.' She reached down and picked up the refill pad that lay on the pillow.

'What's in it?'

'He's been stalking Sienna. He talks about her meeting up with a man at cafés mostly. Oh goodness.'

'What is it?'

She cleared her throat and began to read. 'It says, "That bitch. She's nothing but a cheap whore and to think I thought I could marry that. She's not going to get away with what she did to me, and she lied. All that time she was with him too. The plan. Make her pay. Follow her, fuck with her head. She deserves it." Then—'

'What is it?'

Gina realised she was staring at the emoji. 'There's a doodle of a gun. He wanted her dead.' She read the passage again and it almost took her breath away. From what Gina had heard, they'd had a whirlwind romance that resulted in Sienna moving in with Gerard without giving it much thought. He must have started out charming to make her move that quick and to think, all he wanted to do was trap her, own her and take her money to solve his own problems.

She gasped a little. It sounded much like the start of her relationship with Terry all those years ago. What is visible on the surface is nothing like what is going on in their heads. These manipulators always have a plan. They know how to erode self-worth and to control. Sienna had escaped him at the onset, but he'd lingered around and stalked her, refusing to let her go.

'Let's run through this theory. Sienna met up with someone earlier that day and went to the wine shop. Maybe it was Robbie, maybe it wasn't. At some point, she had sex, but we don't know who she had sex with. Sienna goes to see Robbie at the bungalow as soon as Lauren has left. Maybe they had sex.

Maybe she then tried to pressure Robbie to tell Lauren about their daughter. In a state, he popped out to clear his head and get some wine, leaving her at the bungalow. Frustrated and furious, he smashed the bottle in a temper. On returning, he found that Hale was already there and that he'd killed Sienna. We know that Hale was following Sienna. The address of the bungalow is written on his board. Maybe Hale watched Robbie leave and in a fit of jealously knocked on the door. Sienna might have thought that Robbie had forgotten his key. Hale then entered and killed her. Robbie then returned to the chaos and he's in the way so maybe Hale locked him in the cupboard while he finished with Sienna. After, he knocked Robbie out and wrapped him in the rug. Hale could have used Robbie's car to deliver the body to his own car before returning the car to the drive. The mustard-coloured fibres in Robbie's boot show that the rug had been in there. Hale knew time was running out and that he'd have to deal with Robbie later, so he quickly cleaned the bits of the car he used. He didn't leave much evidence. There were no fingerprints so I'm guessing he knew what to do. He gloved up, kept his hair under a hat. It was a calculated attack.'

'And there was someone lurking at the property when Lauren arrived back from her night out.' Wyre opened one of the cupboards as she spoke.

'He may have come back to look for the nail file and on hearing her, scurried off. He didn't hurt her because she didn't see him, and she wasn't his target.'

'What about the case of Tiffany Crawford? How does Hale fit in?'

Gina exhaled. 'I wonder if she knew Hale. That's a link we're going to have to investigate, see where the evidence leads.'

Wyre pulled out a folded pile of clothes that looked like they belonged to Hale's mother, then her hand got caught in a pair of tights and a scarf. She opened the next cupboard and there were more scarves, all silky and decorated with beautiful animal and botanical prints. 'Guv, there are scarves, and lots of them.'

'Do we know where his mother lives?'

'Not offhand but the man who runs the site will have her details for billing as she and Gerard are joint owners.'

'We need to speak to her. I know we have this link with the flowery scarf and Tiffany Crawford's attack, but we can't rule out that one of Ms Hale's scarves was used to strangle Sienna. It is possible that she owned the same scarf. We need to ask her if she recognises the print, if it was hers and if it is and it's missing. If she answers yes, we have him.'

TWENTY-SEVEN

TIFFANY

She's watching him from afar but it's like she's above him, looking down. Maybe she's flying. For some reason, she has it in her head that he has all the answers but when she tries to scrunch her eyes to focus, all she can see is a shadow. Chills run through her, a bit like when she had the flu that one time. She can't stop shaking. She closes her eyes, not wanting to be taken down this path again. There's nothing she can do to stop it; however hard she fights the fear bursts from her ribcage. Silence surrounds her. It's not right. She was in a town. There were cars and the sound of people out and about, walking at night. Slowly, she prises her eyes open. That's when she sees him. He's above her and she sees the blue flowers, but she can't breathe as she drowns in them. So many flowers.

Panic floods her body. She closes her eyes again. That's when she hears Kieron shouting at her to stop. Hands taut; she screams out. On opening her eyes, she sees blood, lots of blood. She's killed him.

'Tiffany, stop it.'

'What, where am I?' She scrunched her brow and stared up at the moon.

'Ouch.' Kieron holds his hand under his bleeding nose.

'What happened?'

'I know I shouldn't approach you when you're sleepwalking, but you were about to step in that broken glass. You hit me in the face.'

She glanced down at her hand to see blood dripping from her fingers. 'I'm so sorry. I can't believe—' She didn't know what to say. She hadn't meant to hurt him again.

'It's okay, Tiff. It was an accident. You were asleep and my nose will be okay. It's not as bad as it looks.' He removed his hand. The bleeding had at least stopped but that didn't make her feel any better about herself.

What was she doing around the back of the flats, next to the dustbins? 'How did I get here.' She trembled and hugged herself as she stood in her pyjamas. On looking down, she could see that a blackened banana skin had worked its way between her toes. She kicked out and let out a slight scream as it hit the fence.

'It's okay, darling. Come here.' Kieron pulled off his coat and threw it over her shoulders.

That's when she noticed that he was in his lounge pants and bed T-shirt. 'Were we in bed? What time is it?'

'It's two in the morning.' He tried to lead her back towards their flat.

She shrugged him off.

'Tiff, come inside. It's cold. You'll get hypothermia.'

She shook her head, a few strands of her hair sticking to her cold damp cheek. 'My brain, it's trying to tell me something, but I can't work out what. I don't know what's going on.' Tears slid down her face.

'It's just a nightmare and you sleepwalked. That's all. Tiff, I'm freezing, and you have nothing on your feet.'

She glanced around and stared at the chinks of broken glass on the pavement. Lifting one of her feet up, she checked for any cuts but all she could see was dirt. She nodded and reached out to hold his hand, allowing him to lead her back into the warmth. A small sob escaped her lips. 'It was him. I saw him and he was trying to kill me. I thought you were him before I woke up. I'm losing my mind.'

Once in the flat, he helped her to a chair in the living room and kneeled in front of her. He took her bed socks from the couch and put them on her icy cold feet. 'There. Let's get you warmed up. Do you want a tea or hot chocolate?'

She nodded. 'Hot chocolate.' As soon as he left, she lifted her feet onto the chair and pulled them close to her body as she trembled away. She tried to think back over the evening, but as hard as she tried, she couldn't remember getting to bed. That's when she saw the empty wine glass on the coffee table and the blister pack of diazepam tablets. As she went to grab it, Kieron came back in and took it off her. 'Please don't. I am so worried about you at the moment, it hurts.'

'I wasn't.' She paused. 'When did you get home from work?'

He shrugged and placed the hot chocolate on the table. 'The usual time, about six. When I got back, I saw those.' He pointed to the wine and tablets.

'I only had one.'

He raised his brows. 'The pills are screwing you up because you're taking too many and I'm scared one day I'll come home and find you—' He took a deep breath.

She knew he was making sense. It had been stupid to drink with them. That's why she had no recollection of the evening. She'd been all woozy and sleepy, but she was sure she hadn't drunk the whole bottle of wine. She only had a glass. 'Did you say empty bottle?'

He nodded.

'I only had a glass.'

Kieron sighed. 'We're going to get through this okay. We're going to get you the help you need, I promise.'

'I can't just get through this,' she snapped, tears falling down her cheeks. 'Every time I close my eyes, I see him in our bedroom trying to strangle me to death. And now, we have this stupid panic button because even the police think he might come back. You don't understand. You never have done, and you never will.' In an instant, she regretted saying all that to Kieron. He had been her rock. He'd nursed her on days when the pain got too much, when her physical health had been at its worst. He'd been reassuring during her anxiety attacks. He tried to encourage her to eat wholesome healthy food and to make sure she took her vitamins. She had violently attacked him twice now, and still he stood by her, always believing that she could and would get better. 'I'm sorry. That was a horrible thing to say.'

He sat on the arm of the chair and placed an arm around her. 'I love you, Tiff. I know what you went through was horrendous, but wine won't help, tablets won't help and not looking after yourself won't help. The police will catch him and when they do, everything will be better, and I'll always be here for you. Promise me, no more abusing your body. This can't happen again.'

'I promise.' She reached out, picked up the cup of hot chocolate and took a sip. It was lovely and milky. After gulping it all down, she popped the cup back on the table.

'Shall we go to bed now, try to get a bit more sleep. I have work in the morning, and I don't want to go in looking like a zombie.'

Work, she knew he had to go, and she hated him leaving her, but they couldn't afford for him to stay at home. 'Yes, and I'll try not to escape out the door again or hurt you. Is your nose okay?'

He shrugged. 'It was just a little knock. I pulled the chain across before coming to bed but somehow you managed to remove it, so I'll put a chair against the bedroom door when we go back to bed. If you try to leave, I'll hear you moving it.'

'Can we get some more locks for the front door? I don't want this to happen again, and we can't go to bed every night with a chair against the door.'

He kissed her head as they reached the bedroom. 'I'll sort it this week if you think it's for the best. Can't have the love of my life stepping onto glass or getting mown down by a car, can we? I do worry.'

She knew the pressure she was putting on him was immense and she was grateful for all of his help. How he'd stuck by her, she'd never know. After washing the blood off her hands, they were tucked up in bed. She lay there listening to Kieron's gentle snores. Her heart hammered away as she stared at the ceiling in the dark. The loss of control she was experiencing was scarier than her attack ever was. As hard as she tried, she couldn't remember drinking all that wine, she couldn't remember going to bed and she couldn't remember how she got to the bins. Palpitations filled her chest, and her throat began to throb with the ferocity of them. Her muscles itched to be moved and her stomach began to churn. She could remember something; her weird dream had triggered a memory. She knew she had walked to Lauren and Robbie's bungalow on the night of the murder. At first it only felt like a dream, but now, she was certain it was real. Images of her strangler began to further intrude on her thoughts. He'd made her the way she was but had he turned her into some sort of monster? What the hell had she done?

TWENTY-EIGHT

Tuesday, 31 January

Gina yawned as she ate a cereal bar in her office, washed down with a cup of black coffee. Briggs had been true to his word. She'd returned home late, but he'd waited up and served her a dinner of cheese omelette and oven chips. He was no chef, but the food and company had been most welcome as had the cuddles with Jessie. She had wanted nothing more than to remain in her warm bed with him, but duty called. They had Hale's mother to visit, and it had to be first thing.

'Guv, I'm ready when you are.' Wyre smiled in the door-way. 'I'll wait in the incident room.'

Gina flinched as she moved in her chair. The hard landing on the mud last night had left her with a bruised side, whereas Wyre looked bright and ready to go. She stood and stretched before throwing her wrapper in the wire bin. Ambling down the corridor, she heard a voice she recognised. It was Jacob acknowledging the desk sergeant. Their visit to see Ms Hale would have to wait a short while. She'd made a promise to Briggs that she'd speak with him. She glanced at her watch. It was only a little past seven in the morning. He'd arrived way earlier than expected.

'Jacob? We've all been so worried about you.' For the first time ever, her colleague and friend looked distant, unkempt, and there was a smell about him. He obviously hadn't showered. The creased hooded sweater hung down over his loose jeans.

Jacob stood still and leaned against the wall. He went to open his mouth but couldn't speak.

'Jacob, come through to my office. We can talk there.' He didn't acknowledge what she was saying. He flinched as she placed a hand on his elbow and carefully led him out.

He didn't object. He simply followed her. In all their years of knowing each other, she'd never seen him looking so broken. She knew that Jennifer was staying in Bernard's spare room and that something major had happened between the couple. 'Have a seat. Can I get you a drink?' He looked like he needed something stronger than coffee.

He shook his head.

'I heard that Jennifer is staying in Bernard's spare room. I'm so sorry. You must be devastated.'

She saw his Adam's apple bob as he swallowed. 'I love her so much, guv, but she doesn't want me. With all that happened after she got run over and lost the baby; things have never been the same. She said she wasn't sure anymore, about us. I've tried so hard to keep us together, to plan the wedding on my own and to be there for her.' He wiped his damp eyes and took a deep breath as he tried to hold his emotions back. 'We finished just before Christmas, but I didn't want to say anything at work. I hoped that she'd come round, and that it was just a blip. We tried sharing the house, but we'd bicker, then she moved in temporarily with Bernard and she hasn't come home since. We decided not to say anything to anyone for the time being and again I hoped that she'd come back, but now she wants to sell the house.'

'I wish you'd confided in me, Jacob. We're friends and you know I'm always here for you. We've missed you. Tell me you're not leaving. You love this job.'

He shrugged. 'I do love this job. I have loved every minute of working here, with you and everyone else.'

'Loved, what are you talking about? We need you on the case. Like I said, we miss you.'

He swallowed again. 'I've blown it, guv. I've literally blown everything.'

'It wasn't your fault. Trauma can affect people differently and what Jennifer went through with the hit-and-run was awful. Losing the baby was a blow to both of you and I can't imagine what you've both suffered. You can get through this. Maybe Jennifer just needs a bit more space to process everything.'

'Maybe, but once done, some things cannot be undone. We can't go back.' His voice became raised. 'There is no going back.'

'I don't understand.' What he was saying didn't make any sense. She knew Jacob loved Jennifer to bits, but she'd also seen the end of previous relationships he'd had, and he'd never been this bad.

'I'm really in it and I don't know what to do.' He ran his shaky fingers through his hair.

Something told Gina there was more to it than a regular split. 'What is it, Jacob? Please talk to me. I want to help you, but I can't help if I don't know what's wrong.' She tilted her head.

He took a deep breath. 'I met someone else. Well, sort of.'

'Okay.' That wasn't what she'd expected to hear but she wasn't about to judge him.

'I dated her years ago, when I was in my twenties, she was nineteen at the time. I didn't intend for anything to happen. She was being harassed, and I tried to get her to report him, but she wouldn't. Anyway, I met up with her a few times over the Christmas period and after. We became good friends, that was all.'

'It's okay to want to help someone.'

'I slept with her, and it shouldn't have happened. We're not in love or anything like that. It was a huge mistake. We were just a bit lonely. All I wanted was for Jennifer to take me back and, as for her, I'm not sure what she wanted. Maybe she was hoping that we could be more. She did want more, and I didn't. I was so confused.'

Gina studied his pale face. 'Please don't beat yourself up about it. We all make mistakes. You didn't cheat on Jennifer, she left you.'

'I know all that.'

'So why are you so worried? I'm seriously beyond concerned for you right now and I say that with love. You look like you haven't eaten or slept.'

'I haven't. Because every time I close my eyes, I see her.'

'The woman you slept with?' Gina felt her own nerves twitching as Jacob fidgeted.

'I have a confession to make.'

Gina felt her heart rate increasing.

'On Saturday, I slept with Sienna Moorcroft. It only happened that once. I have no alibi for the whole day. I should have said something when we got called out early Sunday morning, but I was in shock, guv. I didn't expect to see Sienna's dead body in that bed. It's like that whole day was a blur.' He broke down. 'I know you'll have to read me my rights next. I know my DNA is in her and on her so it's only a matter of time before what I say is confirmed, but I swear on my life, I didn't kill her. You have to help me, guv.'

Gina's heart sunk. She stood and stared out of her window at the car park. She spotted Jacob's black saloon, and it was splashed with mud at the rear. She knew now that the case was going to get bigger than Cleevesford Police. Jacob would be held on suspicion of murder at another police station with no connection to them. Even if bailed post interview, he'd be suspended from duty and, given the current climate, the press would be all over them if his arrest was leaked. She glanced back at Jacob who was staring into thin air.

'You do believe me, guv? Please say you do.'

'I'll fight with everything I've got to find whoever did this. You have my word.' A part of her wondered if she could trust him, her dear friend. Why had he waited this long to tell her?

TWENTY-NINE

Gina glanced at her phone. She should be on her way to Ms Hale's so that she could find Gerard and bring him in. She nervously bit her nails as they all waited in the incident room for Briggs to enter and let them know how they were going to proceed. It had to be Gerard. In Gina's mind, there was no way on earth the murderer was Jacob. Gerard must have followed Sienna and therefore known about her seeing Jacob. Maybe he'd purposely tried to frame Jacob, knowing that he'd come under suspicion too. Her mind flashed back to the witness, Mr Sallis who worked at Happy Drinker's. He described Sienna arguing with someone after they kissed. That person had to be Jacob. She had to believe that Jacob could not possibly have murdered Sienna and Robbie, despite any argument.

The room was silent even though the core team were sitting around the table. The open packet of biscuits remained untouched. O'Connor hadn't even eaten his cold toast and Wyre had bitten the end of her pen down. Kapoor kept glaring at the table as if she didn't know what to say or who to look at.

Gina stared at the boards and really took in the crime scene photos of Sienna. In her mind, she tried to picture Jacob stabbing her, then using the scarf in the other photo to strangle her. Then there was Tiffany Crawford's attack. Had he been creeping around in her bedroom in the dead of night, planning to kill her? Were they still working on the idea that the cases were linked? The flowery scarf was too much of a coincidence.

The door swung open, and Briggs entered, a solemn expression on his face. 'As you are all now aware, DS Driscoll came in this morning. You are all aware of what he said on a need-to-know basis and that he is claiming to be innocent, so I want a thorough investigation. But things are going to be different with this case. The IOPC have been informed.'

Gina knew that he'd have to contact the Independent Office for Police Conduct, but she wasn't quite sure what the outcome of that communication would have been. It's not like one of their own got implicated in a crime every day. 'Does that mean we're still on the case?'

He nodded. 'Yes, but we're going to have outside help, in fact, they've insisted on it, and I expected that would happen. To avoid any suggestion of bias, we are having a SIO from Hereford. Detective Superintendent Sullivan is on her way, and she'll be bringing a DI with her, DI Collier. You will all report to the super, and she will be overseeing the case. As from now, DS Driscoll has been suspended until further notice. They will be arresting DS Driscoll and sending him to Hereford to be interviewed. He may be released on bail after that, but we won't know for a while.'

'Can I see Jacob?' Gina asked. 'He'll be terrified. He needs us right now. We're not just colleagues, he's our friend.'

Briggs paused and worry lines spread across his forehead. 'I'm afraid not. I know it's a lot to take in, but my hands are tied. This is the way it will happen and there are no ifs or buts. Detective Superintendent Sullivan has made it clear that we are not to communicate with him. My role will be to back up the superintendent.'

Gina felt her stomach turn at the mention of Sullivan. They had met before and she wasn't looking forward to meeting her again, let alone working under her. The woman had made her life as a trainee miserable and she'd hoped never to see her again.

She puffed up her cheeks and slowly blew out a breath while she digested everything. Gina would no longer be Senior Investigating Officer. She would have to run everything through DI Collier, and Collier would communicate directly with Sullivan. She wondered if the super would look down on her with suspicion too. Were they going to be watched and have their every move reported back to the IOPC? She had always run a tight team when it came to dotting the i's and crossing the t's but right now, she was going to have to work ten times harder. 'Someone must have seen Hale. We need to find him and bring him in. And what about the woman in the pyjamas who the witness saw near Robbie and Lauren's at the time of Sienna's murder? We need to do this, for Jacob. We will follow that evidence and he'll be cleared; I know it.'

Briggs nodded. 'But first, we need to wait for the super. She will be issuing you with instructions. In all likelihood, it will be to follow the same investigation path, but she has to lead.' He checked his watch. 'Right, this is the plan we will run by her. Gina, you and DI Collier will still head over to Ms Hale's. You're right in that we need to find Gerard Hale. He is our main suspect, and we need him at the station. The super will want to watch the interview. As for the woman in pyjamas, I will get her mentioned again on today's news. Someone else has to have noticed a woman walking around at night wearing pyjamas and hopefully they can give us a more detailed description of her. She's a key witness so finding her is a priority. Again, if it's okay with the super, O'Connor, Wyre and Kapoor, I think we will need the area canvassed again. Knock on doors and dig a little deeper.'

'How about Robbie Shields's post-mortem?' Gina asked.

'That will happen this afternoon. Again, if it's okay with the super, you and DI Collier will go. There is another thing.'

O'Connor threw his untouched toast in the bin and Wyre placed his chewed pen on the table. Gina swallowed.

Briggs continued. 'The press. Very soon the Hereford team will come here and take DS Driscoll. They're all out there and with the best will in the world when it comes to discretion, reporters are not stupid. They know something's wrong as I haven't given my planned briefing this morning and they're circling the station like vultures. We're trying to arrange for Jacob to go out the back but when I last looked, one of the *Warwickshire Herald*'s reporters was out there. It's going to get out. Our job is to resolve this before too much damage to us as a department can be done. Public trust is at an all-time low given that the IOPC are currently investigating many claims of racism, misogyny and homophobia within the police. We are not trusted, and I don't want to give the people of Cleevesford any room to mistrust us. This is not who we are here. It never has been, and it never will be. We will get through this.' He spoke those words with confidence, but Gina could tell he was nervous.

Gina wondered if they could recover. If it turned out that Jacob had... No, she couldn't even allow her thoughts to go there. They needed to continue investigating the case and see where it led. Their only option was to carry out an unbiased investigation, but she wasn't looking forward to working with the super. Sullivan had been her DI when she was a trainee DC in Birmingham and, for some reason, she'd never taken to Gina. Yes, Gina had been awkward and had lacked self-confidence in the role for a while, but even when she did a good job, the woman had never looked pleased, let alone gave her any credit when she'd been right, and her criticism of everything made Gina feel as though she'd been walking on eggshells.

Gina heard the sound of clonking shoes coming down the corridor, then a tall woman, grey hair in a bun and black skirt suit as sharp as a razor, walked through the door. Gina's gaze locked on Sullivan's. She took a deep breath and hoped with all she had that the super had changed for the better.

Sullivan nodded once at Briggs and stood next to him. 'For those who don't know, I'm Detective Superintendent Sullivan. I've been appointed to the case. I will be running the investigation and I expect your full support and cooperation. I am SIO so everything, and I mean everything, will need to be run through me. Anyone who does not cooperate will be off the case.' Sullivan paused and her stare made Gina grind her back teeth, a habit she'd mostly kicked after working with Sullivan. The super knew she had the power to make Gina shrink and she was using it from the off. 'Are we all good with that?' Gina flinched and Sullivan smirked.

There was a hum of yesses in the room, Gina included. She had to comply, for Jacob. 'I'll be talking to DCI Briggs in a moment to come up with a plan of action while we wait for DI Collier to arrive, and I'll be reviewing what we have to date. You will then be issued with your duties. I run a tight ship and refer to me as ma'am, are we all clear?' Sullivan said.

'Yes, ma'am,' Gina chimed in with the chorus. Nothing had changed. Gina loved what they had at Cleevesford. She had a friendly team that operated on mutual respect, not fear. They had always worked well together but Sullivan didn't have a warm bone in her body. Gina glanced at the woman, her deep-lined eyes and thin lips. She hadn't changed much, only aged. She might not like Sullivan, but they had to work together to get to the bottom of the case. Despite her hostile stare, maybe it was time to put their past aside. Gina was prepared for the past to stay there as long as Sullivan was.

The super scrutinised the small team and stopped at Gina. 'DC Harte? I never forget a face. It's been a long time.'

'DI, ma'am. I'm a DI now.'

Sullivan let out a huff and stretched out her arms before leaving the room. Briggs obediently followed.

Gina took a deep breath. Just as she thought things couldn't get worse, Sullivan was once again her superior and she definitely hadn't changed one bit.

THIRTY

NANCY

'Mum.'

Nancy opened her eyes, and her daughter placed a tray of coffee and toast on her bedside table. She rubbed her aching elbow and the side of her head. She'd come down on the earth hard last night. 'Thanks.' Fifi ran in yapping and dived on her bed, getting her claws caught in the crocheted bedspread.

'I know you refused to go to A&E last night, but I really think you should ring your doctor and get checked out. The side of your face was bleeding.'

She shook her head. 'No, I'm okay. It was just a stupid fall. I should have been more careful.'

Lauren stared right at her in disbelief. 'I saw that message on your phone.'

Taking a deep breath, Nancy flinched and let out a faint ouch as she sat up in bed. The message. *Scream Bitch. Scream.* It must have shocked Lauren to the core to see that when she came out and found Nancy in such a state.

'Mum, who sent you that message?'

She shrugged. 'I don't want to talk about it.' Fifi nudged her head under Nancy's arm and began licking her neck. 'You have enough on your plate without me adding to your stress. That message really isn't anything to worry about. Why don't you tell me how you are? Did you speak to your friends?'

Lauren nodded. 'Yes, finally they both accepted my friend requests, and I called them. They're both really shocked, and work know I won't be in for a while, but the signal was bad both times. I got cut off. I also called the police to see if I could go back to the bungalow, but they said no. I know Robbie wasn't who I thought he was. He was cheating on me, and he lied to me, but he and Sienna didn't deserve what happened. I keep thinking about Dora. I've been like an aunt to that little girl. Robbie was her dad and he abandoned her. I don't know how he could do something like that.' Her daughter swallowed and sat on the bed. 'But I loved him, Mum. I still do and I don't know what I'm going to do without him. All I can think about is how I found Sienna. I feel dirty, like really dirty, I've never been that close to death before and when I saw you last night slumped over that rock and the blood...' Tears slipped down Lauren's cheeks. 'I freaked out. I thought you were dead.' She gasped for breath.

'But I wasn't. It's all okay, I promise. That message was nothing and we're fine. I'm glad you found Fifi. Come here, you little rascal.' She kissed the dog's head, then gently nudged Fifi away. She'd had enough of being licked, even though her kind little dog was only doing it out of love. Grabbing her cup of coffee, she took a sip. The hot liquid was most welcome. Last night, she'd felt a touch nauseous after the fall but now her appetite was returning, and she wanted nothing more than to sit alone eating and not have to explain the message to her daughter. It's a good job she'd deleted the others otherwise Lauren would have the police over and she didn't want to end up on their radar.

'When I found you, you were mumbling and telling me to get away from you. At one point you begged me not to hurt you.

Then you came round. Who did you think I was, Mum? I'm not going to shut up about the message either. Was someone there? Did someone hurt you? You need to tell me.'

Nancy shook her head. 'No, it happened like I told you. I tripped over my slipper while looking for Fifi. I'm an idiot, that's all. I saw that message and things were a bit muddled in my head. No one was there.' She knew there had been a manly figure dressed in dark clothes. Whoever it was hadn't stuck around. As soon as Lauren had called out for her, he fled.

'Okay, I believe you. Who is the messenger? I keep thinking that whoever killed Sienna and Robbie will come for me, or even you. When I saw that message, I panicked.'

'I told you it was nothing.'

'How can you say that?' Lauren sniffled.

The whole conversation was getting tedious. Her messenger had nothing at all to do with her daughter.

'There's something you're not telling me. What is it?' Lauren wiped her eyes with her dressing gown sleeve.

There was no point lying. Lauren could tell she was holding back. 'I've been getting into trouble and I—'

'What is it?'

'You know the protests I've been attending?'

'The environmental protests?'

She nodded. 'We just want the water companies to stop dumping sewage into the rivers and seas.'

'What have you done, Mum?'

She rubbed her sore head. 'Oh, so many things. Too many to count but last week, I broke into a water company's head office. I'm not mentioning any names. Do you know how much sewage they've pumped into the sea?'

'Don't deflect. I'm on your side but I don't know if I'm going to like what you did. What was it, graffiti or a bit of vandalism?'

Nancy nodded. 'That and more. I graffitied obscenities all over their glossy boardroom and I meant it. I was so angry. We took a shedload of bleach, mustard, garlic paste, old cheese, bags full of old veg peelings. Anything and everything we could get our hands on got ingrained into their offices, into their couches. We smeared them over everything, put things in the air conditioning system, poured bleach into all the computers. We wanted the place to stink and break, so they would get a feel for what they were doing to the sea.'

'You say we. Who are the others?'

'Just my friends, the other activists. Anyway, that's why I can't tell the police. They will link the destruction to me and, so far, I'm not even a suspect, which means I can carry on the good work.'

'It's not one of your friends, is it?'

'No. Why would they send me messages like that when we're all on the same side?'

'Well, who then?'

'A few months ago, we clashed with some drivers while holding up a dual carriageway. It got heated, well that's an understatement. One of them went for me and tried to drag me by my hair, so I hit him in the face with my placard. Later that day, he started harassing me on social media which is why I came off. My phone number was used as a contact on the leaflets that day. That's how he has my name and number.'

'So, you think it's him?' Her daughter stroked Fifi as she waited for an answer.

'It must be. The messages are horrible, but you can rest assured that he has no idea where I live. I'm literally off-grid as you know. No one ever comes here, ever.'

'What if he followed you from one of your protests?'

A day ago, Nancy wouldn't have believed that to be true but now she was sure he'd been there last night. Her daughter was right. He could have followed her home after any protest since. She'd seen him lurking and mocking her. 'Listen, I just know and all this, it doesn't matter. What matters is you and all that you've been through. I chose this fight and I'm not going to stop, not until I feel like humanity has a future. Okay?'

'Not okay, Mum. I don't want you to get hurt, end up in prison, or worse get killed by a weirdo stalker. I don't want any more people I love to get hurt.'

Nancy shook her head. 'You don't get to choose what I do. I do it for you and for any children that you may have one day. Someone has to make these companies accountable, and the government are doing stuff all.' She smiled and stroked her daughter's cheek.

Lauren waited while Nancy took a swig of coffee and a bite of toast. 'What will you do if he messages again?'

It was time to come clean. Maybe bottling up the messages wasn't the right thing to do. Lauren now understood why the police couldn't be involved. 'He's been messaging me for weeks. At first, I answered, calling him all the names under the sun, but now I just delete them. He'll get fed up.'

'Or he'll do something bigger to command your attention. Don't mess with people like this, Mum. You don't know who you're dealing with.'

'No, they don't know who they're dealing with, sweetheart. I always win in the end, and I will win this one too. Don't you worry about me.' She ate the toast like she hadn't eaten for a week. She meant every word of what she'd said. It wouldn't be the first or last time she took matters into her own hands. Her life had been filled with doing what it took to protect Lauren and she was ready for anything.

THIRTY-ONE

For once, Gina wasn't driving. She wondered if DI Collier was going to say anything, but he'd kept his gaze on the damp road ahead. As for his thoughts, who knows where they were right now. She noticed that the collar of his crisp white shirt had been starched stiff. He reached up and poked a finger down it to loosen it away from his dark brown skin. Gina remembered those moments well when working with Sullivan. She was a stickler for smartness and heavily critical of anything out of place and that was truly reflected in how perfectly Collier was dressed.

'It's this turning.' She pointed to Bay Road.

'Thank you.' As he turned the wheel, the low morning sun glinted off his wedding ring.

And that was it. No talk of the witness or how they were going to approach the interview. All she knew was that she was going to lead, and he was going to be monitoring her every word and reporting back to Sullivan. Was he friend or foe? She still had to find that out.

He turned and glanced at her as he pulled into a parking space opposite Hale's mother's house. His expression gave nothing away. 'Right, I'm okay with you leading but stick to what we discussed. You know the case better than me, but I will try to catch up with everything between the briefing at the station and attending the post-mortem later.' He pushed his horn-rimmed glasses further up his nose and got out of the car.

'We have another briefing that soon?' She knew they'd barely have time to even nip to the loo, let along wedge in another briefing.

He cleared his throat. 'I have. The super requires that I report back at regular intervals, and she wants me there in person.'

Gina was grateful to remain on the case but if every move was monitored to the nth degree, it would take forever to catch the murderer. 'Great, let's go and see what Ms Hale has to say. We have backup on standby just in case Gerard Hale turns up. Uniform is positioned less than a minute away should we need them. Keeping them out of sight for now is the best way to approach as I'm hoping she'll open up. I'd say we're ready to go.' Gina opened the passenger door and stepped out onto the pavement.

DI Collier took his large grey overcoat off the back seat and put it on before following her towards the house. Gina stopped at the edge of the block-paved drive while he pulled his satchel across his chest and hurried over. She took in the three storey Victorian terrace with its huge bay ground-floor window. Thick nets stopped them from seeing inside. She wondered if Hale was holed up in one of the many rooms, hoping that he'd never be found. A nervous flutter stemmed from her stomach to her throat, and acid threatened to rise. She'd never felt such pressure in her life. Jacob needed her to get this right. If she didn't, he could end up being charged and his life would be over. She couldn't get the image of his face out of her mind as she replayed their last conversation in her head. He was broken.

A woman opened the bottle-green front door and stepped

out with a fat ball on a piece of string. 'Can I help you?' She proceeded to the bare blossom tree and hung it on a low hanging branch. Gina spotted a friendly robin, obviously a regular visitor waiting for its meal.

'I'm DI Harte, this is DI Collier.' They held up their identification.

Ms Hale walked over, pulled her glasses from her pocket and scrutinised their IDs. 'Oh, it's you. I'm still not happy that you all went into our caravan without my permission. Can I go there yet?'

Gina stepped forward as the stout woman pulled her thick brown cardigan across her chest. She didn't want to remind the woman that the caravan was co-owned by Ms Hale and her son, and the officer who called by the previous evening had explained that they had a search warrant. 'May we come inside to speak?'

Ms Hale blew out a breath and her shoulders dropped. 'I suppose.' She turned her back and led them into the tiled hallway with a high ceiling. Their footsteps echoed until they reached a carpeted sitting room, surrounded by bookshelves and a desk. 'Take a seat in my study.'

Gina glanced at the books on rocks, minerals and tectonic plates that covered the walls from floor to ceiling. A masters certificate hung proudly on the wall behind her large leather-studded desk. Adina Hale was an earth sciences expert. 'I guess you're looking for Gerard. I can tell you something. He's not here and I haven't seen him at all since Saturday night. Pull up a seat, both of you.'

DI Collier passed Gina a chair and pulled one up for himself. They sat and she pulled out her notes. He began heading up a page with the interview details.

Gina cleared her throat. Adina Hale claimed that she'd seen her son on Saturday night. She needed to get to the bottom of that. She also had to consider whether she could trust her as an alibi for her son.

'What is it you think my son has done?'

'We're investigating a serious crime and your son's name has come up.' It was obvious that Hale's mother had not linked the murders on the news to Gerard. Gina noticed the vein on the woman's head twitching as she looked away. Adina Hale knew more than she was letting on. 'You mention that you saw your son on Saturday night. Where were you when you saw him?'

'I was here. He came over for dinner and stayed the night. He didn't want to stay at the caravan. It was cold.'

Damn, if that was true and he didn't leave the house, he had an alibi. But would his mother lie to protect him? That's what Gina needed to establish. 'What time did he arrive at yours?'

'Around five. We had dinner about six and watched a film on Netflix. Later I went into the kitchen and called my sister. When I went back into the living room, he had fallen asleep in front of the TV, so I left him on the settee and went up to bed to watch something else.'

'What time was this?'

'About eight thirty, I guess. It was early but I know he hasn't been comfortable in the caravan, and he isn't really meant to be there until March.'

Gina waited for DI Collier to catch up. 'Why was he staying there and not with you?'

She pressed her lips together in thought before continuing. 'I love my son, I really do, but I find him hard to live with. He's messy, he can be snappy and he's lazy. I don't want to spend all day picking up after him. We agreed that it would be best if he stayed in the caravan after losing his house. I guess it's only a matter of time before that gets sold off as an asset so they can get their hands on his share, but he's using it for now.'

'You say you went up to bed about half eight on Saturday. Could he have woken up and gone back out?'

'I'd have heard him.'

'Where do you sleep?'

She swallowed and scrunched her brow. 'On the second floor.'

Gina just wanted to clarify. 'So, you could have heard him leaving from all the way up there?'

'Yes, I'm sure I would have.'

Gina knew that Gerard didn't have the perfect alibi in his mother, and she saw DI Collier write a question mark where he'd noted Hale's whereabouts.

'Did he mention his previous relationship?'

She shrugged. 'I know he was seeing someone, and she moved in with him for a couple of weeks, but he wouldn't tell me much. I don't even know what her name was. I only know he worked with her. He said he wanted to see how things went. Most of his relationships don't work out so I didn't hold out much hope for that one.'

'Do you know why that is?'

'Like I said, he's hard to live with. Messy and lazy. It wouldn't have taken the poor woman long to find out. You saw his room in the caravan. Is that why you're here?' Ms Hale looked into her hands. 'I was a bit concerned when I saw those boards, but Gerard assured me he was over her and he was going to get rid of them. He said he was just missing her, and all that stuff would be gone next time I visited.'

Now Gina wondered if Ms Hale was in denial over the red flags her son was displaying. 'Do you know where he is now? It's important that we find him and speak to him.'

'He got the train to London on Sunday morning. He said he was visiting some old uni friends for a few days and that he had some holiday from work. He wanted to go abroad to Magaluf with a few friends but didn't have enough money. I know that much as he tried to borrow some off me.'

'Do you have a name for the friends he met up with in

London, or do you know which part of London he was heading to?'

She shook her head. 'I dropped him off at Birmingham on Sunday lunchtime, by the coach station at Digbeth. That's all I know.'

Gina sat back. He could literally be anywhere. 'Do you know when he's due back?'

'He said he'd be back today and that he didn't need me to pick him up. It is still early, maybe he'll be back later. I've tried to call him to check, but his phone is off and keeps going to answerphone, then you turned up. Should I be worried? Do you think something has happened to him?'

Gina couldn't answer that. Either he was hurt, or he was on the run. She had no idea which. 'If you hear anything from him, can you call us straight away? It's highly important that we speak to him as a matter of urgency.' Gina placed her card on the desk.

The woman took it and placed it in her desk drawer.

Gina pulled a photo of the blue flowery scarf that was found at the scene of Sienna Moorcroft's murder. 'Do you recognise this scarf?'

Adina Hale took the photo. 'I think I do. I have so many. I'm a bit of an obsessive collector of scarves and I'm sure I have one like this.'

'Do you have it here? Could you check?'

'It's either here or at the caravan. My collection is all over the place. Yes, I'll have a look.' She left the room and hurried up the two flights of stairs. A few moments later she returned. 'It's at the caravan, it has to be as I can't find it with my others in the wardrobe. I'm sure I left it there.'

Gina glanced at DI Collier. When she and Wyre searched through the scarves at the caravan, there was no blue flowery scarf there at all. Gerard Hale was still firmly in the picture for the murder of Sienna and Robbie.

THIRTY-TWO

TIFFANY

With a fuzzy brain, Tiffany went into the kitchen and reached into the cupboard for her diazepam, but it wasn't there. She ran into the living room and the bathroom, but again, her tablets were nowhere to be seen. Last night, Kieron put the tablets away. Her hands began to shake. She needed her tablets now. All night, she'd lain awake with rushing thoughts and palpitations. All she wanted was for her skin to stop crawling and her innards to stop partying away. She grabbed her phone and punched out a message.

Where the hell are my tablets?

The reply came back instantly, like he was waiting for her message.

Please, Tiff. I'm worried about you. I have them here. I can't risk a repeat of yesterday. I love you so much. Please understand. I am so scared of coming home and finding you dead one day. When I get home, we'll book an appointment with the doctor. This needs sorting. I've left you a healthy fruit salad in the fridge. XXX

Fruit salad! That was meant to help in this situation. Right now, she hated Kieron. Her heart rate was through the roof and her stomach was churning away like nothing she'd ever experienced. For the past hour, she'd been in and out the loo like she had a stomach bug. Her irritable bowel was playing up like never before and now she couldn't even take a chill pill for her anxiety.

She ran to the door to check that the chain was on. It was. Kieron's alarm had gone off about six. While she still lay awake, he'd quietly got dressed and left after kissing her goodbye and telling her that he loved her. She clenched her fists. Around that time, he probably had her tablets in his bag. As she'd finally drifted off a sense of peace filled her, but that was short-lived.

Tiff, are you eating the fruit salad? Love you. X

She hurried back to the kitchen, opened the fridge and pulled out the bowl of berries. Lifting it up, she went to hurl the fruit at the wall but then she took a deep breath. Slowly she placed the bowl on the worktop and burst into a huge sobbing mess. Tears fell and her nose began to fill. Kieron was wrong to take her tablets, but she could see where he was coming from now that the red mist was clearing. He loved her and he'd left her a healthy meal and sent her such a loving message. What was wrong with her? She would eat the berries but not yet, not until her stomach had calmed down. Right now, she would have nothing but water and sit in front of the television until the jitteriness subsided. With every step, she felt a deep muscular ache, like her whole body was made of lead. She slumped into her chair and pressed the remote.

The look on Kieron's face the night before flashed through her mind. She had hurt him for a second time. No longer did she know or trust herself. That horrible dream was a message. It was her brain trying to unlock the memories of all the bad things she'd done. She swigged her water and spilled a few drops on her pyjama top. She shivered as the cold water reached her skin.

Last night, her mind showed her that she had walked to Lauren's on the night of Sienna's murder. She had been there, so why couldn't she remember it properly? Why was her brain only giving her cryptic snippets? The fog wasn't lifting. She slammed the glass down on the coffee table and screamed into a cushion repeatedly until she was dizzy.

Her phone rang. It was Kieron. There was no way she could speak to him at this moment. She let her answerphone pick it up. When she calmed down, she'd drop him a message. She didn't want him to leave work to check on her. His boss wouldn't be pleased as it had happened too often. *Breathe in, breathe out,* she kept telling herself as her stomach growled.

The local news flashed up on the TV screen. She turned the volume up and stared at it intently until the newsreader finished speaking. They were looking for a woman who was seen close to Lauren's bungalow on the night of the murder. They described a blonde woman wearing pyjamas with lemons printed on them. Her mind flashed back to Kieron bleeding after she hurt him, then it darted to Lauren and a whirl of other thoughts, jumbled and not making sense. Her feet had been gritty on the night of Sienna's murder. She was now certain she had been standing on Bell Road.

All the bad things happening had to be down to her attacker. He was playing with her mind, and she was certain he was enjoying every moment. He must have seen her there because, however much she thought she could hurt someone, she knew she wasn't capable of murder. With weak, trembling legs, she crept to the front door and checked the chain again. It was still on. She glanced through the kitchen door. The panic button was on the table. She crept towards the kitchen window and peered out. A man walked past and grinned at her, then another did the same. Then another followed. They were everywhere. After rubbing her eyes, the men had gone. There were no men. She fell to the floor and hugged her knees, wishing it would all stop, then she scratched at her neck and chest.

Maybe she should call the police, or an ambulance. She felt so ill. Or should she shut up and remain still until Kieron returned? The men weren't real. Her mind was playing tricks on her. Maybe there was just one grinning man or none. There may have been no one. She shook her head frantically. There was definitely one. While her attacker was still out there, he would always be in her mind. He never left, ever. It was like he'd crawled under her skin and was living in her body, battling to take her mind for his own. Not content with attacking her and nearly killing her, he wanted to drive her insane.

She wondered if she should call the police and confess to being outside Lauren's bungalow on the night of the murder. She couldn't remember anything, but she had been there. How many other women could be out and barefoot on that night? She glanced down at the exact pyjamas the news reporter had described, and she traced one of the lemons with her index finger.

Her phone rang again, and her hands began to tremble with relief as she remembered that she'd dropped a tablet in her bag about a month ago. She'd have to turf out all the old tissues and bits of make-up, but it was in there somewhere. After running to the kitchen, she grabbed her bag from the chair and began tipping it upside down. Knees digging into the cold floor, she rummaged through the clutter until her fingers fell upon not only a tablet but a whole strip of them.

On standing, the shock of what she saw made her chest tighten. She gasped for breath as she came face to face with a man in a balaclava at the kitchen window. Her attacker was back.

THIRTY-THREE

Gina held on to the passenger seat as DI Collier took a corner faster than expected. She doubted that Sullivan would approve of his driving right now. As soon as Briggs called her with the news that Tiffany Crawford had pressed her panic button, they were on their way. Collier pulled up behind the police car that was parked up on the road outside the block of flats. PC Smith and another officer were already searching around the area. Gina hurried out of the car and ran towards them, wasting no time waiting for DI Collier. 'What happened?'

PC Smith held his side and took a few deep breaths before speaking while the other officer continued searching the bushes to the side of the building. 'We arrived about ten minutes ago. Mrs Crawford said that a man wearing a balaclava was staring through her window, that's when she pressed the button. We've searched the building and down a few side streets, but we haven't seen anyone around. If he scarpered when the button was pressed, he could be anywhere by now, especially if he had a car parked up in another street. She's shaken, but we haven't had time to properly speak to her yet.'

'That's okay, we'll do that now. Keep looking. Can you

please arrange for a few officers to assist with knocking on neighbours' doors. One of them might have seen this person acting suspiciously or hanging around, or they may have seen which direction he ran in. Also organise for an officer to remain outside these flats for the foreseeable. She needs more than drive-bys. Given all that is happening, we need to ensure her safety. Have the downstairs flats got back doors?'

DI Collier joined her and began punching out a message, no doubt keeping Sullivan fully updated. He glanced up as if scrutinising how Gina was handling the situation before continuing with his message.

'No, so that's less of a worry.' PC Smith hurried back towards the other officer and then began talking on his radio.

'What has Tiffany Crawford got to do with the case? I was rushed in this morning, so I'm not fully up to date. The super has filled me in on the two murders, and I know that DS Driscoll and Gerard Hale are the main suspects. I've read those case notes.' DI Collier waited for her to explain.

She almost shuddered at those words mentioned together – DS Driscoll and suspect. 'A few years ago, Tiffany was attacked in her own home. Her attacker weirdly stabbed her in the back of the neck with an earring at the scene and then attempted to strangle her with her scarf.'

'I see, that's why you asked Ms Hale about the scarf?'

Gina nodded. He really didn't know the case that well at all. He shouldn't be working it with her and he knew it. Her first thought was to call Briggs and see if she could have Wyre or O'Connor assisting but she knew that Sullivan would cause more trouble for her, so she would remain on the case with her spy by her side, and she would play the game, for now.

'Yes. Then that exact same design of scarf was used to kill Sienna Moorcroft. We are working on the theory that the attacker uses something from the previous attack in the current attack, although we can't prove that yet. We haven't come across a past case of strangulation where an earring was taken, so right now it's a working theory. When we attended the scene of Sienna's murder, we found that she wasn't wearing underpants. We know there was a pair of underpants found in Robbie's pocket when we found his body. They looked to be Sienna's size but right now we can't prove that they are Sienna's until the lab have finished their job. The killer is playing with us.'

He looked confused while he thought through what Gina had said. 'Right, I see.'

Gina swallowed. She knew that officers would be going through all of Jacob's personal belongings as they searched for anything and everything that connected him to Sienna. That was a side of the investigation she wouldn't hear about until it was over. Being kept in the dark would make everything harder. Only Sullivan would have the whole story for now, unless Collier had heard something. 'Have you heard anything about the search of Jacob's house?'

He raised his brows. 'Yes. You shouldn't be asking me questions like that, DI Harte.'

Tiffany opened her front door, breaking the tension. 'Hello. Did you catch him? Tell me you did.'

Gina walked past the shoulder height shrubs outside Tiffany's front door and followed the short path with DI Collier in tow. 'The officers are still looking, and they will be conducting door-to-doors where your neighbours will be asked if they've seen anyone suspicious.'

The young woman tucked her blonde curls behind her ears and put her hands into her sweatshirt pockets. 'So, he's still out there, ready to terrorise me again.'

'May we come and speak with you? This is DI Collier and I'm DI Harte, we met before.'

She opened the door. 'Come through.'

Gina followed the woman through to the living room. The large window led the eye to a square garden, dotted with washing lines and a bin store at the far end. Once seated, she waited for DI Collier to get his notebook ready. 'Can you talk me through what happened this morning?'

Tiffany wiped her nose with a creased-up tissue, then placed it in her pocket. 'I err, was just about to have my breakfast about eleven. When I stood at the window, he was there.'

'He? Do you know him?'

'My attacker. The one who tried to strangle me four years ago. He was wearing a balaclava back then, so I know it was him. He stared at me through the window, and I grabbed that panic button and pressed it. I hid on the kitchen floor and I think he was trying to open my front door.' Tiffany began to rock back and forth in her chair while biting her nails.

Gina knew from the previous interview that Tiffany was poorly, but they didn't know what illness she suffered with. She certainly looked pale and clammy. 'Can you describe anything about him that might help us. Eye colour, height, build?'

Tiffany scrunched her brow as if in thought. 'I didn't look for long enough to catch his eye colour. I felt his stare on me and it was angry, maybe manic. He was definitely taller than me, but most people are, and he was of average build, I think. I saw him for a couple of seconds so it's really hard to think.'

'You're doing really well. I appreciate how difficult this is for you. How about clothing. Did you see what he was wearing?'

'All I saw was that balaclava. He must have had a jumper or coat on, but it was as if nothing else existed around him. I was so scared, I literally dropped to the floor, out of sight. When I eventually got back up, he'd gone.'

The young woman looked to the side then cleared her throat. For a second, Gina thought she might say something. She opened her mouth and held her breath.

'Is there something you want to tell me? Is something worrying you?'

Tiffany didn't answer and began fiddling with her cuffs. 'No, just please catch him. I'm sick of living in fear. No one understands what it's like with him out there. I don't speak to my parents anymore. Can you believe they accused me of malingering? If my mother had experienced what I had, she'd be the same, I know she would. Everyone thinks that I should be over it by now. I've lost friends, jobs. If he is caught, I feel like I might stand a chance at a normal life again. Please promise me you'll catch him.'

Gina took a deep breath. She couldn't begin to imagine how Tiffany was feeling but she couldn't make a firm promise. More than anything, she wanted to bring the perpetrator in, but she couldn't guarantee it. All they had linking the recent murders and Tiffany's attack was a scarf. Was it enough to convict the perp of Tiffany's attack? She didn't know the answer to that question yet. 'I am going to do everything I can.' That's all she could say to Tiffany for now. 'Have you noticed anything else? Maybe someone loitering around.'

She shook her head. 'No, but it's as if I can feel him. I find myself waking up in a sweat after reliving the attack. I feel as though he gets off on that. I don't know why, but I keep thinking he's close, but my feelings aren't what you need, are they?'

'We want to do everything we can for you so if you see or hear anything, don't hesitate to press that panic button again. Another officer will pop in shortly to take a formal statement. If you remember anything after we've left, call me straight away, any time, okay?' Gina placed a card on the coffee table.

'Or you can call me.' Collier placed his card next to Gina's. Gina let a breath out slowly, trying not to reveal her irritation.

Tiffany nodded. 'I will, thank you. And thank you for not treating me like I'm mad. My doctor treats me like I'm mad.' She waved a hand. 'Thank you, that's all.' Her eyes welled up.

The young woman looked so vulnerable; Gina wondered if

she should be alone. 'Do you know anyone who will sit with you for a while?'

'I need to call my husband. He tried ringing earlier while all this was going on and my phone died. I'll call him as soon as you go.'

Gina and DI Collier stood. 'For your protection, a police car will be stationed outside your flat at all times. You have your panic button and our numbers. They will have shift changeovers, but you won't be left without them for long.'

'Thank you again.'

A loud knock at the door made Gina's heart jump slightly. All the talk of the creepy man at the window had sent a slight chill through her. Tiffany passed Gina and hurried to open the door. 'Hello, Mrs Crawford. Is DI Harte still there?'

Gina heard PC Smith and hurried to the door where she and DI Collier left. DI Collier packed his notepad into his satchel as they followed the PC to the roadside.

'Have you found anything?' Collier asked before she could speak.

PC Smith nodded. He held an evidence bag up. 'We found this caught on a tree, just over there.' He pointed to a line of shrubs and trees that lined the path at the back of the flats. 'We can't be sure if this black wool came from a balaclava but there was a fair bit of it. It could have caught on a branch and unwound before the perp snapped the thread or it could just be anyone's jumper or scarf. If it did belong to him, it means he would have escaped that way.'

'What's behind those trees?'

PC Smith stared in that direction. 'If I remember rightly, there's a bit of shrubbery, then a lane. If you cross the lane, you come to a quiet road that leads to a few fields and the river. He could have followed the lane for a while then headed back into the estate, or he could have been parked up on one of the smaller roads. We've got officers checking these out as we speak.'

'Thank you. While you're doing the door-to-doors, if anyone has CCTV, that too will be most helpful. Can you please go over the area where you found this wool, and cordon it off? Make sure no one disturbs any cigarette ends, drink cans, bits of paper, fibres or footprints. I'll call Bernard so that one of his team can head over and assist.'

'Will do. I'll head over and cordon it off.'

'Thank you.' She grabbed her phone and quickly called Bernard.

A man pulled up on the road and ran over. 'Tiff, Tiff,' he called as he ran past Gina.

She turned to face him. 'Are you Mr Crawford?'

The man stood there, a confused look spreading across his face. 'What's happened? I've been trying to call her. I got worried. Is everything okay? Where is she?' As he walked across the path, he removed his company yellow jacket and rolled it up.

Tiffany came out and hurried towards him. Gina watched as she threw her arms around him. 'I'm okay, but he was here, Kieron. He was watching me through the kitchen window, wearing that same balaclava. He won't stop until I'm dead.' She burst into tears.

'Are you sure he was here, Tiff?'

'Yes. Do you think I'd make it up?'

'No, I never said that, I just—'

'I know what you meant, and I thought you were on my side.'

'I am. Of course I am.' Kieron broke their embrace and awkwardly turned back to Gina. 'You have to find this man and put him behind bars. We've already moved once from our Redditch house because my wife lived in fear every day. Please.' He turned back to his wife. 'I'm never going to let anyone hurt you, I promise. I'm here now. Let's get you inside, in the warm before you freeze to death.'

'He's going to come back and he's going to kill me, don't say I didn't warn you,' Tiffany yelled just before Kieron closed the door.

THIRTY-FOUR

Following DI Collier's private briefing with Sullivan back at the station, he and Gina were once again hurrying to their next appointment – Robbie Shields's post-mortem.

'I'm not good at this so I may need to leave at some point. Just warning you,' Collier said as he stared at the huge glass-fronted building. 'If I can get past the Y-incision and the removal of the bowels, I'll be okay.' He shuddered.

They walked to the reception door. 'That's okay. If you need to leave the room, I understand. It's better you take five minutes and get some air rather than faint.'

'Thanks.'

The receptionist smiled from behind her desk as they entered. 'Please take a seat, and we'll call you through in a moment. It's DI Harte, isn't it?'

Gina nodded. 'Yes, and this is DI Collier.' The woman turned back to her work while they sat on the couch by the floor-to-ceiling window.

'The super said you used to work at Birmingham, when you were a DC.'

Gina nodded. 'Is that all she said?'

He paused and began to twiddle his fingers. 'There may have been other things.'

'I bet there were,' Gina muttered. She glanced at Collier and knew that Sullivan had enjoyed telling him how incompetent Gina had been. Of course, it was all lies but Sullivan had singled her out from the pack on day one, encouraging the rest of the team to come down hard on her, give her the tricky shifts, deny her holiday leave and make nasty comments under their breath.

'Did DS Driscoll ever mention the victim to you or how he's been over the past few weeks? You worked closely with him. You must have sensed something. I mean, he was having a fling behind his partner's back. If you knew him as well as you say you did, then you'd be a bad detective to not know.'

It was one hundred per cent obvious that Sullivan had set Collier against her, just like the good old days. She felt her heart begin to pound as she clenched her teeth. That's why the super wanted to speak to him. He'd been tasked to push and push until she released a small nugget of information that could be used against Jacob. Superintendent Sullivan also wanted nothing more than to drive Gina off the case and she was using Collier to do that.

'Jacob is the gentlest person ever. He would never hurt anyone. The quicker we can follow all these leads and find the real culprit, the better.' Gina paused. 'That wasn't subtle at all – you, asking me about him. I know the real reason for the briefing was to gear you up to getting information out of me. There is nothing to tell. It wasn't Jacob.'

Collier shrugged. 'DCI Briggs was in the meeting too and we were discussing if you should even be on the case. You really should say if you know something and you're holding back on us, but Sullivan said you weren't a team player. You know that withholding information—'

'Don't patronise me, DI Collier. I know the consequences and that's not what's happening here. I don't need your threats.'

'Merely reminding you of the law.' He smirked. 'Just think hard, DI Harte. You don't want your career to go down the pan, do you?'

She shuffled in her seat, feeling more uncomfortable by the second. 'I will categorically say, Jacob is not the murderer and he's not the strangler.' She felt a line of sweat forming under her hairline. 'And don't think you can bully me like she did. I won't take it so you can keep your threats and snidey comments to yourself.'

He glared at her for a few uncomfortable seconds. 'You know, I believe that you believe he didn't do it.'

She stared at the man, refusing to break eye contact. 'Patronising me again, DI Collier? Report this back to Sullivan. I am going to prove that Jacob didn't do it and I'm going to catch who did. I will do it if it kills me.'

'You won't because he did it. We all know he did.'

'You know sod all.' She stood, turned her back to him and stared out at the car park. Emotion was building up and her eyes began to water. Collier couldn't see her cry. If he reported that back to Sullivan, the super would be laughing. She missed working with Jacob and right now, she couldn't imagine spending the rest of her working life without him by her side. She'd worked in other police stations, but none were ever as special as Cleevesford. The people made it what it was, and things would never be the same again. All she could think was that he better not have killed those people. What if she was wrong? Sullivan and Collier would have a field day in bringing her down.

'The Home Office pathologist is ready for you now.' Gina wiped her eyes, turned around and acknowledged the receptionist. 'Thank you.' She would not let Collier see how upset she was just so that it could be used against her later.

THIRTY-FIVE

Gina sat rigid on a tall stool behind the viewing screen with Collier to her left, still livid from their conversation in reception. His face mask disguised any expression that he had, and his eyes gave nothing away. He was clearly as bad as Sullivan and still today, she was training a pack of workplace bullies. She took a deep breath and tried to shift her focus onto the task in hand.

The post-mortem team were all in place. The script writer was ready. Another forensic-suited figure stood poised with a camera. Another camera was set up on a tripod which would film everything, and the same crime scene assistant was also ready to press go on that. A couple of others waited next to the pathologist – all togged up from head to toe.

Gina glanced at the young man lying on the large metal tray, all life drained from the bits of him she could see. The bag that had been placed over his head at the scene remained in place, as did the others covering his hands and feet. His clothes soiled from secretions that had escaped his body made Gina shudder. Death was ugly in all ways, yet it came to every single person.

She caught the smell, just slightly as one of the CSIs slammed a door and it made her baulk. It would coat her nostrils for the whole day at least, not a thought she relished. She glanced at DI Collier who stared at his feet. At least he was experiencing some discomfort after what he'd just put her through.

The victim had been described as a charmer and a lot of his neighbours had liked him. He was a father. Not that he wanted to be a father, but little Dora would now grow up without him or her mother. Gina thought of Lauren, an innocent person caught up in all this, and she hoped that Gerard Hale would flag up on their radar soon.

The pathologist continued by removing the bag from Robbie's head. The victim's dark wavy hair had stuck across his face. Then off came the hand and feet bags, each one carefully being entered into evidence. Then his T-shirt was cut and removed, followed by his jeans and his underpants. Each item was described for the recording. Gina read the text on his T-shirt which said, 'Body of a God' on the front of it. She pictured him wearing it as Sienna arrived to discuss their daughter. Sienna had arrived all dressed up as she'd been with Jacob earlier where they'd had sex. She tried to push Jacob out of her mind. In normal circumstances, she'd think it possible that Jacob followed her there and had a jealous fit, but it had to be Hale. Jacob did not have those tendencies. Or did he? Maybe she didn't know him as well as she thought she did and Collier was right. Confusion whirred through her mind and all she wanted to do was shut herself in a soundproof room and scream until she passed out.

Blood had matted the victim's hair and a brownish smear of it had stained his forehead. She pictured something solid coming down, the initial blow that rendered him unconscious or badly injured. That was before he'd been rolled up in his own rug and dumped in his own boot, while Sienna lay dead in his bed. It would take a strong person to do all that on their own. Had the killer seen them through a window, in the bedroom together just before the red mist of anger burst out?

The laceration mark was severe, caused by the coarse rope being pulled around his neck until he took his last breath. The killer deviated from using a scarf as the murder weapon, but the method remained the same.

'As you can all see, there is bruising to his torso and his right bicep, and there is a cut to his ankle. The skin on his arms is covered in scrapes and what we can see is consistent with resistance wounds. He saw that rope coming and put his arms up to block it. There are tiny fragments of rope fibre caught in his skin. There is also evidence of petechial haemorrhage. You can see these red dots. Cause of death, strangulation.'

Gina now pictured Robbie defending himself as best he could. He saw the rope coming and he fought with all he had but his attacker had been stronger, and his head injury had rendered him much weaker. For just a second, she pictured Jacob coming at Robbie with the rope, and she shook that thought away.

'You okay, DI Harte?'

'Yes, are you?' She gave DI Collier a look and she hoped that he couldn't sense what she was thinking.

As one of the CSIs turned Robbie's clothes inside out over a sheet of plastic, she brought something to the pathologist's attention. With the woman's back turned, Gina couldn't see what she was pointing at. Something relevant must have got caught in Robbie's jeans. She wondered if Robbie had known what his fate might entail and, in turn, he placed a clue there for them to find. Her heart rate began to hum as she waited patiently for the pathologist to continue speaking but he muffled some words that she failed to hear.

The pathologist popped the mystery item into a bag.

Time went slow as the team took hair and nail samples, various swabs, and noted every mole and marking down on the form. Only after all that did the pathologist begin with the Y-incision. Gina turned to look at DI Collier as the cut started behind the ear and drew all the way down to the pubis. 'I need five.' He swallowed.

Gina ignored him. As DI Collier left, she continued to watch as the bowels were removed. Then the other organs came out, ready for weighing and sample taking.

DI Collier returned just as the body was being sewn back up. 'You okay?' she snapped, still angry with him.

'Yeah. I had to call the super anyway.'

Gina shook her head and turned away from him. Shortly after, the pathologist called them over and led them to a room where all three took a seat. Gina couldn't wait any longer to find out what his team had bagged. It might be the one item that proved Jacob's innocence. 'I couldn't see what was found in the victim's jeans.'

'It was a gold wedding ring,' the pathologist replied.

Robbie and Lauren hadn't married so it wasn't likely that it was Robbie's ring. The killer was either missing a wedding ring, or the ring had some relevance to the case.

The pathologist continued. 'It is inscribed with the words, forever mine. There are visible partial fingerprints on the inside and outside of the ring along with bloody smears, so that, amongst other things, will be sent straight to the lab.'

'That's great. We'll need that fast-tracked.' Gina felt her excitement building. Just one of those fingerprints could belong to the killer and that might be all that was needed to prove Jacob innocent and bring the perp in. Her phone rang. 'I just need to take this, it's my DCI.' She stepped out of the room leaving DI Collier with the pathologist. 'Sir.'

'Gerard Hale is back. And we've got him.'

As soon as the call ended, she punched the air. The truth was surfacing and she needed to get back to see Sullivan's face as it unfolded.

THIRTY-SIX

NANCY

Nancy let out a snore and Fifi's wet tongue on her cheek told her she'd accidentally fallen asleep. Where had that last three hours gone? She rubbed her side and legs. That fall had knocked her sick. Grabbing her phone, she checked to see if she'd had any more horrible texts, but her inbox was empty. Lauren's words had been whirring through her head earlier and still they were as loud as ever. Calling the police wasn't an option but there was something she could do. She reached under her mattress, pulled out her old iPad and wiped the smeary cracked screen with her dressing gown sleeve. She had to reactivate her Facebook account and warn him off. Snatching the charger from her bottom drawer, she plugged it in, then she hid the gadget under her pillow. Maybe it had been wrong telling Lauren she had nothing to connect to the internet on, but she took the decision to keep Lauren away from social media and away from all the online chatter that would have upset her even more. She'd hate for Lauren to see that she did still have her iPad.

The house seemed silent, and her heart began to pound. If Lauren had left, she might be in danger. It was a good twenty-minute walk down a creepy lane to reach the nearest bus stop and then she'd have to wait alone for who knows how long. What if her attacker had returned and had watched Lauren leave? Nancy nudged Fifi away and stepped into her slippers. 'Where's your sister, Fifi?' The dog whined and tilted its head. 'Lauren,' she croaked, but there was no answer.

As she walked across the bedroom, everything swayed just a little bit. She shook her head with her eyes closed and gave it a moment before continuing. The dog pawed at the slight crack in the bedroom door, opening it further and Nancy stepped out. 'Lauren.' The dog thundered down the stairs. Nancy stepped across the landing and pushed Lauren's bedroom door open. The bed was unmade, and her clothes were strewn across the floor, but that was nothing unusual. She crept across the landing and nudged the bathroom door open. It was just as she left it, except the shower was dripping. Lauren must have used it a short while ago.

One step at a time led her into her dark hallway. She checked her watch. It was almost four and dusk was already upon Malvern. She rushed to the front door and peered through the spyhole. Her car was still on the drive. Not that she thought her daughter would take it as she'd never passed her test, but why was the house in silence? 'Lauren.'

She heard Lauren say shush from the kitchen. Heart now banging, she crept a few more steps past the lounge door. As she pushed the kitchen door, it bounced back at her. 'Lauren, what's going on?' she asked, in a loud whisper.

'Don't turn the lights on and don't say anything. Get on the floor,' her daughter said in a hushed voice.

Nancy gently lowered herself to the floor until she was on all fours. Fifi wagged her tail and darted through. Only then did Lauren gently push the door open to let her in. That's when Nancy saw Lauren on the floor too. Her eyes wide and her body shaking as she sat in almost darkness. 'My phone is dead so I couldn't try to call you, and I saw someone in the garden. He might still be there. I've been too scared to leave the kitchen floor in case he sees me. We need to call the police because he must have seen you. We're not safe.' Visibly shaking, Lauren ran her hands through her tangled hair. Fifi began nudging Lauren's arm from under the kitchen table.

'I'm going to lean up and look out the window, okay?'

Lauren shook her head. 'No, just crawl to the living room and call the police. He's standing by the gate. I saw his coat flapping in the breeze.'

Nancy held her hand out. 'It's okay. The door is locked. No one can get in. You're safe.'

Lauren shook her head and tears began to slip down her face. 'He's been in the house. I left my phone on the worktop and when I came back into the room, it was on the table.'

'Was the door locked?'

A confused look spread across Lauren's face. 'Yes, but he had to have come in because my phone had moved.'

'Are you sure you didn't move it?'

'Yes. I'm not going mad.'

'Sorry, sweetheart. I know you're not, but I am going to look out that window.' She shuffled closer to it and leaned up on her knees.

Lauren tugged the bottom of her dressing gown. 'Don't, please.'

Too late. Nancy pressed her nose on the cold glass and peered across the dusky garden, right into the corner where Lauren said the man had been standing. She stood.

'Mum, get down. What are you doing?'

She held out a hand to help her daughter up. 'Stand up, Lauren. It's okay.' She glanced at her garden patio set where the plastic covering had come off. It had blown from the table and ended up caught in the corner by the gate where it remained flapping in the breeze.

Slowly, Lauren got to her feet and gazed out. 'There was a man.'

The lock was still slid across the gate. Nancy reached down and pressed the door handle. The door was locked, and the keys were hung up next to the door. Her daughter had merely let her fear get the better of her. Nancy was used to an isolated life, but this environment was proving no good for her daughter. 'I know that text message scared you and with all that has happened, I understand you must be terrified. I'm going to deal with it, okay?' As she pressed a little harder on the window, it nudged forward slightly. The catch was off. She closed the window properly as Fifi distracted Lauren. No one would have known it was open and there was no man in the garden.

'How will you deal with it? You won't call the police. You won't let me call them.' Lauren frowned and flicked the kitchen light on.

'No, but I have a plan. I have a friend who will have a word with him for me. I'm going to call this friend, and I'll sort this. There will be no more texts, I promise.'

Lauren exhaled. 'Whatever. I can't live like this. This place is sending me mad. My fiancé and best friend have just been murdered; I need my other friends and I can't see them. Not one of them has offered to come to me. I even tried to call Robbie's brother but he's not answering either. I've never felt so alone.' She burst into tears.

'Come here. You're not alone, you have me.' Nancy held her daughter as she cried on her shoulder. 'Do you want a chamomile tea? It might help you relax?'

'No, Mum. I don't need tea! I need to escape this limbo. I need to know what I've done to deserve such crap friends.'

She rubbed her daughter's back. 'It's not you. Please never think that. People can be odd in circumstances like this. They don't know what to say or do. Just give it time.'

'Don't make excuses for them. Please don't.'

Lauren was right. Her closest friends were nowhere to be seen. 'You've always got me. I will always be here for you.'

Lauren pulled away and wiped her eyes. 'Thanks, Mum. Sorry about what just happened. I got scared, but I really thought I'd seen someone but maybe it was just that sheet of plastic. Promise me that no one attacked you last night and that scary man doesn't know where you live.'

'I cross my heart and I'd never lie to you, ever. I fell, that was all. We're safe here. I promise.' She almost choked on her lie and hoped that Lauren didn't notice. Her daughter had been right earlier. Nancy knew that she could have easily been followed home and she saw the shadow of a man, but it wasn't the murderer. The man she knew was far too much of a coward to do anything more than provide a few minor scares. Reaching across the kitchen, she pulled the blinds down. 'There, we're all cocooned in. I'll close the lounge curtains, double-check all the locks and we're as safe as safe can be. Now go and charge your phone.'

'Thanks. I'm just going to watch a bit of TV. It might keep my mind from coming up with all kinds of crazy.' Lauren snatched her phone from the table and left for the lounge.

'Great. I'll freshen up and then I'll put some dinner on.'

Fifi followed Lauren into the living room. Nancy pulled two slats apart on the blind and tried to see into the dark corners of the garden. The plastic still flapped, and the gate was still locked. She swallowed, knowing she had no choice but to confront what was happening and that meant hashing all this out with the man who was behind all this, Preston Hemming. She hurried back upstairs and pulled her partly charged iPad from under the pillow. Within seconds, she'd reactivated her Facebook account and sent him the briefest of messages.

You. Me. Grafton's Garden Centre. Tomorrow. Ten in the morning. Be there or I will call the police and I don't care what happens to me.

Maybe it was time to confront her nasty messenger in the safety of a public place. She would record the whole conversation on her phone without him knowing. Yes, they clashed at that protest and, yes, it had got a bit physical but if he was turning up at her house, harassing her and her daughter, it had to stop, and preferably without the police being involved. She wasn't scared. Never was, never would be. Hemming was nothing but a pathetic little boy with an angry streak. Nothing she couldn't handle. In fact, she should have done this a long time ago. Her iPad lit up with a reply.

You're on, bitch. Nice house, by the way.

With anger shaking through her, she turned the tablet off and placed it back under her bed. *You're on, Preston.* She turned off her light and gave her eyes a moment to adjust. Staring out of her bedroom window at the back garden and beyond, she wondered if he was out there watching. No, she knew he was out there watching. He might scare Lauren, but he didn't scare her. After she'd finished with him, he'd wish he'd never been born.

THIRTY-SEVEN

Gina tapped her fingernails on her desk while waiting for Collier to get back from another mini briefing with Sullivan. They had Hale in interview room two and the clock was ticking. He'd been arrested at the station, so they had twenty-four hours in which to charge him otherwise they had to let him go. Wyre knocked on her office door and entered. 'Thought you might appreciate this.' She placed the steaming hot cup of coffee on her desk.

'I've never needed this more. Thank you so much.' She brought the cup to her lips, blew the steam away and took a sip of the dark liquid in the hope that it would bring her back to life. 'I feel like we're wasting precious time while they have another one of their secret meetings.'

'I know.' Wyre nodded. 'One good thing though, he said he doesn't need a solicitor so at least there's no hold up there.' She paused. 'They told me to leave the incident room, so I thought I'd see how you were.' Wyre sat.

'Who's they?'

'Sullivan, Hale and Briggs.'

'Briggs?'

'I guess this is how it will be for this case. They talk first, share information about what's been gathered on Jacob, then they decide what they want to tell us after.'

Gina leaned back in her chair. 'He didn't do it. We have Hale in an interview room. All is going to become clear soon and Jacob will be off the hook, even though Sullivan and Collier are doing their best to prove he did it before we've even spoken to Hale.'

Wyre played with a strand of her hair. 'I just want everything to go back to normal.'

'How have things been today, while I was out with Collier?'

'You know I'm like a neat freak?'

Gina nodded. Wyre never normally had anything out of place. She was smart, fit, great at her job, a real credit to the station.

'Well, Sullivan told me that my boots were dirty, and I had to clean them. She said that you might run a slack department but while she was heading the case, she wouldn't. I literally had a leaf stuck to my boots after being out and working like a dog all day. It's not so much what she said, it was the smug look on her face as she said it.'

Gina bit her bottom lip and sighed. 'It's nothing personal against you. She doesn't like me. That was a dig at the way I run things. She just chips away at people. Hopefully we'll get this case sewn up and she'll be out of our hair, along with her sidekick. I worked with her for two years and hated every moment of it. Soon she'll just buzz off back to Hereford and just make her own staff miserable.'

Collier cleared his throat as he stood at the door.

Gina felt her face begin to redden and heat up. Had he heard everything she'd just said? She wondered if she even cared after the conversation they'd had earlier.

Wyre stood, recognising the awkwardness of the situation. 'I best get back to it, guv.' Her colleague left.

'How long were you standing there?'

'Long enough. What does it matter? It's good to know where we all stand with each other. We're ready to interview Hale. As before, you lead as you usually would and I'll back you up.'

She took a long swig of the coffee that Wyre had made and stood, ready to start.

'Your shirt has come untucked. If Sullivan sees that—'

'I know, I know.' She pushed her shirt into place and followed him along the corridor. 'Did she say anything about Jacob?'

He stopped and turned. 'You know I can't say anything. If Sullivan wants you to know what's happening on that side, she'll tell you.'

'I'm worried about him, that's all. I care about my team.'

'Okay, I'll tell you this.' He glanced up and down the corridor. 'They were processing his bail but something came up and they've kept him in. In fact, it's not looking brilliant for him. He'll need one hell of a solicitor. That's all I'm going to say.'

'What does that mean?'

He ignored her and walked off towards the interview room. She hit the wall as hard as she could and held in the yell that was dying to escape. All she could think about was her colleague, stewing in a cell and hurtling towards a murder charge. She recalled how disturbed he looked following their visit to the scene of Sienna's murder. All day he looked as sick as a dog, and she couldn't shrug off the thought that he had come face to face with his crime.

Sullivan's heels clacked along the corridor. She stopped and stared at Gina, a smirk forming on her lips. 'Gina, Gina, Gina, look at you. A murderer right under your nose and you don't even see it. You really should have quit all those years ago. You really don't have what it takes to keep your cases out of your head. You never did and look at you now. It has me questioning whether you're up to this.'

Gina took a deep breath and continued down the corridor. Sullivan breezed past, shoulder banging Gina as she hurried to the viewing room.

THIRTY-EIGHT

Sullivan wanted Gina to bite, to get angry and be taken off the case. Holding her tense hands by her sides, she took a deep breath. If Sullivan caught wind that she'd upset Gina, it would make her day. She continued down the corridor and around the corner to reach the interview room where Collier was waiting outside for her. How she wished it wasn't him and that it was Jacob who was with her on the case, and that he hadn't just been refused bail. She opened the door and let Collier go in first so that he could sit next to the recording machine. Gina closed the door and tried to quell the nausea that was building in the pit of her stomach because Sullivan was about to judge her every move from the viewing room.

While Collier introduced them for the tape, Gina observed the suspect. His teeth were whiter than fresh snow and the colour of his ice-blond crew cut was faker than a display of Armani bags being sold out of the boot of a car. His tight jacket showed how ripped he was. He looked like he had the strength to move Robbie Shields's body on his own. 'Can you confirm your full name for the tape?'

'Gerard Elliot Hale.' He leaned back and folded his arms.

'Date of birth.'

'Twelfth of March, nineteen ninety.'

Gina thought he looked more to be in his mid-twenties, rather than his thirties. There was an immaturity about the man.

'You've waived your right to legal representation. If anything changes and you want a solicitor, just let us know.'

He sniffed. 'I don't need one because I haven't done anything.'

'Tell me about your relationship with Sienna Moorcroft?'

He looked to the right and pressed his lips together for a second before speaking. 'We had a thing. It was fast, intense and she ended up moving in with me early December. She and her daughter stayed for two weeks, and we realised we'd moved too fast, so she moved back in with her landlady, Patsy, who she rented a room off.'

'How did that make you feel?'

He swallowed. 'I didn't want her to leave. This might sound stupid but as soon as I met her, I knew we were meant to be together. We got on well and I thought her moving in would turn my life around but after that, everything went downhill. My house got repossessed. I knew it was coming but I was living in denial. I even thought, with Sienna's wage coming in and her savings, I could pay them off and keep the house, and that we'd all live happily together in it and in return, I'd put her name on the house. It was a pipe dream. I know that now. She found out about my financial situation, we argued, and she stormed out. I did everything I could to win her back. I begged, I pleaded, but she didn't want me.'

Gina took the file off Collier and began to read through the notes. She'd been told that Sienna had left him because of his possessiveness and that he'd harassed her after. There was more to the story than Hale was letting on. She'd seen that much for herself. 'Tell me about the caravan.' Gina laid the photos of his

boards and the note on the table while she described them for
the tape. 'We found photos of Sienna Moorcroft, photos of
Robbie Shields and a log of their whereabouts. The note says,
"that bitch. She's nothing but a cheap whore and to think, I
thought I could marry that. She's not going to get away with
what she did to me, and she lied. All that time she was with him
too. The plan. Make her pay. Follow her, fuck with her head.
She deserves it." All this is followed by a doodle of a gun. This
shows us that you were stalking her and were planning to kill
her and then, we find her murdered.'

'I can explain.' He scrunched his brows.

'Please do.'

'I was angry, in fact, I knew there was a reason she'd left me,
and I suspected it was because she was seeing someone else. I
did follow her. I wrote all those horrible things, but I didn't kill
her. My head was in a real funny place, and I thought by
writing my feelings down, it would help. I'd lost my home and
she walked out on me. My own mother wouldn't let me stay
with her and she made me sneak into that cold, damp caravan
when the site was shut. Everything was going wrong at once
and I stupidly blamed Sienna. I'm not proud of my behaviour.
That's why I went to London to see my old uni mates. I needed
to clear my head. Really, I needed to take responsibility too, so
it's important that I tell you the truth. I will admit to following
Sienna a little bit. Not all the time. It's not like I tailed her
twenty-four seven. Just when I pined for her, or I was a bit
lonely – you have me there. I'm guilty of being a nuisance to
Sienna, but I did not murder her or Robbie. On that night I was
staying with my mother. I was there all night.'

'Your mother said she went to bed early because you fell
asleep on the settee. You had opportunity and you have a
motive. She rejected you and you couldn't handle it, could you?
You needed her money as you were about to lose your home.
That's why you followed her. Your mother didn't hear you

leave. You saw Sienna go to Robbie Shields's house and you killed her, didn't you?'

'No.' He slammed his open palm on the table and tilted his head. His bottom lip quivered, and he looked like he might cry. 'That's not what happened. I didn't follow her that night and I've never been violent.'

'And how about Robbie? He popped out and when he came back, he saw what you'd done to Sienna. Tell me what you did to him?'

'I didn't do anything.'

'Forensics have samples from Robbie Shields's car. We will know if they belong to you so it's in your interest to tell us now.'

'I have nothing to tell.' His chin and cheeks began to turn crimson. 'You really are barking up the wrong tree.'

'Do you ever go to Redditch?'

He scrunched up his nose. 'What has that got to do with anything?'

'Please answer the question.'

'I've been to the shopping centre, but I tend to go to Birmingham more. I have a friend who lives in Redditch, but I last went a few years ago.'

Tiffany had been strangled in her home four years ago. Gina wondered if he'd mention Tiffany's name. 'What is your friend's name?'

'Seriously?'

'We just need a name.'

'Janice Grant. We went to school together and I used to hang out with her brother. He died so I visited her a few times. We didn't date or have a relationship. I just went to see if she was okay.'

Flicking through the file, she pulled out the photo of the ring that the pathologist had emailed to her. 'Have you ever seen the ring in this photo?'

'No, it's not mine. I've never been married.'

Gina placed another photo on the table. 'For the tape, I'm showing Mr Hale a photo of the scarf which was used to strangle Sienna Moorcroft to death.'

He shrugged. 'What's that?'

'Your mother owns a scarf with blue flowers on it.'

'She owns a million scarves. Every drawer is stuffed with them. She hoards them like some crazy person.'

'Except her scarf like this one is missing.'

His shaking got more erratic. 'This is a fit up. I've never seen that scarf in my life. In fact, I've changed my mind. I didn't want a solicitor because I knew what I'd done and I wanted to own up and do the right thing, but I'm not having you lot falsely charge me with a double murder. I. Did. Not. Kill. Anyone. I was at my mother's house all night on Saturday the twenty-eighth. I'm sure there will be a way of me being able to confirm that. Ask some of the neighbours if they saw me go out. There's a nosy bastard who lives next door, his name is Amos Jeffrey. Ask him. Do your job.'

Gina collected up all the photos and passed them to DI Collier, who placed them back in the file. She went to speak.

'Don't ask another question. I'm taking my right to silence. Don't waste your breath.' He made a zip motion across his mouth with his fingers and folded his arms again.

Gina fired several more questions at him but true to his word, he replied with no comment after each one.

'Actually, I do have one more thing to say. Well two. I realise I have a problem. Those photos I took, that horrible note I wrote, following Sienna in the hope that I could drive her back to me somehow, that was messed up. I see it and I'm going to get help for that. I don't want to be that person anymore. I know I've said that already, but I want it noted.'

'What is the second thing?'

'I don't remember dates or times, but I followed Sienna about two weeks ago, she was with a man in a dark saloon car. I didn't take a photo. As soon as she got out of his car and went into her house, he was on the phone arguing with someone and he sat there for half an hour, staring at the door she'd just gone through like some obsessive nutter, then he literally lost it in his car. He hit the steering wheel. He got out and kicked his tyres and he was clenching his fists while talking to himself. You need to find that angry bastard. He did it because it wasn't me.'

Gina pictured Jacob arguing on his phone, parked up while Hale watched on. It wasn't looking good if Hale was telling the truth, but she had no way of determining if he'd just fed them a pack of lies. Speaking to his mother's neighbour, Amos Jeffrey, would be a good start. She needed to know if Hale left the house that night, or if anyone saw him driving away. She wanted nothing more than to call Jacob up and ask him what the hell was going on but that was never going to happen, not while he was still in custody. She saw O'Connor through the little square of glass in the door, so she instructed Collier to wrap the interview up. Hurrying out, she walked a little further down the corridor. Sullivan slammed the viewing room door to join them just as O'Connor was going to speak. 'Stand aside, Harte.'

She blew out a breath and it sickened her to comply, but the smallest of wrong moves would have Sullivan laughing as she was dropped from the case and sent home. 'Yes, ma'am.'

'What is it?' Sullivan sniffed and pressed her lips together as she stared at O'Connor. 'You report to me first.'

'Yes, ma'am,' O'Connor said. 'I've been scouring all previous strangling cases similar to that of Tiffany Crawford.'

'And?'

'There's an unsolved case. A woman was attacked in her home in Kidderminster, but she now lives in Tardebigge, which is just outside Redditch.'

Sullivan scrunched her face. 'I know where Tardebigge is.'

'Okay, there are similarities in the cases, and she claims to be missing an earring after the attack. There is a photo of the remaining earring in the file and it's identical to the one found at the scene of Tiffany Crawford's attack.'

'We need to speak to her, now.' Gina glanced back as Collier got relieved by a PC who would take Hale to a cell while he waited for a solicitor.

O'Connor glanced at Sullivan and Sullivan glanced at Collier. 'Collier, go with her and report directly to me and DCI Briggs straight away.'

Gina exhaled as Sullivan turned away from them and headed back to the incident room.

'That's good news isn't it, guv. That link is solid.' O'Connor smiled.

She nodded. 'Our serial strangler theory holds. We need to get to the bottom of this before he strikes again.' With two suspects in custody, they'd normally feel secure that no more attacks would take place, but one was Jacob, and she wasn't sure about Hale. He was disturbed, he was dangerously creepy, but was he a murderer? 'O'Connor?'

'Guv.'

'Could you please call the victim and let her know that we need to speak to her and that we're on our way?'

He nodded and left her with Collier. She swallowed. Something about the whole case wasn't adding up. The only people who could really want Sienna and Robbie dead were Gerard Hale or Jacob. Gina couldn't put her finger on that niggle at the back of her mind, the niggle she couldn't unravel. A sick feeling in her gut told her to not be complacent and that the murderer could still be out there, and time was her enemy.

THIRTY-NINE

'It's about time you found who did this to me. What's going on?'
Gina recognised the woman from the case file as the victim,
Hazel Becker, now Blackford, since she got married. The security light lit up the huge frontage. To the right of the house was
a canal and to the left, a dense thicket. Gina and Collier had
spent several minutes driving along the snaking roads to find the
house that was barely visible in the dark.

'May we come in?'

Hazel opened the door to reveal a wide hallway. It sported
only one open door and that led to a room with a bar at one end
and a pool table in the middle. Benches against the wall made
the room look a bit like a cosy pub. 'Take a seat but do try to be
quiet. My wife is in the kitchen trying to get our baby to sleep.'

'Of course. How old is your little one?' Gina asked.

'Six months. She barely sleeps as you can see from my eye
bags, but I forgive her because she's so cute.'

Collier sat next to Gina on the bench and Hazel pulled out
a stool and sat opposite them on the ends of her long black hair.
It shone a little blue and green under the light in the same way
that a raven's feathers did.

'So, what do you have? The officer I spoke to on the phone said you'd explain everything.' She bit a nail. 'Have you caught him?'

Gina shook her head. 'Last Saturday night a woman was murdered in Cleevesford and there are some similarities to your attack. We're also linking your attack to another one that took place in Redditch four years ago.'

'Jeez, murdered? And there are two other victims?'

Gina swallowed. 'Three actually. One woman was strangled in her own home, very much like your attack, and another where the woman was murdered.'

'He's escalating, isn't he? He wanted to kill me so badly, but I fought, and he hated it. Who was number four?'

'A man who was with the third victim that evening.'

Hazel scrunched her brow. 'That doesn't fit his pattern, obviously. I'm gathering he got in the way.'

Gina nodded. 'It looks that way, although we can't be certain yet. It sounds like you've spent a lot of time analysing your attack.'

She nodded and opened her brown eyes wide. Gina had seen a past photo of Hazel on file and she had blue eyes. Gina knew she had to be wearing coloured contact lenses. 'I did and I still do, well attacks and murders in general. I love true crime programmes.' She cleared her throat. 'The first couple of years were a fuzzy blur. I thought he was everywhere, that he was watching me, so I read and researched everything I could so that I could understand him better. Know your enemy, that was the idea. I thought, the more I could learn about his type, the more of a chance I had of recognising him if he came into my life again.'

'And do you feel as though he's come into your life again at any point?'

She shrugged. 'I didn't feel safe in that house anymore, so we moved. Since then, I stay off social media, I work from home, and I rarely go out. I finally feel as though he doesn't know where I am. I told the police this on the night and I've repeated this many times since, but he had to have been stalking me. He attacked me when Karin was away, so he had to know our routine. One week per month, Karin had to work in the New York office. It was an inconvenience, but she loved that job. He must have known I was alone in the house.'

Gina waited for Collier to scrawl a few notes. She made a mental note that Tiffany Crawford's attack was the same in that her husband was away at the time, on a stag night. Sienna's attack was different though. It didn't follow the same pattern, but the scarf linked Sienna and Tiffany. Also, Sienna was never home alone, she lived with her landlady. Was that why he changed his pattern? 'Do you remember seeing anyone in the run up to her leaving for New York or during the weeks before?'

She nodded. 'I told the police. It was as if someone was there all the time, but I could never see who. Things got moved around the house and I could sense someone was maybe watching me through the windows. I'd catch movement out of the corner of my eye and as soon as I turned, there would be nothing or no one there.' She paused and let out a laugh. 'I dismissed it, wrote it off as stress and me being nervous when I was home alone. Anyway, when he came into my house, I was asleep, but he knew his way around. He knew where I slept because while I slept, he came into my room and took my phone. I lie awake imagining him watching me sleep, waiting for his moment.'

'Can you talk me through that night, as you remember it?'

Hazel looked down and bit her nail.

'We're really sorry for putting you through this. If you'd rather not, that's okay.' The last thing Gina wanted to do was re-traumatise Hazel but there was a killer on the loose. She hoped Hazel would continue. 'But he is still out there, and we want him caught. It might be the smallest thing that helps us to catch him.'

She took a deep breath and let it out slowly. 'At first, I heard the noise, just a tap maybe. I can't really remember but it woke me up. My phone wasn't on my bedside table, and I panicked. I knew I left it there and I could hear someone approaching. I was too slow to block the door with some furniture and before I had a chance to think, he opened it and stood there. He was taller than me, wore dark clothes and a balaclava. All I could see was these intense staring eyes in the dark and I knew he was going to kill me. The room lit up. He had my phone in his hand. I pleaded with him, begged him to take my bag and car but he wasn't interested in those things. I knew then that it was me he wanted so I ran at him. I remember falling back. Maybe he pushed me, or I tripped. I'm not sure. When I was down, I kicked him directly in the balls. While he was groaning in pain, I got up and ran to the stairs.' She stopped and took a few deep breaths.

Hazel's knee began banging the table and her hands shook.

'I know this is hard and I'm sorry we're asking you to talk us through it again. You're now at the stairs.'

'I ran down and I think I slipped down a couple. I remember thinking if I fell, I'd die because he was so close. I raced him to the front door and just as I was about to open it, he hit me with something. My earring fell out and then he tried to strangle me with one of my own scarves. Not once did I give up. We had an umbrella stand by the door. I grabbed one and I jabbed him with the end of a golf umbrella. I'm not sure where I caught him or how much damage I did but he keeled over. I opened the door, and I ran barefoot with the scarf still flapping round my neck. I ran in the dark until I reached the care home down the road. I banged on the door, they let me in, and the police turned up. When they went to the house, he'd gone. He did bleed but I've been told he's not on your files, so they've never been able to identify him from that.'

'The report seems to show a lack of suspects. I think one of your colleagues was cleared as he had a firm alibi.'

She nodded. 'That's right. I can't think of anyone who would have wanted to kill me, yet the attack seemed so personal. I've been through every person I know, racking my brains.'

'How long had you and your now wife been in a relationship then?'

'A couple of years, at least. I'd had other partners, two men and a woman, but I hadn't been in contact with any of them for ages. All my break-ups have been civil. No weird neighbours or friends either. I really don't think it's anyone I knew. I think he targeted me, but I don't know why. Maybe I was an easy target, living in the country, being alone sometimes. Maybe that's the only reason he chose me.'

Gina watched Collier write slowly and then continued as he finished his sentence with a full stop. 'I haven't seen anything in your report that suggests this but as far as you were aware, was anything left behind that didn't belong to you?'

'No.'

Gina pondered that information. If the pattern was correct, they had found the strangler's first victim. She was the intended, not like Robbie Shields. The perp had watched her, planned his attack meticulously, then he messed up and got hurt resulting in his blood being left behind. That screamed early attempt. There was no blood left after Tiffany's attack, but she too managed to fight him off. Sienna wasn't so lucky. By then, he was experienced in how they fight back, and he was ready with a weapon which was used to stun her first.

Gina pulled a paper file from her bag and removed a photo. She showed Hazel the earring. 'This was found at the scene of the second attack. He jabbed the victim with it.'

'And you know that's my missing earring so it must be him. Let me guess. He takes something from one attack and incorporates it into his next attack and the same happened for attack number three. As nothing was left at my scene, I was the first.'

Gina nodded. 'Please don't mention that information to anyone. We're keeping it out of the public domain as it may be the very thing that catches the killer.'

'I won't and I understand why. It's been a long time since I've slept well at night even though I've moved and have a different surname. My job has changed, everything about me has changed. I'm naturally blonde and my eyes are blue. I spend ages disguising the old me and I'd like her back one day. I'd like to live again. I'd like to have a Facebook account and be able to post my holiday snaps like normal people. I don't want to walk into a shop and think he's the man in the queue behind me.' She stood, walked over to her bar and poured herself a brandy with her shaking hands. For all her bravado, Gina could tell that Hazel was trying to bottle her fear up. 'Do you want one?'

'No, we're good, thank you,' Gina replied on behalf of her and Collier.

'There's something I didn't mention and now that I think of it, I should have. I'd been to the hairdressers that day and didn't think much of it, but you said it might be in the detail. It might be nothing.'

Gina raised her brows. 'Please go on.'

'There was a strip of my hair missing, underneath. About an inch wide and two inches long. I thought the hairdresser slipped, and I had so much hair, it didn't matter. I'd used a student at the college to save a bit of money.'

Gina made a mental note to ask Tiffany about her hair. She observed Hazel for a second longer as she tried to picture her back then with long blonde hair and the blue eyes. She then imagined Hazel carrying another couple of stone and in her mind, she could almost see Tiffany. She too had blonde hair and blue eyes.

The baby began to cry, and Hazel's wife knocked and entered. 'She needs feeding and that's something I can't do as we forgot to express, sorry, love.' She passed the baby to Hazel.

Gina stood and they wrapped up the interview.

'Please let me know what you find out,' Hazel said as she pulled her sweater up to feed the baby.

Gina assured her that they would.

As they headed to the car, thoughts kept whirring through Gina's mind. He had a type when it came to Hazel and Tiffany, but Sienna didn't fit the picture. He'd certainly broken his pattern and not only by murdering Robbie. She wondered if the hair was the trophy. As far as she was aware, Bernard or the pathologist hadn't mentioned a chunk of hair missing from Sienna's head. That would have flagged up during the post-mortem.

'That's confused things even more,' Collier said as he got into the car.

All she could do was nod. She had no words for him, especially as he'd already decided it was Jacob. Collier was now in this to close all other avenues. It wasn't how it should be but that's how it was. 'We've got time to visit Amos Jeffrey. Can you clear it with Sullivan?' Here she was, playing by the rules.

He nodded and pulled his phone out. They had Hale in custody. If it was him, she was going to make sure he never left.

FORTY

Gina knocked on Amos Jeffrey's door again. Collier stood on the step behind her. Ms Hale next door peered through her window. As soon as Gina spotted her, she pulled the curtain across. A frail man using a walking frame opened the door several minutes later. 'Sorry, my old bones won't let me move any faster. Who are you?' He looked at each of them in turn. Gina spotted the camera housed in a black dome above his door.

'I'm DI Harte, this is DI Collier. May we come in?'

He shrugged. 'I guess. It's always nice to have visitors. Although, I do have a woman coming over soon, so you best be quick.'

'Are you Mr Jeffrey?'

He nodded. 'Amos.'

'We'll try not to take up too much of your time.'

He turned his back, slowly shuffling with the help of a walking frame. Gina led the way and Collier closed the door. He turned into the dining room, laid neatly with place mats and candles.

'Date night.' He nodded for them to sit. 'Make sure you don't mess the table up. Right, what can I help you with?'

Gina sat and smiled. 'I need to ask you a couple of questions and I'd appreciate it if you didn't mention them to anyone else for the time being as we're currently investigating some serious crimes.'

'Sounds intriguing. Go ahead. Discretion is my middle name. I see all but say nothing. Sorry, I don't have a lot to do and I'm the only one on the road with CCTV.' He dabbed his bald head with a serviette as the log burner roared away. 'Sorry about the heat, she's always cold.'

'We need to speak about Saturday night.'

'Okay, I was in. As you can gather, I don't get out much, especially in the evenings. My dancing days are non-existent.' He let out a laugh.

'Would you have your CCTV from that night?'

He shook his head. 'No, it's written over after forty-eight hours.' He leaned back on the kitchen chair and pressed his lips together. 'I was sitting in here though, with the curtains open. I like to watch the world go by. It makes me feel less lonely.'

'Do you know Mr Hale, your neighbour's son?'

'Oh him.'

Gina noticed that Amos's expression changed from cheery to a frown. 'He was a little shit in his teens. He scratched my car, threw a firework at my shed and graffitied my back wall. But that was a long time ago. I hear him arguing with his mother here and there and I heard them arguing on Saturday but that was earlier in the day.'

'Did you hear what they were arguing about?'

He shook his head. 'No. The walls are thick. I could just tell by the tone and the fact that they were shouting over each other that something was going on. Saying that, it could have been the telly.'

'Do you remember seeing him leave the house on Saturday night?' She knew that he'd been using his own car and his mother's saloon car.

'No.'

'Did you notice either his car or Ms Hale's car missing?'

He slowly blew out a breath. 'No, sorry.'

Someone rang the bell.

'You couldn't be a darling and get that for me, could you?' He pointed to the walking frame.

Gina smiled. 'I'm sure DI Collier would be happy to.' Collier cleared his throat and hurried to the door. A woman made a bit of small talk as she asked for Amos, then she shuffled into the dining room.

'Ah, Margaret. The DIs have come to ask a few questions. Have a seat. The takeaway will be here in about half an hour so we're okay for time.'

The woman removed her duffel coat and sat next to Amos. 'DIs? Has something happened, Amos? Are you okay?'

He nodded. 'Yes, it's not me. The police just wanted to know if I saw Gerard leaving his mother's house on Saturday night. I didn't see anything though. Maybe you did. Did you clock both cars being on the road that night when you walked Polly. Polly's her dog.' He turned to Gina.

'You know me, I only walk up and down the path under the street lamps but when I was walking, both cars were there. I did see Gerard. It was about eleven, maybe eleven thirty. He stood at the window, yawning and rubbing his eyes like he'd just woken up. I waved but he didn't see me. Then he closed the curtains. I was outside for about ten minutes more while I waited for Polly to do her business, then I went in.'

Gina felt her warm body boiling up as she fidgeted out of the way of the fire. Her phone beeped with a message. It was from O'Connor.

I thought you should know, guv. Gerard Hale's mother sent us an email with a photo attached. She's found her missing scarf. Apparently, it got caught at the back of her drawers. The scarf is nothing like the one used to murder Sienna Moorcroft. It has completely different flowers on it.

The room began to close in on her. With Margaret claiming to have seen Hale at the time of Sienna's murder, he was out of the frame. And that only left one suspect. Jacob.

FORTY-ONE

TIFFANY

Wednesday, 1 February

She prised a sticky eye open and waited for her vision to focus on the time. It was just after three in the morning and her head was pounding like never before. It was like the weight of everything had hit her and... she couldn't remember the evening again. The police went. Her heart went from relaxed to banging within a second. She jumped out of bed and opened the curtain just a little and she saw the police car parked up outside. An officer was reassuringly stuffing a sandwich into his mouth. She was safe, for now.

Grabbing her phone, she used it to light up the room. Kieron wasn't in bed. She listened intently and there were voices coming from the living room. After opening the door, she stepped out onto the hall carpet and shivered. The heating would have gone off hours ago. 'Kieron,' she called.

He ran into the hallway and led her into the lounge. The

stark main light made her wince, and her legs began to wobble. 'Here, sit down.'

'What's going on?'

He stared at her blankly and the uniformed officer sat on the settee, pen in one hand, pad in another. 'Can't you remember?' His eyes pleaded with her to think.

Bursting into tears, she knew she'd been wandering again. Her tablet packet was on the table next to an empty tumbler. A bottle of sherry that they'd had for years in the cupboard had been left under the table. She tried to think back. The news had been on but what had happened next? The room had been spinning and she'd closed her eyes, then opened them again as Kieron led her to bed. There had been an argument and she'd tried to push him. He'd moaned that he'd only gone to take a bath and when he came out... she must have drunk the sherry and taken her tablets. That's why the night wasn't making much sense. 'I'm sorry.'

He stood and held his arms open. She sank into them. 'I don't think my wife is up to making a statement tonight. Can we do it tomorrow?'

The police officer stood and nodded. Tiffany caught a glimpse of an evidence bag. 'What's that?' She pulled away from Kieron and pointed at the bag. 'Get that out of my flat now.' It wasn't the scarf that he strangled her with, but it was similar enough to make her skin crawl. It looked like one of her scarves, the ones she never wore anymore following the attack.

'We're entering it into evidence, Mrs Crawford.' The officer began walking to the living room door. 'I think your husband is right. We can interview you tomorrow. We'll make sure that an officer remains outside all night.'

With that he left her with Kieron. As the front door slammed shut, she sat. 'How did the scarf get here?'

'You said you found it.'

'I what?'

'You weren't in bed. It was about an hour ago. You moved the chair away from the door and went outside in your sleep. You came back in with it. I asked you where you got it from, and you pointed out the bedroom window at the bushes.'

She leaned down and pulled a dead leaf from between her toes. 'Didn't the police see who left it there?'

'They were on a changeover. I'm so worried about you, Tiff. I think you need to see a doctor and you need to be honest about this.' He grabbed the half-empty bottle of sherry and the pills. 'This can't go on. I know you're worried, and I know he's trying to scare you, but you'll end up accidentally killing yourself. I don't know what to do anymore.' Tears began to run down his cheeks. 'I need you. I need the old Tiff back. Please, I'm begging you. I just want it to be like it was before the attack.' He fell onto the settee and sobbed.

She'd never seen Kieron like this. He'd always been the strong one in the relationship, but she'd broken him. She hurried over and went to hug him, but he flinched. 'Kieron, what's up.'

He stared at her and wiped his eyes. 'Isn't it obvious?'

More tears rolled down her cheeks.

'I'm scared for you and...' He hesitated. 'I'm scared of you.'

FORTY-TWO

Gina got out of the shower and began to dry herself, then she stopped as she heard Briggs talking downstairs. She wrapped a towel over her dripping hair and pulled her bathrobe on. Ebony began to rub herself against Gina's damp leg, depositing cat hairs all over her. She lifted the cat up and began to quietly walk down the stairs while she listened to Briggs speaking on the phone.

'No, I want her on the case. Your DI didn't even read the whole file. From what I heard she had to fill him in on the historical strangulation. Not a problem, he came in cold and was sent straight out after the quickest of briefings, but he can't handle it alone.' He paused. 'I know it's not ideal and it's looking likely that he'll be charged, but for now DI Harte stays. We'll talk again when I get into the office.'

She sat on the step, knowing full well that Sullivan was on the other end of the call. For now – what did that mean? Were they all working on a way to get Collier up to speed so that they could push her out?

'No, she stays.'

He paced up and down the kitchen.

He paused. 'No, she's not sloppy in her job and just because I'm saying that it doesn't mean I'm soft on her so please stop insinuating that I am. I will do what is necessary for the case but only when the time is right.'

Ebony meowed so she let her go.

'I've got to go. Yes, okay. A briefing at ten with you and Collier. I'll be there.'

She hurried down the rest of the stairs and pressed her lips together as he looked across at her. 'When have you and Sullivan decided is the right time to ditch me off the case? I heard you say that I'm staying on it, for now.'

He slammed his phone on the table. 'I'm doing what I need to do to keep you on the case.'

'Which is wait until Collier is up to speed then let me go, because that's what it sounded like. You know, that woman is the reason I missed Hannah in school plays and sports days and now, look how that's come back to bite me. We have the worst mother daughter relationship ever. Sullivan told me the job had to come before everything and I so badly wanted to prove myself, I believed her. I did everything I could to please her, yet I never did, and I still rightly or wrongly put the job before everything else like some institutionalised robot.' Gina paused. 'Thanks for nothing. You know I need to stay on this case, for Jacob.'

'It's not like that, Gina, it really isn't. I'm trying my best to stay on it myself so please don't doubt me, not now. Jacob may have been your right hand, but you are mine. Our department sticks together, and I will not hear a bad word said against you. I've never met anyone more committed to the job, but it saddens me to know that she took advantage of that in the past. Let's get this case wrapped up and then we can send Collier and Sullivan packing.'

'Thanks and I'm sorry, I know you're stuck in the middle. Any developments on the case?' It saddened her that Sullivan was coming between her and Briggs. As if things couldn't get any worse. She hoped that he was being truthful with her.

He nodded. 'There was a callout in the night at the Crawford household.'

'Has something happened to Tiffany?'

'Tiffany sleepwalks. Her husband found her coming back into the flat with a scarf. He said he thinks she pulled it from the bush outside their bedroom window.'

'Are we thinking that the man came back? But the police were outside.'

He nodded. 'The officer watching their flat was desperate for the loo. He popped to the garage and just after there was a staff changeover.'

'I see.'

'The scarf has been entered into evidence and is on its way to the lab. Another officer is going to take a statement today. She wasn't up to it last night. Apparently, she'd taken a couple of diazepam and had a couple of sherries. She was disorientated and dopey.'

Gina swallowed. Tiffany was having a tough time of it.

'And get this.'

'What?'

'The scarf was one of Tiffany's. Tiffany recognised it and her husband confirmed it. It wasn't missing and no one has been in the flat.'

'Are we thinking that she went out with the scarf and came back in with it?'

Briggs nodded. 'That's the thinking but I don't want to be too quick to doubt her. It's just something to keep in mind. It may well be the stress of it all.'

'I need to speak to her today. I'll go with Collier and ask her about the hair, whether her attacker may have cut a little off. There may or may not be a connection. It wasn't mentioned in her file but it's worth an ask.' Gina's phone rang. She grabbed it off the table. 'Hello.'

She listened to Wyre speak and hung up.

'Has there been a development?'

Half-running towards the stairs, Gina turned as she pulled the towel from her hair. 'Maybe. Robbie Shields's brother has called, and he wants to speak to someone. He said he has something to tell us and he's coming in later.'

FORTY-THREE

NANCY

Nancy ordered her second cup of mint tea and stared out the window at the patio furniture. A toddler fought with his parents in a battle to see if he could escape the highchair. A woman sat reading a saucy romance and a couple ate a huge fry up that stank of death. How people could eat meat was beyond her. She checked her messages to see if Preston had something to say but there was nothing. The coward had stood her up. She nervously ambled through the pet section and the household plants before exiting the huge shop. That's when she saw him by the back of her car. He was late, that was all. Purposely, of course.

Hurrying back in, Nancy sat back where her empty cup still adorned the table and she waited. Within a couple of minutes, he was standing in the queue. His cheesecloth shirt was buttoned up to the neck and tucked into his pale-blue jeans. Droplets of rain glistened on his shaven head. His gaze met hers and it lingered for a few seconds, sending a shiver through her. She would not look away though. The woman behind the counter passed him a can, forcing him to break their stares. One nil to her. Before he turned back, she pressed record on her phone.

He clomped over in his army-style boots and slammed his energy drink onto the table, making her teacup jump and clatter in the saucer. Good job it was empty otherwise she'd be wearing it. 'So, we meet again.'

'Why are you harassing me?'

He grinned and took a swig out of the can. A sickly aroma filled the air. 'It's typical of the commie bitch to accuse me of all sorts. I wouldn't dream of harassing a lady, or you, come to think of it.' He leaned forward. 'People like you make me laugh with your holier than thou attitude. You think the world is coming to an end. This environmental crisis, it's nothing. All bullshit invented by our leaders to turn us into good little people and you, you lap it all up.' He smirked and leaned back, his legs apart. 'People like you hold up traffic and people like me hate you. I really hate you.'

'Finished?'

He stared at her again. All of his twenty-five years were plastered across the baby-faced man boy. 'You've got a nerve. Just remember, you went for me first. One of my mates recorded it so I can prove that you assaulted me, but I chose to let it go. We were all fired up and God it was fun dragging you out of that road.'

She remembered that day well. She and her fellow activists were blocking the bypass when Preston got out of his car and went for her like some deranged monster. For a moment, she could almost feel her scalp burning as he dragged her through the crowd by her hair. She had struck him because he'd come right up to her, his nose almost touching hers. What she set out to do was push him but instead she punched him. Yes, she'd started the physical violence, but he instigated it by threatening her and the threats had continued. 'Preston, the messages have to stop.'

'Any other demands because, you know, I always do what bitches like you tell me to do.'

She felt her clenched fists tensing up. So far, recording him had just ascertained that she struck him first that day, and that he had a recording. 'Leave my daughter alone.'

He laughed. 'She's a beauty, not like you. You really should have checked your privacy settings on social media. Those leaflets you were handing out, you even put your phone number on them. How stupid can a person get? The moment you lot cleared off, I knew your group name, your name, your phone number. Within minutes, I found your unprotected profile on Facebook, Instagram and Twitter. Didn't find you on TikTok but I guess that's an age thing, grandma.'

Right now, she wanted to reach over and punch the man. It would so be worth getting arrested to see his bloody face, especially as he'd threatened her. Now, it appears, he'd seen Lauren on her social media. He knew that Lauren was her daughter. He'd insinuated that he'd been to her home. 'What were you doing at my house the other night?'

He stared, took a long swig of his drink and belched.

'You think attacking me was clever. I saw you, Preston.'

'Saw me, did you?' He plonked his can down and folded his arms. 'This gets more hilarious by the second.'

'I took a photo of all those messages that you sent me on Facebook before I deactivated my account. If you'd have hurt me that night, the police would have found them. They would have known it was you.'

'Really?' He began to laugh.

'And now you've got yourself a new phone and you think it's clever to try and scare me again. I tell you something, I'm not scared of a mummy's basement dweller like you. I pity you, the stupid little incel that you are. You're nothing but a troll, someone who likes to find a fight wherever he can. You get off on it. I saw the glee in your eyes when you were dragging me by my hair.'

'You really are something, Nancy. Think you're really clever.'

She smiled sarcastically. 'The problem is you think you're clever. You're probably just another flat earth idiot because you sure are a total science denier. Leave me alone and leave my daughter alone.'

He smirked. 'Or what?'

She reached into her pocket and pressed the off button on her phone. 'I will kill you. You won't know when it's coming or how, but that is a promise. No one and I mean no one threatens my daughter.'

He burst into laughter.

She kicked his shin under the table. She'd barely caught him but still, it must have hurt a little.

The couple with the toddler glanced over at his reddening face. 'What the hell? What is wrong with you, you insane bitch?' They quickly turned back to their little one.

'Stay away from me and stay away from my daughter.'

He shook his head and frowned.

The table slid. He jumped back and walked out of the café. She hurried, chasing him out onto the car park. 'You hear me, stay away from us. I meant everything I said.'

He stopped and walked right back towards her, his nose almost touching hers. 'There's a camera there. You hit me now and the police will be involved, and I will get you down for assault this time. Okay, I'm done with playing this game. Looks like you've royally pissed someone else off. I can see why someone would want to attack you. Good on them. I hope they succeed in killing you next time. Don't contact me again or I'll call the police and tell them that you're harassing me. I never want to see you again.' He turned to walk away.

'So, you've never been to my house?' she shouted.

'Why would I?'

'How about the messages you sent to my phone over the past few days?'

He shrugged. 'Not me. Not me at all. Believe me, if I did attack you or sent you some creepo messages, I'd be thrilled to tell you. I'd wear that moment like a badge of honour. Just go back to your sad little life and your stupid bimbo daughter and stop harassing me. I'll see you at the next demo. Bloody loony lefty.'

With that, he jumped into his battered Land Rover and drove off, sticking two fingers up as he passed her. She ran over to her car and searched underneath the back bumper. She lay on the floor. What had he been doing by her car? Planting a tracker. Had he done something to make it dangerous? She wondered if she'd crash as soon as she turned onto the main road. She grabbed her hair with both hands and her body began to shake as she reran the last few minutes in her mind. Yes, she'd held her nerve and she'd managed to get her message across, but she could prove nothing. He'd toyed with her and denied everything, and the worst thing was, she believed he was telling the truth.

She walked around to the back of the car and then she saw what he'd done. The word bitch was scrawled in the dirt on her back window. Using her index finger, she rubbed it away and wiped her hand on her jeans.

Her phone beeped. Another message.

Revenge is the sweetest thing. I hope you liked my parting words.

She replied to his message.

Consider yourself blocked, Preston.

She hit the block button. He could no longer taunt her with messages. With jellied legs, she got into her car and started the engine. Her phone beeped again with another message. She sighed and grabbed it.

Mum, I've just called a taxi. I'm going to visit Tiff. Something's happened. She needs me. Fifi is fine. I've fed her and she's been out. X

She called Lauren and her daughter answered. 'What, Mum?'

'I'm on my way back. Please don't go, love. You should stay in. It's not safe, not with the killer out there. I'm on my way home. At least wait until I get back.'

'Please tell me you sorted that weirdo out?'

'Yes, I mean I think so.' She knew she hadn't. She exhaled. What if Preston had been telling the truth? What if the messenger wasn't Preston? She thought back to all the incidents she'd been involved in. She'd upset someone else, but who?

'What do you mean you think so?'

'I did, yes. He won't bother me again. We've agreed to disagree.'

'So, all is good. You worry too much, Mum. Anyway, I spoke to the police. They've made an arrest. They're not telling me much yet but that's good news. Right now, I need to be with a friend and Tiff needs me. I'll see you later.' With that, Lauren hung up.

Nancy roared and shook her phone. All she wanted was to keep Lauren at home, wrap her up, protect her. She'd done bad things, but it was always for the love of her daughter. Why couldn't Lauren see that? It was the phone. Nancy knew that getting her a phone had resulted in Lauren leaving. She swallowed. A part of her wanted the police to never release Lauren's bungalow. She wanted to keep her daughter forever and protect her from all the bad people out there, just like she'd always done. Only a mother could do that, and she wasn't about to give up. She slammed the car into first and angrily revved it out of the garden centre. The driver she cut up beeped his horn, but she didn't care. All that mattered was Lauren. Like always.

FORTY-FOUR

Sullivan stood at the head of the room and waited for the hum of noise to calm down and for everyone to gather around the main table. Gina scraped a seat on the floor and sat next to Collier, knowing she was no longer needed at the front. Wyre, O'Connor and Kapoor remained together at the one side of the large table. There were no pastries or biscuits and the look on O'Connor's face told Gina that Sullivan had probably banned them. A couple of detectives sat together at the other side. Like Collier, they were pristinely dressed. The only person missing was Jacob and Gina felt his absence. Sullivan tapped the board with her fingernails. 'Good to have you all here. I have an announcement to make but first I want a catch up. Collier, can you talk us through yesterday? I know we can all look on the system, but I feel as though we need to all catch up.'

Collier walked to the front. 'Yes, ma'am.' His attention turned to the table. 'I've liaised with forensics, and we can confirm that there is nothing from their side to link Gerard Hale to any of the attacks or murder scenes. The blood logged at the scene of Hazel Blackford's attack is not a match to Hale's and that was a key piece of evidence taken from the scene.'

'Is it a match to Jacob's?' Gina asked.

'We're still waiting to confirm that,' Collier added.

'Please don't interrupt again, Harte, or I will have to ask you to leave the room. DI Collier, continue.'

Collier cleared his throat. 'He has an alibi for the time of Sienna's murder. He is no longer a suspect.'

Gina held up a hand and spoke. 'But he has admitted to stalking Sienna.'

Sullivan turned to Gina. 'Yes, and he will be charged for that. The murders and historical attacks are our priority so let's stick to talking about them. Go on, DI Collier. Maybe you can speak without interruption, this time.' She shook her head at Gina as Collier continued.

'We can confirm that the earring found at the scene of Tiffany Crawford's attack belonged to victim one, Hazel Blackford. We also know that nothing out of place was left behind at Hazel's attack so we're working on the theory that she was his first. Both victims had similar features at the time of their attacks, suggesting that our perpetrator has a type. They have blue eyes and blonde hair.'

Gina held a hand up again.

'DI Harte.' Collier exhaled and raised his eyebrows.

'We still need to speak to Tiffany Crawford. We need to know if she suspected that she had any hair missing following the attack.'

He nodded. 'Yes, it may be that he's taking a trophy and I agree that we should speak to her next.'

Gina interrupted again. 'We also know that he didn't take any of Sienna's hair and she was a brunette.'

Collier rolled his eyes. 'I was just getting to that if you give me a chance to speak.'

She held her hands up. 'Sorry.' Sullivan cut her a look and at that moment, she didn't care as having her say in the case was more important than anything else. Gina moved her attention to the table and listened so that she didn't have to see Sullivan's angry stare.

After a pause, Collier continued. 'DS Driscoll is now our only suspect. We have applied for an extension to keep him in custody while we investigate further, and it's been granted.'

Gina shook her head and pressed her lips together. He didn't do it. Her lovely colleague could never strangle and murder people, but they obviously had something on him that they weren't telling her side of the team. If she got even a whiff of what was happening, she'd follow it up alone, without Briggs's or Sullivan's permission. She swallowed her rage down. Briggs quietly entered from the back. He'd claimed that he knew as much as she did but she knew he was lying. He'd been present for all the extra briefings and right now, she considered him one of them.

Her mind wandered while Collier went over all the facts they already knew relating to forensics, the wedding ring found on Robbie and the scarves. The fingerprints on the paint can at the bungalow belonged to Robbie, as did the blood in the cupboard. After that, the room went silent as Collier finished speaking.

Superintendent Sullivan stepped forward. 'For the announcement. I feel that we need to partially share the other side of the investigation with you.'

Gina sat bolt upright. Finally, they were going to let her team in on what they had.

As she spoke, Sullivan stared at Gina, her mouthed curved in a smile. 'A key piece of evidence has come to light. At the time of Hazel Blackford's attack we can confirm that DS Driscoll was also living in Kidderminster with his parents. That gives him opportunity.'

Gina gasped for breath, and she glanced at the shocked faces in the room.

Gaze still on Gina, Sullivan continued. 'It's looking likely that he will be charged. Right, DI Harte, you and Collier will visit Tiffany Crawford to discuss last night. As we know, DS Driscoll was in custody so he can't have been there but there is a question as to whether Mrs Crawford actually saw anyone in the day or last night. We've since heard that she'd taken a concoction of strong prescription drugs and had drunk a lot of alcohol. She is prone to sleepwalking too.'

Gina kicked the table leg and clenched her fists under the table. She didn't know what was angering her more, the fact they were dismissing Tiffany because the poor traumatised woman needed something to block out the memories of her hideous attack, or the fact that it felt like they were trying to pin everything onto Jacob. Sullivan would love nothing more than to bring Gina's team down and the grin on her face confirmed that.

'Did you find anything to link Jacob to the attacks when you searched his house?' Gina asked.

Sullivan took a deep breath and exhaled in a relaxed manner. 'I'm not at liberty to share the answer to your question at the moment. Interview Tiffany Crawford and then see what Robbie Shields's brother has to say. We are now collecting evidence to present the case to the CPS so that we can charge DS Driscoll.'

FORTY-FIVE

As Gina and Collier left the station, they drove through a group of protesters that had gathered outside, each with a placard claiming that they had no confidence in the police. They knew that a detective had been arrested and Gina knew of only one person who would leak that kind of information. She'd never be able to prove it, but it had to be Sullivan, or maybe she put Collier up to it. Ever since Sullivan saw that Gina was running the case, she'd been looking for a way to bring her down. Her nasty streak had lasted all those years. A reporter banged his hands on the passenger window and Gina flinched. 'Is it true that a detective at Cleevesford station has been arrested for the murders of Robbie Shields and Sienna Moorcroft?' Collier continued driving and soon they were leaving the chaos behind.

Less than twenty minutes later, Collier pulled up on the road outside Tiffany's flat. Gina spotted PC Ahmed stationed outside in his car. The young officer nodded and buzzed his window down as they got out. 'If you're going to be here for a while, is it okay if I leave to grab a sandwich?'

'Of course. We'll be about half an hour.'

'Great. Husband went to work around seven and she has a

friend over. Nothing else has happened.' PC Ahmed smiled and drove off. Gina had been in his position many times in the past and she didn't envy anyone who was on sentry duty. Also, the chill in the air was bitter with occasional rain showers. Turning his engine on would give him a chance to warm up a bit.

They walked down the path and Gina spotted Tiffany at the kitchen window. Within a few seconds the woman had answered. 'I'm just making a drink; do you want one?'

'That would be lovely.' After not even having a coffee at the station, Gina was parched, and she knew that Collier probably needed one too.

'Take a seat in the living room. Lauren has come to visit.'

Gina led the way and as she entered the small room, she saw that Lauren was biting her nails. Her tired eyes and bitten down nails told Gina that she was struggling. For a second, Gina thought about Sienna and her daughter. Lauren had found out so much about Robbie in such a short space of time. She couldn't begin to imagine the level of shock that she was going through. She was glad that Lauren and Tiffany were offering each other some support.

'I heard about the arrest. When is someone going to tell me more and when can I go back to my bungalow?' Lauren asked in a quiet, broken voice.

Gina sat on the settee next to Collier. 'We'll be able to release it soon and hopefully we will have some news to share with you then.' She hoped that Lauren couldn't see the lump in her throat. How could she handle visiting Lauren later to tell her that it was her colleague who had been charged with killing her fiancé and her friend? Her heart rate began to pick up. It couldn't be Jacob. It wasn't Jacob.

'Are you okay?' Collier asked.

Gina unclenched her hands and closed her mouth. Her heart began to bang even louder, and she wondered if Lauren could hear it. She nodded. 'I'm fine, thank you.' She wanted to yell no. Everything was not okay, but she wouldn't upset Lauren and she wouldn't let Collier know that he'd got to her.

Tiffany walked in with four cups of coffee, a bag of sugar and a carton of milk. She placed the tray on the coffee table. Gina took one of the drinks, a hit of caffeine being the only thing she needed. 'Someone said you were coming to talk to me about last night?'

Gina glanced at Lauren. Although Lauren was a part of the case, she needed to speak to Tiffany alone. 'Lauren, I'm sorry to have to ask you this, but would you please give us a few minutes?'

The woman nodded and stood. 'I'll go out and get a bit of fresh air. Give me a shout when I can come back in.' With that, she left out the front door.

'She could have stayed. I've told her everything that happened to me, so I have no secrets from Lauren. I know about Saturday too. She told me how she got home and found Sienna. Can she please come back in?'

'We need to ask you something about your attack all those years ago and I'd prefer to ask you alone.'

Tiffany's brows furrowed. 'I've told you everything.'

'It may be nothing but something else has come to light and we need to ask you about it.'

'Okay.' Tiffany's trembling fingers reached for her coffee, and she blew on the hot liquid.

'After your attack, did you notice anything different with your hair, anything that may have seemed irrelevant at the time?'

'What like?'

Gina didn't want to put words into Tiffany's mouth. That would make Collier and Sullivan's day if she slipped up. 'Just anything.'

Tiffany sipped her drink and began to bite the inside of her cheek.

'Did you have long hair at the time?'

She nodded. 'It was as curly as it is now, but it was way down my back. This might sound ridiculous...'

'Or it might help.' Gina waited for her to continue.

'I think that during the attack, I must have lost a clump of hair, but I thought it was because I fought him.'

Gina looked at the curls on her head. If her attacker had cut a piece off, she wouldn't have noticed so easily as it curled and frizzed up, not like Hazel's straight hair.

'It was at the nape of my neck. It just felt a little different, but I can't see how that would help. The police at the time didn't mention my hair and I only noticed it after. What's happening?'

Gina sat forward. 'Another victim who we believe was attacked first claims that a chunk of her hair was missing.'

Tiffany's cup began to judder, and liquid slopped over the top and into her lap. Gina stood, took the cup and placed it on the tray. 'How many times has he done this?' Tears slid down her cheeks. 'How many lives has he ruined?'

Gina wished she could offer some comfort.

'I want Lauren to come back in now.'

'I'll go and let her know that we're finishing up.' Gina walked toward the hall, passing the framed photos on the wall. She took in Tiffany on her wedding day. Tiffany lying on a patch of lush grass smiling up at the camera without a care in the world. She continued to the door and as she opened it, she saw that Lauren was talking on her phone.

'Mum, I'm okay. Please leave it out. I'll be back when I'm back.' Lauren ended the call and placed the phone in her pocket.

'Thanks, Lauren. You can come back in now.'

Lauren stomped over, looking slightly red.

'I'm totally upset about everything but most of all, right now, I'm struggling with my mother. It's all getting too much.

She's wrapping me up in cotton wool like I'm a baby.' She wiped a stray tear from her eye.

'She's worried about you, that's all.'

'I know.' As Lauren hurried in, she paused for a moment at the photo wall and her gaze lingered on the wedding photo. 'I don't know what I'm going to do without him. A part of me hates him for what he did to me with Sienna. I mostly feel sorry for Dora. That little girl deserved more.' A tear drizzled down her cheek. 'I was so excited to be marrying him but right now, I feel nothing.' She stared at a photo of the huge cut bark in the middle of some woodland and furrowed her brow.

'Are you okay?' Gina wondered where her mind had wandered too.

'Huh, yes.'

'Do you recognise that place?'

'Everyone does. That large stump is a bit of a feature at Bluebell Woods. Loads of people Instagram a photo of themselves there.' Lauren cleared her throat and wiped her eye. 'I hoped that Robbie and I would get a dog and walk it there. You know when you dream about nice things, and you hope those dreams come true?' Lauren glanced at the photos one more time and turned to the living room. 'None of us are okay but we keep going.'

Gina glanced at the photos again, especially the one of the tree stump, then she shook her head. Her phone beeped. She read the message from Briggs.

Mr Shields is at the station, and he looks really worried.

FORTY-SIX

Gina trailed behind Collier to the interview room. As Jacob hadn't yet been charged, there was still a chance. Sullivan came from the opposite direction through the corridor, then she nodded to Collier to enter the interview room alone.

'What?' Gina asked, sick of keeping up a pretence. She had no time for Sullivan and Sullivan had no time for her.

'He did it, you know. You might be living in denial, but I've interviewed him myself and I know a killer when I see one. They're often the nicest of people. You know that.'

Gina shook her head. 'So what if he lived in the area at the time of Hazel Blackford's attack and he had opportunity when it came to Sienna's and Robbie's murders, but you don't know him like I do.'

Sullivan led her into the room next door and slammed the door. 'Gina, Gina, Gina. Juries can be convinced to deliver a guilty verdict if the circumstantial evidence is strong enough. In this case it's there and it's strong.'

'But the blood at Hazel Blackford's house. Did it match Jacob's?'

Sullivan didn't answer. 'I know about your case, your past.

You lost your husband when your daughter was a baby. Tragic accident. I read all the details.'

Gina swallowed. She allowed Terry to die after nudging him down the stairs when he was about to hit her. The moment he first attacked her flashed through her mind, a back-handed slap across her face that landed so hard, she flew across the kitchen floor.

'People are capable of more than you think. We both know that.'

'What are you trying to say?'

'Nothing. Just that you had it hard, I realise that. I respect how far you've come but look at you. When you worked for me, you were sloppy, and it's the same right now. You can't see a killer when he's staring you in the face. I see right through them.'

Sullivan's stare reached right into Gina's heart. What was the woman trying to tell her? Could she see that Gina had let Terry die?

Thoughts flashed through her mind. In her nightmares, Terry still taunted her, and everyone knew what she did. They kept saying that her past would catch up with her just like Jacob's was catching up with him now. She saw her ex-mother-in-law, Hetty, telling her that she'd never see her granddaughter again and how Gina had ruined both of her sons. She saw Terry's brother, Stephen, as he vowed to kill her one day for sending him to prison and threatening to frame him for another crime. Did Sullivan really see all that?

'I see right through you, Harte.' Sullivan opened the door and walked out.

What did she see? Gina wanted to shout after her, but the sound of her heels had disappeared around a corner and Robbie Shields's brother was waiting to be interviewed. She took deep breaths and leaned against the wall while composing herself.

She walked into the interview room and saw Collier waiting, ready to start the recorder while perusing the file full of notes in front of him. Mr Shields tapped his fingers on the table. He couldn't have been more different to his brother, Robbie. He wore an old tracksuit covered in splashes of paint and his rugged, acne-scarred face was framed by a mound of dark shaggy hair. She caught sight of the notes in front of Collier as he pulled them out of the file. The man's name was Damon Shields, and he was married with four children. Collier started the recorder and made all the introductions.

Gina cleared her throat and began. 'I'd like to express our condolences. We're really sorry for your loss.'

Mr Shields nodded and did the zip up on his tracksuit top. 'Thank you. You can't believe how much we miss him. My kids are gutted, and it hasn't sunk in yet that Uncle Robbie is gone. Of course, I haven't told them what happened. It's too much and they're so young.'

He pulled his phone from his pocket and turned it around to reveal a photo of two boys holding fishing rods. 'That's me and Robbie. I was five years older, and I had friends my own age, but on this day, I told them I was hanging out with my little brother. We went fishing at the canal and just before we left, our mum took this photo. He had this infectious laugh and people loved him. I guess he was a little cheeky chappie. He grew into a teen who people loved too, not like me, I was a grumpy teen who lived in my room and got into trouble at school. Robbie swept people's drives and worked in their gardens for hardly any money. He was like that, he liked to help the community and really thrived on making people happy.' Damon Shields paused. 'That's why I can't get his fling out of my head. I knew about Sienna.' He paused.

'What did you know about Sienna?'

Collier began to take notes.

'He had a slip up. Lauren and Robbie had been through a

bit of a bad patch. That's why he slept with Sienna. He wasn't a serial cheat.'

Gina wondered what he was getting at. She also wondered if Damon Shields knew about Robbie's holiday fling too.

'When it happened, Robbie told me about the pregnancy. He asked me what he should do, and I had a go at him, told him what an idiot he'd been. I mean, Sienna was Lauren's best friend. He later told me that Sienna agreed that they should never tell Lauren, after all Sienna didn't want to lose her best friend either. Anyway, several months later Sienna has a daughter, and he knew the little girl was his but still, Sienna came up with this story about a soldier she'd been seeing, and they agreed that they would stick to it as long as Robbie paid her monthly maintenance. I have children and I know that children need the truth. Dora still needs the truth. I made it my mission to work on Sienna to get that truth out there as I knew Robbie was too gutless to face it.'

Gina wondered how well he knew Sienna. 'Did you speak to Sienna without Robbie being present?'

Damon Shields nodded. 'I met up with her a few times because I really wanted to see my niece. My youngest is the same age and all I could think of was my kids getting to know Dora. I wanted them to play together as cousins and grow up close, like me and Robbie did, so I told Sienna this. Dora has Robbie's blood and I thought she deserved to have a father who would be present in her life. I didn't know if his forthcoming marriage would survive the truth coming out, but I also told Robbie separately, this little girl is your daughter. She means more than anything and if your marriage can't withstand your mistake, it wasn't meant to be.'

'How did they react to what you were saying?'

He began to pick dried paint from his arm and he flicked a bit onto the floor. 'Sienna was on board. She was fed up with the lie and she knew Dora deserved more. Robbie hated the idea and I know that on Saturday night, she was planning on speaking to him about it. He wasn't looking forward to her coming over at all, but he planned it for that night as he knew Lauren wouldn't be back for hours.'

What Mr Shields was telling them fit with what they already knew. 'When did you last see Sienna Moorcroft?'

He bit the inside of his mouth and frowned. 'Maybe a week before. I saw her in the supermarket, and we spoke outside.'

'What did you talk about?'

'Not much, there was a man waiting for her in a car, a dark saloon car. I asked her if he was her new man as I knew she'd not long come out of a bad but short relationship.'

Gina felt her stomach roll. He was describing Jacob's car, and she had to do her job, even though it might hurt Jacob. 'Can you describe that man?'

He shrugged. 'It was dark, but he was parked under a street-lamp. Maybe short hair, clean shaven, the registration ended in SA.'

That fit Jacob's description and car.

Collier raised his eyebrows.

Gina continued. 'So, you asked her about her new relationship?'

He nodded. 'She seemed hesitant to say anything so maybe they hadn't been together long. She said he was nice, and they got on well. Then she hurried over to him, got into the car and he drove off. That's the last time I saw her. Where's Dora staying?'

'With Sienna's family, up north.'

He pressed his lips together. 'There is something else, which is why I came. I thought you should know everything.'

Gina sat up. 'What is it you want to tell us?'

'It's about Lauren. Robbie slept with Sienna because Lauren had a fling. It was an immature move, I know, but that's why he did what he did. I don't know who Lauren slept with, but Robbie did say it was an ex. Robbie wasn't a bad man. He was upset, he was angry and sleeping with Sienna had been a stupid, impulsive mistake. All he wanted was to settle down and grow old with Lauren and she shattered him. Time passed and he decided to forgive her.'

'What's happened since to make you believe Lauren's past has something to do with Robbie's murder?'

'Robbie told me something over Christmas. When he came home from work on Christmas Eve morning, he saw a wrapped-up package on the step. It was addressed to Lauren. She was meant to have had the day off work, but she'd been called in as one of her colleagues was off sick. Robbie was also meant to be working until five, but his boss let him out early. Robbie took the hand-delivered parcel into the bungalow and opened it.'

'What was in it?'

'A box of what he described as beautifully crafted hand-made chocolates. He never told her they arrived, and he binned the chocolates and the card. About a week later, he found something in her side of the wardrobe, a very sexy blue chemise. He knew that Lauren had never bought it for herself, and it was in a box, wrapped in tissue paper like it had been gifted. Robbie thought that Lauren was having an affair and the gifts were from a lover. She used to go out a lot, with the excuse of just nipping to the shops or popping into Redditch to do some shopping, but she often never came back with anything.'

'So, you think Lauren was having an affair and that had something to do with Sienna and Robbie's murders?'

'That's exactly what I'm saying.'

Gina thought back to the argument in the road that Lauren denied having. One of the neighbours had seen her. Had she been trying to tell her lover that it was over, or had they been arguing because Lauren was still with him? 'Did Robbie suspect anyone he knew of having an affair with her?'

'He accused me. He said that I'd been trying to break him

and Lauren up by telling Sienna to confess to Lauren about their one-night stand. I knew this would come out so I thought I should come here and tell you everything.'

Gina observed the scruffy man's features and his slightly crooked nose as she tried to picture him cleaned up and standing next to the woman who presented make-up demos on TikTok. Robbie was described as charming, but Damon seemed quiet and unkempt.

'I know what you're thinking. Me and Lauren, what a joke? You're right. Robbie was out of his mind accusing me and I was at the pub with my friends on Saturday night. I'm probably on CCTV and I went to the chip shop after where I talked to several people in the queue. Elouise at the Angel Arms will vouch for me too, so I'm not worried. What I am worried about is the man I saw Sienna with outside the supermarket. Maybe he was jealous of Robbie and angry at Sienna for going to see him on Saturday. You need to find him, and you need to charge him with murdering my brother. Either that, or it has to be Lauren's bit on the side, whoever he is. Ask Lauren. You have to talk to her, okay? Maybe Lauren was out that night, but have you considered she might have been trying to get rid of Robbie? Maybe she knew about his fling with Sienna and about their daughter. I might be jumping to conclusions, but maybe Sienna's new man was Lauren's lover and they planned this together as an act of revenge for what Sienna and Robbie did to her.' He paused. 'I don't know. I'm getting confused now. All I know is that I don't trust Lauren or Sienna's new man.'

They needed to speak to Lauren, and they needed to do it now. If she was still at Tiffany Crawford's house, they could call PC Ahmed and hope she'd come in voluntarily for an interview. The hole was getting deeper by the minute for Jacob and Gina knew that Sullivan was enjoying seeing her team's downfall. Gina felt the room sway slightly. Jacob lived near the first victim, Hazel. He's always stayed close enough to Redditch, which puts him in the area for Tiffany's attack, and now Sienna. He was in a relationship with her and there was some tension between them. The more she denied he could be their perp, the more her stomach turned. She couldn't deny that the evidence was piling up and that Jacob could be heading for a life sentence if charged with double murder.

FORTY-SEVEN

NANCY

Nancy threw her bag on the sofa, still shaken from her encounter with Preston. 'Lauren,' she called, but her daughter still wasn't home. Fifi yapped and jumped around her legs, almost tripping her up. 'Down, girl.' Confusion filled her mind. Was it Preston? If it wasn't then who was sending the messages and trying to attack her? She'd been so sure it was him. Running into the kitchen, she checked the back door and the window. Both were locked. She grabbed her phone from her pocket and to her relief she saw that there were no more messages in her inbox. She placed the phone on the kitchen table. Taking a deep breath, she slumped against the worktop, turning the tap on. She lathered up her hands, wanting to wash away the day. Fifi snuffled at the back door. 'You want to go out.' She dried her hands and let the dog into the garden.

Fifi bounded over the stumps of grass, barking at the trees swaying in the breeze. Her gaze fell upon a strip of white material caught on a branch that danced away as the breeze caught it. She stepped out onto the slabs and hurried over. As she traced the delicate material with her index finger, she checked the garden again before snatching it off the tree. She held it in her hands and for a second, she thought she recognised it. No, there was no way it could be what she thought it was. No way at all. That train of thought was absurd.

She hurried to the back of the garden and lifted the lid off the wheelie bin. After taking one more look at the lacy veil, she dropped it into the bin, happy to see the back of it. Maybe Lauren had kept it all those years as a memory. The breeze picked up again and the patio set cover still flapped at the back gate. She walked over and scooped it up. That's when she noticed that the gate was unlocked. Heart banging, she slid the lock across and ran back into the kitchen. 'Fifi,' she called as she dropped the plastic onto the floor, but the dog ignored her and wagged its tail. 'Fifi, Mummy said get in, now.' The dog barked and began to nudge a ball with its nose. Nancy didn't want to play; she wanted Fifi to do as she was told.

Someone rang the doorbell. She froze and held her breath. A heavy knock made her flinch. Her pulse quickened. She pulled the kitchen door closed and left the dog playing in the garden. Hurrying to the living room, she peered from behind the curtain to see who was calling but she couldn't see anyone. There was something on the paving stones. Maybe the edge of a mauve-coloured box. She wasn't expecting a delivery. Maybe Lauren had ordered something. She held a hand over her thrumming heart, knowing she'd have to check. Glancing through the window, up and down the road, she couldn't see any cars parked up and no one was around. On occasion, walkers would take the route past her cottage to climb the Malvern Hills, but not today. Today, there was no one at all. It was safe to open the door. The delivery person had long gone.

As she placed her hand on the lock, she paused, wondering if it was a good idea to open the door. Maybe the caller was hiding in the porchway. She couldn't see that from the lounge window. She made a mental note to get a peephole fitted. After pulling the chain across, she gently opened the door and exhaled as she held her hand over her beating heart. There was no one there but there was a bunch of red and pink roses in a mauve box. She removed the chain and opened the door, listening for the sound of a cough, a footstep or any noise that would tell her that someone was lurking around. There was nothing, only the sound of the howling breeze. She reached down and picked up the flower box. Water sloshed inside the sealed bag at the stems as she carried it into the hallway and placed it on the floor. They had to be for Lauren. She pulled the card out and opened the envelope. As she slid it, she read the only two words on the embossed paper. *Forever mine*. Those words almost took her breath away.

Fifi began to bark and scratch at the back door. She threw the card onto the floor, hurried to the kitchen and flung the back door open, letting Fifi in. Her mind swam with memories and thoughts as the enormity of all that had happened hit her. It wasn't Preston. He had nothing to do with those messages or her attack. She knew exactly who was behind it all and she knew why. She also knew that there was worse to come. Turning the key in the back door, she stared out at the back gate which was now flapping open and closed. There was no time to waste. She reached for her phone on the kitchen table, but her hand brushed on nothing but wood. Heart in mouth, she knew he had it and he was coming for her. Then she heard footsteps in the hallway, and she knew she wasn't going to live another day and worse, he would take the one person who was more precious to her than anything. 'Fifi,' she called, and the dog shook as it hid under the table.

Tears fell down her cheeks. All she could think of was Lauren and the terrible thing she did. All these years, Nancy had done everything she could to protect her daughter but now she was powerless, and she was to blame. She went to unlock the back door, but it was too late. She felt his warm, slow breaths on her neck, and she knew it was over.

FORTY-EIGHT

'Guv, Lauren Cross is waiting in interview room one. PC Ahmed has just brought her in and headed off on his break.' O'Connor stood at the entrance to her office.

She closed the emails she'd been staring at for the past ten minutes. By some miracle, she lived in hope that new evidence would surface, and it would clear Jacob but that hadn't happened. 'How does she seem?'

'Confused. She only knows that we want to speak to her about the case.'

'Is there someone watching Tiffany's place?'

He nodded. 'Yes, PC Smith turned up and relieved PC Ahmed. Right, I best get back to it. Collier said he was on his way.'

'Great,' Gina replied, sarcastically and O'Connor raised his brows.

'I can't stop thinking about Jacob, guv. Do you think he did it?'

She stood and looked through the slats in her blind, watching the protesters in the car park. 'They've already convicted him.' She paused. 'I can see why this is happening.'

She pointed at the mob. 'You only have to turn the news on and there's yet another report of a police officer charged with a sex offence. Public trust in us is at an all-time low but Jacob – no way. He's always been respectful and never discriminatory. He is not one of the bad apples and I'm going to prove it, even if it kills me.' Turning back, she saw O'Connor swallow.

'No, guv. He's not one of them.'

They both wanted to believe that so badly but that niggle in the back of her mind was turning into a thumping pain. Sullivan's heels clipped down the corridor. Gina and O'Connor stood straight, as if conditioned by her presence.

'Harte and O'Connor. I have news. Unless something big comes up before teatime today your colleague, Jacob Driscoll, is set to be charged for the murders of Robbie Shields and Sienna Moorcroft. He is also set to be charged with the two previous attacks. Just thought I'd let you know.'

Gina felt heat prickling her chest and neck as her fists clenched. 'He didn't do it.'

'Oh, Gina, letting emotion rule the case again. When the evidence points in a direction, we have to follow it and at the moment it's all pointing to Mr Driscoll.'

'DS Driscoll.'

Sullivan shook her head. 'Mister. Right, get back to it. Collier has updated me, and you don't want to keep Lauren waiting. I don't know why you brought her in. We already have our perp.' She paused. 'Have you seen all the protesters in the car park?'

Gina nodded.

'They need us to do the right thing. They'll get their update when the press come back at teatime. That's five this evening, by the way. Set your alarms, don't want you to miss it.' Sullivan smiled broadly, turned and left.

Gina grabbed her mug of coffee and flung it at the corner of the room.

'I'm sorry.' O'Connor had remained rooted to the spot the whole time the superintendent was in the small room.

'She wants us to fall apart but that isn't going to happen.' Gina slammed her hand on the windowsill and closed the blinds to the world outside.

'We have until five. There's still time.'

She glanced at her watch. 'What? Four hours? And we're here, hoping that an interview with Lauren will suddenly fix everything while Jacob is rotting in a cell. I need to do more, but what?' She tapped the side of her head as thoughts whirred around. There had to be a way and if it meant going alone, she would.

O'Connor shrugged, not knowing what to say.

'I'm sorry,' she said. 'You shouldn't have seen my display of anger.' She took a deep breath and retied her hair in a ponytail.

'I feel the same so don't apologise. You've got this,' O'Connor replied with a smile. 'There has to be a way, guv.'

'You're right. There is and I'm going to find it.' She left the room, feeling the weight of the pressure like never before. If Jacob was charged and later convicted, her whole team would come under scrutiny, herself included and Sullivan was waiting to throw the final punch. The end of an era was about to fall upon them all. One thing was certain though, Sullivan had underestimated her and she wasn't going down without a fight.

FORTY-NINE

Lauren was sitting opposite Collier when Gina entered. Slightly hunched forward as if hugging herself, she looked up at Gina. Her TikTok videos showed an ultra-glamorous woman who had instructed people on how to apply topliner with wings, or create that perfect complexion with only two products, all available from her counter at the beauty outlet. Right now, it looked like she was wearing her mother's joggers and sweater, her talons were cracked and her face pale and puffy, like she'd spent the week crying.

'I need to know when I can go back to the bungalow, and Robbie needs a funeral.'

'We should have news for you soon.' Gina knew that forensics were finished, and the scene release would follow but she didn't have a date for Lauren, not yet.

'So, I'm not here about that?'

'Sorry.' Gina pressed her lips together for a second. 'We need to speak to you, regarding the case.'

'But I don't know anything. I came home and I found Sienna murdered in my bed.'

'I know and I'm sorry to have to do this as I know it's distressing for you.'

Lauren shrugged and leaned back. 'They said this was a voluntary interview.'

Gina nodded and Collier got out his notebook in readiness. 'We will be taping the interview. Is that okay?'

Eyebrows furrowing, Lauren tensed. 'Why, do I need a solicitor?'

'You're more than welcome to have a solicitor if you want one but you're not under arrest. You can leave at any time.'

She glanced into her hands. 'Okay.'

Collier started the tape and made the introductions. It was now one thirty and time was slipping through their fingers. Gina knew she needed to get through her questions swiftly. 'We need to go back to the night the neighbour saw you arguing with someone at the end of your road on either the evening of the nineteenth or twentieth of January.'

'I've already told you. I bumped into a drunken idiot on the path. That was all. There was no argument.' Lauren glanced to the left and failed to meet Gina's eye.

'How about the gifts?'

'What gifts?'

'The blue chemise.'

Lauren went to open her mouth but closed it again. 'I, err, it's nothing. It was a wrong delivery but there was no return address.'

'Were you having an affair?'

'No. Robbie was having the affair. I've never cheated on Robbie.' Lauren's bottom lip began to wobble.

'How about years ago, around the time when your boyfriend, Robbie Shields, would have had his affair with your friend, Sienna Moorcroft? Were you having an affair back then?'

She huffed. 'Damon said that, didn't he? The man is transfixed, even told Robbie he should finish with me. I wasn't sleeping with anyone else. Even if I was, it was a long time ago and unless you can charge me with cheating, I'm not answering any more questions like this. I will say again, I was not cheating on Robbie. He was cheating on me, with Sienna. Either her crazy ex, Gerard, killed them both, or her new boyfriend did. I feel like I'm on trial here.'

The room fell silent. Gina's mouth began to dry up. She took a sip of water and placed the glass down. She considered what Lauren had said. Gerard couldn't possibly have murdered Sienna which only left Jacob in the picture.

'Did you meet Sienna's new boyfriend?' Gina hoped that the woman would describe anyone but Jacob. She knew that Lauren would have seen Jacob just after Sienna's murder as he came to the scene with her. Surely Sienna would have discussed her new boyfriend with her best friend. She sat on her trembling hands under the table as Collier turned a page in his notebook.

'No, I never met him, but she told me about him. Some sad case who was still in love with a woman who dumped him. He wasn't really her boyfriend, just someone she'd meet up with and talked to. She said he was helping her to deal with Gerard and that he was trying to persuade her to report him. You know Gerard was stalking her? The man is a lunatic. He'd just be sat in his car outside where she lived. It was him, it had to be. He watched her turn up...' Lauren swallowed, and Gina could see the pain on her face as she relayed her theory. 'He saw her go into my bedroom with Robbie, he got jealous and killed her, and then he took Robbie from the bungalow, and he killed Robbie. It's obvious.'

Gina shook her head. 'Gerard Hale has an alibi, and he couldn't have murdered Sienna.'

Lauren's brows furrowed and she remained open-mouthed for a moment before licking her dry lips. 'The man she was seeing, she said he was a policeman or someone who worked for the police. That's why the protestors are outside, isn't it? It's him. He killed her, didn't he? You don't want it to be him so you're inventing a scenario. I'm not stupid. You think I was having an affair and that I knew about Sienna and Robbie. You think I planned their murders, don't you?' She stood, pushing the chair back against the wall. 'I tell you what, I'm going. You said I was free to leave at any time. I'm not under arrest and you know what, I don't want to be here. Call me when Robbie's body is released, and I can go home. Until then, I don't want to hear from you.' Lauren walked out of the interview room and left. Collier chased after her while Gina described what was happening for the tape.

'Well, that was a success,' Sullivan said as she entered.

'You were watching?'

She laughed. 'I'm always watching.' She pointed at the clock on the wall. 'Time is ticking and I'm looking forward to getting this case wrapped up so we can all go home.' Sullivan pointed two fingers at her eyes, then pointed them at Gina before leaving the room.

Gina glanced down at a stray hair on the table, and she picked it up and pulled it taught. The ombre, brown at the tip, blonde at the other end. It was a beautiful transition of colour. Her mind kept going back to Hazel and Tiffany. She dropped the hair and her heart rate sped up. What if they'd been looking at the case all wrong. Hurrying out of the interview room, she burst into the incident room. She ran to the board and snatched up a pen with her clammy hands, crossed a name from the victim list and added another. The whole room went silent.

Sullivan shook her head. She took the pen and rewrote the original name on the list and crossed out Gina's suggestion, dismissing her theory instantly. 'DI Harte, you have been warned more than once. Leave it out. We have our murderer.'

'But, ma'am.'

'Don't, Harte. Let's not do this. You're embarrassing yourself now and I won't hesitate to throw you off the case. DCI Briggs and I were just talking about you and he agrees, you're too close.'

Before she said something she'd regret, Gina stormed out of the room. She knew she'd blown it but if Sullivan wasn't going to take her theory seriously, then she'd had it. For the first time in her career, she was going it alone. She would not let Jacob down by leaving stones unturned. Wyre and O'Connor followed her into the corridor.

After clearing her throat, Wyre spoke. 'We're with you, guv.'

Sullivan breezed past. 'Briefing in ten. I expect you all to be there, including you, Harte.' She disappeared around a corner.

They all went obediently back into the room, ready to play Sullivan's game. As soon as the briefing was over, they were alone on the case without the support of the department. Gina knew it could cost her everything, but it no longer mattered.

FIFTY

TIFFANY

Tiffany wobbled slightly to the kitchen. Something wasn't right. It was as if the room was tilting back and forth, only slightly. Her stomach growled. Hunger or nausea?

She poured a glass of filtered water from the fridge and took her tablets. Maybe she felt so rough because she hadn't taken them. She took another swig of the liquid and felt like heaving. Maybe she was dehydrated. Her head began to throb. What she'd really like is a glass of wine, then she could sleep and forget everything. She slammed the glass down. Some crazed killer was out there, and he was coming for her, and she was expected to get by on water and... She paused and pulled out the bowl of lunch that her husband had prepared for her. Egg salad. She grabbed a fork and heaved as she forced a few leaves down her gullet before bouncing the bowl on the draining board. It had tasted funny. In fact, everything tasted odd. Maybe she was coming down with a virus.

Reaching into her pocket, she grabbed the blister pack of diazepam that she'd kept close all day. She'd happily kept them hidden from Kieron since finding them in her bag.

Her chat with Lauren had seemed a bit weird and Tiffany didn't know if her friend had meant to tell her that she knew about Robbie and Sienna's fling, and for a short while, Lauren had stared into thin air. On the way out, Lauren had been so consumed by her thoughts, she accidentally brushed into Tiffany's photos on the hall wall, smashing a couple of frames.

Tiffany ran a hand through her hair and imagined her strangler taking a chunk as a trophy. Did he smell it and play with it? Maybe it turned him on as he relived his attacks? On the night of Sienna and Robbie's murder, Tiffany had wandered out. She'd gone to the house as Lauren's neighbours had reported seeing a woman wearing pyjamas hanging around. At first, she'd thought that she might have done the unthinkable, but now she wondered if the murderer had seen her, which is why he'd been terrorising her.

She popped a couple of pills out of the blister pack onto the worktop and stared at them. Kieron wouldn't be happy, but they made her happy. She wanted to feel sleepy and numb until he got home so that she could forget about the strangler. Maybe Kieron would come home earlier if he knew the police had been but then again, she'd texted him to tell him, and he hadn't even read the message. Her phone lit up on the table. It was Kieron.

Sorry, love. I was tied up with the boss. I can't get home early. I did ask but they're already fed up that I've had to leave a few times. I can't afford to lose this job. We need the money. I'll be home soon. You're safe with the police officer outside. Love you loads. XXX

She threw her phone onto the table narrowly missing the broken frames and the panic button. She picked up her wedding photo and felt a tear springing from one of her eyes. Then, she held the photo of the cut log in Bluebell Woods.

Kieron had proposed to her there. He'd got down on one knee after treating her to an amazing picnic and he'd asked her to marry him. She remembered jumping up and down before flinging her arms around him. They'd been happy. She had been happy. Then she got attacked and neither of them had been happy since. Her heart ached for him to come home.

She glanced at the message again, but her vision was getting blurry. This week had been one of the worst ever and Kieron would not stand up to his boss and say he needed to be with her. She popped the tablets into her mouth and swallowed them down with the rest of her water. As she went to put the jug back into the fridge, she glanced through the kitchen window and gasped. The police car had gone. Her heart began to race, and she dropped the jug on the floor.

She ran to the door, flinging it open. Maybe the officer had parked a little way down the road. But why would he? Hurrying to the edge of the path, she stared up and down but there was no sign of a police car. Her front door slammed shut, leaving her outside with no shoes on. The breeze must have caught it. She spotted a brown scarf tied to the dense bushes outside her bedroom, then a breeze caught it, and it was gone. She stared a while longer and it didn't come back. She shook her head, wondering if she'd imagined it. Taking a step towards her front door for a better view of the bush, she swayed while watching an empty pop can as it hurtled along the road in a gust of wind. No, she wasn't going anywhere near the bushes. There was no scarf. She'd humiliated herself enough with all the other outbursts. Hurrying around the back of the block, she hoped that one of the windows wasn't properly closed and that she could climb in. When Lauren was there it had got a bit stuffy, so she'd opened the window while Lauren had made them another drink. She nudged the back gate open. As she passed the bin area, she avoided stepping on the broken glass that still littered the area. When she reached the window, she prised her finger-nails into the tiniest gap and pulled it open. After falling through it, she closed it properly, brushed off her clothes and staggered back into the kitchen. She leaned over the sink to catch a glimpse of the bush. There was no scarf.

Yawning, she knew she needed to sit down before she fell. Diazepam never affected her in this way before now. Kieron had nagged her to visit her doctor again. When the whole night-mare was over, she was going to do just that. Sinking into the chair, she felt her eyelids getting heavy as the room spun. *Fight it*, her mind kept telling her. She could do without being a total zombie today. But fighting it was impossible. As she half drifted, she imagined a huge glass of wine slipping down her throat.

She prised an eye open and wondered if she'd nodded off briefly as the room was a little darker. She must have and she'd walked in her sleep again. On the table in front of her was an open bottle of wine and a glass already poured. Down the front of her top were red splash marks. She shivered and grabbed a blanket from the back of the chair, then she topped up the glass and drank the liquid down in one.

'Sleep, my lovely, sleep.'

Was that a voice in her head or had someone said that to her? She wanted to turn, but the pull of sleep was too strong. It was all in her imagination anyway. Maybe her strangler hadn't come back. Maybe there had been no man at the window. The police would be back soon anyway. If anyone was lurking about, they'd catch him. The voice had all been in her head. She was half awake and hallucinating. It was the wine. It was the tablets. It was her.

'It'll soon be over.'

That voice again. Was she remembering something that had been said or was there someone else in the room? She wanted her nightmare to be over and she trusted the voice as it carried her to such beautiful dreams. The hands on her forehead were soft and warm. Were they a dream too?

Her limbs turned to lead, and she began to gently snore as soft lips kissed her cheek.

'Goodnight forever.'

'Goodnight,' she mumbled as a snore escaped her mouth.

FIFTY-ONE

Gina sat through the briefing, fingers twitching as she itched to leave. They should have seen the connection earlier.

Gina wouldn't normally have missed something so obvious, especially after she and Collier had spoken to Hazel Blackford.

She put her hand up, wanting to give Sullivan one more chance before she went rogue, but the woman dismissed her and continued talking about how Jacob had opportunity in all four cases. Sullivan revealed that Jacob had a burner phone that he'd been using to message Sienna on. He'd argued with her as Sienna had moaned at him to forget Jennifer and he couldn't. No one believed him when he told them that the burner phone was only bought as he didn't want to give Sienna his phone number, because he wasn't sure what was going on in his life.

Briggs glanced over at her, and Gina could see that even he wasn't even going to attempt to challenge Sullivan's authority. He was merely getting primed for the big press release later that day. If he knew that she was going to follow up on her theory, he might try to stop her. Gina wouldn't let that happen. Sometimes a person has to choose between doing what they were ordered to do and doing what was right and this was her moment.

'Harte, you're alright to manage that, are you?' Sullivan waited with raised eyebrows for her to answer.

'Huh?' She stopped chewing the bottom of her pen and placed it on the table. Wyre glanced at her as if trying to convey a message with her eyes, but it was lost on Gina. Sullivan cleared her throat.

'The crowd. You and your team can manage the crowd alongside uniform when the announcement goes out. Okay?'

'But, ma'am, uniform will be handling that.' Uniform had always effectively kept things like that under control. She needed to be out there finding the killer and proving Jacob's innocence.

Sullivan shrugged. 'Are you saying it's beneath you? You will be required to back uniform up. It's going to be explosive when the news hits, so you all need to get your gear on and be a team player. That is an order.'

'But, ma'am, we need to talk about Lauren. I'm not letting this go.' She felt her hands shake. She'd always treated her superiors with respect, and she'd prided herself on being a team player. It wasn't sitting well in her gut and for a second, she felt like she might heave.

'Step down, Harte. Are you challenging my authority again? DCI Briggs and I won't stand for this level of insubordination.' Sullivan glanced over at Briggs, and he looked away from her. Briggs must know she was onto something and that ignoring this lead could also be a nail in the coffin for the department. If he was on her side, he wasn't showing it.

Gina stood and slammed her palms down on the table. 'Can we put our differences aside and think about the case and about Lauren. Everything has changed. We've been looking at the case in the wrong way, which is why we haven't solved it yet.'

'Harte. Sienna was murdered, not Lauren.'

'But Lauren fits his type which leads me to believe that the killer went there to kill Lauren, but he accidentally killed

Sienna instead. Lauren has long blonde hair and blue eyes, just like Hazel and Tiffany. It's dyed but that's how it is naturally. Both Sienna and Lauren were wearing little black dresses on the night of the murder, once again, I'm suggesting that the killer could have mistaken the two women.'

'His type, there were two attacks, that's hardly enough to prove a type.'

'But Robbie came home and got in the way, which is why he too was murdered. Robbie wasn't planned. Don't dismiss it, you can't dismiss it. It's too big.' Gina unbuttoned the top of her shirt, letting the heat escape that had been radiating from her chest.

'Get out. Go and wait in my office.' Sullivan pointed to the door. Briggs stood to follow her out as she stormed across the room. 'Get back, DCI Briggs.' He did exactly what he was told, leaving Gina to battle Sullivan's unreasonableness alone.

Hurrying along the corridor towards Briggs's office, she saw the spare room next door, adorned with Sullivan's temporary nameplate on it. She passed it and hurried down the fire escape, taking two steps at a time. No way was she wasting another minute in that building while Lauren's life might be at risk and her colleague was facing such accusations. She sent a quick message to Wyre, letting her know what she was doing but she doubted that Wyre would be out of that briefing anytime soon. As she crossed the car park, the crowds chanted words of vitriol against her team and all police. Too busy focusing on the entrance, they missed Gina as she slipped into her car and drove out of the car park, but then another crowd formed and stopped her in the middle of the road. More protestors with banners. She hit the steering wheel. Lauren, she had to warn her. She instructed her hands-free to call the woman. The call went straight to voicemail and cut her off before she could leave a message. She pulled over and began typing out a text.

Please go to your mum's and wait for me. I have reason to believe you might be in danger and I'm coming straight over. DI Harte.

She hit send and started the car up again. Pipping her horn, she hoped the crowd would disperse but even after edging through them, a backlog of traffic had caused a jam. Her actions were going against all protocol, but she had to do all she could. If Lauren was the intended victim, he was coming for her.

FIFTY-TWO

NANCY

Head stabbing in agony after the blow, Nancy came around and tried to wriggle out of her binds but there was no escape; he'd made sure of that. She had no idea how many times he'd wrapped the twine around her wrists and ankles, then he'd tied both together behind her back. She tried to rock back and forth, but nothing was happening. If he hadn't blindfolded her with a scarf or rammed a sock in her mouth before taping across the top, she'd at least have her sight and voice.

What if Lauren had returned and he'd hurt her too?

The material against her eyes began to dampen as her tears fell.

How?

Think.

She'd received the flowers and there was a note. Written on it were two words. *Forever mine.* He must have entered while she'd been outside looking up and down the road for a car.

Pain flashed from her shoulder to her wrist as she wiggled again. It felt as though she'd pulled a muscle. Her stiff neck wouldn't budge, and the sock was damp with drool and all she could do was cry and fill her stuffy nose up even more.

A wet tongue drew a short line up her arm, then it happened again. The little dog barked and nudged her with its nose. Fifi was safe and all Nancy wanted to do was hug her. She felt a tremor in her knees as she thought of her daughter again. Was she also tied up in the same room? Maybe she was unconscious and unable to move.

Just before knocking her out, she'd felt his presence, the warmth of his breath on her neck as she fell to the floor. Then she caught sight of his reflection in the stainless-steel water bowl that Fifi drank from. She remembered his words as he dragged her up the stairs and trussed her up. He was coming back and both she and Lauren would pay for everything. His words rang through her head. *You just couldn't leave things alone, could you? You were everywhere, in my face all the time and you're an angry little bitch. You thought I just went away but you were wrong. I've been waiting for this moment.* For ages, he'd been watching her as she waved her placards and held up traffic. He'd been watching her house and he'd enjoyed scaring her the other night. But she'd started it and now she was paying the ultimate price. Nancy needed to find a way out of her binds so she could warn her daughter. He was going for her next. It was always about Lauren.

She heard the back door slamming and all her muscles froze. The dog yapped and ran down the stairs. Nancy rolled onto her side and her hip jutted into the threadbare carpet. Her legs, she couldn't feel her legs.

She hyperventilated as she heard his heavy footsteps banging up the stairs, perspiration dripping down her face. He was finally coming to finish the job and there wasn't a single thing she could do about it.

More tears spilled from her eyes and the blindfold was now sodden. If only she could talk to him, tell him that she was sorry, and reason with him. If she could go back in time, she wondered if there was anything she'd do differently. She'd never have encouraged Lauren to go to one of her wellness and meditation sessions. He was there for the same reason as she was, to find inner peace and Lauren had fallen for him. That was where it all started. Nancy was solely responsible for their introduction.

'I see you're still where I left you. That's good,' he whispered. 'Don't worry, you won't be there for much longer because Lauren and I, we're leaving. We love each other and there's nothing at all you can do about it.'

She wanted to yell that Lauren didn't love him, that she never had. Nancy saw through him all those years ago, that's why she did that bad thing. He pretended to care, and he was a good actor but Nancy wasn't fooled.

'We're going back to the beginning, starting again and reliving our love. You.' She felt him prod her side. 'You are just pond scum. We don't need you anymore. Lauren hates you, but you know that already. We talk about you. She tells me everything.' He paused. 'The others, they were nothing but Lauren, she's special. At first, I wanted her dead, but I've sat back and made a better plan. I wanted the others dead, but I want her, and I will have her. I always get what I want eventually, and she was never going to marry Robbie. I was going to make sure of that. She's mine.' He slapped his lips. 'All I wanted back then was for you to like me, to accept me.' He laughed. 'We could have been friends too. I could have got on board with your activism, joined in, but you drove me away.'

Lauren turned her key in the front door. Nancy went to bang her head on the floor to warn her daughter, but he grabbed it. Then, she felt his rough hands feeding a length of material around her neck and she jerked.

'I suggest you keep still. You wouldn't want to strangle yourself now, would you? Don't make me. I would love to strangle you.'

She remained still, knowing that Lauren wouldn't hear her

over the sound of Fifi's barking. After slamming the front door, Lauren called out. 'Mum, I'm back.' The dog began to bark.

Please Fifi, don't run upstairs. If the dog came up, her daughter would be led straight to her death.

The dog darted up the stairs and straight into the bedroom, licking Nancy's face.

'Mum?' Lauren called again. 'Are you upstairs?'

Nancy heard her daughter take the first creaky step. It was no good, either she made some noise to alert Lauren, hoping that she understood that something was wrong, or she did nothing, and Lauren would come up to her death.

Her daughter took a few more steps. 'Mum? Fifi? What is it, girl?'

Nancy thrust her head back, pulling a tendon as she hit it against the radiator, then she let out a muffled scream. He tightened the material around her neck, and she heard her daughter shrieking. White-hot pain seared through her face as something sharp hit her. It was over, he had won, and it had all been Nancy's fault. Now they were both going to die. What had she started?

FIFTY-THREE

Gina finally got through the traffic queue and past the temporary lights that had held everyone up. Cars full of parents leaving a school added to the chaos. Her phone rang. It was PC Smith. 'Hello.'

'Guv, Shaf and I just did a shift change. As soon as I got here, I could see something was wrong.'

'What was it?'

'A scarf was caught in the undergrowth a little way down the path. A brown one that was almost camouflaged by the mud. Given what Tiffany had reported, I thought I should knock to see if she was okay.'

'And?' Gina indicated and took a right onto the carriageway.

'There was no answer. I ran around the back, and I saw her sleeping in a chair, at least I thought she was sleeping, then I saw the empty blister packs. She's taken an overdose, guv. Paramedics have just arrived, and I don't know how it's looking yet. I smashed the door to get in, called it in and waited for the ambulance to arrive. I'm on my own here until someone arrives but I thought I should let you know. We didn't mean to leave her alone. She was okay when I left. She had a friend with her, and we thought she'd be okay for a short while.' He paused, and she heard him exhale. 'If we'd have planned it better, this might not have happened.' She heard PC Smith's voice cracking.

'Smith, it's not your fault.'

'I stopped off for some snacks from the garage. I knew it was going to be a long night.' He paused. 'Hold on, they're bringing her out.'

'I'm going to put the phone down in a minute. Just to warn you, I'm not meant to be out, and you need to report this direct to DI Collier. I'm meant to be at the station.'

'I've done that already. Guv, are you in trouble?'

'Listen. Just tell me how Tiffany is. Can you see anything?'

'The paramedics have just wheeled her into an ambulance and DI Collier has just pulled up with DC Wyre. Tiffany looks dead.' He paused.

'Did the scene look suspicious?'

'Yes, I've also reported that too. There was mud over the windowsill and a footprint which was odd. The kitchen was covered in water and there was a shattered jug on the floor. They're sending someone over to take a look. We've called her husband and he said he's heading to the hospital. There's also a typed-up suicide note.'

Gina swallowed. 'What does it say?'

'I have it here in an evidence bag. It says, "I'm sorry but I couldn't go on. Every day I live in fear and that's no way to live a life. I can't carry this pain any longer. Kieron, if you found me, please know that it's not your fault. You did everything you could. I'm sorry for all the times I hurt you, all the times I wandered out in my sleep and stressed you out, and I'm sorry for all the drinking. Please forgive me and don't hate me for what I've done. Tiff. X"'

'Shit.' Gina wiped a stray tear from her eye.

'Collier and Wyre are about to approach. Should I tell them that I've spoken to you?'

'Just tell them the truth.' She couldn't bear for him to get into any trouble and if she was wrong about everything, they'd see his phone records anyway. She hung up and drove straight towards Malvern. As she pulled onto the winding country road in darkness at the base of the hills, she couldn't help but think about Tiffany. She should never have been left alone. The trauma she'd gone through had broken her. She didn't care what Sullivan and Collier thought; Tiffany wasn't making things up and Jacob had not killed anyone. Gina thought of the pain that Tiffany would have been in as she took those tablets.

Swallowing her upset down, she pulled up next to Nancy's cottage. Nancy's car was parked outside the house. Collier's name flashed up on her phone as it rang. She pressed end on the call. Just as a message came through from Sullivan, her phone battery ran out but not before glancing at the two words Sullivan had sent. They almost took her breath away.

You're suspended.

FIFTY-FOUR

Gina stood at Nancy's front door and rang the bell as dusk created shadows everywhere. It chimed from behind the hallway and the dog barked. There was no other sign of life coming from the cottage. She banged on the door. 'Police.' If she had to, she'd say that she'd never received that message from Sullivan and her phone was now dead. As far as she was concerned, she knew nothing of her suspension. She'd continue standing at Nancy's door and call out the word 'Police'. Until she knew that Lauren was safe, she was staying on the case.

Gina lifted the letter box. 'Nancy, it's DI Harte. Please open the door.' She dropped the flap and wondered if Nancy had popped out for a walk, then the dog began to yap and snuffle again at the bottom of the door. She couldn't imagine that the woman had gone for a walk up the hills and not taken her dog.

She lifted the letter box again and stared through the tiny slit, waiting for her eyes to adjust to the dark interior. There was a bunch of flowers in a box on the floor, at least they looked to be the shape of flowers. Her line of vision continued along the hall and through the downstairs where the faint light from a kitchen gadget showed her the open back door. It began to creak as a gust of wind caught it. Her heart began to hum and the cold chill in the air reached out and touched the back of her neck. Something wasn't right. Gina shook her head. Maybe Nancy was in the garden and couldn't hear her knocking and calling. But why would she be in the garden when it was almost dark? The dog sprinted along the hall and ran through the back door. That's when Gina heard a tinny banging noise coming from upstairs. 'Nancy.' The bang came again.

Without hesitating, Gina ran from the front door. She pushed the bushes away that were dense along the side of the cottage as she followed the path to the back garden. Shivering, she glanced around at the trees and hills beyond. No one would hear if anything went wrong. Gina felt her hands tremble slightly, knowing that there was no place to run to out here. No houses, shops, people. She was alone.

On reaching the back gate, she stepped into the garden. The breeze whipped up a pile of dead branches and leaves. The dog darted towards her. 'Nancy,' she called. She pulled her phone from her pocket and confirmed that she had no charge at all. She'd never felt so alone while entering a potential crime scene, but it was the only way. She knew that the intended target was Lauren and none of Sullivan's team were listening. She stared at the lit-up hands of her watch, and she could see that it was almost five. Within minutes, the news would go out that Jacob had been charged with the most horrific of crimes.

She hurried down the garden path as the little dog whined while running circles around her. As she approached the door, she placed a pair of latex gloves over her hands and pulled some shoe covers over her boots. 'Nancy?' she called as she flicked the light switch. This time, she couldn't hear the tinny noise and for a moment, she wondered if it was no more than the heating system crackling. She kicked the sheet of plastic that lay crumpled on the kitchen floor and continued past the table.

The dog yapped at the bottom of the stairs. Gina walked through to the hallway where she saw the bunch of mixed flowers. A card lay on the floor, and she shivered as she held the note up towards the light. *Forever mine.* That same message had been engraved inside the wedding ring found in Robbie Shields's clothing. She turned the card over; they were addressed to Lauren. She had been right all along and here was her evidence. The flowers had been sent by Bill's Blossoms, a florist in Worcester. All they had to do now was trace the sender and they had their killer. If the flowers had been sent while Jacob was in custody, they'd have to let him go.

Another tinny bang came from above. Gina peered into the lounge but there was nothing amiss there. She snatched the cordless phone and placed it in her pocket. Taking the first creaky step, she continued up. 'Nancy?' Her breaths were shallow, and her heart banged.

The dog ran past her and began barking from one of the bedrooms. Gina hurried up to the landing, pushing open the first door, which showed her that the bathroom was empty. She turned the landing light on. On passing the first bedroom, she saw the dog's tail wagging at the base of the double bed. As she stepped in, she flinched, the sight in front her sending her gasping. Glancing in all directions, Gina wondered if the killer was in the house. There was no movement, apart from that in front of her. She ran over to the woman who lay on her front. Her legs had been secured behind her back to her arms. A scarf around her neck that had been tied to a hook above. If Nancy had slipped or fallen unconscious, she'd have been instantly strangled.

Running over, Gina removed the noose from the woman's neck and began to untie her binds. Her hands flopped forward, and her feet slammed onto the floor. With shaky fingers, Gina pulled the scarf from the woman's eyes away and the tape off her mouth. Nancy spat the sock out and inhaled so deep, it sounded like she was sucking the air out of the room. The dog began to jump all over her as she lay with her face in the carpet.

'You're safe now. I'm going to call for help.' Gina grabbed a pillow from the bed and placed it under Nancy's head as she pulled the cordless phone out her pocket. She dialled one of the only numbers she knew by heart and Briggs answered immediately. 'Gina where the hell are you?'

'I'm at Nancy Cross's house. I've just found her in the bedroom, tied up. Please call an ambulance and get a team down here immediately.'

'What number are you calling on?'

'This is Nancy's home phone. I have no charge.'

'So, you didn't get the message. Just to let you know, Sullivan has sus—'

Before he could finish his sentence, she ended the call. 'Help is on its way. Can I get you some water?'

The woman coughed and spluttered, then shook her head. 'Lauren.'

'What about Lauren? Do you know where she is?'

'He has her and he drugged me. He wanted me to fall asleep so that I'd strangle myself.' Her eyelids half closed as she fought it.

'Who has her?'

Nancy whispered his name under her breath. Gina pulled a blanket from the bed and wrapped her up in it. 'Do you know where I can find him?'

'Where they...' She coughed again. 'Engaged. Please bring her home, she's so scared. He will kill her. Please, hurry.' Nancy struggled to say as her eyes half closed.

'Where do I need to go?' Gina's tensed jaw made her head throb as Nancy began to drift into a world of her own as whatever he'd drugged her with took over. 'Nancy, please listen to me. Where can I find Lauren? Where did he take her?' Gina caught sight of the sock that had been in Nancy's mouth, and she recognised it from the post-mortem. It was Robbie's missing sock.

Nancy began to shiver erratically just as Gina heard ambulance sirens coming up the road. 'Help is here, Nancy. I'm going to let them in.' She ran down the stairs as fast as she could until she reached the front door, and a paramedic was about to knock. 'She's upstairs, first bedroom. She's been tied up and drugged. I don't know what with.' As she said those words, a thought came to mind. Tiffany. She called Briggs again.

'Gina, I'm about to lead the press conference. I can't speak yet.'

'Don't do it. Jacob didn't do it. I have proof right here.' He went to interrupt. 'Don't speak, I have too much to tell you and no time.' She blurted everything she knew out to him. That way, they could secure Tiffany and Kieron's flat as a scene. She had a theory about where Lauren had been taken too but it was only that. Without the team to bounce things off, she was alone, and she only had minutes before uniform would arrive. She needed to be gone. 'And, Chris?'

'Yes?'

'Please tell Hereford all this so that they can let Jacob go now. He couldn't possibly have attacked Nancy and taken Lauren. He's in the clear.'

She threw the phone onto the settee and ran out of the house, leaving Nancy in the capable hands of the paramedics. Nancy would want nothing more than for Gina to find her daughter and bring her home safely. Gina wasn't about to sit around being questioned and reprimanded all evening, wasting valuable time while their killer had Lauren. As it stood, Sullivan was about to call an end to investigating the case and was prepared to allow Jacob to take the blame. Sullivan was right, Gina had a heart, and she was emotional because she cared and that was Sullivan's downfall. Sullivan had no heart.

Running to her car, she got in, did a three-point-turn and

headed past the ambulance down the windy road back towards Malvern. She plugged her phone in to charge but turned it off immediately. She had no need for messages or calls, Lauren was running out of time. Large trees loomed over her, casting shadows across the road from the backlighting of the street lamps. O'Connor's car came the other way and for a moment, she wondered if he'd stop but he smiled at her as she drove past. She exhaled knowing that this was just the beginning. She was still alone, and she was yet to confront the killer and if her theory was right, she was dancing with death, but she was also Lauren's only hope.

FIFTY-FIVE

TIFFANY

Tiffany leaned over towards the cardboard dish and vomited. The nurse looked on sympathetically as she took the bowl. Tiffany felt the weight of her head fixing her to the pillow. In fact, her whole body was like lead. She lay on her side and hugged herself as her stomach spasmed again. She was living in some kind of hell. The beeping sound of machines made her head spin and pound. She pulled the sheet up a little further so that it covered her eyes. How had she got here? She moved her arm a little and felt a sting as the cannula caught in the sheet. They were pumping something into her, and she'd heard the word overdose mentioned when a doctor had been in. That was nonsense. She hadn't taken an overdose, she'd taken her usual tablets and she grimaced, there was the wine. She remembered something about wine and then there was a voice.

The nurse was saying something sweet and soothing, but the words weren't registering. It was as if they were in some sort of echoey chamber and the sound was bouncing off the walls.

'Is my husband here?' she said, in a wavering voice that was hoarse from heaving.

'I'll find out for you.'

Tiffany remembered drinking water and being so tired, she couldn't keep her eyes open. After Lauren's visit, she'd panicked. The police weren't outside and... what happened then? It was like a veil was dampening her thoughts. With shaky hands, Tiffany pulled the sheet from her face and grabbed a tissue off the table. She wiped her mouth before taking the tiniest sip of water.

A flash of jumbled memories made her shudder. The smashed photos, the scarf hanging on the bush, the balaclava, his outline in the darkness. The man at the window, he had been real. Her problems were a result of trauma but all everyone wanted to do was use her mental health against her. She knew her mind and knew she'd seen a man at her window. It was an easy box to put her in, the hysterical woman. No more. She grabbed the plastic glass and threw it onto the floor, but the satisfying crash didn't come, making her feel more powerless. Why did they keep mentioning the word suicide? She hadn't been trying to kill herself.

As the realisation hit her, she began to gasp for air. She knew exactly what had happened, but she wondered if anyone would even believe her. She had to get out before they did something unthinkable, like section her. She knew how it worked. Hysterical woman won't leave house, drinks too much, takes drugs for her mental health, never believed, husband tells everyone she's crazy, no one takes her physical symptoms seriously anymore and they think she makes them all up.

Sliding one leg out of the bed, she shuffled to the edge and rolled off, landing in a heap. The cannula came loose. Every part of her body ached or felt weak. The room filled as an alarm sounded. The nurse ran back in and was followed by someone in a white coat. 'I don't consent, no more drugs. Don't you dare sedate me, or I will sue the hell out of you,' Tiffany called out. 'I want the police. Someone tried to kill me. Please believe me.'

Terror rained down on her as the white coats came closer.

She closed her eyes and waited for a jab. That's when she felt someone taking her under the arms and helping her up. She sobbed like never before. Maybe, just maybe they believed her. 'Your blood results will be back soon, Mrs Crawford, but we need you to stay in bed. You're far too weak to walk around.' The white-coated man smiled, and she dared to believe that she could trust him.

She glanced up and saw a woman with a shiny black pony-tail looking through the tiny window in the door. It was all coming back now. That night, while she'd been wandering in her pyjamas, she'd seen the murderer and the murderer had seen her. The whole puzzle had clicked into place. Finally, she was free.

'Police, I need the police. I know who attacked me and I want to give a statement.'

The nurse waved the woman in. 'This is DC Wyre from Cleevesford Police.'

However hard she tried to control her sobs, it was impossible, but she managed to get her sentence out as she heaved and cried. 'He killed Sienna, too. I was there. I saw him.'

FIFTY-SIX

Gina drove through every ANPR camera she could find as she whizzed through Cleevesford. She wanted the police on her tail, and they were her only hope should she be right. She checked her phone, and it showed ten per cent charge. She took a left out of the town and followed the dark country lanes for the next mile. The fields were nothing more than different shades of grey blocks. There were no more cameras to automatically recognise her registration now. She was alone and heading for the woods. If she went in without backup, she could end up dead.

She thought of Hannah, the daughter she barely got on with, and her little granddaughter, Gracie. Families had a way of working through their problems and despite their differences, Hannah would be beside herself if Gina was killed in the woods tonight. She thought of Briggs and she knew she wasn't ready to stare death in the face, despite him not keeping her fully in the picture. She turned her phone on and commanded the hands-free to call Briggs.

'Gina, seriously, where are you? I'm worried sick,' he said in a hushed voice.

Gina listened to the sounds of the incident room and Sullivan spoke. 'Her registration has just been picked up. Cleevesford High Street, by the bus stop. Get uniform out there.'

'They're coming, Gina.' Briggs cleared his throat.

'It's okay. I'm no longer there and I won't be flagging up on any more ANPR. I wish I was because I feel as though I'm about to walk into the dragon's cave.' She took a right into the car park that led to the woodland walk. Her signal dipped. 'I don't even know if I'm right, but Sullivan doesn't want to know my theories so I'm alone. I can't ignore this lead and let Lauren die.'

'I let you down. I should have said more, been more vocal but I've been shot down too.'

'I know and I'm glad you're still there but you could have trusted me with what was being said in those briefings,' Gina replied. She paused.

'I know and I'm sorry.'

Gina peered out into the darkness.

'What's happening?'

The wind howled and a branch hit her windscreen. 'His car is parked up. I've just spotted it at the back of the car park, almost backed into the bushes. He's here and he has Lauren. He came back to his familiar place.'

'What familiar place, Gina? You're not making any sense.'

'Nancy was mumbling something about Lauren getting engaged years ago. Forever mine, he was never going to let her go, she was the one and not only that, he took the next woman he proposed to, to the exact same place. Maybe he wanted to capture that same magic but never could. Tiffany didn't take an overdose, he tried to kill her and now he's trying to kill Lauren. He went to the bungalow to kill Lauren and he killed Sienna instead.'

'Gina, where are you? Don't do this alone.'

Her phone began to beep, telling her that her charge was running low again. 'Bluebell Woods. The blue flowers on the scarf, they're bluebells. He chose this place. You're looking for the huge stump of an oak tree. I think I know where it is. I've brought Gracie here to play in the past.'

'Where is it?'

'I can't explain. Just follow the walking trail and hurry. Don't veer off. I'm heading down there before it's too late.' With shaky hands Gina ended the call. She grabbed her torch from the boot and ran as fast as she could up the muddy slope that led to a dense mass of trees. She swallowed while crunching on branches below. Eerie shadows were cast from her torchlight, each one a finger pointing to tree upon tree. That's when she heard a loud piercing scream.

'Lauren,' Gina called as she ran as fast as she could.

FIFTY-SEVEN

TIFFANY

'Are you able to speak?' DC Wyre asked again. This time her words sunk in.

Tiffany nodded. 'Yes, but I feel as though my tongue is too big for my mouth,' she slurred.

'Just do your best and if at any time it gets too much, just say.' The detective smiled warmly and took a seat next to Tiffany's bed.

'I didn't try to kill myself. They said I did.'

'What happened?'

'I drank some water out of the fridge and took my tablets, then, I don't know. My dinner tasted funny. Everything tastes funny. I felt weird and woozy. I was scared as the police officer was gone and then I managed to shut myself out of the flat.' She scrunched her brows. 'I went around the back and climbed in through the window.' She shook her head. 'I don't know if I'm telling you all this in the right order.'

DC Wyre scribbled a few notes. 'That's okay. We can go through it all again, when you're feeling a little better.'

'I nodded off, then I woke up and saw the wine on the table, so I drank it. I couldn't remember opening a bottle of wine but I was convinced I had. Then I got worse. My head was fuzzier, and I heard a voice as I drifted off. Someone was there, behind me.'

'Who?'

'I'm coming to that. I know who killed Sienna Moorcroft. I was there.' She cleared her throat as she tried to recall her mixed up half dreams. 'I was the woman on her street that you're looking for, the one in pyjamas. I'd sleepwalked and I thought you'd blame me because I couldn't remember anything. I think I followed him.'

'Who?'

Tiffany ignored that question, needing to get her thoughts out as they were coming to her. 'The front door was on the catch, and he went in. Then I'm not sure what I was doing but Robbie then returned. This is when it gets patchy. After that, I remember Kieron's hand holding mine as he led me back into our flat.' Tears fell down her cheeks. 'All this time, I thought he loved me, but he's been hurting me.'

'Your husband?'

Tiffany nodded. 'Yes, it was Kieron. He killed Sienna and he's going to try to say that I'm mad and shouldn't be believed. He'll say that it's the tablets and the wine, but I didn't pour the wine, he gave it to me. And he prepares all my tablets. He makes all my food. I wanted to cook once, but he wouldn't let me. He said I was too unsafe in the kitchen, but I think he's been trying to slowly kill me.' The detective stopped writing and waited for more. 'Something clicked when Lauren came earlier. She'd never been to my place, and she'd never met Kieron, or so I thought. She kept staring at my wedding photos and the tree stump, where he proposed to me, she took those words out of my mouth as if she knew, but I'd never told her. At first, I thought I'd imagined it but later after she'd left, I heard a whisper, and the voice told me it would all be over soon and the last words I heard before waking up here were, goodnight forever. My own husband tried to strangle me all those years ago. He must have left that stag party, attacked me, and drove right back. I think he's been drugging me and controlling me ever since. Please don't make me go back to him, please. I'm not mad. It's the truth.' Tiffany couldn't hold back the sobs.

FIFTY-EIGHT

As Gina followed the screaming, her hands shook. She flinched as a fox darted from behind a tree before vanishing off behind another. She clambered over the stony floor and slipped as she stepped on a bit of slimy moss. The wind whipped up, distorting the sound of Lauren's cries, sending an eerie wailing through the woods. She checked her phone and again, the charge had gone. Although, she doubted she'd even have a signal anyway.

As she reached a run of hard, flat, mud, she began to jog closer to Lauren. A faint light bled through the trees. She turned her torch off and crept closer and closer until she reached the clearing with the tree stump.

'You're just the same as all the rest,' he yelled as he pushed Lauren to the stick covered ground. Then he dropped to his knees and pulled his belt off. He dragged it around Lauren's neck and sat behind her.

'Please, don't hurt me. You don't want to do this.' Lauren sobbed and tried to pull at the belt.

'Oh, but I do. I want to hurt you so bad. I want to tighten this belt and watch your eyes pop out of their sockets. And I'll

laugh as you beg me to stop, while your hands flail but ulti-
mately, you are powerless.'

'I thought you loved me,' Lauren managed to blurt out.

Gina fought the sickening feeling rising in her gullet and
stepped out from behind a tree. Lauren had been having an
affair with Kieron and it had led to this moment. He'd meant to
kill her, not Sienna. Had she rejected him in favour of
remaining with Robbie. Or maybe it was her marriage
announcement that started it. She couldn't wait for backup. If
she waited a moment longer, Lauren would be throttled. Her
gargling attempts at crying made Gina shudder.

'Kieron, it's over. You're surrounded.' That was a lie, but she
had to commit now. She couldn't let him know that she was
alone. 'Please, let Lauren go.'

He huffed. 'Let this bitch go, never. I'm prepared to go
down for her.' He lifted her up using the belt like it was a lead.
Now, Lauren was in front of him, and he was using her as a
shield.

'Kieron, there is no way out. We've found your car. Lauren's
mum, Nancy, told us everything.'

He furrowed his brows. 'Hear that, Mummy has been
rubbishing me again.' He looked back at Gina, and he glanced
beyond. 'There's no one out there, is there. You're all alone. If
there was, they wouldn't let me do this.' He wrenched the belt
and Lauren began to flail, trying to grab him but not even being
close.

'It's over.' Gina pressed her lips together and took a step
closer to him.

'Get the hell back or I swear I'll snap her neck off clean.'

She held her hands up and stepped back again. 'Okay, I'm
stepping back.'

Lauren's fearful stare met Gina's and she could see how low
Lauren's hand was. She was going to reach for his groin. They

had no choice but to fight him because Kieron was right, no one else was going to help.

'I tell you what,' he said. 'I'll kill her, then I'll kill you. I can have you both because fucking women are all liars. Each and every one of you. You all deserve to die.'

'Is that why you hurt Tiffany?' She had to keep him talking until Lauren gave her a signal. What that signal might be, she had no idea yet.

He let out a laugh. 'I've never hurt her. All I ever do is look after her, care for her, feed her and make sure she's safe but in the end, we needed her out of our life, didn't we Lauren, so that we could try again?'

Try again, that suggested he and Lauren had history. Had he been the man she had an affair with early on in her and Robbie's relationship, or did they go back further? Lauren emitted a roar just before the belt tightened again. She brought her hand to his groin and squeezed with gritted teeth. Instead of letting go, he yelled in agony as he tightened the belt.

Gina ran over but as she approached, he kept using Lauren as a barrier between her and him. 'Kieron, let her go.'

'Nah.'

Gina nodded and smirked as trainee DC Kapoor and two uniformed officers came up behind him and fought the belt from his hands. Within seconds, they had the man on the ground, and he was being cuffed and read his rights. Gina threw herself to the ground and loosened the belt from around Lauren's neck and the woman gasped for air. 'You're safe, Lauren. It's over.'

FIFTY-NINE

As Gina drove back to the station, all she could think about was the trouble she was going to be in. It wasn't over for her yet.

She wondered if Jacob was being processed for release. She pulled into the car park relieved that the protesters had thinned out. She turned on her partly charged phone and clicked onto the *Warwickshire Herald*. There was no mention at all of Jacob's arrest. She headed over to their social media where they normally shared any breaking news, again, there was nothing. She leaned back in the driver's seat and exhaled, exhaustion setting in. She hurried into the incident room.

'Well, well, well, Harte returns.' Sullivan shook her head slowly. 'You put yourself in danger. That was clever.'

Gina shrugged. 'You put me in danger. You refused to look at where the evidence was leading, and you forced me to go alone.'

'You're suspended, Harte.'

Briggs stepped forward. 'No, she's right. The team failed her and without DI Harte's intervention, we'd have another body on our hands and if you suspend her, you'll have all that to explain.'

Sullivan bit the skin on the inside of her mouth, suppressing her rage.

Briggs continued. 'DS Driscoll is no longer a suspect and I've just been informed that he's being prepared for release from custody on no charge. You're not needed here anymore. Our team has successfully apprehended the suspect, we will be interviewing him, and we will be charging him. I'll be sending a full report on how this was all handled to your superior. I'm sure there will be a full enquiry.'

Sullivan shook her head and Gina felt her knees trembling. She'd never seen such a stand-off in her career, and she had no idea where it would end. She raised her eyebrows. Gina couldn't help the tiny smile that formed on her lips.

'And I'll be reporting all this insubordination.' Sullivan walked over to Gina. 'You're still as lost as you always were, Gina. You might be smiling but you can't fool me.'

Gina had given up wondering what Sullivan might think of her or what she might think she knew about her. What will be, will be. There was nothing more she could do, and she had no more fight in her. She could think of a million sarcastic quips to come back at her with, but they would do her no good. She'd won. Jacob was free and the real offender had been caught. That was a win, and she wasn't going to let Sullivan ruin the moment.

'You're still like a lost little bird. Lost birds fly into windows. Just before they hit the glass, they see their own terrified reflections as their lives flash in front of them. I know things haunt you, Harte. You take all that baggage home, and you keep it, like some hoarder who can't let go. What would you see, little bird, if you stared into that death window?'

Now Sullivan was showing her true self in front of someone else for a change.

Briggs broke the silent tension as Gina clenched her teeth. 'Now, that's enou—'

Gina held a hand up and Briggs stopped talking. 'I got this.' She was thankful that Briggs was on her side, but it was her battle. 'I'd see my team, a happy and loyal team, who work together well. I don't need to bully them or make them feel infe-rior. I trust them to do their jobs, I care about them, I'm there for them, I'd do anything for any one of them. I'd go to the ends of the earth for them. They'd do the same for me. I have that, all that. And it's everything I've ever wanted. Now, I'm going to say goodbye and I'm going to continue doing my job. Is that okay, sir?' She turned to Briggs.

Briggs nodded. 'Wyre is with Kieron Crawford. He's been charged and booked in, so I'd say he's ready to interview. There is a duty solicitor waiting. We're all set to go. I'd like you to lead the interview.'

'Thanks, sir.' With that, Gina walked past Sullivan, knowing that the woman who'd made her training years a misery would now be investigated for gross misconduct. Failing to consider her team's input had led Gina into a dangerous situ-ation, without backup and that was unforgivable. She thought of trainee DC Kapoor, and she hoped to do nothing but nurture her. Sullivan went to speak but stopped.

The mighty had fallen.

SIXTY

Kieron Crawford remained tight-lipped as they'd started the tape and made all the introductions.

'Mr Crawford. You have been arrested for the attempted murders of Hazel Blackford, Tiffany Crawford, Nancy Cross and Lauren Cross; and for the murders of Sienna Moorcroft and Robbie Shields. Also, you've been arrested for controlling and coercive behaviour, and administering a noxious substance to Tiffany Crawford.'

Kieron whispered something to his solicitor, and she shook her head.

'Where were you between seven on Saturday night and one on Sunday morning?'

'No comment.'

'Why did you kill Sienna Moorcroft?'

'No comment.'

Gina went through all their questions but for every one he answered no comment.

'Mr Crawford, this evening, I found you strangling Lauren Cross. Is that what you did to Hazel Blackford and Tiffany Crawford?'

'No comment.' He stared into the lap of his standard-issue track bottoms. 'No comment, no comment, no comment.'

'Mr Crawford. We have a blood sample found at the scene of Hazel Blackford's attack. Your DNA has now gone to the lab. It's your blood, isn't it?'

'No bloody comment.' His fingers began to shake.

'We have word that the tablets your wife thought were vitamins were heavy sedatives. Also, there was residue of that sedative found in Mrs Crawford's water, in her food and in her wine glass. Other things in your medicine cabinet, caffeine pills that had been crushed into a powder. The one pill your wife describes as a probiotic, turned out to be a strong laxative. Have you been purposely making Tiffany Crawford ill to the point she doubted her every move?'

'You didn't have to live with her.' He slammed his fist on the table, making the cups jump. Gina leaned back. She'd cracked him. His solicitor whispered in his ear, and he dismissed her. 'It's no good, that blood is mine.' He let out a laugh.

Gina's muscles tightened. Was that a confession? 'Are you saying that the blood left behind on Hazel Blackford's door is your blood?'

'Yes.'

'Are you saying that you broke into her house and attacked her?'

'Yes. That bitch deserved everything she got.'

Gina's heart began to thrum as she imagined Hazel fighting for her life. She wanted to reach over the table and make him pay but, as always, she remained still and calm. 'Why did you try to kill her?'

'She let me down like they all do. You know, my mother was an evil bitch, and Hazel knew that. She knew how hard I'd had it and she told me that no one would ever hurt me again. She said she'd never leave me. I was so happy that I'd found this angel with her long blonde hair and piercing blue eyes. She told me she loved me, and I fell for her deeply. Then out of the blue, she dumped me. I was upset and, at first, I wondered if it was because there was someone else, but she didn't pick up with anyone, not for a year or two. Then, I noticed on her social media that she was in a relationship with a woman. I was never going to be enough for her and she'd led me on and spat me out. I couldn't get her deceit out of my head. I went to her workplace to speak to her, but I couldn't approach her, so I followed her home. That's when I saw the nice house, the perfect everything and...' He clenched his fist.

'So, you attempted to kill her because she rejected you?'

He slammed his hand on the table. 'They rejected me. You know, even though my heartless bitch of a mother never loved me, I cared for her up until the day she died. I bathed her, fed her, administered her medicine. In the end, she was in so much pain, she begged me to end it, but I made her suffer to the end while I watched the bitch die. Before you ask, no I didn't kill her or help her to end it.'

'Why did you strangle Tiffany? She was your wife.'

The solicitor began to whisper to Kieron Crawford. 'Oh, zip it. She knows, they know.'

'Tiffany?' Gina waited and hoped that he'd continue against the advice of his solicitor.

'At first it was hearts and roses. I fell for her quick and we drove to Cleevesford one day and stopped at the Bluebell Woods. I proposed to her, and she said yes. I was so happy.'

'What changed?'

'I couldn't stop thinking about how happy I thought I was when I was with Hazel so I made sure the same thing wouldn't happen again.'

'How?'

'I knew that if I scared her, she'd want me to be with her. I didn't want to go to that stag do, I wanted to stay with her, but she insisted, like she wanted me to go out so she could get rid of me. A part of me wondered if she was seeing someone else and I couldn't bear for her to leave me. After the night I had her scrawny neck in my hands, she never wanted me to leave her side.'

'Why Lauren?'

'After I'd got over Hazel, I met Lauren, it was before Tiff but I bet you never knew that.' Kieron Crawford looked almost smug in telling them everything, like somehow he was the winner for outsmarting them for so long. 'We had a whirlwind romance going on. I didn't want to hurt anyone again in the way I'd hurt Hazel, so I tried to get out more and meet more people. That's when I met the witch.'

'The witch?'

'Nancy. Lauren's mum. I'd started meditating, trying to keep myself calm and happy and I met Nancy at a wellness centre. One time she brought Lauren along and the moment I saw her, I was besotted. And when she agreed to go out with me, Hazel was in the past. I loved Lauren with everything I had and soon we were engaged. But something was off with Nancy, she just didn't like me.'

Gina wondered if the woman could sense danger around Kieron.

'She kept telling Lauren that she shouldn't be tied down so young and that marriage at such a young age was a mistake. Of course, we ignored her. But on our big day, Lauren dumped me. Apparently, Nancy had told her that she saw a text on my phone, one that suggested I'd been sleeping with someone else. Lauren demanded to see it, so I showed her because I wasn't cheating, I knew there was no text. You can imagine how I felt when there was a text on my phone. Nancy had obviously sent it from a burner, and it was enough for Lauren to call the wedding off and dump me. Nancy then told me that I was never going to be enough for Lauren and that there was something about me that she didn't like and that she'd do everything in her power to keep us apart. I just wanted to be happy, and the witch ruined it. After that I met Tiff. Now you can see why I couldn't bear for her to leave me. I wasn't going to get hurt a third time.'

'Why did you try to kill her?'

'I didn't.'

'But you repeatedly drugged her.'

'I didn't try to kill her though. I only strangled her to scare her, and I never fed her that many tablets, just enough to keep her under control.'

'She was found with enough in her system to kill her. We found drugged wine, water and residue on another cup in your flat.'

'I left her the wine because I thought she might find it, but I didn't drug the wine or the tea.'

Gina exhaled and leaned back. 'Who did then?'

He shrugged. 'Ask another question.'

'Tell me about you and Lauren.'

He let out a laugh. 'Have I or have I not been cooperative?'

'You have,' Gina replied, hoping that he'd continue.

'Just so you have it on record too, I went over to Nancy's cottage today, and I tied her up.'

'Then you took Lauren.'

'There's so much more you need to know, and it is going to blow your mind. Lauren and I hooked up again. She was always the one, forever mine, that's what I used to say to her. That's what we had engraved in our wedding rings, the ones we never got to swap. We were seeing each other.'

'But she had just announced that she was going to marry Robbie Shields.'

Kieron balled his hands into fists. 'That's why we argued. I went over a few days before and I had to talk sense into her. She was torn and I couldn't lose her again. She said that Robbie would never let her go and she was upset. She'd found out that her little bitch friend had been screwing Robbie and that he'd fathered her daughter.'

Gina scrunched her brows. Lauren knew all this time that Dora was Robbie's daughter.

Kieron grinned. 'I can see those cogs turning, Detective. Don't you see now? Isn't it all as clear as air. I first proposed to Lauren at Bluebell Woods and then I took Tiff there too. All the time I pretended that Tiff was Lauren. Weird maybe. When I told Lauren that, she was so flattered, and she couldn't keep her hands off me. She took a lot of convincing when it came to her mum lying about that text, but, of course, I'd been telling the truth. There was no point carrying such a lie for so long so she could see I was being honest. That's when we made a plan. Lauren wanted Sienna and Robbie to pay, and I wanted Tiffany gone. All went well my end. Sienna and Robbie were easy. I even went back to check on the bungalow just before you lot came. I even hung around to watch those stupid kids find Robbie. I thought Lauren and I had everything running smoothly. I bet you're wondering why I'm dumping her in it.'

Gina didn't say a word. While Kieron Crawford was in full flow, why would she interrupt.

'The bitch changed her mind when she saw what I'd done to Nancy. What psycho lets me kill her best friend and her fiancé, then gets all het up about a mother who is a complete lying cow? She went for me at that point like a rabid dog and I couldn't help it, I laughed and shoved her in my car. She was no match for me.'

'So, you took her to the woods where you intended to kill her?'

'I took her back to where it all started. We had the best day of our lives by that stump, and I felt she should end her life there too. See, I even thought about that after she turned on me. Always thinking of other people who never put me first.' He paused. 'You know how Lauren planned to end Tiff? She was going to pop over, make her some tea and open up. They were going to chat away like they were best buddies, each other's supportive friend and then Lauren was going to make sure there was a fair few crushed up tablets in that tea. I fed Tiffany the usual number of pills she was used to. Yes, she felt rough, but she was never about to die. With what Lauren gave her on top of those, it was inevitable she'd overdose. I wrote the note though, thought it might be more convincing. All Lauren had to do was sneak in, set everything up and leave the note. We knew that leaving the wine out too would entice Tiff to drink it. She was just a woman who couldn't say no to a drink or a pill.' He paused. 'Lauren let me down and now she's going down with me. It's funny really.' His bellowing laughs filled the room.

Gina's heart banged away as she thought of all that Tiffany had been through. Kieron, the man she trusted more than any one had treated her so cruelly and as for Lauren, Tiffany believed she was going over to talk and befriend her, but she too had deceived her. Gina wondered if Tiffany would ever be able to trust again. Gina knew she had to be the one to confront Lauren who was at present playing the role of victim and being treated in hospital.

SIXTY-ONE

NANCY

Every bone in Nancy's body ached as the nurse pushed her to the room that Lauren had been settled into. They'd both escaped with their lives and for that she was thankful, but she needed to hurry up, get better and get out. Fifi was waiting for her, and Lauren needed her. As soon as her daughter was well enough and the police had left her house, they'd be able to go home.

'I'll just see if it's okay for you to go in now,' the nurse said as she knocked on the door. Another nurse left and nodded. 'I'll be back in ten minutes to return you to the ward.'

'Thank you.' The nurse went to push the chair into the room, but Nancy held a hand up. 'I'm okay to walk.' On shaky legs, she stood and hobbled over to her daughter's bedside. Her eyes filled with tears as she saw the red mark around Lauren's neck. Her mascara-streaked face and the vacant look in her eyes told her that she was still in shock. Nancy had been told that they'd had to rescue her from Kieron Crawford's grip. She sat on a plastic chair and stroked Lauren's arm.

'He was killing me, Mum.'

She leaned up and hugged Lauren, allowing her daughter to let it all out. 'They have him now. He can't hurt you ever again.'

Lauren's sobs died down. 'I know about the text that you sent him, on our wedding day.'

Nancy stared open-mouthed.

'It's your fault, all of it. If you hadn't interfered, I'd have been happy. You did this. You did it all,' Lauren screamed. 'I hate you. You ruined my life.'

'Lauren, stop. Where is this coming from? Kieron was and still is a dangerous man. Yes, I sent the stupid text but there was something about him that set my hair on end when he spoke. Everything I did was to protect you. You're all I have.'

Lauren shook her head. 'You wanted to control me. You didn't like anyone I ever fell for. You hated Kieron. You didn't like Robbie.'

'And look what a cheat and liar he turned out to be.' Nancy instantly regretted speaking up. Her daughter was upset, and she was venting. As a mother, she should have let her get all her upset and anger out of her system.

Lauren wiped her eyes and paused. 'Kieron was right. I should have let him kill you today.'

'Lauren don't say that. What are you talking about?'

'Ms Cross, will you please step away so that DC Wyre and I can talk to Lauren?'

The detective who saved her, DI Harte, stood at the door.

'Err, what's going on?' Nancy hobbled out of the way and swapped places with the two detectives.

Lauren looked up at them, a flash of panic in her eyes. Nancy swallowed. 'What's going on?'

'He's lying,' Lauren said, all upset gone from her voice.

Nancy had never seen her daughter looking so cold and calm. It's as if she'd been replaced with another person. 'Lauren.'

The detective sat on the chair and looked directly at Lauren. Nancy felt her hands trembling and her heart booming. 'Lauren Cross, you are under arrest for the attempted murder of Tiffany Crawford and the conspiracy to murder Robbie Shields and Sienna Moorcroft. You do not have to say anything. But it may harm your defence if you do not mention when questioned something which you later rely on in court. Anything you do say may be given in evidence.'

'Stop, that can't be right. He tried to kill Lauren. You've got it wrong.' The stare that Lauren gave her told her that she didn't know her daughter anymore. Her legs gave way and DC Wyre ran over to help her out of the room. A uniformed officer came down the corridor and headed in, leaving Nancy with the detective. 'This isn't happening,' Nancy cried out. But she knew it was. She knew from seeing Lauren right there and then, that she was guilty. Lauren had it plastered all over her face. Nancy cried and screamed as self-blame took over. If only she'd never taken Lauren with her to the well-being class. If only she hadn't made up that text to split Lauren and Kieron up. If only, if only, if only...

She pierced the air in the corridor with her scream and the detective came over. No pain she'd ever felt had come as close as this. 'Ms Cross, I'm so sorry.' DI Harte stood beside her.

'No, I'm sorry. I failed as a mother. I failed.'

The detective tilted her head and bit her bottom lip before speaking. 'You haven't failed, please don't blame yourself.'

Nancy huffed. 'I will always blame myself.' It was over. Nancy wanted to go home. In fact, she was going to sign herself out and leave to go and be with Fifi. That was all she had left. She left the detective and walked away, knowing that life would never be the same again. She'd be dutiful. She'd visit Lauren in prison when she could, but she'd never understand how her daughter could do what she did. Ever.

All she'd ever wanted in life was to make the world a better place and instead, she'd reared a killer. She'd wanted nothing more than to save the earth but what for? When her main reason for saving it was as contaminated and polluting as the companies she despised.

SIXTY-TWO

Gina paused at the end of yet another hospital ward while she waited for Wyre to finish up with Lauren. There was one more person she wanted to see before she headed back to the station to get on with the paperwork. She glanced at her phone and saw a message from Jacob.

> *Guv, I wish I could call and talk to you, but I just don't have the words at the moment. I'm exhausted. I need to go to bed, and I guess I need to process everything. I wanted to say thank you for all that you did. DCI Briggs told me about you going rogue. I owe everything to you and the team and I'm coming back on that team. I don't know where I'd be now without you. Anyway, end of message because my emotions are all over the place. Speak tomorrow. J.*

She wiped away the tear that was threatening to spring.

'Right, are we going to see Tiffany then?' Wyre asked as she hurried over.

Gina nodded. 'I had a message from Jacob. He's not leaving us.'

Wyre smiled. 'That's the best news.'

They reached the ward that Tiffany was recovering on, and Gina pressed the buzzer. The nurse recognised her from a previous visit and released the door. 'Have you come to see Tiffany Crawford?'

'We have,' Gina replied.

'Last room on the left. She's tired but good to talk.' The nurse smiled and sat behind the desk at the nurses' station.

She knocked on the open door and Tiffany opened her eyes and glanced over at her and Wyre. 'Are there any updates?'

Gina nodded. The only way to deliver the news about Kieron Crawford was straight. 'We've arrested your husband for the murders of Sienna Moorcroft and Robbie Shields. We've also arrested him for attempting to murder you, controlling and coercive behaviour, and administering a noxious substance.'

She pushed her body up in the bed. 'What? Because he was drugging me?'

Gina sat beside her bed. 'Your husband was the man who strangled you.' Gina gave it a few moments for the news to sink in. She had so much more to tell Tiffany, but some things could wait. She'd have to explain about Hazel at some point and also about Kieron's past and current relationship with Lauren.

'I... err...' She paused. 'It's over.'

Gina nodded. 'There is more you need to know.'

'Okay.' Tiffany blinked hard and rubbed her tired eyes.

'We've also arrested Lauren Cross for your attempted murder.'

'But she came to see me earlier.'

'We have reason to believe she drugged you and she left the wine for you to drink and the note.'

Tiffany shook her head and wiped her damp eyes. 'I trusted her. I let her into my home and... Was it Kieron? Did he put her up to it? Were they...?'

Gina nodded. 'I'm sorry.'

She paused and began to massage her temples. 'Don't be. Finally, things make sense. Am I even ill?'

Gina shrugged.

'All these years, wasted. How do I get past this? How?' Huge sobs filled the room as Tiffany let it all out. Gina remained beside her for the next half an hour until the nurse thought it best that she and Wyre left. 'Tiffany, you're safe now. I know it's not easy, but it will get easier, I promise.' Gina headed towards the door. 'I'll come back tomorrow after you've had some more rest. Okay?'

Tiffany nodded and Gina left with Wyre. The case was presentable to the CPS, but it was far from over. There would be months of waiting while it went to court. Tiffany would be called as a witness and Gina knew she'd be there to support her through it. She wasn't Sullivan. She did have a heart and she always would have. Better to feel and be hurt in life than to exist as a stone. She wondered what Sullivan would see as she crashed into the window that was about to end her career. The super's life was now shattered, and Gina had been forced through a wringer, but she had her team back.

EPILOGUE

Friday, 3 February

Gina drove down the country lane to the Drunken Duck, and she pulled into the car park. What a week it had been. A rock dabbed in dried-up blood and two neatly preserved strips of blonde hair had been found in the door panel of Kieron's car which had provided more evidence towards his conviction.

She was still tense from explaining everything again to Hazel Blackford but it was over. The woman finally knew who had tried to strangle her and she was more than happy about being a witness in court. On leaving, Gina had watched through their games room window as Hazel hugged her partner and tiny baby. She too could now get back to living.

As for Tiffany, Gina had managed to find her mother who was ready and willing to rush down from Nottingham to be with her daughter. It appeared that Kieron had pulled her away from her family and all this time they'd been waiting and hoping that one day, Tiffany would come back to them. The reunion had caused Gina to rush to her car and sob her heart out. She missed her own mother terribly and maybe over the weekend, she'd go and take some flowers to her grave. She closed her eyes and leaned back in the driver's seat, in darkness as she fought the tears away. What an emotional week it had been? It was one she never wished to repeat.

A thud on her car window made her jolt up and gasp. Briggs opened the car door. 'We're all waiting for you before we order. What are you doing out here?'

She went to speak but tears flooded down her face.

'Come here.' He bent over and held her as best he could through the open window.

'I'm okay. It's just been—'

'You don't have to explain. I understand.'

And he did. He knew her like no one else. He was also feeling the pain of the last few days, the whole department were. All that time Briggs had been trying to keep Gina on the team even though she did doubt him. He was really stuck in the middle and trying to cling onto his position within the investigation. She missed Jacob so much and she was ready to see him now. She wiped her face, fanned it dry and smiled. 'Pull yourself together, Harte,' she said.

Briggs stepped back and she got out of the car. He opened the door, and she entered the pub to laughter and hugs. Jacob was in the centre of it all. Wyre turned and saw her, then O'Connor put his drink down. She noticed how many soft drinks they were all holding because most of them could be called in at any time. Kapoor and PC Ahmed stood together. PC Smith swivelled around on a bar stool and grinned as he held a green cocktail. Jacob smiled at her and walked over. 'I have missed you, guv. I've missed you all.' He flung his arms around Gina, she hugged him back.

'Speech,' PC Smith called out, obviously having had more than one drink. 'Come on Briggsy.'

Gina laughed as she wondered what Sullivan would make of this scene. She wanted to laugh even more when she'd heard that Sullivan had handed in her notice and opted to finally retire. If she'd have heard Briggs being called Briggsy by a drunken PC she'd have made sure he'd been fired, but Briggs was a good person to work for and not just because Gina loved him.

'I don't do speeches. You'll have to settle for glad to have you back on the team, Jacob. You've been through the absolute pits, and I can't even pretend to understand how you must feel but what I can tell you is, we are all here for you and that's a promise. If you need to talk, well there's always Smith.'

The crowd laughed as Smith put his miniature cocktail umbrella between his teeth and gurned.

'Seriously, we missed you. Onwards and upwards, as they say. Right, let's drink to Jacob.'

Everyone roared and cheered.

'And congratulations to trainee DC Jhanvi Kapoor and PC Shafiq Ahmed who will be assisting major crimes.' He turned to Shaf. 'Whatever you do don't turn out like him.' Briggs nodded to Smith who smiled widely, showing his stained green lips. Shaf laughed. 'Right, it has to be time to grab our table and order some food before we all wilt like the delicate little flowers that we are.'

As everyone made their way through the busy pub to the reserved table, Gina remained at the bar waiting to be served. Briggs ambled over. 'Great job, Gina.'

'Yay, let's do it all again tomorrow.' She let out a laugh but inside, she wanted to weep. Everyone was happy but the last few days had really knocked her sideways. When she finally settled tonight, she would give a thought to everyone whose lives were ruined by Kieron and Lauren. The road to recovery was infinite. The trauma would rear its ugly head at the most inconvenient of times and at other times, life just might feel normal for a while. She knew that it never left. It remained dormant, waiting for an excuse to pop back up and say hi.

'What do you want to drink?'

She stared at the optics. 'You know, I'm not on call tonight and I think I'll come back to yours. Make it a fruity gin and tonic.' Why not. Life was for living and tonight, she was going to live a little.

A LETTER FROM CARLA

Dear Reader,

I'm so thankful that you decided to read *Her Hidden Shadow*. I enjoyed exploring Tiffany and Nancy's separate stories and situations, and I hope you enjoyed unravelling Gina's latest case, too.

If you enjoyed *Her Hidden Shadow* and would like to keep up to date with all my latest releases, just sign up at the following link. Your email address will never be shared and you can unsubscribe at any time.

www.bookouture.com/carla-kovach

The idea for Tiffany's story came from the fact that I prepare all my husband, Nigel's, vitamin tablets every day and I realise that a controlling and dangerous person could totally exploit that situation.

Thankfully all I give Nigel is his vitamins. I did tell him about my Tiffany character as I wrote the book and swiftly asked him if he wanted to organise his own tablets. He said no and I'm still happily balancing our ever-changing vitamin needs – haha. On a serious note, if you're ever worried about medication that someone else is giving you, do check it with a chemist or buy another bottle of that vitamin pill and compare them to what you're being given.

As for Nancy, I found her to be a colourful character with

her activism and her motherly interference in Lauren's life. It does sadden me that raw sewage ends up in our waterways. I felt this was a current issue and I wanted to touch upon it.

Whether you are a reader, tweeter, blogger, Facebooker, TikTok user or reviewer, I really am grateful of all that you do and as a writer, this is where I hope you'll leave me a review or say a few words about my book.

Again, thank you so much. I'm active on social media so please feel free to contact me on Twitter, Instagram or through my Facebook page.

Thank you,

Carla Kovach

facebook.com/CarlaKovachAuthor
twitter.com/CKovachAuthor
instagram.com/carla_kovach

ACKNOWLEDGEMENTS

I'd like to say a mahoosive thank you to everyone who has helped bring to life *Her Hidden Shadow*. Editors, cover designers, people working in every aspect of publishing from admin to management are all a part of this big team and I'm so grateful and proud to be a part of team Bookouture.

Helen Jenner, my super editor, is fabulous and I couldn't do all this without her. I say super as I don't know how she does it each time. Her edits make my books the best they can be.

Thank you to Lisa Brewster for the cover design. It's gorgeous!

The Bookouture publicity team are the best. Noelle Holten, Kim Nash, Jess Readett and Sarah Hardy make publication day mega special. I'm grateful to you all.

I'm always in awe of how generous the blogger and reviewer community are and I remain grateful to the bloggers who chose to read my book.

Huge thanks to the Fiction Café Book Club. I love what they do for authors. The Facebook lives and publication day fanfares are generous. I can appreciate the time the admins give to keeping this group as awesome as it is.

I'm also thrilled to be a member of the supportive Bookouture author family. Thank you, you're all amazing. My other author friends are fabulous too. Authors are just the best.

My beta readers, Derek Coleman, Su Biela, Jamie-Lee Brooke, Anna Wallace and Vanessa Morgan, are all lovely and I'm grateful that they read my work at different stages before publication. Special thanks to Jamie-Lee Brooke (again), Julia Sutton, Abigail Osborne and Phil Price. We have an author support group that keeps me happy and motivated. Love you all, 'Hot Dog Cringey Crew'. Big apologies but this is an in joke. Thanks also to author, James Marx, who joins our Cringey Crew on our Thursday pub writing sessions. It really does help to have drinks and food on tap while working with other authors.

I'd like to give special thanks to Stuart Gibbon of Gib Consultancy. He answers my policing questions and without his knowledge, I'd definitely be making a mess of the police procedures and charges. Any inaccuracies are definitely my own.

Lastly, thank you to my husband, Nigel Buckley, for the cups of coffee and being there for me throughout the whole process.